MANITOU CANYON

A NOVEL

WILLIAM KENT KRUEGER

ATRIA PAPERBACK

New York London Toronto Sydney New Delhi

ATRIA
PAPERBACK

An Imprint of Simon & Schuster, LLC
1230 Avenue of the Americas
New York, NY 10020

First Atria Paperback edition May 2017

ATRIA PAPERBACK and colophon are trademarks of Simon & Schuster, LLC

For information about special discounts for bulk purchases, please contact Simon & Schuster Special Sales at 1-866-506-1949 or business@simonandschuster.com.

The Simon & Schuster Speakers Bureau can bring authors to your live event. For more information or to book an event, contact the Simon & Schuster Speakers Bureau at 1-866-248-3049 or visit our website at www.simonspeakers.com.

Interior design by Esther Paradelo

Manufactured in the United States of America

20 19 18 17 16 15 14 13 12

The Library of Congress has cataloged the hardcover edition as follows:

Names: Krueger, William Kent, author.
Title: Manitou Canyon : a novel / William Kent Krueger.
Description: First Atria Books hardcover edition. | New York City :
Atria Books, 2016. | Series: Cork O'Connor mystery series
Identifiers: LCCN 2016013735 (print) | LCCN 2016020714 (ebook) | ISBN 9781476749266 (hardcover) | ISBN 9781476749280 (ebook)
Subjects: LCSH: O'Connor, Cork (Fictitious character)—Fiction. | Private investigators—Minnesota—Fiction. | Missing persons—Investigation—Fiction. | Ojibwa Indians—Fiction. | BISAC: FICTION / Mystery & Detective / General. | FICTION / Suspense. | FICTION / General. | GSAFD: Suspense fiction. | Mystery fiction.
Classification: LCC PS3561.R766 M36 2016 (print) |
LCC PS3561.R766 (ebook) |
DDC 813/.54—dc23

LC record available at https://lccn.loc.gov/2016013735

ISBN 978-1-4767-4926-6
ISBN 978-1-4767-4927-3 (pbk)
ISBN 978-1-4767-4928-0 (ebook)

To all those who work for and
with the Ain Dah Yung Center and the
Minnesota Indian Women's Resource Center.
Every day, these great hearts save Native lives.

ACKNOWLEDGMENTS

My thanks to Dave Rydeen, formerly of the U.S. Army Corps of Engineers, who shook his head at my stupidity when I told him the story I wanted to write, but nonetheless helped me immensely in my understanding of dams.

Thanks, as always, to those early readers whose comments and insights improved the work tremendously—Danielle Egan-Miller, Joanna MacKenzie, Alec MacDonald, Abby Saul, and Libby Hellmann. *Chi migwech* to Deb Foster, who has been so generous in sharing her thoughts on the Native elements of this story.

A shout-out to those wonderful coffee shops who tolerated my long presences while this novel was being written—the Como Park Grill, the Underground Music Cafe, and Caribou Coffee.

And finally, acknowledgment of a great debt of gratitude to my longtime editor, Sarah Branham, whose insights have been indispensable in crafting so many of my stories. I'll miss you, Sarah, and I wish you nothing but good fortune on the new path you're traveling.

CHAPTER 1

In the gray of early afternoon, the canoes drew up to the shoreline of the island. The paddles were stowed. The woman in the bow of the first canoe and the kid in the bow of the second stepped onto the rocks. They held the canoes steady while the men in the stern of each disembarked and joined them. The kid grabbed a rifle from the center of the canoe he'd come in, then lifted a pack. He studied the island and the great stand of red pines that grew there.

"Where to?" he said.

"First, we hide the canoes," the man who was the oldest and tallest said.

They carried the crafts from the lake a dozen yards into the trees. The tall man in the lead and the woman with him set their canoe behind a fallen pine, and the kid and the other man did the same.

"Want to cover them with boughs or something?" the kid asked.

"Break off boughs and someone will know we were here," the tall man said. "This'll do."

They returned to the shore where they'd left their gear. The kid grabbed his rifle and reached for a pack.

The woman said, "I'll carry that. You see to your rifle."

She shouldered the pack, and the tall man started toward the interior of the island. The others followed, wordless and in single file.

On some maps, the island was called by its Ojibwe name: Miskominag. On others, it was called Raspberry. Words in different languages that meant the same thing. They walked inland through the pines, passed bushes that in summer would have been full of berries, but it was the first day of November, and all the plants except the evergreens were bare. They came to a great upthrust of rock, a kind of wall across the island, and the tall man began to climb. The others spread out and found their own ways up. The top of the outcropping stood above the crowns of the trees. From there, they could see the whole of the lake, a two-mile-long, horseshoe-shaped body of water three-quarters of a mile across at its widest point. The water of the lake was the same dismal color of both the sky above them and the rock outcropping on which they stood. The gray of despair.

"Where will he come from?" the kid asked, his eyes taking in all that water and shoreline.

"The south," the tall man said. "Over there." He pointed toward a spot across the lake.

The kid looked and said, "All I see is trees."

"Try these." The tall man unshouldered the pack he'd carried, set it down, and drew out a pair of binoculars. He handed them to the kid, who spent a minute adjusting the lenses.

"Got it. A portage," the kid said. He returned the binoculars to the man. "What now?"

"We wait."

The others unburdened themselves of their packs. The shorter of the two men—he had a nose that was like a blob of clay plopped in the middle of his face—took a satellite phone from his pack and walked away from the others.

The woman said to the kid, "Hungry?"

"Famished."

She pulled deer jerky and an orange from her pack and offered them.

"Wouldn't mind some hot soup," the kid said.

"No fires," the tall man told him.

"He won't be here for a long time," the kid said.

"The smoke would be visible for miles. And the smell would carry, too," the tall man said.

The kid laughed. "Think there's anybody besides us way the hell out here this time of year?"

"Out here, you never know. Enjoy your jerky and orange."

The tall man walked away, studying the whole of the lake below. The wall fell off in a vertical cliff face, a tall palisade several hundred yards long. A few aspen had taken root and clung miraculously to the hard, bare rock, but they didn't obscure the view. There was nowhere on the lake that wasn't visible from that vantage. The woman followed him.

"He's too young," she said with a note of gall. "I told you."

"He's strong in the right ways. And a far better shot than me or you, if it comes to that."

He looked back at the kid, who'd already eaten his jerky and was peeling the orange while intently studying the place along the shoreline where the trees opened onto the portage. The woman was right. He was young. Seventeen. He'd never killed a man, but that's what he was there for. To do this thing, if necessary.

"When the time comes," the tall man said, "if he has to do it, he'll be fine." He turned from the woman and rejoined the others.

The man with the formless nose said, "Sat phone's a problem. These clouds."

"Did you get through?"

"Only enough to say we made it. Then I lost the signal."

"That'll do."

The kid sat on a rock and cradled his rifle in his lap. He leaned forward and looked at the lake, the trees, the shoreline, the place where the man would come.

"Does he have a name?" the kid asked.

"What difference does it make?" the woman said.

"I don't know. Just wondered."

"Everyone has a name," the woman said.

"So what's his?"

"Probably better you don't know. That way, he's just a target."

The tall man said, "His name's O'Connor. Cork O'Connor."

The kid lifted his rifle, sighted at the shoreline.

Behind him, the woman whispered, "Bang."

CHAPTER 2

April is the cruelest month. Some poet said that. Robert Frost was the only poet whose work Cork was familiar with, and it wasn't Frost. Whoever it was, he was dead wrong. Corcoran O'Connor knew that November was the bastard of all months. Anyone who thought different had never been in Minnesota's North Country in November.

He couldn't remember the last time he'd seen the sun. Every day was like the one before it, the sky a hopeless gray, the hard-woods stripped of color, the water of Iron Lake flat and dull as an old tin roof. It felt as if all life had deserted Tamarack County, even the wind, and every morning dawned with the same dismal promise.

Some of this feeling, he knew, was because of his own unhappy history with that month. His father, who'd been sheriff of Tama-rack County four decades earlier, had been mortally wounded in the last week of October, had lingered for two days, and had finally succumbed in the first hour of the first day of a long-ago Novem-ber. His wife had gone missing and, for all intents and purposes, was dead to him in a November not so long ago. His good and true friend George LeDuc had been murdered in that same November. For Cork, it wasn't just a dreary month. It was a deadly one. Every year when it came around, it brought with it ghosts and regret.

"April, my ass," he mumbled. Then he heard the car approaching.

He looked down from atop the ladder where he perched with

a wire brush in his hand. He'd been cleaning dirt from an area on the roof of an old Quonset hut, which had been converted into a burger joint called Sam's Place. He'd owned it for more than fifteen years. The Quonset hut stood on the shore of Iron Lake, at the edge of the small town of Aurora, in the deep Northwoods, in that part of Minnesota called the Arrowhead. There was a leak in the roof of the hut, and Cork wanted to get it patched before the snow came. He'd already cut a square of steel sheeting. On top of his toolbox on the ground at the base of the ladder lay a roll of double-sided butyl tape, his cordless Black & Decker drill, and a small box of metal screws.

He watched the car, a black Lexus, pull into the gravel lot and park. His visitors got out and walked to the ladder. They were a young couple, man and woman. He realized that he knew them. Or knew who they were anyway, though they'd never actually met.

"We're looking for Cork O'Connor," the woman called up to him.

Even if he hadn't known them, he would have guessed that they were family, guessed brother and sister, probably even guessed twins, their features were so similar. Both were slender, had light brown hair, and were quite good looking. Very early twenties. She appeared to be a good deal more robust than her brother, whose complexion seemed pale in comparison. But maybe that was just the effect November had on the young man. Cork could understand.

"I'm O'Connor," he said.

The young woman craned her neck upward. "Can we talk?"

"Give me a minute."

Cork swept the roof with his gloved hand and was satisfied that the area was ready for the patch. He glanced up at the sky, a mottled gray that reminded him of bread mold, and started down the ladder.

"Lindsay Harris," the woman said even before he'd finished descending. "And this is my brother, Trevor."

Cork got his feet on the ground and turned to them. He pulled off his gloves and accepted the hand each of them offered.

"John Harris's grandchildren," he said.

The young woman nodded. "That's right."

"What can I do for you?"

"Find our grandfather," her brother said.

Cork dropped his gloves on the toolbox. "I already tried. Me and a lot of other good people. I'm part of Tamarack County Search and Rescue."

"We know that," the sister said.

"So what is it you think I can do that hasn't already been done?"

She wore a green down vest with a gold turtleneck beneath, jeans, good hiking boots. Her brother wore a dark gray car coat that looked expensive. The pants that showed beneath were gray slacks with a sharp crease. His shoes were black and polished and soft and out of place in the North Country.

"Could we go somewhere to talk?" the young woman asked.

"Inside." Cork led the way.

In the early sixties, a man named Sam Winter Moon had bought the Quonset hut and revamped it into a place that became known for the quality of its food—burgers and fries, mostly, but also hot dogs and good, thick milk shakes. The Sam's Special was renowned in Tamarack County, Minnesota. On his untimely death, Sam had willed the property to Cork, and the onetime lawman, whose badge had been taken from him, turned to flipping burgers. It was a vocation he'd come to love and a business he'd brought his children into. But he'd kept a finger in law enforcement in a way. He'd gotten himself a private investigator's license.

The front of the Quonset hut had been given over to the food business, but the rear Cork had kept as a kind of office in which he conducted much of his security and investigation work. Before beginning his repair of the roof that morning, he'd made a pot of coffee, and there was still plenty left to offer his visitors. He poured mugs for them all, and they sat at the old, round, wooden table where he often met with clients.

"Your sign outside says 'closed for the season,'" Trevor Harris said.

"That's just for Sam's Place," Cork told him. "A lot of us who cater to tourists close up in November. Once the color's gone, the flow of leaf peepers dries up. After the snow comes, we'll get snowmobilers and cross-country skiers, but for a while, things'll be pretty quiet here in Aurora. What you've come to me for, that business is open year-round." Cork took a long swill of his coffee. "We looked for your grandfather for two weeks solid. Tamarack County Search and Rescue. The U.S. Forest Service. We brought in trackers from the Border Patrol, K-9s, cadaver dogs. So I'll ask again, what do you think I can do to find him that hasn't already been done?"

Cork had been right about the brother. Under the car coat, he looked dressed for a date or church or a funeral. In the Twin Cities, he'd have been just fine for a business meeting. But in this neck of the woods, he stood out like a peacock in a chicken coop.

"We've read about you," the young woman said. "Your wife went missing, but you didn't give up looking, and you found her."

"If you know that much, then you know that when I found her she was dead." Although their bringing up the incident had caught him by surprise and made his gut twitch with that November regret, he kept his tone flat.

"It must have been hard," she went on quickly, as if sensing the thin ice onto which she'd ventured. "But at least you had closure. At least you know. We've been left with nothing but questions."

In the middle of October, John W. Harris, head of Harris International, one of the largest construction design firms in the country, had entered the Boundary Waters Canoe Area Wilderness with his two grown grandchildren and a local guide. The second day out, on a lake called Raspberry, John Harris had disappeared. That morning, grandfather and grandson had gone on some kind of fishing competition, each taking his own canoe and heading in a different direction. Lindsay Harris and the guide, a kid named Dwight Kohler, had stayed behind at the campsite. Trevor Harris had returned an hour later with a near-trophy walleye. His grandfather never returned.

The grandchildren and the guide went looking. They found his empty canoe floating in the middle of the lake, all his fishing gear still in it, but no sign of Harris. They checked the whole of the shoreline and the big island that rose near the center of the lake. There was only a single portage, which was a trail for carrying canoes between lakes, going in and another going out. They followed the portages and checked the lakes at either end. They waited a night, spent the next day searching again all the areas they'd already covered. Then Dwight Kohler went back to the entry point, a graveled lot where they'd parked their cars and launched themselves into the wilderness, driven into Aurora, and alerted the Tamarack County Sheriff's Department. Because of who John W. Harris was, the resulting search was one of the most thorough Cork had ever been a part of. Two days ago, the sheriff had called an official end to the effort.

"And just because I found my wife, you think I can find your grandfather?" Cork said.

"We don't want to give up on him," Lindsay said. "And we've heard you didn't want to either. We heard that you didn't agree with the decision to end the search. You don't think my grandfather just vanished out there. Is that true?"

"Who'd you hear that from?"

"That doesn't matter. What matters is if it's true. Is it?"

Cork scratched an eyebrow, considering. "You do the best you can in a search effort. But there's always a limit to the resources, the time, the manpower, the budget. The sheriff decided she'd exhausted all of those. It wasn't an unreasonable decision. In her place, I might have done the same."

"But it's true that you didn't agree with it?"

"In my opinion, there were still too many unanswered questions." Cork sipped his coffee. "Your grandfather grew up in Aurora."

Lindsay nodded, a piece of information not new to her. "Did you know him?"

"He lived across the street from my house. He was kind of like the big brother I never had. I had a feeling even then that he was destined for great things."

"He never talks about his childhood here," Trevor said.

There was good reason for that, Cork knew. But this wasn't the time to go into it.

"You said there were still too many unanswered questions," Lindsay said. "Like what?"

"Okay, one of the speculations was that he had a heart attack and fell into the water. We went over that lake bottom with divers. Nothing. And that takes care of another speculation, that he committed suicide. If he did, where's the body? Here's another speculation, that he had some kind of stroke and wandered off. If that was the case, why didn't the dogs pick up and follow his scent? And here's another one, off the wall, maybe, but not unheard of. A man sometimes gets to some dark point in his life when he might think that just ending it is the answer. Or rather, ending what his life is and starting over somewhere as someone different, burying himself somewhere where no one expects anything of him. Your grandfather's a very wealthy man. If he wanted a new life for himself, I imagine he could arrange that. When I knew him forty years ago, he didn't strike me as a guy who'd run from trouble and try to hide. Has he changed?"

"Grandpa John run?" Trevor said. "Christ, no. Not from anything."

"Someone could have done something to him," Lindsay suggested.

"Maybe," Cork said. "Did you see anyone else on Raspberry Lake?"

"Not a soul."

"And the sheriff's people found no evidence of foul play," Cork said.

Lindsay frowned. "So what happened to him?"

"I don't know. But I do know that something out there wasn't right. I just couldn't put my finger on it."

Lindsay glanced at her brother again, a furtive look. "There's something else."

She waited, as if expecting her brother to pick up the thread. Trevor Harris took a deep breath.

"It's going to sound weird, I know," he began. "The night the search ended, I had a dream, the strangest I've ever had. If it weren't for my grandfather's situation, I probably would have written it off as— What is it that Scrooge blames his vision of the ghosts on? A piece of undigested beef?" He laughed weakly and turned his mug nervously on the tabletop. "In this dream, I was in a desert of some kind. Like in the Southwest. It was night, big moon in the sky. I was all alone, stumbling around. I think I was lost. I know I was scared, that was the big thing. Then all of a sudden, there's this figure in front of me. He just kind of pops up. I can't see him clearly because the moon's behind him and the front of him, his face and all, is in shadow. He speaks to me. He says, 'I have a message from two fathers.' Then, honest to God, he quotes Shakespeare: 'Mark me. Lend thy serious hearing to what I shall unfold. But that I am forbid to tell the secrets of my prison house, I could a tale unfold whose lightest word would freeze thy young blood.'"

"You're kidding me," Cork said.

"No. Dead serious," young Harris said. "Are you familiar with *Hamlet*?"

"Not since high school."

"That quote is a kind of mash-up of the speech the ghost of Hamlet's father delivers to his son in Act One."

"And you remembered all that from the dream?"

"I'm an actor. Remembering dialogue is what I do."

"Two fathers," Cork said. "Your father's father speaking through the ghost of Hamlet's father?"

"I can't think of another meaning. And my grandfather is a huge fan of Shakespeare."

"That's all there was to the dream?"

"No. This figure said he had something for me, too. He said, 'Seek and ye shall find.'"

"The New Testament and Shakespeare. Quite a dream."

"That's not all," his sister said.

Cork looked at the brother and waited.

Trevor said, "I asked this messenger or whatever his name."

"And?"

"He told me it was O'Connor. Stephen O'Connor."

Cork was about to take another sip of his coffee, but he stopped in midmove and stared over the rim of his cup.

"He said one more thing before he vanished and the dream ended, something I still don't understand," Trevor went on. "He said, 'There are monthterth under the bed.' He said it like a kid with a kind of speech impediment. I don't understand what that was all about."

But Cork did. When his son, Stephen, who was eighteen now, was very young and still called Stevie, he had trouble pronouncing words that included an *s*. The *s* sound came out like *th*. Like lots of children, he'd been afraid of "monthterth" under his bed and in his closet. Stephen also had unusual, portentous dreams. In one of those dreams, he'd seen the exact details of his mother's death, years before that tragedy occurred. Stephen still sometimes dreamed in this way, but these days he called them visions.

Lindsay said, "We asked around. Your son is named Stephen. And folks here say he has . . ." She hesitated. "Special gifts."

"This dream seemed to take place in the Southwest?" Cork said.

"Or a place very like it," Trevor said.

"Any idea why that particular landscape?"

"None. Except I live in Las Vegas, so it's a landscape I'm familiar with."

"Dreams often take place in landscapes familiar to the dreamer," his sister offered. When Cork eyed her, she said, "Psychology minor."

Cork sipped his coffee, openly studied them both, thought it over, and finally said, "There's paperwork we'll need to take care of."

"You'll do it?" Lindsay seemed a little surprised and clearly pleased.

"I'll do my best, but I have to tell you up front that I don't think there are any stones left unturned."

"So what's the plan?" Trevor asked.

"I'll start by going back into the Boundary Waters to see if there's anything we didn't see before."

The young woman said, "If you do that, Mr. O'Connor, I'm coming with you."

Cork gave a nod. "We'll have to leave right away, first thing tomorrow morning. We're right at the edge of winter up here, and if we wait, snow might cover every clue we hope to find. Also, my daughter's getting married in two weeks, so we need to be in and out quickly." He looked at her brother. "You coming with us?"

"The Boundary Waters isn't really my thing," Trevor said. "I only went in the first place to please Grandpa John, and that didn't work out so well. Believe me, I'd only be in the way."

Cork glanced at his sister, and she gave a little nod of agreement.

"But I'll say a prayer or two while you're there," he said with a smile. "Never been very good at that either, but it's the best I can offer."

Lindsay Harris put a hand over her brother's. "We must accept finite disappointment, but never lose infinite hope."

Both men looked at her curiously.

She gave a little shrug. "Martin Luther King, Jr."

"You know the poem that begins 'We dance round in a ring and suppose'?" Cork said.

Lindsay thought a moment. "And the next line is about something that sits in the middle and knows, right?"

"Yes," Cork said. "The Secret."

"Who wrote it?" Trevor Harris asked.

Cork stared out the window at the cold, gray November sky, and said, "Frost."

CHAPTER 3

Cork parked on Oak Street in front of the State Bank of Aurora to deposit the retainer check John Harris's grandchildren had given him. More than forty years earlier, on a gray day not unlike this one, his father and some deputies had been involved in a gun battle here, exchanging fire with some escaped convicts who'd just robbed the bank. An old woman, deaf and oblivious, had wandered into the shoot-out. Cork's father, in grabbing her and bringing her to safety, had taken a fatal bullet. Cork generally didn't reflect much on his father's death, except in this bleakest of months.

After he finished his business in the bank, he walked to the Tamarack County Sheriff's Office, just a couple of blocks away. He could smell the aroma of deep-fry coming from Johnny's Pinewood Broiler. He walked past North Star Notions, where the window had already been stripped of Halloween decorations and now sported turkeys and cornucopias and other symbols of Thanksgiving, more than three weeks away. He waved to Ardith Kane, who stood inside amid aisles and shelves filled with pine-scented candles and toy stuffed moose and dream catchers and Minnetonka Mocassins, and she waved back. He turned the corner at Pflugleman's Rexall Drugs and walked another block to the Sheriff's Department and County Jail. Behind the thick glass of the public contact desk, Kathy Engesser, who was a civilian employee and usually worked dispatch, sat bent over the *St. Paul Pioneer Press*, working that day's *New York Times* crossword puzzle. With a pen. She looked up and smiled.

"Hey, handsome," she said into the microphone. She had dark blond hair with a few solidly gray streaks. She pushed back a tress that had fallen over one eye. "Long time, no see. Where you been hiding yourself?"

"Closing up Sam's Place today, Kathy."

"Already? Time does fly. What can we do for you?"

"Is the sheriff in?"

"She's here. Want to talk to her?"

"If she's free."

"Working on year-end budget stuff. Wouldn't take much to pull her off that, I'm guessing. I'll let her know you're here."

She lifted her phone and punched a button. Cork watched her lips move. She nodded, put the phone down, and bent to the microphone. "She says, and I quote, 'God yes, let him in.'" Kathy reached below the desk and buzzed Cork through the security door.

He found Sheriff Marsha Dross at her desk, awash in a sea of paperwork. She had her elbows propped on the desk and her head in her hands. She looked as miserable as Cork had ever been when he'd worn the badge that was now hers.

"We're broke," she said hopelessly.

Cork sat down on the other side of the desk and smiled at her across the chaos of documents. "You'll find a way. You always do."

"We're driving cruisers that desperately need replacement. Our radio equipment is from the eighteenth century. Because of all the overtime on the Klein case last spring and the search for John Harris, my personnel budget is a disaster. In two weeks, I'm going to have to go to the commissioners and tell them that if they want a police force in this county at Christmas, they've got to give me more money. Frankly, I'd rather shoot myself."

"They'll probably do it for you."

"If I'm lucky. Old Nickerson has never liked having a female sheriff." She finally smiled, wanly. "What's up?"

"In fact, it's John Harris."

Dross was in her early forties, a not unattractive woman who kept her brown hair cut short and her body in good shape. She'd been the first woman to wear a Tamarack County sheriff's deputy uniform, and it was Cork who'd brought her onto the force.

"You found him?" she asked with a tired smile.

"I've been hired to give it another shot."

"Hired by who?" Now she was serious.

"His grandchildren."

She nodded, as if it didn't surprise her. "They weren't happy when I pulled the plug on the search." She eyed him. "You weren't either."

"But I understood."

"What do they want you to do that we didn't do before?"

"Like I said, find him."

"Christ, we did everything but consult a Ouija board. You have some brilliant idea that escaped us?"

"Not yet. I'm going to begin by talking to Henry Meloux. Then I'm going back into the Boundary Waters, back to Raspberry Lake."

"This time of year? Good luck. Good chance you'll just get yourself snowed in."

"Me and Lindsay Harris both."

"His granddaughter's going with you? You're actually taking her?"

"She wants to go and she's footing the bill."

Dross seemed impressed. "Lot of pluck in that girl." She eyed him. "I understand her. But you? You don't think we did a good enough job in our search effort?"

"I think I owe it to her grandfather to give it one more shot. We were pretty good friends once."

"Long time ago."

"There's a statute of limitations on friendship?"

"When are you planning to put in?"

"Tomorrow morning. If he's still out there, the chances of finding him alive are pretty slim. But the longer we wait, the slimmer they get."

"Jenny's wedding is in less than two weeks, Cork. Aren't there responsibilities you're supposed to be seeing to?"

"We'll spend two, maybe three nights on Raspberry Lake. If I don't find anything, I'll call it."

"And if you do find something?"

"I'll cross that bridge when I come to it."

Dross sat back and ran a hand through her disheveled hair. "That whole thing still leaves a bad taste in my mouth. No worrisome medical history. No evidence of foul play. No reasonable suspect in a thousand miles who might have wanted him dead."

"Maybe his grandchildren, the only heirs to his fortune?"

"Dwight Kohler, their guide, supplied them with rock-solid alibis. And you know Dwight. That kid couldn't lie if his life depended on it. Besides, if they had anything to do with their grandfather's disappearance, why hire you to keep the search going? And if they want an inheritance, they'll have to wait a good long while before he's declared legally dead. So, yeah, I considered them, mostly because I had to, but I couldn't really see it. You?"

"I don't know them well enough, but in your shoes I'd probably be looking somewhere else, too."

"We considered kidnapping, of course, but there hasn't been a ransom demand, so where's the motive?" Dross shook her head. "Not a single goddamn lead. Not even a body. The man just disappeared into thin air."

"Maybe you really should have used that Ouija board."

"Not funny," she said. "Why are you here, Cork? What do you need from me?"

"Nothing. Just a courtesy call to let you know what's up."

"Do you actually think you can find him?"

His reply was a noncommittal shrug. "There's something else you should know. The brother, Trevor, claims to have had a vision. That's what's sparked all this."

"What kind of vision?"

"Hold on to your hat. Stephen came to him in a dream, spoke some blather from Shakespeare, then quoted Matthew: 'Seek and ye shall find.'"

"Your Stephen? Seriously? And you bought it?"

"There were some elements of the dream that were pretty compelling and not broadly known. Enough for me to take it seriously. Anyway, I've been hired. Just wanted you to know."

He stood and looked down at the work she had before her. "All things considered, I'd much rather be doing what I'm doing than what you've got on your plate."

"Tell me about it," she said. "Look, do me a favor. On your way out, have Azevedo give you one of our satellite phones. Then promise me you'll check in regular while you're out there."

"What are you worried about?"

"Let's not call it worry. Let's call it due diligence. And, hell, it'll make me feel better, okay?" As he turned to leave, she added, "Why Meloux? Why talk to Henry about this? He wasn't involved in any of it."

"Maybe not," Cork said. "But he's the nearest thing I have to a Ouija board."

CHAPTER 4

The O'Connor house had been built on Gooseberry Lane long before Cork was born. His grandparents had lived there, then his parents, and now it was his. He thought of it as his second heart. It contained several lifetimes of wonderful memories, was haunted by familiar ghosts, and held the firm promise of happiness yet to come. It was large, two-story, clapboard painted white with green shutters. A covered porch ran the length of the front, and the swing that hung there was a favorite nesting place for the O'Connor clan. Taking down that swing was always one of the last of Cork's preparations for winter. In his thinking, it nailed the coffin shut for the next five months on any hope of balmy weather. He hadn't taken the swing down yet.

He parked in the driveway beside his daughter's Forester. Then he stood for a while staring across the street at the house where John Harris had once lived. The O'Loughlins lived there now, had for years. It was a nice home, brick, a good place to raise a family. But Cork knew that John Harris had never been happy there.

He entered the house through the kitchen. The place smelled of freshly baked cookies, one of the best defenses against the gloom of the dismal season. He heard a child's laughter from the living room, hung his coat on a peg by the door, and went to see what was up, although he had a pretty good idea. He found his daughter, Jenny, playing with his grandson, Waaboo, who was four years old. The boy's real name was Aaron Smalldog O'Connor, but his nickname was Waaboozoons, an Ojibwe word that meant "little rabbit." Mostly, everybody called him Waaboo. He was half Anishinaabe and was Jenny's adopted and beloved son. They were playing soccer with a Nerf ball, the goals created with pillows from the sofa and the chairs.

Waaboo saw Cork enter and cried, "Baa-baa!" which was the name he'd called Cork ever since he could first speak but hadn't been able to pronounce "Grandpa." It had come out Baa-baa, and so it had remained, even though Waaboo could speak quite well now.

"Who's winning?" Cork asked. Though he was pretty sure of the answer. Waaboo was not a good loser, and right now he was beaming.

"Me," Waaboo said.

Jenny laughed. "I'm too old for this."

"You play with me, Baa-baa," Waaboo insisted.

"How about we take a milk and cookie break?" Cork suggested.

Which was an idea they all thought was grand. They sat at the kitchen table, and Waaboo chattered about the kids in his preschool class, and Cork listened with pleasure.

When Waaboo finished his milk and cookie, he said, "Can we play now?"

"Why don't you go practice while I talk to your mother?" Cork suggested.

"Okay. But you come soon." Waaboo got down off his booster chair and ran from the kitchen.

Jenny eyed her father and said, "What's up?"

"What do you mean?"

"You're stiff as a broom handle. I can see you're holding something inside, Dad. What is it?"

His daughter was twenty-seven, blond and tall. She was a writer, could call herself that legitimately because she'd sold the manuscript for a novel titled *Downwind of the Devil*. It was a fictionalized account of the true rescue of a young Ojibwe girl from the hands of sex traders. Both Jenny and Cork had been at the heart of that rescue. There was no publication date for the novel yet, but in those hours when Waaboo was away at preschool or when he'd gone to bed for the night, Jenny was hard at work on her next project.

Cork said, "I took on a couple of new clients this afternoon. John Harris's grandkids hired me to find him."

"You already looked for him pretty thoroughly, didn't you? You and just about everyone else in this county?"

"They want me to have another go."

"What do you think?"

"Probably be pissing in the wind, but it's their money."

"I know you didn't agree with the decision to pull the plug on the search. But is there something else now that's reason enough to go back out there?"

"Yeah," he said and filled her in on Trevor Harris's dream.

She took a small bite of what was left of her cookie and considered as she chewed. "I admit it seems compelling on the surface. But before he went into the desert, Stephen posted all about it on his Facebook page. Pretty much anybody interested could have seen it."

"Agreed. Do you remember him and his 'monthterth' under the bed?"

"Sure, that speech thing he had when he was kid. And, boy, was he always afraid of monsters."

"According to Trevor Harris, Stephen told him, and I quote 'There are monthterth under the bed.' What do you make of that?"

She sipped her milk. "It does get curiouser. You'd have to know us pretty well to know that. Still, they could have done their homework."

"To what end? They clearly want me to find their grandfather. And they're willing to pay me good money to try. If it's a manipulation, I can't see the dark twist to it. They just seem like grandchildren very concerned about their grandfather. And maybe I owe it to Johnny Do."

"Johnny Do?"

"That's what I called him when he lived across the street. He was a hardworking kid, had himself a little enterprise. He hired out to do anything, any odd job. Called his business Johnny Do-All. He tacked up business cards all over town. I just called him Johnny Do."

"You didn't talk much about any of this while you were searching for him."

"No reason to, really. He and his mother left Aurora a long time ago, after his father died. They moved to California, and I lost track of him."

In fact, until Harris disappeared, Cork hadn't known much about the life of Johnny Do after Aurora, except for the result, which had been wealth and world renown. The news accounts, in covering the search effort, had filled him in quite well.

Harris had married young, only a year after leaving Aurora, and had become a father almost immediately thereafter. Although it was never spelled out, it sounded like a shotgun wedding. He put himself through night school, supporting his family by working heavy construction during the day. He was an exceptional student and went on to the Stanford graduate School of Engineering on a full scholarship. As a geotechnical engineer, he'd joined the firm of Alwon and Gale, a large construction company based in San Francisco that specialized in big projects—roads, bridges, dams. Very early on, Harris had designed what had been considered an impossible road across one of the most rugged sections of the Andes. He'd gone on to specialize in creating the designs for projects others considered impossible—roads, dams, bridges in some of the most remote areas of the world. At age thirty, he'd founded Harris International, and his star had done nothing but rise. Although a great success in business, he had a difficult personal life. His projects kept him away from home for long periods of time, and when his daughter was ten, his wife had divorced him. He'd never remarried. By all accounts, his daughter had been a rather wild and reckless youth, married, like her father, in her teens, and a mother before she was twenty. She'd been killed in an auto accident, along with her equally wild and reckless husband, who'd been driving drunk. In his late forties, John Harris had become the guardian of two young grandchildren.

"What are you going to do?"

"Go back into the Boundary Waters, to Raspberry Lake, see what I can find."

Jenny looked a little disturbed. "When?"

"We leave tomorrow."

"We? You and Harris's grandkids?"

"Just his granddaughter."

"Dad, do I have to remind you that you're walking me down the aisle in two weeks?"

"I'll go in, stay a couple of days, then come out. I'll be back in time for the nuptials."

Her face was one huge scowl. "So you agreed to all of this just for the sake of good old Johnny Do, a man you haven't seen in, what, forty years?"

"He's the only family these two kids have, Jenny. Remember when your mother went missing, all the hell we went through not knowing what had happened to her? I imagine that's what these folks are feeling right now, don't you?" He saw her relax just a bit, relent. "I probably won't find anything that we didn't find before, but I have to try, and it has to be now. If I wait, the snow's bound to come, and it'll cover every trace that might still be out there." He pushed away from the table. "I'm heading to Crow Point. I want to talk to Henry."

"Why? He was involved in the search?"

"No, but he understands those woods better than any man I know. Maybe he can give me a clue to what I ought to be looking for, something we all might have missed."

"Back for dinner?"

"Yeah. I'll need to pack the gear for tomorrow. By the way, where's Rose?"

He was speaking of his sister-in-law, who'd come from Evanston, Illinois, to help with the wedding preparations. In the absence of Jenny's mother, Rose had often stepped in to fill the matriarchal shoes.

"Working out at Curves. She says she wants to look svelte for the wedding."

"But it's all about the bride, isn't it?"

"Oh, you are so male."

"Come on, Baa-baa," Waaboo cried from the other room.

"I'll explain to him," Jenny said. "You go do what you have to do."

Cork said, "I can spare fifteen minutes for my grandson." He stood to take care of the most pleasant business he'd seen to in that whole dismal day.

CHAPTER 5

Henry Meloux lived on a point of land well north of Aurora, at the very edge of the Iron Lake Reservation. To reach it, Cork parked his Expedition along a gravel county road, near a double-trunk birch that marked the beginning of a trail through a forest of mixed hardwood, spruce, and pine. He locked his vehicle, tugged on his gloves, turned up the collar of his leather jacket against a chill wind that had risen, and set off down the well-worn path. It was a hike of nearly two miles, one that, over the course of his life, Cork had taken more times than he could count or ever hope to remember.

The trees lining the path felt like dark walls that day, and the narrow strip of sky above was like a ribbon torn from some soiled and shabby fabric. Cork hunched his shoulders and walked, lost in brooding thought, oblivious to the beauty that, in a different mood, he might have appreciated. He was thinking now of his daughter's impending marriage, which he greatly approved of. He liked the man she'd chosen and who'd chosen her. He liked that Waaboo would have a father. What he didn't like was that they'd chosen to wed in November, a month that promised nothing but disappointment and, if he allowed himself to sink into melodrama, doom.

Had he said anything to Jenny about his concern? No. It wasn't his place. The wedding was theirs, and the date they set was a decision that belonged to them alone. But it was a thorn in all his thinking. Just one of many these days. And it seemed to him as if they'd all begun to fester at once. As he walked the path toward Crow Point, he felt the poison in every part of him.

"We have a visitor, Niece," the old man said. "Corcoran O'Connor."

Rainy Bisonette had been making bread at the table in her great-uncle's cabin. She looked up from her floured hands, out the window, across the dead grass of the meadow where the trail broke from the trees. She saw nothing but the emptiness of a land preparing for the long sleep of winter. November—*Gashkadino-Giizis*, which meant the Freezing Over Moon in the language of her people, who were called Anishinaabe or Ojibwe—was always a busy month for her and for Henry. Their cabins on Crow Point had no electricity or running water. The little structures were heated by cast-iron stoves and lit by propane lanterns. There were important preparations to complete before the deep snow of winter began its work of isolation. Cord after cord of cut and dried wood had been laid up. The roof of Henry's cabin, which had been constructed nearly a century earlier, had been repaired with new cedar shakes. The herbs that both the old man and Rainy would need for the medicines they prepared had been gathered and dried and stored. They were Mide, members of the Grand Medicine Society, traditional healers. Even in winter, even with snow as deep as a man's thigh and cold so bitter that it froze your eyeballs, the people who needed their skills would come to them.

This year the month of the Freezing Over Moon had special meaning. Daniel English, Rainy's nephew, and Jenny O'Connor, Cork's daughter, were to be married. The wedding was going to be held in the house on Gooseberry Lane. It would be a ceremony drawn from two traditions—Anishinaabe and Catholic. Father Ted Green from St. Agnes in Aurora would preside over the Catholic part; Henry was to handle the traditional Ojibwe elements. Rainy's spirits were running high. The prospect of the marriage excited her, and she was happy for Daniel and Jenny, two people she loved fiercely. She also happened to love Jenny's father pretty fiercely, too. And so, when Henry spoke his name, she watched for him happily out the window. But he didn't appear.

"I don't see him, Uncle," she said, though she knew that when the old man predicted a visitation of this kind he was seldom wrong. She'd asked him time and again how he knew this thing, but his only answer was "I listen to the spirits."

She had no doubt that he did.

Henry Meloux was a hundred years old, give or take a couple of years. His hair was long and as white as moonbeams. His face was as cracked as dried desert mud. His eyes were dark brown, but there was no hardness to them. They were eyes in which you could lose yourself and let go of all fear, eyes soft with understanding.

Henry was grinding herbs with a pestle in a clay bowl. Ember, an old Irish setter whose former owner Cork had helped put an end to, and whom Henry, out of pity, had adopted, lay at his feet, drowsing. Without looking up from his work, Henry said, "He is slow. He comes like a turtle in the mud, with no energy. Expect him to be no lover, Niece. This cabin is the only thing he will enter today."

"Uncle Henry!" she said.

The old man laughed and went on grinding.

She saw him then, just as her great-uncle had predicted, trudging out of the woods, crossing the meadow. He wasn't looking her way. His head was down, his eyes on the worn path. She could see from his whole aspect that he carried some crushing weight. And she thought that maybe Henry was wrong about one thing. Maybe she would take this burdened man to her bed, and in that ancient, carnal way, offer him some comfort.

She opened the door before he arrived, and before he could say a word, she kissed him.

"*Boozhoo*, love," she said in greeting and with such enthusiasm she hoped it would light a warming fire in him.

He smiled, but not with his heart, she could see. "Is Henry here?"

"Come into my home, Corcoran O'Connor," the old man spoke from inside. "You and whatever trouble you bring."

Cork stepped into the doorway. "What makes you think I've brought trouble, Henry?"

"You hold yourself stiff, like a wary deer. But come inside. I do not mind your trouble."

Cork did as the old man said, and Rainy closed the door. Ember struggled up and trotted to meet the visitor. Cork gave him a halfhearted patting, and the Irish setter went back to his place at Henry's feet.

"Would you like some coffee, Cork? It's a chilly day out there," Rainy said.

"No, thanks. I just need to talk."

"Not yet," the old man said. "Sage, Niece. We will smudge this troubled man and this place where he has brought his trouble."

Rainy took a sage bundle from the store in one of Henry's cupboards, dropped it into a shallow clay bowl, lit it with a match, and waved the cleansing smoke over Cork, Henry, herself, and around the cabin saying, "*Migwech, Nimishoomis.* Thank you, Grandfather. *Migwech, Nokomis.* Thank you, Grandmother, for the beauty of this day, for the life you have given us, and for the wisdom that comes when we listen to your voices on the wind and in the water and singing among the trees. We pray for guidance from the Creator and the spirits. Let our hearts be open to all you offer us."

When she'd finished, her great-uncle brought out one of his pipes and a pouch of tobacco. He filled the pipe, then offered tobacco to the spirits of the four directions. He put a match flame to the tobacco, and they sat together at his table and shared the pipe.

Only when they'd completed these preparations did Henry finally say, "And what is this trouble you bring, Corcoran O'Connor?"

Cork explained about the two clients he'd just taken on and about the vision Trevor Harris claimed to have experienced and about what he intended to do.

The old man nodded but said nothing.

Rainy said, "Jenny and Daniel's wedding is coming up fast, Cork."

"I'll be in and out, Rainy. I don't imagine I'll find anything at Raspberry Lake that wasn't found before."

"Then why go?"

"They need help."

"No, they need comfort, closure. If you find nothing, which is what you seem to be expecting, how does that help them?"

"I'm not convinced we won't find anything. The whole time we were out there, I had the feeling we were missing something. I still can't quite put my finger on it. There's no harm in giving it one more try."

"Is this really about them, Cork?"

He looked surprised. "I sort of think it is."

"Are you sure it's not more about you?"

"Well, I'm certainly a part of it." His voice was hard, which was unusual for this man she knew and loved.

"I'm only pointing out that if in the end you really can't offer them any comfort in this way, you're only delaying the inevitable."

"And the inevitable would be?"

"Acceptance. Opening their hearts to the pain and the grief. And then to the healing."

"They want to be sure. I can understand that."

"And if you don't find him, how will that help them to be sure?"

Meloux had been quiet, but now he spoke to Cork. "Your father found his father."

Rainy looked confused. "What have I missed?"

"Many years ago, the father of John Harris disappeared in much the same way that he has now. Liam O'Connor found him, Niece."

"I thought his father died in a boating accident," Rainy said. "That's what I read in the papers when Harris disappeared."

Cork shrugged. "There were things the papers missed, back then and now."

"So what really happened?"

"They discovered his empty boat run aground," Cork said.

"They searched the whole of Iron Lake but couldn't find him. Dad was sheriff then. He finally pulled the plug, but he didn't give up looking. A week or so later, he located the body. It was tangled in the anchor rope of Harris's boat in ten feet of water off Little Bear Island. He'd most probably killed himself, but that part never made it into the papers. Not then, not now."

"And you're going to find John Harris, just like your father found his father?"

"I can try."

"I thought they searched every inch of Raspberry Lake. Used divers, right?"

"Maybe his body's not in the lake. Maybe there is no body. Maybe he's still out there wandering around in those woods. Or maybe there's an explanation that will reveal itself to me."

It was clear his mind was made up, and she didn't want to argue, so she said, "What have you come for?"

Cork looked at the old man. "Henry's advice. And yours, Rainy. What do you think about Trevor Harris's vision?"

Henry said nothing and looked instead to Rainy.

She said, "Are you wondering if it's real? How can we say? Stephen's in the middle of the Arizona desert. Is it possible that his spirit communicated with Trevor Harris? Your son's remarkable in many ways, so maybe. Have you asked him?"

"He's incommunicado," Cork said. "No cell phone out there while he's seeking whatever he's seeking."

Nearly two years earlier, when Stephen was seventeen, a madman had put two bullets into him. One of them had damaged his spinal cord, and whether he'd ever walk again had been a serious concern. He'd spent a long time in rehabilitation, and the work of his therapists and his own determination had yielded great results. He did, indeed, walk. With crutches at first, then a cane, and finally with nothing except a very noticeable residual limp. He would never be an Olympic runner, he was fond of saying, but he'd never wanted to be one anyway. He was supposed to have entered college in September, but he'd put that on hold, and instead had decided on a kind of pilgrimage, a solitary sojourn in the emptiness of the Arizona desert.

"He isn't seeking, Cork. Nothing has been lost to him. He's just trying to open himself to what's always been inside him. His own strength, his own knowledge."

"Okay, so let's leave Stephen out of the equation. What if Harris's vision is real, how should it be interpreted?"

"That's up to the dreamer, Cork."

"The dream seems pretty clear to me."

"Seems, yes."

"You sound skeptical."

"Does it really matter what I think or Uncle Henry? You've already decided to go. So what is it you really want?"

He looked from her to the old man. "I want to know what we missed. I want to know what I'm looking for. How can a man just disappear and leave no trace, not even his scent for a dog to find?"

"Why do you ask me, Corcoran O'Connor?" Henry said. "I was not a part of your search for this man."

"You understand more about hunting in those woods than anyone I know."

The old man lapsed again into silence, and the whole of that tiny cabin seemed consumed by it. Rainy could feel, just as Henry had said, the wariness in Cork and could plainly see how rigidly he held himself. She wanted very much to be able to offer him something that would help.

"Do not look for an answer out there, Corcoran O'Connor," her great-uncle finally said. "Let the answer find you."

"How do I do that, Henry?" His voice was harsh, urgent. "Are you suggesting I just go out there and sit?"

"Not sit. Sift. Sift all that comes to you. The answer is what is left in your hands after everything else has slipped through your fingers."

"That's it, Henry? That's all you've got?"

"As my niece has said, finding is never about seeking. It is about opening yourself to what is already there."

Cork stood and pulled on his jacket. "*Migwech*," he said. Thank you. But Rainy could tell from his tone that he didn't mean it.

"Don't leave so soon, Cork," she said.

"I've got a lot to do to get ready for tomorrow."

Rainy drew on her own coat and said, "Let me walk with you a bit, then."

Outside, under the gray canopy of the sky, they walked together, past Rainy's small cabin and onto the path through the stiff, browned meadow grass and the dry stalks of dead wildflowers. Dead only to the eye, Rainy knew. They would rise again in the spring. She took Cork's arm and could feel his resistance.

"What's going on, Cork? Why are you so hard, so impatient? It's not like you."

"I love him dearly, Rainy, but sometimes he frustrates the hell out of me. Why does he have to speak in riddles? Why can't he ever just give me a straight answer?"

"This isn't about Henry."

He was quiet a long time, and she let him be with his thoughts.

"November," he finally said.

She knew his history with that month, knew that for him the darkness of *Gashkadino-Giizis* wasn't about the clouds or the cold or even the bitter winter that would follow.

"Ghosts," she said. "You need to let them go."

"They come to me. I don't go looking."

She stopped suddenly and turned to him. "Let me or Uncle Henry do a sweat with you before you go. It would be so good for you, and I'd feel better."

"Like I told Henry, a lot to do to get ready for tomorrow."

"Then go and get ready, but come back."

He looked away from her, his eyes taking in the low, ragged clouds. "When this is done," he said and walked away toward the line of trees where the path disappeared.

Though it tore her heart, she let him go.

CHAPTER 6

In the dark of early morning, he left his bed and dressed. Downstairs he found a light on in the kitchen, coffee dripping into the pot, his sister-in-law, Rose, at the stove. She wore a red robe and white slippers and was scrambling eggs.

"Bread's toasting," she said.

Long ago, she'd been a part of the O'Connor household, helping to care for her sister's children and contemplating a life as a nun when that responsibility was finished. But she'd met a man, Mal Thorne, a priest who'd lost his way. As they both were fond of saying, God gave them a new life together. She wasn't a classic beauty, but Cork thought her beautiful in many ways. Not the least of which was that generosity of spirit which had always been at the heart of who she was. When her sister, Jo O'Connor, was killed, she'd stepped in and had often filled the maternal shoes. Now, with Jenny's wedding so near, she'd come from her home in Evanston, mostly to help cover Waaboo while Jenny directed her energies toward the nuptials. Her husband, Mal, who ran a shelter for the homeless in Chicago, was planning to arrive just in time for the wedding.

"You didn't have to do this, Rose," Cork said.

"Were you going to eat before you left?" she asked without turning from the stove.

"Figured I'd grab coffee and a breakfast sandwich from the Gas 'N Go."

"You really want heartburn out there in the Boundary Waters? Pour yourself a cup of coffee, get a plate and silverware, and sit down. The eggs are almost ready."

He did as she'd instructed.

"Two days," she said. "Right?"

"Two days, maybe three."

"Unless you find something."

"Unless I find something."

Rose began transferring the eggs to a serving bowl. "So you'll be back in plenty of time for the wedding."

"Absolutely."

"Good."

She set the steaming eggs on the table. She'd mixed in onion, peppers, mushrooms, and cheddar cheese. The toast popped up. She pulled out the pieces and set them on his plate, then poured coffee for herself and sat down. She hadn't brushed her hair yet. and in places it sprang out from her head in rust-colored splashes.

"I looked at the ten-day forecast. Snow possible by Thursday."

"They're predicting only flurries."

"I'll offer up a few prayers in that direction."

Jenny came into the kitchen, looking sleepy. She'd thrown on a robe over her pajamas, but her feet were bare.

"You didn't have to get up," Cork said.

"Smelled the coffee."

She yawned, poured herself a cup, and joined them at the table. They sat together in the bright light of the O'Connor kitchen. Beyond the windows, the world was still nothing but darkness.

"I don't know what to hope for," Jenny said. "If you find something, I suppose that would be a good thing. But it'll keep you out there longer."

"There's no way I'm going to miss the wedding," Cork said. "I promise."

"And you're nothing if not a man who keeps his promises."

Cork heard her biting tone. "Suppose it was me out there and you really believed there was a chance I was still alive," he said. "Wouldn't you want someone looking?"

"I suppose," she admitted.

He finished his meal, took his plate and silverware, and set them in the dishwasher.

"Time?" Jenny said.

"Time," he replied.

He took his leather jacket from where it hung on a peg next to the door. Jenny stood up and gave her father a hug.

"Come back as soon as you can, Dad. And be safe."

"Give that grandson of mine a hug for me. Tell him I'll be back soon."

"I'll do that."

Rose took him in her arms. Into his ear, she whispered, "Godspeed."

Lindsay Harris was waiting for him in front of the Four Seasons, the best hotel in town. It overlooked the marina and Iron Lake, a view totally unimpressive in the dark at six o'clock on an overcast November morning. As he'd instructed her, she had a full pack with a sleeping bag rolled and secured atop it. He took her gear and hefted it into the back of his Expedition.

"Your brother not bothering to see you off?" Cork asked.

"He's a late sleeper. And a little bit of a monster if you wake him too early."

She wore a sweater under a quilted vest, long pants, Timberland boots, and an odd stocking cap, red and white striped, straight out of *Where's Waldo?*

"That stocking cap is something else," he said.

She gave a little shrug. "A gift from my grandfather. Goofy, I know, but well, you understand."

"Did you eat?"

"I arranged with the hotel for an early meal. Pretty hearty."

"All right, then."

Cork got in behind the wheel. Lindsay took the passenger side. He drove away from the lights of the hotel, down Oak Street, which was empty except for his Expedition. They were out of town in five minutes, rolling southeast along the shoreline of the lake.

"I don't think I slept a wink last night," Lindsay said.

"Worried?"

"Troubled, I'd say."

"By what?"

"Thinking this will be nothing but a wild-goose chase."

"Then why go?"

"Trevor's dream. It sounds crazy, I know, but it's got to mean something. Right? I mean it was so specific. Stephen O'Connor. Did you talk to him about it?"

"Stephen's in Arizona, somewhere on Navaho land, hiking in the desert. No way to reach him."

"Just like in Trevor's dream." She sounded amazed and re-lieved. "I was ready to give up, and then that dream. I didn't know if you'd believe us. But then you're Indian, right? And Indians know about visions."

"My grandmother was true-blood Iron Lake Anishinaabe. But there's a lot of stubborn Irish in my heritage, too, and I've never had a vision, so I'm more than a little skeptical." Cork slowed in an area he knew to be a favorite crossing for deer. "I'll tell you up front that I don't think we'll find anything. So many of us went over the area so thoroughly."

"But what about Trevor's dream? And that feeling you said you had that something wasn't right?"

"Maybe that's what the dream means. Maybe not. We've got a couple days to find out."

They drove for an hour and a half, most of it on a gravel road that skirted the Iron Lake Reservation and took them north. A rat-gray light slowly suffused the sky and the thick ceiling of clouds. The Northwoods, dark and damp and forbidding, gradually emerged around them. Cork pulled into the parking area for their entry into the Boundary Waters. It was no surprise to him that his Expedition was the sole vehicle there. The Boundary Waters Canoe Area Wilderness was a vast tract, more than a million acres of unbroken forest, pristine lakes, fast rivers, and no human settle-ment. On the other side of the Canadian border was the Quetico Provincial Park, another million acres of the same wilderness.

People sometimes got lost out there. In summer, they had a decent chance of surviving until they were found. November and beyond, the odds became daunting.

They unloaded their packs and provisions, then Lindsay helped Cork slide the canoe from where it had been secured atop the Expedition. They carried it together down a short path to a small lake and set it in the water. They returned to the parking area, grabbed the paddles and the rest of their things, and loaded the canoe. Cork directed her to the bow. He took the stern and shoved them off.

It was a cold morning, but not bitterly so. The overcast moderated the temperature. The air was still, the water a perfect mirror of the gray sky. The lake was long and narrow, with a wall of dark rock running along the far side. In summer, the lake would have been home to loons and ducks and Canada geese, but all those birds had wisely fled long ago. The lake was silent now, except for the dip and swirl and occasional splash of their paddles.

Lindsay Harris was in good shape and knew her way around a canoe. In the stern, Cork guided them toward the first portage. There would be several more lakes and portages before they reached Raspberry. He tried to look ahead, wondering what they might find when they arrived, what they might see this time that had been missed before, and wondering deeply about the true meaning of the dream that was bringing them back to that place.

Rainy Bisonette woke with a start. She lay on her bed in her little cabin, beneath her blankets, shaken by a fear so sudden and deep that it had startled her from sleep. She stared up into a dark that showed no hint of morning yet. Her first thought was of Cork. She would have loved nothing more than to have him with her in that bed, each of them warmed by the nearness of the other. It was often that way. Cork was a regular visitor to Crow Point. He used to come mostly to see Henry, but now when he made that long hike in, it was more often for her.

His visit the day before had been troubling in so many ways.

She'd seen him recently growing more and more taciturn, staring into the fires she or Henry built on Crow Point in the sacred ring, gone someplace he wouldn't allow her or anyone else to follow. Some of it, she suspected, was the season. Late fall. The approach of November. She knew about his terrible history with that month. But there was more to it, something that gnawed at his spirit, that little by little, over a long time, had eaten away a part of his heart. She'd tried to probe him gently, but he pretended that he had no idea what she was talking about. She and Jenny—and Rose, too, now that she'd come to help with the wedding—had discussed the darkness they all saw in him lately. She'd asked her great-uncle for his advice. Henry, as usual, had offered her only a riddle.

"When he is gone, he is in a place he must go alone. There is a battle coming, Niece. He prepares himself."

"A battle, Uncle Henry? Who with? Why hasn't he said anything?"

"Because he does not realize it yet."

"Have you warned him?"

"I do not know when this battle will come. I only know that I see him preparing. No one can help him until he sees this himself."

"If I sweated and asked the spirits, would they tell me?"

"Only the spirits can answer that."

And so she'd wrung the sweat from her body in great rivers, asked for answers, prayed for guidance, but the spirits had remained silent.

In the end, there was nothing for her but to wait.

As she lay awake in the dark of that morning, afraid for the man she loved, she whispered her desperate prayer:

"Creator, in this battle he's preparing for, give him strength and courage and wisdom. And when this battle is over, Creator, bring him back to me. Bring him back whole in heart, in mind, in body, and in spirit."

And because she'd been raised Episcopalian on her home reservation in Wisconsin, she added something from her Christian tradition as well. She said, "Amen."

CHAPTER 7

The mist descended, a wet, gray curtain that blotted out the distant landscape. Shorelines loomed dark and vague, and if Cork hadn't had such a good sense of the country, he might have been easily lost. But he'd been this way many times, both before John Harris disappeared and during the weeks of searching afterward.

They put on their rain gear and ate lunch on an island in Bear Lake at one of the official Boundary Waters campsites Cork knew well. He recalled a summer day on the island when his children were young and Jo was alive. Stephen—Stevie, in those days—had caught his first walleye. The photo of him holding it proudly, like a whale in his little hands, hung on the wall in Sam's Place.

Cork tried the satellite phone Deputy Azevedo had given him, per the sheriff's request. It wasn't really necessary. They didn't expect him to check in until that evening. Mostly, he wanted to make sure the unit was functioning correctly. It wasn't.

"No signal?" Lindsay Harris asked.

Cork shook his head. "The clouds maybe. Maybe this particular location. Sat phones can be tricky. I'll try again tonight. You doing okay?"

"Fine," she said.

"You're good with a canoe."

"After my parents died, I pretty much grew up in a boarding school in the Twin Cities. But summers in high school, I worked at a YMCA camp at the edge of the Boundary Waters, a place called

Widjiwagan. My grandfather came to visit me there one of those summers. That's always been a special memory for me."

"When I knew your grandfather, he was too busy to enjoy the Boundary Waters," Cork said. "He was a lot older than me, but he kind of took me under his wing. Called me Corky. I called him Johnny Do. When I was ten, I helped him rebuild a vintage 1934 Packard Eight. Sweetest car you ever saw."

"I never heard him talk about his childhood, his life here in Aurora."

Cork knew there was good reason for that.

The trouble had happened the summer Cork was twelve. John Harris had just graduated from high school. Harris's father was an attorney. Cork remembered him as a gruff man who seldom smiled and always seemed to smell of whiskey. There was some kind of business trouble, serious questioning of how the man had handled his clients' monies. Suits were pending, and maybe criminal charges as well. Cork recalled how quiet Johnny Do was in that time. Then one day Mr. Harris went out fishing and never came back. His boat was found nudged against the shoreline of Iron Lake, empty, the electric trawling motor still running, an open bottle of Jim Beam among the gear. Also, the boat's anchor was missing. The search had been exhaustive, but Iron Lake was large and Cork's father had finally called an end to the effort. Rumors floated. Because the man had recently increased his life insurance policy substantially, there was a good deal of speculation about suicide. But the suicide provision would have made that policy useless. Mrs. Harris and Johnny Do kept to themselves, talking to no one. Then a couple of weeks later, Cork's father located the body. Publicly, he said it was dumb luck. But Cork had overheard his father explain to his mother how he'd gone about it.

His father, like everyone else, believed the man had killed himself. And he thought if that was the case, and he were Harris and concerned about the well-being of his family, he'd try to hide the fact of the suicide. Which meant doing the deed somewhere out of sight. The trawling motor had been fixed with rope so that it would travel in a straight line. Cork's father simply followed that line across Iron Lake, island to island, and finally found the body in ten feet of crystal-clear water off Bear Island. Publicly, he said he'd discovered the body tangled in the anchor line, clearly an accident, probably as a result of judgment badly impaired by the Jim Beam. The coroner, who at that time was also the town's mortician, ruled the death accidental drowning. The widow, Mrs. Harris, was paid the life insurance. Shortly thereafter, she and her son left Aurora, and Cork had not seen Johnny Do since.

When John Harris had first gone missing, suicide had, of course, been one of the speculations. But there'd been no evidence of any personal or business difficulties or any history of suicidal ideation. His grandchildren claimed to have seen no indication of any mental distress when they'd gone into the Boundary Waters. So pretty much that possibility had gone to the bottom of the list. Apparently Harris had never seen any reason to talk to his grandchildren about his father's death, so Cork decided that, at the moment, there was no reason for him to go into it either.

"It was a long time ago, and why would he talk about Aurora anyway?" Cork said. "A small memory in a life that's been full of large accomplishment." Cork took a big bite of a Saltine heaped with tuna fish and cheese and spoke while he chewed. "When I heard he was back in Aurora, I hoped we might connect. But he went straight out into the Boundary Waters with you and Trevor, and, then, well . . ." He didn't say what was obvious. "What about your brother?"

"What about him?"

"He doesn't seem much interested in roughing it."

"Never his thing. He was always into more self-indulgent pursuits." There was a bitter edge to her words.

"And you? What are you into?"

"Tree hugging." She smiled. "I graduated from Northland College with a specialty in environmental humanities. I'm doing graduate work at McGill in Canada."

"You're in pretty good shape for an academic."

"I hike a lot, camp out, canoe. Some of it for pleasure, some because of my studies. It all helps to keep me healthy."

"Then you know you should drink a lot of water out here. You may not feel like it now, but you can easily dehydrate."

"You sound like my grandfather."

"Sorry. Didn't mean to."

"That's okay." She took his advice and drank deeply from her water bottle. She looked up into the gray mist that fell. "We were supposed to be here the first week of September. My favorite time in the Boundary Waters."

"Mine, too," Cork said. "No people, no bugs, and the color's gorgeous. What happened?"

"Grandpa John had to cancel. Dam business. His great African project." She said it without trying to hide her sarcasm. "There's always been some project more important than me and Trevor. In a stupid way, I hoped our time together out here might change that."

For a few moments, she sat in the gray quiet, her eyes taking in that dismal scene.

"The truth is that I don't really have family. My grandmother was an alcoholic, drank herself to death before I was old enough to really know her. Both my parents were alcoholics. Killed themselves driving drunk."

"As I understand it, there can be a genetic component to addiction."

"Trevor got that gene. He struggles." She capped her water bottle, slipped it into her pack. "We're not really close, my brother and I, not like siblings should be. And Grandpa John's always been distant. So this"—and she opened her arms to everything around her—"this is home to me. This is family. Better than family. It never makes irrational demands. Never disappoints. It can be harsh, but never cruel. If you know how to accept it, even when it's the most challenging, it's still so awesome, so beautiful, so generous. You know?"

Cork understood. And he thought that if John Harris hadn't

vanished, who knew what gift the wilderness might have given them all?

When they broke from the portage that led to Raspberry Lake, they couldn't see anything of the far shore or of the big island that normally would have dominated the scene. The water, flat and hard-looking as burnished steel, disappeared into the mist that was both a very light drizzle and fog. They set the canoe on the lake, reloaded the gear, and Cork shoved them off.

"It feels forbidding," Lindsay said.

"The mist?"

"The whole place. This is where he disappeared. Just vanished. I saw a tabloid headline that said aliens abducted him, another that said only an alien could have designed the projects he's built and he disappeared because he's gone back to his home planet. Stupid bullshit."

Cork had heard of folks who claimed to have seen UFOs hovering above the Boundary Waters. There were photographs of fuzzy, dark objects. He'd seen a lot of inexplicable things in the wilderness, but nothing like that. Long ago, when Cork was very young, Henry Meloux had offered him this sage observation: *There are more things in these woods than a man can see with his eyes. More things than he can ever hope to understand.* Things of this earth, Cork thought, or of the spirit world, maybe. But not from outer space. Whatever had happened to John Harris, it had nothing to do with extraterrestrials.

As if reading his thoughts, Lindsay said, "But if it wasn't aliens, where did he go?"

She wasn't really asking him. It was a question directed more to that dismal curtain hiding everything around them.

Cork led them unerringly to the site where Harris, his grandchildren, and Dwight Kohler, their guide, had set up camp when the man vanished. They unloaded their gear, erected their tents, and stowed their packs inside, except for the bear bag with the food in it. Cork walked a few yards away from the campsite and tied the bag to the trunk of a fallen pine.

"Shouldn't you hang that?" Lindsay asked.

"Ursack bear bag," Cork said. "It's got a liner that seals in the smells. It's tough, too. A bear could play soccer with it for hours and not get at the food inside. But I doubt bears will be a problem. Most of them have probably already found somewhere to hibernate."

"What now?" Lindsay asked, looking toward the lake.

"With the clouds and the mist, dark'll come early. We'll be lucky if we have a couple of hours of light. Best get started."

Cork headed toward the canoe, which they'd tipped on the shoreline. They each grabbed an end and settled the craft back on the water. Once again, Lindsay took the bow and Cork the stern, and they shoved off.

"Where to first?" Lindsay asked over her shoulder.

"West. That's where he went when he disappeared."

He guided them in that direction. It wasn't long before a great dark shape loomed to their left, behind the dim curtain.

As they passed, Lindsay said, "Shouldn't we check the island?"

"Tomorrow," Cork replied. "We'll have to do some climbing. I'd rather wait for more light and maybe a little drier conditions. Those rocks can be treacherous when they're wet."

They swung around to the north end of the horseshoe-shaped lake. Cork lifted his paddle from the water and laid it across the gunwales. When she realized what he'd done, Lindsay followed his lead. They drifted silently until their momentum dissipated, then they sat dead in the water.

Lindsay said, "This is where we found his canoe."

"Yes."

"Is there a reason we're just sitting here?"

"I'm waiting for something to come to me," Cork said.

"You mean like an inspiration?"

"A man I know and trust told me not to look for an answer here. His advice was to let the answer come to me."

She held to silence for a few minutes, then said, with a clear note of impatience, "So, we just sit here?"

"A lot of eyes went over this lake already, every inch of it. We had divers in the water, cadaver dogs on the shore. We brought in the Border Patrol, some of the best trackers you'll find anywhere. I'm thinking there may be a better way to find what we're looking for."

She said, "So you're what? Listening?"

"Sensing is more like it. The Ojibwe believe that everything is invested with spirit. This lake has spirit, and spirit is awareness. Spirit remembers. If something happened to your grandfather here, the spirit knows."

"And will the spirit here speak to you?"

He thought she was suppressing a smile, and he understood. "I guess we'll find out."

After a while, he said, "Do you smell it?"

"What?"

"Orange."

"The fruit?"

"Yes."

She lifted her nose high into the air. "I get nothing."

"Orange," Cork said, mostly to himself and in a puzzled way.

"I don't know that I believe in spirits," the young woman said. "But what I do believe is that in the absence of sufficient stimulation, the senses can fool themselves."

"Hallucinations?"

"Mirages, that kind of thing."

"Like oranges in the middle of the wilderness?" Cork laughed quietly. "Maybe you're right. Let's go."

They paddled until they reached a place where the lake fed out in a little stream. The stream meandered through a boggy area full of tamaracks. When the search for John Harris had first begun, the needles had been bright yellow, and every tamarack was like a flaming torch. Now the needles had been shed and the trees had become skeletal.

"They searched that bog," Lindsay said.

"A man can disappear in a bog and never be found."

"And searchers, if they're not careful, can disappear there, too. You're not planning to go in, are you?"

"No. And I don't think your grandfather went in either. At least not of his own accord."

"What does that mean exactly?"

"That from everything I know about him, he was a pretty savvy guy. And savvy guys don't go strolling in dangerous bogs."

"Unless?"

"That's what I'm trying to figure out."

She turned and looked at him. "You have a mind like my grandfather."

"Meaning?"

"He looks at a situation from all the usual angles, then he steps back and considers the unusual. It's part of what's made him so successful, I think."

The mist and fog had turned everything around them the color of ash from a fire. Cork said, "We should be getting back to camp. It'll be dark soon. We'll go over this whole lake tomorrow."

"Sensing?"

"Until I have a better idea."

They swung the canoe around and headed back the way they'd come. When they passed the island, Lindsay paused in her paddling and studied the great gray shape.

"Makes me think of some kind of prehistoric place where monsters lurk, like in *King Kong*," she said.

"No monsters there," Cork assured her. Then added, "Or monthterth either."

CHAPTER 8

Rose Thorne stood at the kitchen counter, at work on the roasted potatoes that would go with the meat loaf she already had in the oven. From the living room came the sound of Waaboo and his mother reading a story together. Waaboo loved to read and be read to. Currently, he was into a Junie B. Jones. Before that, it had been trains. And before that, monsters, thanks to Maurice Sendak. He'd passed out of that phase, but Rose supposed he would come back to even scarier things at some point, ghosts and werewolves and the other creatures that went bump in the night. Maybe boys were especially prone to that. She remembered Stephen going through a period when he was about Waaboo's age during which he clamored for a scary story every night. They'd given him nightmares. Or that's what she'd thought then. Later, she thought the nightmares, at least some of them, had come from a different place.

The telephone rang, and she called, "I'll get it."

As if she'd conjured him with her thinking, it was Stephen on the other end of the line.

"Aunt Rose!" His voice was scratchy, as if he were speaking to her from the moon.

"Stephen! Where are you?"

"Chinle, Arizona. The nearest place I could get a phone signal."

"Are you all right?"

"I'm fine, Aunt Rose. How are things there?"

"We're all good."

"You're sure? Everyone's okay?"

"Stephen, what's this all about?"

"Look, Aunt Rose, I've had this feeling I can't shake that something's wrong. It's really become oppressive. I came to the desert to unburden and suddenly all I'm feeling is this big weight. Is Dad there?"

"No, Stephen, he's not. He's in the Boundary Waters. We think he'll be back by Tuesday."

"The Boundary Waters? What's he doing out there?"

"Looking for John W. Harris."

"The search is still going on?"

"The official search ended a few days ago. His family hired your father to go back in and take another look."

Stephen's end of the line fell silent.

"Are you still there?" Rose asked.

"When did he go in?"

"This morning."

"Has anyone heard from him?"

"He's got a satellite phone, and he's supposed to be checking in with the sheriff."

"Has he checked in?"

"I don't know."

"Could you find out, Aunt Rose?"

"I'll try."

"Then call me back. I'll be waiting."

"Who was it?" Jenny stood in the doorway, a book in her hand.

"Your brother."

"What did he want?"

"He's had one of his feelings."

Jenny said, "That's never good."

"He wants us to find out if Cork's checked in on the satellite phone. You mind making that call?"

"If you'll take over Junie B. Jones."

They read together, Waaboo helping sometimes, Rose doing most of the heavy lifting. She kept an ear to the kitchen, where she could hear some of Jenny's end of the conversation. Five minutes later, Jenny came back out.

"Hey, little guy," she said to Waaboo. "I think it's Lego time."

"We haven't finished reading," he protested.

"Go get your Lego box and bring it down here. We'll build a pirate ship together, okay? But I need to talk to your aunt Rose first."

The pirate ship, one of his favorite constructions, won him over. He jumped from the sofa and hit the stairs at a run.

"What is it?" Rose asked.

"They haven't heard a thing from Dad at the sheriff's office, but they aren't expecting him to check in until this evening. They went ahead and tried to raise him. Nothing. They said the cloud cover's heavy and that can interfere. They said not to worry."

"You should call Stephen."

"I already did. I told him about the vision Trevor Harris had. I thought maybe that might explain the heaviness he's feeling. He's pretty freaked out. He's heading to Phoenix, and he'll catch the first flight home."

"Seems a little extreme, doesn't it?"

"If we hear from Dad tonight, we'll let him know. But, Aunt Rose, don't forget that before he was shot, Stephen had a vision of the man who would do it. If this dark feeling has him worried, I don't care what the people at the sheriff's office say. I'm worried, too."

Although her great-uncle thought it odd and unnecessary, Rainy kept her cell phone with her at all times. She charged it with a small, portable generator that Cork had given her on her last birthday. Cell phone service on Crow Point could still be a bit spotty, but more often than not, the phone kept her in touch with a world that was usually on the far side of Iron Lake, beyond the wall of the great Northwoods.

She was in Henry's cabin, preparing a stew for dinner that included wild rice, carrots, potatoes, and leeks she'd harvested from the garden she'd planted near her cabin. She'd thrown in some walleye she'd smoked earlier in the fall. Henry was sleeping on the straw-and-wild-grass-filled mattress of his little bed, snoring loud enough to scare off a bear. Ember lay curled beneath the cabin's small table, not sleeping but looking comfortably idle. It was dark beyond the cabin windows, the overcast and drizzle having brought night even earlier in that season of early dark.

She was thinking of Cork, always thinking of Cork these days. Love was a troublesome emotion. She'd been married once and had been in love at the beginning of that disaster. Then she'd watched a good man go down a destructive road. For far too long, she'd stayed by his side. Before they'd all been destroyed, she'd left with her children, but they'd already been terribly wounded. The healing was still going on. Her daughter, Kari Chantelle, had followed her mother into the field of public health and worked as a nurse in an Inuit community in Alaska. Rainy seldom saw her more than once a year, though they texted and talked often. Her son, Peter, battled addictions. He'd been through treatment three times. The last time had been at a clinic in Arizona, and Rainy had left Tamarack County to do what she could to help. In the time she'd been gone, there'd been more than a physical distance between her and Cork, and she'd been afraid that she'd lost him. Somehow they'd held on, held together, and her time with him now she counted among her most blessed days.

Still, the scars from her early marriage sometimes ached, reminding her that the hardest blows came only when you let love lull you into dropping your guard.

Her cell phone rang, a soft chime she used so as not to disturb Henry. She wiped her hands on her jeans, reached into her pocket, and saw it was Jenny calling. She hoped it was to talk about the wedding, but the moment she heard the young woman's voice, she let go of that hope.

"What is it, Jenny?"

"Have you heard from my dad?"

"No. He's in the Boundary Waters. No cell phone service."

"He took a satellite phone, and he was supposed to check in with the sheriff's office. They haven't heard from him. I thought he might have called you."

"He hasn't."

Rainy listened as Jenny explained about her conversation with Stephen.

"One of those dark premonitions of his," Jenny said. "You know how that goes."

"Yes."

"Do you think Henry might have some idea about Stephen's darkness? I mean, would it help if I came out and talked to him?"

"I'm sure Uncle Henry would be willing to talk to you, but I don't know how that will happen tonight. It's too late to be traveling out here now."

"I know the way well," Jenny said. "And I wouldn't mind getting a little, you know, comforting advice."

"It's different here coming at night, particularly in this weather. I think it's best to wait until morning."

It wasn't audible, but Rainy could feel Jenny's deep sigh of regretful acceptance on the other end.

"You're right. And I suppose it's nothing. I just . . ."

"I know," Rainy said. "Tomorrow morning, first light, be here."

She put the phone back into her pocket.

"Much can happen in one night."

She turned and found her great-uncle sitting up on his bunk.

"It was Jenny O'Connor."

"A concerned Jennifer O'Connor," the old man said. "Concerned about her father?"

He rose and Rainy heard the crack of his old bones. He took a moment to straighten himself fully. Then he smiled, and in that moment, he was ageless.

"No one's heard from Cork. And Stephen called. He's sensed something bad. You know Stephen."

Henry gave a nod, then walked to the pot where the stew simmered, leaned into the rising vapor, and took a deep breath.

"You have many things to learn about healing, Niece, but cooking I think you have mastered. When do we eat?"

She knew him well and knew not to press the issue of this disturbing feeling that had descended on Stephen and what it might mean for Cork. She dished the stew and they ate, and then the old man said, "Let us build a fire."

The drizzle that had fallen most of the day had ended, but the sky was still overcast. The clouds blocked any light that might have come from the moon or stars, and Crow Point lay in a darkness so profound that Rainy couldn't see her feet or the ground on which she set them. She brought a flashlight, which she could have used to illuminate their way, but her great-uncle had traveled every inch of Crow Point for almost a hundred years and his own feet knew the way unerringly. He led and she followed and Ember came after them both. The path the old man took cut through a small rock upthrust to a stone ring surrounded with hewn log sections as seating. In the blackness beyond, invisible at the moment, lay Iron Lake.

Her great-uncle stopped and she stood beside him and felt the soft brush of Ember's warm, old body against her leg.

"Crack this darkness a little, Niece," he said.

She turned on the flashlight and the beam lit the scene with a harsh light that felt like a violation and was, in its way. A supply of firewood had been laid up against the rocks and covered with a canvas tarp. Under the tarp, too, was a box full of dry kindling. In ten minutes, Rainy had a good blaze going inside the fire ring.

The old Mide stood in the dancing light and offered tobacco to the spirits of the four directions. He and Rainy smoked tobacco from the pipe he'd brought, and they sat together a long time in silence.

"Stephen O'Connor listens," he finally said. "The heart knows much that the head ignores. If we pay attention, our hearts speak to us. Stephen O'Connor has always listened. His father not so much."

Rainy knew what he meant. Though she loved Cork, Rainy understood that he was often blind to his own feelings, sometimes purposely so. He thought of himself as *ogichidaa*, which was an Ojibwe word that meant "one who stands between evil and his people." It was hard and sometimes required his heart to be like stone. He carried scars all over his body and she knew his spirit was scarred, too. Sometimes when she held him at night in her bed, she could feel his pain so acutely it made her want to cry.

"Does this feeling Stephen has mean something's wrong with Cork?"

"Only Stephen O'Connor knows the true meaning of what his heart has said."

"I'm afraid, Uncle Henry."

"That is what it is to be human, Niece."

"And to love," she said.

The old man nodded. "Sometimes."

CHAPTER 9

In black night, Cork woke to the call of nature. He was warm in his sleeping bag, but it was icy cold in the tent, and he lay there awhile, working up the will to go out to relieve himself.

He hadn't built a fire that evening. With the drizzle, the available wood was wet, and although he could have stripped away the damp bark, doing so was more trouble than he wanted. Their rain gear kept them dry and the wool layers kept them warm. By the light of Cork's old Coleman lantern, they'd eaten a meal of freeze-dried chili that he'd prepared on his one-burner camp stove. He'd made coffee for them, too, which probably accounted for him being awake in the dead of night.

Cork had tried to check in with the sheriff's office on the sat phone, but once again could not get a signal. He knew it might be worrisome to Marsha Dross, but there was nothing he could do about it.

After that, over the coffee, Lindsay Harris had told him a bit more about herself and her grandfather.

"After my folks were killed in the car crash, he tried to do his best. At first, he took us with him when he went to build his dams. But he was mostly gone and we were taken care of by paid housekeepers or sometimes a nanny, and our schooling was sometimes an iffy proposition. Trevor was a handful, always in some kind of trouble. And there were the women. We definitely put a crimp in Grandpa John's love life." She'd sipped from her cup. "This is good."

"Cowboy coffee," Cork had told her.

"Eventually, he decided it was better for everyone if Trevor and I went to boarding school," she'd gone on. "So Trevor got shipped off to Choate, and I went to a Catholic girls' school in the Twin Cities. We saw each other on holidays, and we'd join Grandpa John at one of his houses over the summer. But even then, he'd have to be gone for long periods sometimes. How can you have a family when one of you is never there?"

For that question, Cork had had no answer.

He could no longer put it off, and he unzipped his bag. He unrolled the pants and sweater he'd been using as a pillow and slipped them on, then put on his cold boots. He unzipped the tent and stepped outside.

"Where are you going?" Lindsay asked from the dark of her own tent.

"To see a man about a horse."

"I think I need to see that man, too."

He heard the rustling as she put on her coat, then the growl of the tent zipper, and she stepped outside.

"Okay," she said.

"You'll need a light."

"I've got it."

She turned on the headlamp she'd worn when Cork had finally snuffed the flame of the Coleman lantern.

Lindsay headed for the primitive pit toilet that was a part of every official campsite in the Boundary Waters. Cork picked his way slowly through the dark down the little path that led to the lakeshore. He had a flashlight, but chose not to use it. He relieved himself against the trunk of a pine tree, then stood looking across the lake. Sometime after they'd turned in for the night, the drizzle had finally ended, and now the cloud cover had thinned just enough that the phantom of a nearly full moon was visible. The lake reflected a gray, ghostly light, and far out in the water, Cork could see the black outline of the big island called Raspberry.

As Cork stood watching, his eyes caught a pinpoint of light

high up on the rock ridge that formed a wall on the far side of the island. It was there for only a moment, then gone.

He heard Lindsay returning, but she'd turned off her headlamp and came in the dark.

"Funny how quick your eyes adjust out here, even in the least little light," she said. "And there's something about an artificial beam that feels out of place. Know what I mean?"

He did.

She stood beside him awhile, silent in the same way he was silent. "A beautiful place," she said. "Until it eats someone you love."

"It's not a monster, Lindsay. There's a logical explanation for your grandfather's disappearance. We just haven't found it yet."

"But we will?"

"I try not to make promises I can't keep."

She caught her breath, an audible gasp. "Did you see that?"

"Yes," he said.

The pinpoint of light had come again, then gone.

"What was it?" she said.

"If I don't miss my guess, someone on that island has struck a couple of matches. Maybe to smoke a cigarette or light a pipe."

"We're not alone?"

"We're not alone."

"Who are they?"

"Boundary Waters enthusiasts maybe."

"Why didn't we see them earlier?"

"It was hard to see much of anything in that mist today."

"What time is it?"

Cork pushed the stem on his wristwatch, and the face lit up. "Two-thirty-eight."

"Who'd be up at two-thirty-eight in the morning?"

"Someone seeing a man about a horse, maybe. Or someone just craving a smoke. We'll ask them."

"Tonight?"

"Tomorrow's soon enough."

"I'm going back to my tent," she said. "You coming?"

"In a minute."

He studied the black outline of the island. There was an official BWCAW campsite on the lakeshore, but the two bright pinpricks had come from atop the ridge. He'd climbed that rock wall during the search for John Harris. It was tough even in good light and in good weather. What would anyone be doing atop the rocky ridge in the dead of that kind of night?

As he stood there wondering, clouds once again gobbled the moon. The island vanished from sight and the lake became a black emptiness. Cork felt his way back to his tent. Inside, he pulled off his boots, slipped off his pants and sweater, rolled them again into a pillow, and zipped himself into his bag.

He wondered if Lindsay Harris had gone back to sleep. Probably not, he thought. Probably her brain was pinballing, bouncing among a lot of unanswered questions. He knew there would be no answers that night, so he closed his eyes and let himself sink into oblivion.

"I'd kill for a cup of coffee." Lindsay came from her tent, breathing clouds of gray vapor. She looked like hell, but Cork knew that everyone did first thing in the morning in the Boundary Waters. She wore the red-and-white striped stocking cap that she'd worn the whole trip so far and that Cork couldn't look at without thinking of *Where's Waldo?* In its way, it was kind of cute, and because her grandfather had given it to her, he appreciated its sentimental value.

"No need," he said and handed her a cup.

"How long have you been up?"

"Long enough to make coffee." And although he didn't tell her, long enough to have tried the satellite phone again with the same disappointing result. Then he'd taken out his field glasses and carefully studied the island. He could see the official campsite there, but saw no tents or canoes or any other sign of human life.

The same was true for the top of the ridge where the lights had been.

"Not so grim this morning," Lindsay observed.

"Still gray, but no precipitation. That helps."

She hugged herself as if for warmth. "Must be near freezing."

"It'll warm up."

She took a long drink of her coffee. "Ahhh, that helps. Breakfast?" She nodded toward the pot Cork had on the camp stove burner.

"Oatmeal. Then I'll fry up some bacon and rehydrate some eggs."

"What's the plan?"

"The island first. See if we can track down whoever was over there last night."

"Then?"

"Like I said yesterday, I'm hoping something will come to me."

"That's it? That's your plan? All of it?"

"Do you have a better one?"

She looked disappointed but clearly had nothing of her own to offer.

They ate mostly in silence, and Cork cleaned up from the meal while Lindsay visited the pit toilet. Then they went down to where the canoe lay tipped. A translucent skin of ice had formed around the rocks nearest the shoreline.

"Winter comes early here," Lindsay said, as if it were a sudden revelation.

"That's why we won't be staying long. If the lakes ice over, it'll be hell getting out. Same if it decides to snow much."

"But if we find something?" she said hopefully.

"If we find something, we'll figure what to do then."

They put in to the water and made for the island. Cork guided them to the landing for the BWCAW campsite, a little sandy area edged with rocks. They lifted the canoe from the water and tilted it on the shore. Cork studied the sand.

"No footprints. If someone was on this island yesterday, they didn't land here."

"Where else?"

"A couple of other possibilities, but this landing makes the most sense."

"Hello!" Lindsay called.

The suddenness and volume of her voice startled Cork, and he shot her a look.

She shrugged. "Seemed like the easiest thing."

She was right, and Cork gave a holler. "Hello! Is anyone here?"

"Maybe they can't hear us," she said.

"It's so quiet you can hear bark growing."

"Maybe they left."

"They got off awfully early then. I was up at first light. Let's just have a little look around."

He followed the shoreline to the west side of the island, where there was a break in the rocks just large enough for a canoe to slip up to a spot covered in pine needles. It was out of sight from where he and Lindsay had camped the night before, and if there'd been canoes, he wouldn't necessarily have seen them leave. He knew the spot from the earlier, thorough search for John Harris.

"What are we looking for?" Lindsay asked.

"Any sign someone was here."

"And were they?"

"I can't see any indication."

"You said there were a couple of places."

"The other one's a little tough to get to from here. I've got another idea. Follow me."

He led her back to the first landing and then along a faint trail that cut inland through a thick stand of pines. They came to a place where the rock shot up from the dirt in a long wall sixty feet high.

"They were up there last night?" Lindsay craned her neck toward the low, dirty-looking sky.

"On top. If what we saw is what I think we saw."

"What now?"

"I'm going to climb."

"Me, too," she said without hesitation.

"The rock's wet, bound to be slippery."

"You think you can make it?"

"I do."

"Then so can I," she said gamely and started up the wall. She'd gone only a few feet when her boot slid from under her and she fell to the ground.

"You hurt?"

"Only my dignity." She studied the wall again. "I think I'll wait here."

Cork took his time, choosing his handholds and footholds carefully. In five minutes, he'd mounted the ridge. He walked slowly along the top, which was mostly rock. Some aspens had managed to put down roots, but they were a hardy few. He stood on the ridge, with a good 360-degree view of the lake, and saw no sign of humanity except the campsite on the mainland where he and Lindsay had spent the night.

Then he glanced down. On a flat stone just to the left of where he'd planted his feet, he saw what looked like black ash. He removed his gloves and bent and touched his right index finger to the stone. He lifted the finger to his nose and smelled tobacco char. Someone had smoked there. Whoever it was must have smoked after the rain had stopped or the little fall of ashes would have been washed away. Cork walked along the ridgetop studying the ground more carefully. He found a place between the rocks that in summer had been filled with wild grass. That now dead grass lay pressed down in a long outline that had probably been made by a sleeping bag.

It was an odd place to camp. To haul gear to the top of the ridge wasn't an easy thing. There was no shelter from the inclement weather, and no particularly comfortable places to sleep. The only advantage to being there might be the view. In the dull gray of November, that view was hardly worth the climb.

There were only two ways into and out of Raspberry Lake: the portage to the south, which was how Cork and Lindsay had come the day before, and the portage to the north, a long, difficult trek nearly two miles to the next lake, which was called Baldy. If whoever had been here had canoed the lake to either portage that morning, Cork would have seen them. Which meant that they had left when it was still dark. Or they were still on the island.

Cork went back to the place where he'd climbed up the rock wall. He looked down to where he'd left Lindsay Harris. She was nowhere to be seen. The only evidence of her was the stocking cap she'd been wearing, which was lying on the ground at the bottom of the wall, looking very much like a piece of Waldo that had been severed and left for carrion.

CHAPTER 10

Cork hadn't checked in on the sat phone the next morning, but Marsha Dross again advised patience. The cloud cover, the location, the unreliability of sat phones in general. There could be so many reasons for the silence from the Boundary Waters.

It was barely light out when Rose, Jenny, and Waaboo left the house on Gooseberry Lane and headed north out of Aurora. They passed the turnoff to Sam's Place, and Rose glanced across the railroad tracks at the Quonset hut sitting all alone on the shore of Iron Lake. Although Cork continued to use it in winter as the office for his private investigations, it looked abandoned at the moment, a shell with no life inside. Which was how, these days, she sometimes thought of Cork. Something was missing in him, something vital, something life-giving, and she didn't know what it was exactly and so had no idea how to help him find it.

"I always hate it when we close up Sam's Place for the season," Jenny said. She was behind the wheel. Waaboo, who'd been wakened early, sat glassy-eyed in his car seat in back. "It always feels like a small funeral."

"And then in spring, there's the resurrection," Rose said brightly.

"In November, spring always seems a long way off," Jenny replied.

She turned onto a county road that paralleled the western shoreline of the lake, drove past cabin after abandoned cabin. Tamarack County swelled every summer with seasonal residents, and every winter was deserted except for those hearty few for whom it was home.

"I called Daniel last night," Jenny said. "He's going to meet us on Crow Point."

"Good," Rose said.

She quite liked the man Jenny was to marry. This would be a merger of families and cultures that felt right to Rose and was, in truth, something she'd prayed for.

Near the north end of Iron Lake, they parked next to a double-trunk birch tree that stood at the side of a gravel county road and marked the beginning of the trail through the woods to Crow Point. The sky had lightened, though it was still lidded by thick clouds.

Jenny unbuckled Waaboo from his car seat and lifted him out. As soon as the icy air hit his face, Waaboo seemed to wake up and become energized. He'd been on the path to Crow Point many times, and he was off and running.

"Waaboo!" Rose called after him. "Wait for us."

He slowed, found a long stick of great interest to him, and poked at the fallen leaves that covered the path.

"Everything's all stiff," he said.

"Things froze a little last night," his mother told him. "Winter's coming."

"Snowballs," Waaboo said happily. "And sledding."

"Twenty below," his mother said. "And flu season."

Waaboo walked ahead, his feet crunching the frozen, fallen leaves.

It was two miles to Crow Point, a long walk for a four-year-old, but Waaboo was used to the hike. When they broke from the trees and he saw the two cabins and the smoke that poured from the chimneys, he began to race along the path across the meadow. Because they were expected and welcome, the two women let him go. Rose saw the door of Meloux's cabin open. Rainy stepped out. Little Waaboo ran to her and she caught him up in her arms, and Rose heard his cry of delight. After a good hug, Rainy set him down and he disappeared inside. Rainy closed the door but remained outside, waiting for her visitors.

"Daniel?" Jenny said.

"Here already, inside with Uncle Henry. And now Waaboo."

The women exchanged hugs, and Rainy ushered them in.

Like Rainy, Daniel English was full-blood Lac Courte Oreilles from Wisconsin. He was tall, tawny, handsome, and impossible not to love. When he'd met Jenny, he was working as a game warden for the Wisconsin Department of Natural Resources. They'd fallen in love, and he'd left Wisconsin and his family and moved to the Iron Lake Reservation, where he'd been hired as a tribal game warden. He had an apartment in Allouette, the larger of the two communities on the reservation. After the wedding, as was the tradition in Ojibwe culture, and also because they couldn't really afford to do otherwise, he would move in with his wife's family, joining the O'Connor clan in the house on Gooseberry Lane.

Jenny kissed him hello.

Waaboo was sitting with Rainy's great-uncle on the old man's bunk, and Meloux was showing the boy a wooden flute that he'd carved. Ember sat at Meloux's feet, watching the old Mide and the boy.

"When a young Anishinaabe man wants to woo a young Anishinaabe woman," Meloux explained, "he plays music to her on a flute."

"What's *woo* mean?" the boy asked.

"To win her love," the old man said.

Waaboo looked up at Daniel English. "Is that what you did?"

"I don't play the flute, Waaboo," Daniel said. "I play the accordion."

Jenny laughed. "So he wooed me with polkas and zydeco." She kissed him again.

"I've made coffee," Rainy offered. "And biscuits. And for Waaboo, or anyone who'd care for some, my own wild raspberry tea."

The little cabin smelled wonderful to Rose, filled with the aroma of the biscuits and coffee and raspberry tea. And filled, too, she knew, with the love of family. But there was another sense that underlay these things, a sense of concern, which Henry Meloux soon addressed.

"My niece has told me of this feeling that has so troubled Stephen O'Connor," he said. "I would like to talk to him."

"He's flying in today, Henry," Jenny said. "I could bring him here later."

"Good," the old man said.

"How worried should we be?" Rose asked.

"Airplanes are very safe these days," Meloux replied.

Rose said, "I meant about this feeling Stephen's had and about Cork."

"I know what you meant," the old man said with a smile. "Worry is useless. It takes you nowhere. But a laugh, that is always a good thing."

She wondered how he could joke so easily. Then she realized that he was right. At the moment, except for Stephen's troubling feeling—and who knew what that meant?—they had no real reason to worry. Cork was a capable man who understood the Boundary Waters. He wasn't foolish. And what could possibly threaten him that he would not know how to handle?

Jenny said, "The visions Stephen's had in the past, and these feelings he gets, they've always been right and they've always meant trouble."

Rose knew that a decade before his mother went missing, Stephen had begun to have visions of the place her body would eventually be found. Until the tragedy happened, they'd all thought these were simply a recurring bad dream. Then before he was shot, Stephen had had a vision of the man who would shoot him. Only a year ago, before Cork and Jenny had walked into a deadly showdown outside Williston, North Dakota, Stephen had warned that they would be in danger.

"And Dad still hasn't checked in on the sat phone he took with him," Jenny added.

"I can think of plenty of reasons why the sat phone might not be working," Daniel said. "The clouds, the terrain, the tree cover, the age and quality of the sat phone."

A knock came at the cabin door, which seemed to surprise them all, even Meloux, who was seldom surprised in this way. Rainy opened it up, and in came a woman who was a stranger to Rose.

Rainy stepped back, as if a strong wind had shoved her. "Aunt Leah? What are you doing here?"

The woman was slight but had an imperial bearing. She was also Native, gray-haired and with sharp eyes that took in the cabin and everyone in it. Her gaze settled at last on Henry Meloux.

"Hello, Henry."

"*Boozhoo*, Leah," the old Mide said. "It has been a very long time."

"How did you find this place, Aunt Leah?" Daniel asked.

"I can read a map, even a crude one." She held out a sheet of paper, and Rose could see a penciled drawing. "I asked at the coffee place in Allouette. The woman behind the counter drew this for me. You must be Jenny. You're even lovelier than I imagined."

"Hello, Leah," Jenny said, a little tentatively. She glanced at Daniel.

"This is my great-aunt Leah Duling, Jenny. Who, last I knew, was in Africa. The Congo, maybe?"

"The Central African Republic. It's lovely to see you again, Daniel. You've grown and become quite handsome. And you, Rainy, you seem healthy and happy. How nice for you." She looked at Rose. "And you are?"

"Rose Thorne," Rose said. "I'm Jenny's aunt."

"And this fine young man?" Leah opened her arms wide toward Waaboo as if he were a mountain she wanted to embrace.

"I'm Aaron, but everybody calls me Waaboo. It's short for Waaboozoons."

"Little rabbit," Leah said, smiling as if the name pleased her greatly.

"Did you come for my mom's wedding?"

"I wasn't invited, child," the woman said. "But I came anyway."

In the awkward silence in the room, the question of *why* lay obvious but unasked.

Leah answered it, however. She leveled her sharp, dark eyes on Meloux and said, "I want to make sure this old fraud doesn't screw up your mother's life the way he screwed up mine."

CHAPTER 11

"Lindsay!" Cork called from the top of the ridge. "Lindsay Harris!"

To which he received no reply. There was the sudden caw of a crow startled from the branches of a tree below and the flap of wings as the bird took flight. Cork watched it grow small in the distance, black as an ash against the gray of the sky.

He thought maybe the young woman had gone into the cover of the pines to relieve herself or back to the pit toilet of the island campsite. But there was something else that was a possibility, a thought that came to him because of all the loss he'd suffered due to violence, a thought fed by the mysterious appearance of the lights on the ridge the night before and the mysterious disappearance of whoever had been there. And fed as well by the inexplicable vanishing of John Harris. Someone had taken Lindsay Harris.

He could have climbed down the wall the way he'd come up, but he decided on a different tactic. He moved to the far side of the ridge, the long palisade that fell precipitously to the water. He loped east along the ridgeline until he found a fold in the rock that might hide him as he descended. As carefully and quietly as he could, he made his way down. At the bottom, he found himself in a small copse of aspen, bare in this season, the shed leaves on the ground wet and blessedly silent as he made his passage through the trees. He entered the pines, where the forest floor was a soft, deep bed of brown needles. He crept soundlessly toward the place where Lindsay's Waldo-looking hat had been dropped, a thoughtless oversight maybe. Or maybe a bit of bait to lure him down.

He spotted movement beyond a line of raspberry bushes. Although the thicket was empty of foliage and berries, the combined bramble was too dense to see through clearly. He bent low and crept nearer. He still could barely make out what was on the other side, but he could hear the whisper of voices.

"What's he doing up there? What's taking so long?" A woman's voice, but not Lindsay's.

"Patience." A deeper voice, older, offering a piece of advice that might have come from Henry Meloux.

"When I see him, should I shoot him?" A young voice, male. Afraid or, at the very least, terribly uncertain.

"No." The man again, firmly in charge. "You wait for my say-so."

Cork had brought no weapon, had no way of defending himself or Lindsay. This was not at all what he'd expected. But he wasted no time considering the whys of the situation. He needed a plan. These people had come in canoes—there was no other way—and had probably hidden them somewhere on the island. They'd have to return at some point, and if he could find those canoes, he'd be waiting. He slipped quietly away.

They weren't difficult to locate. As he'd told Lindsay earlier, there were only three good landing places on the island, and they'd already investigated two of them. The third was not far from the fold in the rock wall where he'd made his descent. Just inside the cover of the pines near the shoreline, he found the canoes, two of them, tipped behind a fallen log, hidden from the sight of anyone moving past on the lake.

Which would have been Lindsay and me, he thought. They'd been waiting. But why? What was it about this place or the missing man that was so important people were ready to kill because of it? Were they there to protect something? Take something? Lindsay? Her grandfather had disappeared. Did they mean to make her disappear as well? Cork hadn't seen her with the others or heard her. Had she been able to hide?

He didn't so much hear as sense the danger. He spun, and the man came at him with the knife. Cork reacted instinctively, his mind and body trained across a lifetime of law enforcement. He parried the assailant's thrust with his left forearm and punched his right fist into the man's throat. The man staggered back, still gripping the knife. Cork was on him, and they fell to the ground, grappling. The man's breath came in desperate rasps, rattling through his damaged throat, but he fought with surprising strength and delivered a jolting blow to Cork's jaw. Adrenaline had pumped into every muscle of Cork's body. He barely felt the impact. He battled with the thoughtless instinct of survival. They rolled across the soft mat of pine needles, each in the grip of the other, their bodies twisting. Cork broke away and was on his feet quickly. His assailant rose more slowly, and as he came up, Cork delivered a kick to the side of his head that sent him tumbling. Cork tensed, prepared for the next attack, but it never came. The man lay facedown on the ground, unmoving. Cork was on top of him in an instant. The man made a little sound, like the last bit of air from an emptying balloon, and was still. Carefully, Cork stood up and stepped away. As he watched, a pool of blood spread from beneath the downed man. Cork bent and rolled him to his side. The knife handle protruded from his chest above his heart. As Cork watched, the stranger bled the last of his life out onto the pine needles that were his deathbed.

Cork stood slowly. He felt the ache of his jaw now where the man's fist had connected. His head rang. He staggered a little. He had time for only a few breaths before what felt like the kick of a mule hit the back of his head, and he sank into a blackness empty of everything but one last moment of dread.

He came to gradually. The first words he heard before he opened his eyes were "Kill him now."

They were spoken by a woman, the voice he'd heard from the other side of the raspberry thicket. This time the words weren't whispered.

"No," replied the other voice, the voice that had reminded him of Meloux. "We need him."

Cork opened his eyes and at first saw only the flat, slate sky between the pines. He slowly turned his head, and the others came into his line of vision. A tall man, grayed, powerful-looking, Native. A woman, maybe forty, with murder in her eyes, also Native. A kid, sixteen or seventeen at most, holding a rifle, looking nervous. He, too, was Native. Cork didn't see Lindsay Harris.

"He's awake," the kid said.

The man knelt beside Cork. "Can you hear me?"

"I hear you," Cork said.

"This is how it stands. Do what we tell you or you're dead. It's that simple. Do you understand?"

"I understand."

"Can you get up?"

"I'll try."

"Keep him covered," the man said to the kid.

Cork heard the slide of the bolt on the rifle. He rolled and drew himself up on his hands and knees. His head throbbed and he felt dizzy. He pushed himself up fully, swayed a little, then got his footing.

"Cork?"

At the sound of Lindsay Harris's voice, he turned. She stood near the tipped canoes with her hands bound behind her back.

"You okay?" he asked.

"For now." She eyed their captors in a frightened way.

"What do you want?" Cork asked the strangers.

"Your silence and your muscle," the man said. "Help us get him into a canoe."

He nodded to where the body of the man who'd attacked Cork lay in a pool of blood that had turned the brown pine needles a wet scarlet.

"He touches my brother, I'll kill him," the woman said.

"You'll load him then?" the man asked her.

"With your help." She walked to the dead man and stood over him, her face as hard as the wall Cork had scaled that morning. She looked at the tall man expectantly.

"Put one of the canoes in the water," he instructed Cork. To the kid, he said, "Stay with him. Shoot him if he does anything except what I've asked."

Cork went to the nearest canoe and, even as he bent to the work of lifting it, admired its construction. It was birch bark, handcrafted, light and sturdy and made with no iron fasteners. It rose dramatically at the bow and stern, in the way the Ojibwe had once fashioned their canoes. He lifted it easily onto his shoulders, carried it to the lake, and set it in the water.

"Steady it," the tall man said.

Cork stepped into the lake and did as he was asked.

The woman gripped her brother's legs and the tall man took the shoulders. They carried the body between them to the canoe and laid it in the center.

"Now the other canoe," the tall man said, and Cork obeyed.

"Give me the rifle," the tall man said to the kid. When he held it, he pointed the barrel at Cork and spoke to the woman and the kid both. "Go fetch the gear."

His companions walked into the woods and disappeared, leaving Cork and Lindsay Harris with the tall, graying man.

"What now?" Cork asked.

"You'll see soon enough, O'Connor."

"Should I know you?"

"We've never met."

Cork looked at the canoe where the dead man lay. "He attacked me."

"His job was to watch the canoes."

"You can let her go." Cork nodded at the young woman. "She had nothing to do with this man's death."

"She had everything to do with this man's death."

"Who are you?" Lindsay said. "What do you want?"

"You talk too much," the man said. "It would be best if you said nothing."

"Are you going to kill us?" she asked.

"Only if necessary."

"What would make that necessary?" Cork said.

"You'll know when it happens."

The others returned with packs, which they set in the canoes. From one of the packs the woman took a satellite phone and held it toward the tall man.

"You make the call," she said. "I'll hold the rifle."

The tall man took the sat phone but handed the rifle to the kid. Then he walked away from the others and stood near the lakeshore and made the call.

"Well?" the woman said, when he returned.

"Nothing. Must be the clouds. We'll try again at the next lake. Load up."

The tall man directed Cork to the bow of the canoe that held the dead man.

"I don't want him in the same canoe with Flynn." The woman spat the words, full of venom.

"All right." The tall man nodded toward the bow of the second canoe and told Cork to get in. He cut Lindsay's hands free and put her in the middle of that same canoe with the gear, and he took the stern. When the kid and the woman had taken their places in the canoe that held the dead man, they shoved off.

The morning was windless, the water like glass. They glided easily across the lake, heading toward the place where John Harris's canoe had been found empty and adrift and where the day before Cork had sat in his own canoe, trying to heed Meloux's advice, waiting for something to come to him. And it had. In spades.

CHAPTER 12

"When I was a girl," Rainy said, "my mother would read me the letters that came from Aunt Leah, from exotic-sounding places, talking about the work she and Uncle Lucius were doing, the battles he fought for souls and the ones she fought against disease. In a way, I became a nurse because of her and those letters. I haven't seen her in over a decade. Her husband, Uncle Lucius—did you ever meet him, Uncle Henry?"

The old man was putting on his mackinaw. "No," he said.

"He died a few months ago. I'd heard she might be coming back to Wisconsin, to Lac Courte Oreilles. I figured she might be feeling alone and wanting to connect with home and family. I sure didn't expect her here. Why does she hate you so, Uncle Henry? Why does she believe you ruined her life?"

Rainy and her great-uncle were alone in the cabin. Everyone had gone, left quickly after the arrival of Leah Duling, fleeing, Rainy was certain, from the angry energy Leah had brought with her. She hadn't really explained her presence on Crow Point or her obvious vitriol toward Henry. Daniel had insisted on seeing her back to her car. Rainy was pretty sure he wanted an opportunity to question her about her intentions regarding the wedding.

Henry said, "She once thought she would be my wife."

"Aunt Leah? But you're thirty years older than she is."

"Fifty years ago, Niece, this skin was not spotted, this face was not cracked leather. And she was not the only woman who wanted to share my bed."

Rainy hadn't thought of her great-uncle in this way, a younger, virile man. He was her mentor, her teacher. There was such wisdom in him. He'd always been for her someone who'd somehow transcended the seductions of the flesh.

"What happened?"

"That is a story, Niece, I will save for another time." He pulled on his gloves. "Right now, we have work to do."

"What work?"

"If what we have been told about the vision of this young Harris is true, I believe there is a connection of spirit between him and Stephen O'Connor. We will prepare a sweat for them. Maybe this will help us all understand that connection."

"Stephen will be fine with this, Uncle Henry. But I don't know about Trevor Harris."

"Then you will find him and help him to see what he must do."

"He doesn't know me."

The old man ignored her objection. "After we ready the sweat lodge, you will bring him here."

She knew better than to argue with her great-uncle. She put on her coat, an old flannel-lined jean jacket, and gloves, and followed him outside.

Henry went ahead. Rainy filled a wheelbarrow with firewood from the great stand laid up against her cabin, then she followed. The sweat lodge stood in a tiny clearing in the middle of a grove of birch trees at the very tip of Crow Point. The frame was constructed of aspen boughs, bent and tied together with rawhide prayer strips, and was covered with tarps and blankets. There was one opening, small enough that it required entry on hands and knees. Not far away lay the char from the fires that were built to heat the *mishoomisag*, or Grandfathers, the rocks that would be used in the sweat. Henry was inside the lodge, and Rainy began to unload the wood.

"Aunt Rainy!"

She turned and saw Daniel crossing the meadow.

"Did you escort Aunt Leah back to civilization?" she asked when he'd reached her.

"I took her as far as her car. The whole way she insisted she didn't need my help. Which was probably true. She's one very self-sufficient woman."

"Did you get any more from her about why she's here?"

"She insisted she has no intention of interfering with the wedding. She's fine with that. More, I think, she's intent on making Uncle Henry's life miserable. The wedding is just an excuse to be here. Did Uncle Henry tell you anything about her?"

Before Rainy could answer, her great-uncle crawled out of the lodge.

"*Boozhoo,* Nephew," the old man greeted Daniel. "Leah did not pounce on you and eat your heart?"

"She didn't attack me, Uncle Henry, but she had nothing good to say about you."

"When I knew her a lifetime ago, she was a woman of great passion and little control."

"What did you do that makes her hate you so much?"

"He didn't ask her to marry him," Rainy said.

"Whoa, Uncle Henry. She was in love with you?"

"Do not sound so surprised, Nephew. Even a turtle may be beautiful to another turtle."

"She's no turtle. More like a badger."

"While you stand here and offer only insults about one of your elders," the old man said gruffly, "the work remains undone."

When the lodge had been readied, Rainy asked Daniel's help in finding and fetching Trevor Harris. He agreed.

"Wish us luck," she said as they left.

"If I believed you needed luck," Henry replied, "I would not have sent you."

There were two paths to the cabins on Crow Point. One led through the forest north and was the way usually taken by Cork and his family or anyone else coming from Aurora. The other led east and was the main route for anyone coming from the Iron Lake Reservation. Rainy and Daniel followed this path a mile and a half to a gravel road where Rainy parked her Jeep and where

Daniel had parked his truck. They took the truck. As they drove into Aurora, they talked about the wedding.

"Nervous?" Rainy asked.

"Eager," Daniel said. "Any last-minute advice?"

"Talk to her honestly."

"Do you and Cork do that?"

"He's not one to talk much about his feelings."

"Then Jenny must take after her mom," Daniel said and smiled.

Rainy had known him from birth. Had watched him grow and stumble and find his way. She studied him, considered the man he'd grown into, the fine Ojibwe features of his face, his proud bearing, his deep intelligence, his good heart, and it was so easy for her to see why Jenny would fall for him.

"Mind if I ask you a personal question?" he said.

"Go ahead."

"You and Cork, do you think you'll ever get married?"

"I'm not sure it's in him. When he lost his wife, it left a greater wound than he's willing to admit. I think he still needs to heal."

"You're Mide. You could help him."

"Only when he's ready to ask for my help."

"If he proposed, would you say yes?"

She thought about that one. It wasn't the first time she'd pondered the question.

"I don't know. I've been on my own so long. Raised my children as a single mother. I certainly didn't come to Crow Point looking for a relationship. I'm fine with the way things stand at the moment."

This was not untrue. But there was more to it. She didn't tell Daniel, didn't tell anyone, not even Henry, about all the fear she fought against, about all the demons from her past. If Cork asked her to marry him, would she have the courage to tell him the whole, awful truth? And if she did, would he still love her?

* * *

They drove to the Four Seasons, which was where Cork had said the Harrises were staying. Rainy asked for Trevor Harris at the front desk, and they rang his room. He didn't answer.

The desk clerk, a young woman with a tag that told them her name was Nadia and she was from Romania, said with a surprisingly light accent, "You might try the casino. He's there a lot. And he's very lucky."

"Common knowledge?" Daniel asked.

"He tips well. And he likes to talk."

They headed to the Chippewa Grand Casino, which was on the lakeshore south of Aurora. It had begun nearly twenty years ago as a single, great building, all white stone, glass, and glinting copper. In the years since, an eighteen-hole golf course had been added, along with a 150-room hotel, a large restaurant with a fine wood-fired grill, and an auditorium that could seat a thousand.

Although it was a Monday morning and long past the tourist season, the parking lot was surprisingly full. They walked into the cacophony of bells that rang out false promise and into a world without clocks because time was not an encouraged consideration in a casino. Nor was restraint. Casino profits had brought marvelous things for the Iron Lake Reservation: a good water and sewer system, paved roads, a new community and government center, a health clinic, and a number of economic initiatives. But Rainy was a healer. She was dismayed that these good things sometimes came from preying on those who battled a gambling addiction, or those who should be using their money instead to pay rent or buy food and medications.

"What's he look like?" Daniel asked.

"Oh, crap," Rainy said. Because it wasn't something she'd thought of. She'd figured Trevor Harris would just come down to meet them at the Four Seasons, and the difficult part would be convincing him to do the sweat. She had no idea who to look for inside a lively casino.

She was saved by fate, although she knew that Henry might have said it was something else.

"Hey, Rainy. Hello, Daniel."

Ernie Champoux approached them. He was a relative, one of Meloux's great-nephews. He worked at the casino in some capacity that Rainy never quite understood. Something technical.

"Never figured you for a gambler, Rainy."

"I'm not here to lose money, Ernie. I'm looking for someone."

"Anybody I know?"

"A man named Trevor Harris."

Champoux was square-built and square-faced with black hair that he wore in a crew cut. "Harris? Sure. Follow me." He started down one of the aisles between two rows of slot machines. "How're the wedding plans going, Daniel?"

"Good."

"You've hooked a good woman in Jenny. I've known Cork and that family my whole life. Fine people. And little Waaboo? Icing on the cake."

"Are you coming to the reception, Ernie?" Daniel asked.

"Wouldn't miss it." Ernie stopped abruptly. "There. That's him."

He pointed toward a blackjack table, where a slender young man sat with an impressive stack of chips before him.

"Looks like he's winning," Daniel said.

"Seems to happen a lot for him," Ernie replied. "One lucky son of a gun. Gotta get back to work. I'll see you both at the wedding reception."

Rainy and Daniel headed to the blackjack table, where the young man sat hunched over his cards and chips.

"Trevor Harris?"

He turned his head and looked at them. His eyes were blue and a little unfocused. At his elbow sat a glass with the last of what looked like it had been a Bloody Mary. "Yes?"

"Could we talk to you?"

"I'm in the middle of something here."

"It's about your vision."

"I can see fine."

"The vision you had about Stephen O'Connor."

He stared at them. "Who are you?"

"My name is Rainy Bisonette. This is my nephew Daniel English. We're friends of the O'Connor family."

"Oh, sure."

"Could we talk somewhere else?" Rainy said.

"Of course. Hang on a minute."

He finished the hand, slid a blue chip across the table as a tip to the woman who'd been dealing, and gathered his winnings.

"How about the bar?" he suggested.

"That would be fine," Rainy said.

It was still early and the Boundary Waters Lounge was quiet. They sat at a table. A waitress came and took their orders: iced tea for Rainy, a Coke for Daniel, a Bloody Mary for Harris. Although Rainy knew that it would have been better for the young man not to be drinking alcohol if he was going to agree to the sweat, she said nothing.

When their drinks had been delivered, Harris took a long sip, folded his hands on the table, and smiled at them. "All right."

"Cork told us about the vision you had," Rainy said. "I wonder if you'd mind sharing it with us."

"Why?"

Rainy said, "Do you know anything about the Grand Medicine Society?"

"Never heard of it. Is it like the AMA?"

"Not exactly, but they're healers. Ojibwe healers."

"Okay. So?"

"I'm a member of the Grand Medicine Society. A Mide. My great-uncle, a man named Henry Meloux, is also Mide. Cork told us about your vision. But we'd like to hear it from you firsthand."

"Because?"

"In the hope of understanding it better and maybe helping you to understand it better."

"I understand it fine."

"There's something else, Trevor, something you don't know."

He waited.

"In your vision, as I understand it, Stephen O'Connor spoke to you."

"Yes, that's true."

"Stephen is on his way here now. He's had a kind of dark premonition. He gets them sometimes. We've learned to pay attention."

"Premonition about what?"

"We believe it's about Cork."

She saw him tense. "He and my sister are in the Boundary Waters Canoe Area Wilderness right now."

"Yes, we know."

"Hang on," he said. He reached into his pocket, pulled out a cell phone, and made a call. He waited, finally shook his head, and put the phone away. "Lindsay's not answering. Did you try Cork?"

"Yes, but cell phone service is nonexistent in the Boundary Waters."

"So . . ." He seemed lost a moment. "What exactly do you want from me? What do we do?"

"We'd like you to come with us. We'd like you to talk to my great-uncle and take part in a sweat. Do you know what that is?"

"I think so. But why?"

"A sweat can be a way of opening yourself to an awareness that's locked inside you. It might help you understand your vision better. Stephen will also take part in the sweat. We're hoping this might help us understand why he was a part of your vision and maybe what his premonition is all about."

"I don't know. You're Indian, so this is probably normal stuff to you."

"I understand. But consider this. If Cork's in danger, your sister might be, too."

"Yeah." His face looked colorless, his features pinched with concern. "Yeah," he said again, this time to himself. He thought it over some more, then said, "Okay. Why not? What have we got to lose, right?"

"Thank you."

"So, when do we leave?"

"Right now, if you're ready."

"I need to go back to my hotel first. Can you pick me up there? The Four Seasons?"

"Of course."

He looked at his watch. "Would two o'clock be okay?"

"Two o'clock would be fine."

"All right then. Let me cash out and I'm off."

He walked away, and Daniel said, "That wasn't so hard."

Rainy stared where the young man had disappeared amid the maze of machines that sang like sirens to the desperate, the hopeful, the greedy, the lost.

"I'm not sure why exactly," she said, "but I get the feeling that was the easy part."

CHAPTER 13

They canoed the western side of the horseshoe lake until they reached the place where a small stream fed through a line of rushes into the great boggy area filled with tamaracks that they'd seen the day before. In the lead, the tall man threaded his canoe through the reeds and onto the stream. The water was clear and the bottom visible just inches below them. During the search for John Harris, someone had tried to navigate the stream, but it was so shallow and narrow and meandered so pointlessly through the bog that the effort had been quickly abandoned. The slender, handmade birch-bark crafts, however, skimmed along the thread of water without any problem. The way was barely wide enough for their passage. If Cork hadn't been careful, he might have tangled his paddle in the dead reeds that formed a wall on either side.

Not a word had passed between any of them since they'd set off from Raspberry Island. Cork had been trying to put two and two together, but so far his calculations had yielded nothing. When they entered the stream, he made a first, tentative connection. Maps of the Boundary Waters showed only two ways onto and off Raspberry Lake, and both were portages. During the search for John Harris, dogs had been brought in and had gone over those portages and had found no scent of the missing man. They'd also gone along the edges of the bog area, in case Harris had wandered in and been swallowed up, but that, too, had proved fruitless. But if Harris had been taken down the stream, as his granddaughter and Cork were now, the dogs would have had no scent and the man would have seemed to disappear without a trace.

But why? What was it about John Harris, and now his grand-daughter, that would cause anyone to go to such great lengths? That's where all his adding totaled up to nothing. If he could just talk to Lindsay, she might be able to supply an answer. Until then, Cork resigned himself to patience.

He tried to tap his knowledge of the Boundary Waters, accu-mulated across a lifetime, to figure where they might be headed. Although the sky was overcast and there was no sun to help him with directions, he knew they were going roughly northwest. Baldy Lake, which was the way one of the portages led, was a good mile to the northeast. To the west lay the Asemaa River, a long, rough run with several waterfalls, connecting two lakes that were seldom visited, because there were no portages and the Asemaa was a river that would chew up a canoe in no time at all. Hard-core kayakers, he'd heard, sometimes tried the river, but there were other challenging waterways in the Boundary Waters and the Quetico that could be reached much more easily, so the Asemaa was, for the most part, ignored.

Just after noon by Cork's watch, they stopped where a mound of high ground rose next to the little stream and was topped with aspen trees. The water that had been so clear when it spilled from Raspberry Lake had turned a root beer color from the bog seepage along the way. They disembarked and the woman took food from one of the packs—jerky and energy bars and a mix of dried fruits. She also pulled out an orange, which she gave to the kid. Wordless, she handed Cork and Lindsay a water bottle, and they both drank from it deeply.

"How long?" the kid finally asked. He'd peeled his orange, and Cork picked up the sharp aroma on the air in the same way he had the day before. He'd been in the middle of Raspberry Lake, so far from the big island that it made no sense he'd have been able to catch the smell, yet that's exactly what had happened.

More things in these woods than a man can ever hope to un-

derstand. Henry Meloux's wisdom never deserted him, but what good it would do him now, Cork couldn't say.

"Less than an hour, we'll be at the river," the tall man said.

"Should we try the sat phone again?"

The tall man studied the sky. "When we get to the lake."

"If you called him now," the woman said, "he'd be waiting for us."

"In this overcast, he'd have trouble finding the lake," the man said.

"If he doesn't start soon, we'll have to spend another night out here," the woman said.

"We can do that."

The woman looked toward Cork, her eyes like knives. "The sooner we get rid of him, the better."

The tall man didn't reply, but the kid stopped eating his orange and stared at Cork in a way Cork couldn't quite interpret. It might have been fear. Or it might have been regret.

They finished eating and took to the stream again. Cork thought about the hatred with which the woman kept eyeing him, and about the man who was to meet them at some lake still ahead. He had the overpowering sense that his own presence among them would end at that lake, one way or another. He paddled steadily, deeper and deeper into the wilderness, while his brain ran in a dozen directions, seeking a way out.

CHAPTER 14

Stephen was the O'Connor who most showed his Anishinaabe heritage. He was slight of build but wiry. Because he stood straight and proud, most people thought him to be taller than he actually was. His hair was so dark brown that in dim light it appeared black. His eyes were the color of walnut shells, but soft. Unless he was angry. Coming from the secured area of the Duluth airport, he didn't appear to be angry. Concerned, perhaps. But all in all, Rose thought he looked good and tanned and fit. His limp was almost imperceptible.

"Oh God, how I've missed you." Rose gave her nephew a powerful hug.

"It's been less than a year, Aunt Rose," Stephen said.

"It feels like forever. Do you need to pick up luggage?"

"Carry-on." Stephen held up his backpack with his sleeping bag rolled and tied atop. "So, any word from Dad?"

"Nothing. But Daniel and the sheriff keep telling us sat phones can be unreliable. And except for this darkness you've been feeling, we don't really have any reason to be worried."

"I've felt this kind of darkness before, Aunt Rose. It's never good."

"Let's go," Rose suggested. "We can talk in the car."

They rolled out of Duluth and up Highway 61 along the North Shore of Lake Superior. It was gale season for the Great Lakes. The most famous of the lake disasters, the sinking of the *Edmund Fitzgerald,* had occurred in a November storm nearly four decades earlier. But there were plenty of other ships to keep her company two hundred fathoms down. At the moment, the lake the Ojibwe called Kitchigami was as flat as a cookie sheet and graphite gray.

"Big change," Stephen said. He sat eyeing the vast open water that ran unbroken to the horizon.

"What change?" Rose asked.

"In the Arizona desert, water is as rare as diamonds, and the sky is always nearly cloudless. Hot, too. Here the cold can cut right through you."

"Was it good?" Rose asked. "Your time out there?"

"Until this crushing feeling hit me," Stephen said.

"The limp seems better. Is it really?"

"It hurts sometimes. It's like I can still feel the bullet digging into my spine. But I try not to give it power over me. Tell me more about this Trevor Harris and his vision that I was, apparently, a part of."

Rose filled him in fully, about that and everything that had happened since the Harris grandchildren had hired Cork.

Stephen said, "It's odd that I was in this guy's vision without knowing anything about it. All that came to me was this darkness I don't like at all."

"Henry and Rainy are going to help with that," Rose said. She told him about the sweat that was planned.

"Good," Stephen said. "How are the wedding plans coming along?"

Rose braked for a slow-moving logging truck. "There is one small fly in the ointment. Daniel's great-aunt has arrived for the wedding. She's a piece of work. And . . ." Rose passed the logging truck and swung back into her lane.

"And?" Stephen said.

"According to Daniel, she was in love with Henry Meloux ages ago. Thought they would marry."

"Henry?" Stephen said.

"It's clear she still carries a grudge, and maybe a torch. So there might be more to her visit here than simply attending the wedding."

Stephen smiled. "Henry Meloux. That devil."

*   *   *

Jenny was waiting for them at the house on Gooseberry Lane. She wasn't alone. Rainy and Daniel were with her. They hugged all around. Jenny poured coffee, and they sat at the kitchen table and talked. About the wedding, the appearance of Daniel's great-aunt and her history with Henry Meloux, and finally about the sense of dread that so weighed on Stephen.

"I'd been hiking for several days," he told them. "Following a trail that eventually led to the top of a mesa west of Round Rock, an area I'd been told is sacred to the Diné. They call it a place of Nítch'i, the Holy Wind. I was planning to spend a good deal of time there, hoping, you know, to connect, to be in relationship with the spirit, this Holy Wind. But while I was there, this crushing darkness descended. And then all I could think about was Dad."

Rainy asked, "What made you believe it might have to do with Cork?"

"It felt like trouble to me, serious trouble. And you know my father. Where there's trouble, he's usually at the center of it trying to make things right. I just wish I could get this weight off my chest."

"Maybe Uncle Henry can help with that," Rainy said. "He wants you and Trevor Harris to do a sweat with him today."

"Aunt Rose told me. I'd love to hear more about this guy's vision."

Jenny glanced at her watch. "I have to pick up Waaboo. He's got a playdate with little Bennie Degerstrom."

Rainy said, "I need to get back to Crow Point and help Uncle Henry make sure we're ready for the sweat. Daniel, will you pick up Mr. Harris and bring him out?"

"Of course."

"I need a shower," Stephen said. "I've still got desert dust in my hair and sand in every crack in my body."

CHAPTER 15

Cork could hear the Asemaa long before the little stream out of Raspberry Lake spilled itself into that mad rush. Asemaa was an Anishinaabe word that meant "tobacco." The river flowed from Rust Lake, so called because the richness of iron ore in the area gave the water the hue of corroded metal. Add to that the root-beer-colored water feeding in from numerous bog flows, and the river took on the rich darkness of tobacco juice.

They drew their canoes up to the bank and disembarked. They gathered at the edge of the Asemaa and looked north, where the river ran. The course was a rocky one full of white water, and the sound of the river was a dull roar. A fragrance came off the water as it leaped and crashed and foamed around the rocks, the kind of clean smell that had always made Cork think *freedom*. It was an odd thing to be standing there, breathing in that wild scent and knowing that he and Lindsay Harris were anything but free.

It was Lindsay they wanted, that much was clear. As for him, if it weren't for the dead man in the first canoe, Cork was pretty sure he'd have been dead, too. They needed him only to reach the next lake and then he became dispensable. They'd use the sat phone, and Cork suspected that the call would result in a floatplane arriving to quickly extract them from the wilderness. He'd never seen the lake at the other end of the Asemaa River, a lake that on maps was called Mudd. He'd seen the river itself only once before, and that was at its mouth on Rust Lake. He'd heard about the fast water and the numerous falls between Rust and Mudd but had no firsthand knowledge of any of it. If they were going to use the water, it would be rough going. But it wouldn't be any easier if they weren't.

"Okay," the tall man said. "From here, we walk."

"No portage," Cork pointed out.

The tall man ignored him and turned to the kid. "I'll take a pack and the first canoe. You take a pack and the second canoe." He eyed Lindsay Harris. "You look like you can carry a pack." To the woman, he said, "You take the rifle. Don't shoot O'Connor unless you have to."

"What about my brother?" the woman said.

The tall man finally looked at Cork. "You killed him, you carry him."

"I don't want him touching Flynn again," the woman said.

"You want to carry your brother?" the tall man asked.

For a few moments, the woman breathed deeply and angrily and glared first at the tall man, then at Cork. Finally she gave in. "All right. But drop him, O'Connor, and I'll put a bullet in you."

The tall man gave her the rifle and said to Cork, "Let's get him out of the canoe."

Together they lifted and laid the body on the ground. The woman kept the rifle leveled on Cork while the others put on their packs and the two men shouldered the canoes.

"All right," the tall man said. "Pick him up and let's go."

Cork bent and rolled the body onto its stomach. He grabbed the dead man under the armpits and lifted him to a standing position, then maneuvered the body into a fireman's carry over his shoulders, a technique every lawman knew. Cork was grateful that Flynn hadn't been a big man. As it was, it would be a struggle to get him to Mudd without stumbling, and if the woman was true to her word, stumbling was the last thing Cork wanted to do.

The tall man took the lead, with the kid behind him, Lindsay Harris next, then Cork, and finally the woman bringing up the rear. At first they veered away from the river and back into an area of bog that lay not far to the east, a part of the whole system of sluggish flow they'd traveled since leaving Raspberry Lake. Cork realized that although he'd never heard of a portage along the Asemaa River, they were following a path of solid ground that wove in a complex pattern through the marshland. Cork understood that the tall man had a knowledge of the Boundary Waters that even he, across the whole of his lifetime in the North Country, didn't possess.

Who was this guy?

There were other questions that nagged at him. They'd called him O'Connor. Neither he nor Lindsay Harris had told them his name, so how did they know? And how did they know that he and Lindsay would be on Raspberry Lake in the first place, a decision that hadn't been made until the day before they'd entered the Boundary Waters? And circling back always to the question at the heart of it all, what did they want with Lindsay Harris?

Within half an hour, Cork understood only too well what people meant when they said "deadweight." Flynn hadn't been particularly big, but Cork felt as if he were carrying a gorilla. His legs were beginning to weaken, and then things only got worse. The way ahead began to rise, and in the distance, Cork could hear again the little roar of the Asemaa River. The path the tall man took led up a long slope covered with birch trees and rocky protrusions. The birch leaves, fallen weeks earlier, had become a decomposing, slimy mat underfoot. With the added wet from the recent drizzle, the climb was a struggle. Not just for Cork. The kid slipped and went down. The canoe toppled from his grip and he sat holding his knee. Blood welled up between his fingers.

The tall man carefully laid down the canoe he carried. "Let me see," he said to the kid.

Lindsay Harris asked, "Can we sit?"

"Go ahead," the tall man said.

Cork knelt and laid his own burden on the ground. His shoulders ached and his legs quivered. He sat beside Lindsay, grateful for the break.

The woman behind him stepped forward, leaned over the tall man, and stared down at the kid. "Must've cut it on a rock when he fell. Is it bad?"

"Laid it open pretty good. I'm going to clean it," the tall man told the kid. "Then I'm going to stitch it. Okay?"

The kid nodded.

The tall man slipped the pack from his back and dug into a side pocket. He came up with a little box, which he opened. First he took out a small roll of gauze. He unrolled several inches, and used his knife to cut a piece. Next he took out a little white packet and tore it open, releasing the pungent smell of alcohol. He held his knife out toward the woman. "Cut his jeans open some more so I can get in there and work."

The woman glanced warily at Cork, then laid her rifle down, near enough that she could snatch it up if she had to. "Take your hands away," she told the kid. When he did, she quickly cut both sides of the tear.

"A lot of blood," she said.

"We'll fix that."

The tall man folded the gauze and rubbed at the blood, then used the alcohol wipe to clean the wound. He cut another piece of gauze and gave it to the kid. "Hold that over your cut and press hard."

From the pocket of his pack, he pulled another small box. When he snapped it open, Cork saw that it held tiny spools of thread and needles. A compact sewing kit. He closed the case and threaded a needle.

"You ready?" he said.

The kid nodded.

The tall man stretched out the kid's leg along the ground, lifted the bloody gauze away from the wound, and went quickly to work. The kid's head jerked back and his face pinched against the pain, but he made almost no sound. The woman stood stooped over and engrossed in watching the work.

That's when Cork made his move.

Before he'd even thought about it, he was up and running, a mindless flight back into the marshland from which they'd just come. He was already into the tall reeds when the first shot came. He bent low and became invisible and another round clipped through the undergrowth at his back. After he'd run a hundred yards, he dove off the path, through the reeds, and into the mire of the bog. He lay dead still as he sank slowly into the wet muck. He heard the sound of footsteps coming fast. They were light. The woman. With the rifle, he suspected. She passed him and ran on. But still he didn't move, just lay staring up at the low, dull gray of the sky. In a few minutes, she returned, breathing hard. He heard her swear under her breath, and then her footsteps grew distant, heading toward the slope, the birches, the injured kid, the tall man. And Lindsay Harris, who was alone with them now.

Cork eased himself from the muck, crawled through the reeds and back onto solid ground. He was pretty well soaked, but he was layered in wool and didn't worry about the cold getting to him. He was thinking about where the group was headed—Mudd Lake— and he was trying to reconstruct the area from his recollection of the maps he'd studied for years over all his visits to the wilderness. He knew he couldn't make any time going back and circling out of the marsh. His best hope would be to cross the Asemaa and keep to the high ground on that side of the river. Without anything to carry, he'd be traveling light and fast, much faster than the others, with their canoes and probably the dead man. He was sure he could reach Mudd ahead of them. He hunkered low and crept along the narrow, almost invisible path he'd traveled twice already, but he stopped before he broke from the cover of the rushes. He eased himself forward until, through the last of the reeds, he could see the birches on the slope. He caught a glimpse of one of the canoes as it vanished from sight among the trees at the top of the rise.

He was tempted to make a dash for the river, but he heard Meloux's age-old advice in his head: *patience*. He waited nearly half an hour, then followed up the slope into the birches.

They'd left the dead man behind. Just left him, food for wolves and crows. Whatever their purpose, it was important enough to abandon Flynn, their comrade, the woman's brother. Cork knew that if she ever had him in her sights again, she wouldn't miss.

He did his best to put that thought aside and headed west toward the sound of the river.

CHAPTER 16

Rainy watched them come, walking slowly across the meadow, Daniel a little in the lead, Trevor Harris following. Trevor stumbled, caught himself, walked on. He was staring at the ground as if it fascinated him. More likely, she thought with a sinking heart, he was drunk.

There was another reason for her to be concerned. Leah Duling was with them.

"*Boozhoo,*" Rainy called in greeting. "Welcome."

Leah looked beyond her into the empty cabin. "Where's Henry?"

"At the sweat lodge, preparing himself. The others are there, too, tending the fire, heating the Grandfathers. What are you doing here, Aunt Leah?"

"I stumbled onto Daniel in Allouette and he told me about the sweat. It's been a long time since I attended one. I thought it might be interesting."

"All right," Rainy said, but not without misgivings. "If you're ready, Trevor, we'll go there now."

"Yeah," the young man said. "Sure. Whatever."

She led them to the sweat lodge, where Stephen stood by the sacred fire. She introduced him to Leah and Trevor Harris, and there was a cordial exchange.

Then Leah said again, "Where's Henry?"

"He's in the lodge already." Stephen nodded toward the open flap that showed only darkness inside. To Daniel, he said, "Will you take the Grandfathers in?"

Daniel grabbed a pitchfork that leaned against the trunk of a birch. He scooped a red-hot rock from the coals, and Stephen took a cedar broom and brushed away the ashes. One by one Daniel carried the stones inside the lodge.

"Henry says that's enough," he said at last. "It's time to begin."

To Trevor, Rainy said, "You have something cooler on under your clothes, I hope."

"Daniel suggested swim trunks."

Stephen had already begun to remove his clothing. As Trevor worked at dropping his pants and stepping out of them, he almost fell over. Daniel caught him and helped him stand upright.

"Have you been drinking?" Rainy asked.

"Not much," Trevor replied.

"I'm not sure you should do this."

"I want to. I want to try at least."

"All right. There will be several sessions during the sweat. After each session, you may come out of the lodge to cool and refresh yourself. If you feel ill or are having any difficulty at all at any time, I want you to leave immediately. Do you understand?"

"I do."

"Okay, you need to take off your watch and that ring. Nothing goes into the sweat lodge that is unnatural to this place."

"This is a Rolex," Trevor said.

"I'll make sure it's safe," Daniel promised.

From a pouch she carried, Rainy took tobacco and offered it to the spirits. She gave Stephen and Trevor Harris each a little tobacco and explained to Trevor, "Sprinkle it into the sacred fire as an offering and ask for what it is you would like to receive during the sweat."

The young man thought a moment, threw the tobacco into the fire, and said, "I want to know if my sister is safe."

Rainy figured it was a reasonable request, but if he'd asked for her advice, she would have suggested asking instead for the peace of spirit that would help him understand why he was given his vision and what it meant for him and his sister.

Which is what Stephen did: "I thank the spirits for the gift of feeling what can't always be seen with eyes, and I ask them to help me understand and use this gift in the way they have intended."

Rainy explained to Trevor, "After you enter the lodge, you will remain silent unless Henry asks something of you or until it's your time to ask something of the spirits. It will be very hot, maybe uncomfortably so. If you feel at all ill, tell Uncle Henry and he'll give you permission to leave."

"I'm a little nervous," Trevor confessed.

"Everybody is the first time," Stephen assured him. "Ready?"

"As I'll ever be." Trevor gave him a brave smile.

Stephen went first, crawling through the lodge opening. Trevor hesitated a long moment, eyeing the darkness inside, then went down on his hands and knees and followed Stephen. Rainy lowered the covering over the entrance. She heard her great-uncle speak quietly to the two young men. Not long after that, Henry's voice rose in song and prayer, accompanied by the beat of his water drum.

"What now?" Aunt Leah asked.

"We wait and we offer our own prayers," Rainy said.

It was, by then, late afternoon, and the light that filtered through the overcast was fading. Through the bare birch trees beyond the lodge, the surface of Iron Lake had turned the color of charcoal. Rainy believed in the power of the sweat ceremonies, but her heart seemed to reflect the heavy darkness of the lake. She knew exactly where that darkness came from. Fear, pure and simple, and it rose from her concern about Cork's safety.

"Primitive ceremonies," Leah said. The woman sat on a sawed-off section of pine log near the fire. "I've seen every kind there is. Voodoo in Jamaica. Ashanti drumming in Africa. Dukun healing ceremonies in Borneo. Your uncle Lucius dismissed them as heathen. The irony was that he never saw the similarities in his own Christian beliefs."

"And you, Aunt Leah?" Rainy asked. "Do you dismiss them?"

"The first godforsaken place Lucius took me was in the heart of Africa. A disease-ridden Mandinka village. Lucius offered prayers, which as far as I could see, made no difference. Their shamans performed their dances. Same effect. I decided maybe medicine might be worth a try, so I became a nurse. After that, wherever we went, Lucius offered God, and I offered antibiotics. It's always seemed to me that a shot of penicillin does more good than the most fervent prayer or primitive symbols drawn in ash. Or," she said, eyeing the sweat lodge, "ancient rituals."

"But you did sweats when you were young, on the rez."

"Young and foolish. I never had a vision. I never knew anyone who did. You, Rainy, you claim to be a holy person, a Mide. Have you, in all the sweats you've done, ever had a vision?"

"A Mide isn't holy, Aunt Leah, just a healer."

"You didn't answer my question."

"I've never had a vision. But I know others who have," Rainy said. "Stephen, for example. And Henry has had many."

"I don't know about Stephen. But Henry, he's an old charlatan."

Rainy detected more sadness in the words than bitterness. "Aunt Leah, one of the helpful elements of a successful sweat is that the spirit surrounding it is open and positive."

"You want me to leave?"

"Just try to keep an open mind and an open heart."

"I've lived among African natives, South America Indians, primitives in Borneo. I'm nothing if not open-minded."

"Let's take a walk," Rainy said. She wrapped her hand gently around her aunt's arm and drew her up and away from the others.

They went to the lake and stood on the shoreline. A breath of air came across the water, fresh and pungent with the scent of evergreen. Rainy closed her eyes and drew it in and slowly let it out. With it went her anger at her aunt's behavior.

"Would you tell me the story?" she said.

"What story?"

"Of what happened between you and Uncle Henry."

"Not much to tell."

"He hurt you once. Deeply."

"What woman hasn't been hurt deeply by some man?"

"Uncle Henry isn't just some man. When were you last here, on Crow Point?"

"Fifty years ago."

"What brought you?"

The woman stared across the charcoal-colored lake, and Rainy knew that what she was seeing was something at a distance not measured in miles.

"I wasn't quite twenty, still living on the rez, Lac Courte Oreilles. This was even before you were born. My best friend fell ill, terribly ill. Winona Duling. An aunt you never knew. Your family asked Henry to come and do what he could. She died anyway."

"Sometimes what a Mide offers isn't a healing of the body, Aunt Leah."

"I understand. He gave her great comfort in the end." She was quiet, remembering. "There was something unique about him. Mesmerizing. I fell in love with him. I believed he loved me, too."

"When he returned to Crow Point, you followed him," Rainy guessed.

Leah's face took on a sadness that came from a place so powerful in her heart that Rainy felt it in her own. "I discovered I wasn't so special to him. Or special enough that he wanted to take me for his wife." In the next instant, the sadness vanished, and an old, old anger, like an ancient evil spirit, seemed to possess her. "I wasn't the kind of girl to stay in the way he wanted, not if he wasn't my husband."

"So you returned to Lac Courte Oreilles?"

"There was a revival going on in Hayward. Winona's brother, your uncle Lucius, got the spirit and declared that he had received the calling. Oh, did he have a voice like thunder. He'd been in love with me forever. He asked me to marry him. Wasn't the first time. But this time, I said yes. I followed that man all over the earth. I was faithful to him until the end."

"But you never forgot or forgave Henry. Is that it?"

Those hard, dark eyes stared back at her.

"Why are you here, Aunt Leah?"

"It's been a long time since I had a chance to observe a sweat."

"What I mean is why have you come back at all? Why now?"

Leah said slyly, "Maybe I've had my own vision."

Rainy studied her, trying to see beneath the malevolence that so distorted her aunt's face. Before she could press Leah further, get nearer the source of the bitter poison so that she might offer something helpful, something healing, she heard the sound of terrible retching coming from the direction of the sweat lodge. She turned back and saw Trevor Harris bent over among the birch trees, puking his guts out.

CHAPTER 17

There was still light in the day when Cork reached Mudd Lake. Long and narrow, the lake lay between two high ridges of gray rock capped with a mix of pine and aspen. He found where the Asemaa fed in, and he climbed to a place among the trees on the eastern ridge where he could see anyone approaching along the course of the river. Although the whole way there he'd tried to formulate some kind of plan, he'd come up with nothing that had a ghost of a chance of springing Lindsay Harris free. When he'd been taken, they hadn't bothered to frisk him, and he still had the old Barlow pocketknife that his father had given him when he was twelve and that he always carried with him into the Boundary Waters. But what good was a small knife against the rifle they had? And how did one man take on a party of three whose purpose, whatever it was, was so important to them that they would kill or die for it?

His clothes had dried, but he still smelled of the rank muck of the marshland. He was hungry but put that need aside as he lay on a bed of pine needles and carefully watched the Asemaa. All the while, he went over and over in his head all that he knew about Lindsay Harris and her missing grandfather, looking for some clue that would help him understand the why of all this.

John Harris—Johnny Do—had been a kind of hero to Cork, funny, smart, ambitious. Cork had looked up to him like an older brother, in a way. But Harris had left Aurora and not returned, and the man he'd become was a mystery to Cork. However, that he'd found the time to make a trek into the Boundary Waters with his grandchildren said something about him, something good.

When Harris vanished, his grandchildren had insisted on being a part of the search effort to locate him. Even when the search had officially ended, they were clearly not prepared to give up on their grandfather. Which said something about them.

It wasn't much to go on, but there was one possible thread which Cork thought might connect Lindsay's abduction with her grandfather's disappearance. Perhaps there was some vital piece of knowledge that both Harris and his granddaughter possessed that was worth all this bloody effort. If that was it, did this mean that Harris had not given it to the kidnappers, and they hoped Lindsay would? And if Harris hadn't given them what they wanted, did that mean he was dead? And if that was true, what was Lindsay Harris's life worth?

He spotted them coming, portaging along the river. The tall man was in the lead, carrying one of the canoes. Behind came Lindsay Harris, with the other canoe on her shoulders. The kid came next, visibly limping. The woman with the rifle brought up the rear. She also carried a pack. As Cork lay still with his eyes focused on the approaching party, he heard a faint sound at his back. He rolled over quickly and found that he was being scrutinized by two gray wolves. He didn't believe there was any reason to be afraid. He'd spotted wolves before in the Boundary Waters and in other parts of the Northwoods, and he knew they were predators that almost never attacked humans. There was something else, too. The side of Cork's heritage that was Anishinaabe was Ma'iingan, Wolf Clan. These wolves were part of his *dodem*. And so he gazed at them and they gazed back and he said quietly, "*Boozhoo, Ni-sayenyag.*" Hello, my brothers.

The animals turned and slowly trotted away among the trees. Before they were lost completely from his sight, they stopped and looked back. He envied them. They were in their element, and because they had each other and maybe the rest of a pack somewhere near, they weren't alone. He was also grateful because he chose to think of their appearance as a good sign and it gave him hope.

He returned his attention to the people below. They'd stopped at the edge of the lake and unburdened themselves. They sat on the ground, and the way their bodies sagged spoke of their exhaustion. The tall man handed around a water bottle, and they all drank from it. The tall man spoke to the woman, then rose and pulled something from his pack. The sat phone. He moved away from the others and made a call. Or tried, but probably wasn't successful, because he looked at the woman and shook his head. He glanced up at the top of the ridge, where Cork lay. Cork pressed himself to the earth, but kept watching. The tall man spoke to the woman, and she rose with obvious reluctance. She handed the rifle to the kid and said something that must have included Lindsay, because they both looked at her and the kid nodded. Then the woman followed the tall man, who brought the sat phone with him.

They retraced their path along the river, then began to climb the ridge, coming up the same way Cork had come. He slid from the edge and crept away a couple of dozen yards and lay himself flat behind the trunk of a lichen-covered pine that had fallen long ago and was slowly rotting back into the earth. In a few minutes, he could hear their footsteps. They stopped not far from where he'd been watching them. He didn't dare rise to look, but he could hear them clearly as they spoke.

"Let's hope we get something up here," the tall man said. There was a long silence, then: "Isaac? Where's Cheval?" Silence. "Can we get another pilot?" Silence. "All right. We're at Mudd Lake. We'll stay overnight, then head north. I'll check in at noon tomorrow, and let you know where we are. If you've got someone else who can fly us out, we'll figure another pickup point."

Now the woman spoke. "What is it?"

"The RCMP picked up Cheval last night," the tall man said.

"Constable Markham?"

"Yeah, Markham."

"Why?"

"Cheval got drunk and belligerent and Markham arrested him."

"Is Isaac posting bail?"

"He's working on that now, but it won't happen until some-time tomorrow at the earliest."

"So we keep going?"

"O'Connor is on his way out of the Boundary Waters. He can't possibly make it before late tomorrow, but as soon as he does, he'll bring the police back with him. We need to be long gone by then."

"I wish I'd killed him."

"Because it would have helped us, or because of your brother?"

"I owe him payback."

"The balance doesn't work that way."

"Mine does."

"Your brother tried to kill the man. What was he supposed to do?"

The sound of her breathing, fast and angry, carried to Cork. "She better be worth all this trouble."

"We won't know until we get her there."

Cork thought they'd leave then, but he didn't hear any foot-steps.

Finally the tall man spoke, sounding bone-weary. "The weather's beginning to clear. Means it'll be cold tonight. We'd better get ready for it."

Now Cork heard them head away. He lay still for a long time, then slowly raised his head and confirmed that he was alone again. He crept back to the edge of the ridge. He watched as below him the others prepared for the night on the shore of the lake. He looked up and saw that the tall man had been right. The cloud cover was finally beginning to break. In the cleared patches, Cork could see the faded blue of an evening sky.

Like the tall man, he was tired right down to his bones. But he knew he had work to do, and in the quiet of that great wilderness, the closing words of one of his favorite poems came to him:

And miles to go before I sleep,
And miles to go before I sleep.

CHAPTER 18

Rose put Waaboo down for the night. She sat with him on the edge of his bed and read a little Junie B. Jones. When she was finished, Waaboo said, "Do you think Baa-baa will find the goose?"

"What goose?"

"The one he's looking for in the woods."

"What do you mean, Waaboo?"

"Bennie's dad says that Baa-baa's chasing a wild goose in the woods."

"Oh. On a wild-goose chase you mean?"

Rose wasn't surprised that word of Cork's expedition was already abroad. In Aurora, like in all small towns, that kind of information spread with the speed of plague.

"Your grandfather's not looking for a goose, Waaboo. He's looking for a man who's missing."

"Will he find him?"

"I don't know. But I do know that it's important to him that he do his best."

"If I was lost, I would want Baa-baa to look for me."

"What about your mom, or me?"

"Baa-baa's better. He's not afraid of anything."

She kissed his forehead. "If you say so."

"Aunt Rose?"

"Yes?"

"Are you afraid of anything?"

"Lots of things."

"Like what?"

"Spiders."

"Me, too."

"And snakes."

"I don't mind snakes. What about monsters?"

"I don't believe in monsters."

Waaboo thought about it a moment, then said, "Me, either."

"I'm glad. Now good night, you little munchkin. Go to sleep."

She kissed his forehead again, turned out the light, and left the room. But she didn't go downstairs immediately. She stood outside Waaboo's bedroom thinking about his naïve belief that his grandfather was afraid of nothing. She'd known Cork for thirty years, and while he was a good man, a just man, he was not a fearless man. She believed that he'd gone into the Boundary Waters afraid. Not of what might await him there, but of something that shadowed him in. She'd told Waaboo the truth. She didn't believe in monsters, but she thought that Cork did, and the monster he most feared was the one that looked back at him in the mirror every morning and said, *You failed them.*

Downstairs, Jenny was at the kitchen table, working on her laptop. "He's asleep?" she said when Rose appeared.

"On his way."

"Thanks."

Rose went to the coffeepot and poured herself a mug. "What are you working on?"

"My publisher wants a synopsis of my next book."

"I didn't know you were working on another book."

"I'm not. Yet. But since I signed a two-book deal, they want to know what the second book will be."

"Got any ideas?"

"I think I'm going to write the story of how we found Waaboo."

"I've always liked that story."

"You were an important part of it."

"And I love the way it ended," Rose said.

The back door opened, and Stephen came in, bringing cold air with him. He hung his coat on a wall peg near the door.

"Do I smell coffee?" he said.

"I just took the last of it," Rose said. "I'll make a fresh pot. How did the sweat go?"

Stephen went straight to the cookie jar that was shaped like Ernie from *Sesame Street* and that had been in the kitchen of the O'Connor house since he was a child. He took out one of the chocolate chip cookies Rose had made that very afternoon and sat down at the table. "All things considered, pretty awful."

"Why?" Rose asked. "What happened?"

"Trevor Harris came drunk and puked all over the place. And that Aunt Leah woman invited herself along. Her energy was so dark and thick it would've been hard for anything enlightening to get through."

Jenny closed her laptop. "Did Henry lead the sweat?"

"Yeah. He was a lot more optimistic about the whole thing. He said sometimes the mess of a situation is the answer you're looking for."

"What does that mean?"

"Search me. But we've come up with a plan."

The coffee began to drip. Rose took the cookie jar and set it in the middle of the table. "What plan?"

"Rainy, Daniel, and I are going into the Boundary Waters to check on Dad."

Jenny sat back, clearly surprised. "When?"

Stephen wiped crumbs from his lips with the back of his hand. "First thing tomorrow. Daniel called and talked to friends he's got in the Forest Service. They're going to fly us out to Raspberry Lake."

"Through all those clouds? Isn't that dangerous?" Rose asked.

"The clouds are breaking up."

Jenny didn't look happy. "First Dad, now you and Daniel? Pretty soon the Boundary Waters will suck up everyone I love."

"We'll come back," Stephen said with a grin.

"See that you do, and in time for my wedding."

"What about Trevor Harris? Is he going with you?" Rose asked.

"He said he'd leave it to us," Stephen replied. "He was looking pretty green. I dropped him at his hotel and promised to keep him informed."

Rose took a mug from the cupboard and, even before the coffeemaker had finished its work, began pouring. "The puking? What was that all about?"

"He'd been drinking pretty heavily this afternoon," Stephen said. "He was in no shape for a sweat."

"So you don't really know anything more about his vision?"

"Nada," Stephen said. "Or this darkness that's been weighing on me. Henry seemed to think that the way things went was informative."

"How so?" Rose asked, as she delivered the coffee.

"You know Henry. He gives you nothing on a platter."

"Tomorrow you'll know more," Rose said. "Everything will be clearer then."

"I'll drink to that," Stephen said and raised his mug in a mock toast.

Rainy walked the path through the meadow and between the great rocks that hid the fire ring. She carried a flashlight, but didn't turn it on. The clouds had cleared and there was a nearly full moon high in the sky, lighting her way. The North Country had been overcast so long she couldn't remember the last time she'd seen stars, but they were out now, filling the sky like spilled sugar. She went past the char from the last fire in the ring and walked to the edge of the lake. The water was dark, but a mercurial, silver river of reflected moonlight ran toward her across the surface.

Although she hadn't said anything to anyone, the disaster of the sweat that day disturbed her. Henry's take on it had been optimistic. Her own was different, full of foreboding, and she wanted to get down to the source of her fear.

Of course she was afraid for Cork and for Lindsay Harris.

There were troubling aspects to the whole expedition that had nothing to do with Trevor's vision or Stephen's sense of foreboding. The disappearance of John Harris into thin air was a profound mystery. The threat of bad weather that always loomed in that time of year was a concern. And even in the best of conditions, the wilderness could challenge an experienced outdoorsman.

There was something weighing on Cork, too, some terrible heaviness in his heart. "November," he'd said to her the last time she tried to talk to him about it. But it had been there long before the gray of that month set in. As a trained nurse, she wondered if it was something clinical, depression perhaps. She knew that Rose and Jenny believed it could be traced back to the tragic incidents that Cork had been involved in and felt responsible for in a way—the death of his wife, his friends, the shooting of his son. Responsible not because he caused these things but because, despite his best efforts, he couldn't prevent them. He thought of himself as *ogichidaa*. And maybe that in itself was the real failing. How could anyone stand between all evil and the people he loved? That was too much to expect. Even Henry, the wisest person she knew, didn't lay that sense of obligation on his own shoulders. Henry offered people what he believed they might need to face adversity, but he didn't try to be their shield, their protector. So many people came to him, how could he be?

"We often carry the burden of those who come to us burdened, Niece."

She turned, and there was the old man, a silver reflection of moonlight on the other side of the fire ring. He hadn't made a sound in coming.

"I thought you were asleep, Uncle Henry."

A sweat was a ceremony that could drain the strength from even young bodies. Her great-uncle didn't often lead sweats these days, they were so grueling, and whenever he did, she was concerned. But when he insisted, as he had that day, she didn't argue. He'd eaten a bit afterward, and then had laid himself down and gone immediately to sleep. For the night, she'd thought.

"Trouble in the air," he said. He looked up. "It circles like a turkey vulture. You feel it, too."

"I can't help being afraid. I don't like it, but there it is."

"Why do you hold it at such a distance? Better to talk to your fear." He crossed the little clearing and stood beside her.

She stared at the dark water of the lake. "I wish I could tell Cork that, and I wish he would listen."

"Sometimes a man walks into the night and does not understand why he cannot see. He blames himself for the dark he is in. I think that is Corcoran O'Connor."

"I don't know how to help him, Uncle Henry."

"You have offered him a light. He can take it or not. His choice."

"I love him," she said.

"And that is the light," Henry said.

They stood together, and although the fear didn't leave her, she felt great comfort in the old Mide's presence at her side.

"I wish the sweat had gone better." She shook her head. "Aunt Leah."

"She is alone and scared," Henry said. "Just as you were when you came to me. You have learned much in these years. Leah may not know it, but perhaps that is why she has come. Maybe it is her turn now."

Which startled Rainy. "You think she might be here to stay?"

"That will be her choice."

"Is it what you want?"

"I try not to want. I try instead to accept."

Rainy thought that if Leah came to Crow Point for good, it would drive her crazy. Or it would drive her away. This was way too much for her to think about at the moment. She turned back to the most important consideration at hand.

"Cork," she said. "We'll know more tomorrow, won't we?"

Her great-uncle studied the moonlight that fell across the water like a long, quivering finger. He said quietly, "Tomorrow may have a mind of its own."

CHAPTER 19

The moonlight was a gift. And there was another. *Jiibayag niimi'idiwag*. The northern lights. His grandmother Dilsey had told him that the dancing lights were reflections of the fires of Nanaboozhoo, who was both a trickster and a hero in the stories she told him, kindled far to the north. Cork had known better even when he was a child, but he still liked the idea that a great spirit was behind all that beauty.

For hours, he'd watched from the top of the ridge as the people on the shoreline of the lake below him prepared for and gave in to night. They'd allowed themselves a fire, which Cork figured was because they felt they were a safe distance from Raspberry Lake. There were no official BWCAW campsites on Mudd Lake, and they believed they were alone. They cooked over the fire. Even far up on the ridge, he caught the scent of stew. It was probably something rehydrated, but it smelled wonderful and reminded him how hungry he was. They'd shared their meal with Lindsay Harris but had spoken with her very little. He wished he could see her face, get a sense of what she was feeling. Was she scared? Angry? Discouraged? Certainly tired. He watched them lay out their sleeping bags. They'd bound Lindsay's hands with duct tape and put her in a sleeping bag—probably the one that had belonged to the dead man—nearest the water, blocking any escape in that direction. They located themselves roughly in an arc between her and the woods, a kind of barrier should she be tempted to try to slip away in the night. The tall man had banked the fire so there would be coals in the morning, then they'd all crawled into their bags to sleep.

Cork envied them their rest. He would have loved nothing better than to lay his head down and give himself over to sleep. The night grew cold. Although his layered wool kept him warm enough, he thought about home, a shower, a hot meal, a soft bed. He thought about all that was behind him at the moment, comforts he'd taken for granted, people he loved and took for granted, too. Rainy, especially, was heavy on his mind. The night before he left, she'd offered him a sweat to help him clear his spirit and his thinking. She'd offered him her bed as well. He'd turned her down on both counts. The gift she wanted to give him was more than a sweat and a bed. It was the gift of her whole heart, and it scared him.

His wife had been killed. Stephen had been shot, crippled. He wished desperately that he'd been able to put himself between Jo and the bullet that had felled her, between Stephen and the bullet that had lamed him. That was what a man who thought of himself as *ogichidaa* should have done. It was what his father had done, put himself between a bullet and an innocent old woman.

It wasn't until after his father's death that Cork first heard that word, *ogichidaa*. He'd been angry with his father for a long time, angry not only because he felt abandoned but also because of the way it had happened, protecting a woman who'd already lived her life. Meloux had explained about *ogichidaa*, about how Cork's father, although he was not Anishinaabe, had been born to it. He'd looked long at Cork with those eyes from which nothing could be hidden, and he'd said, in a way that had sounded deeply concerned, "You are *ogichidaa*, too." The anger didn't go away immediately, but as he grew into his own manhood, Cork came more and more to understand. And he began to see as well that men like his father and like him walked under a dark cloud and those near them were in danger of being struck by lightning. Long ago, he'd left his job as sheriff of Tamarack County because of the threat to his family. Nothing had changed. He'd finally come to accept that it wasn't the way he lived his life that was to blame. It was who he was, something which had been passed down to him and from which he couldn't turn away, something that would always threaten him and those who loved him and were loved by him.

Rainy was one of those now. And that's what scared him.

More immediately, there was Lindsay Harris, who'd entrusted him with her safety. And what had he done so far but let her down?

When the fire was nothing but a few red coals and those around it were deep in their sleep, he finally rose. His body, prone for hours on the cold ground, ached in every muscle. He stretched, and the crack of his joints was absurdly loud in the quiet of the woods. By the light of the moon, he made his way carefully down the ridge to the rush of the Asemaa River. He crept to the flat at the edge of the lake where the others had made their camp. The noise of the river as it spilled into Mudd Lake was a big help in covering the sound of his approach. The moonlight helped him make out the black forms in their bags. He stepped carefully between them, around the smoldering coals of the fire, and knelt beside Lindsay Harris.

At his touch, she came awake instantly. Her eyes were wide, her mouth thrown open as if to cry out. But she recognized him immediately and relaxed. He put a finger to his lips, then motioned for her to show him her hands. He pulled the Barlow knife from his pocket and cut the tape that bound her wrists, then he put the knife back. She rummaged at the bottom of her sleeping bag and brought out her boots. She slid from her bag and tugged them on. She'd been using her rolled coat as a pillow, and she slipped into that and stood up. Cork led the way. He felt her hesitate, and he turned back and saw her standing, as if paralyzed, fearfully eyeing the unmoving shapes in the other sleeping bags. He reached out and took her hand to guide her through.

They were almost clear when she stumbled. She made an involuntary sound as she went down, and Cork saw the others instantly begin to shed their bags. He drew Lindsay off the ground and cried to her, "Run!" then turned back to face the other three as they came at him.

The tall man was first. Cork lowered his shoulder and lunged and hit him midtorso. They went down together. Cork sprang up quickly, and the kid was on his back. He spun, trying to throw the kid off, but it was like fighting an octopus. The next thing he felt was something like a tree stump shoved into his stomach, and he doubled over and went down.

"Move and I'll kill you," the tall man snapped.

Cork stared up into the barrel of the rifle and went slack. The kid let go his hold and stood up, panting.

"Got her." The woman came into Cork's vision, Lindsay in her grip. "Just shoot him," she said.

"Get up, O'Connor," the tall man said. Then he said to the kid, "There's duct tape in my pack." The kid returned with the roll and the tall man said, "The knife, O'Connor."

Cork handed over his Barlow.

"Hands behind your back. You, too," he said to Lindsay.

They bound them both, and the tall man said to the others, "Try to get some sleep. Dawn's not far away."

"I'll watch him." The woman held out her hand for the rifle.

"No," the tall man said. "I'll watch."

In the moonlight and the flare of the northern lights, Cork could see the disappointment on her face and the hatred as she eyed him once more before turning in.

The kid helped Lindsay off with her boots and into her bag, then he slid back into his own sleeping bag.

"Sit." The tall man nodded toward the coals.

Cork sat down awkwardly beside the smoldering fire and could still feel some of its warmth. The tall man sat cross-legged near him, the rifle resting across his lap. He stared silently at Cork for a good long while. The northern lights were at the tall man's back, but gradually they faded and he was framed by only the night sky, the stars, and the descending moon.

"You could have left her," he said.

"That was one of my choices," Cork replied.

"What is she to you?"

"My client."

"That's it?"

"And a woman in trouble. What is she to you?"

The tall man's face was stone in the moonlight. "Hope," he said.

They spoke no more as they waited for the morning light to come.

CHAPTER 20

The promised de Havilland Beaver floatplane awaited them at the marina when Rainy and her nephew pulled up early the next morning. Stephen was at the end of one of the docks, talking with the pilot, a lean middle-aged man with a balding head and an easy smile.

"Bud Bowers," Daniel said, nodding toward the pilot. "Used to fly F-16s for the Navy."

He pulled his truck into the marina parking lot, which was empty. The boat slips in the marina were empty, too. With the exception of the floatplane, the lake was deserted and would remain that way until the water had frozen thick enough to support the village of shanties and huts that would go up for winter ice fishing, and the trucks and SUVs that would be parked next to them. As it was, the cold of the night before had left a thin, fragile coating of ice on the lake surface very near the shoreline.

The morning was bright and the sky crystal blue in the way it would often be in the winter ahead. The sun had just risen on the far side of Iron Lake, and the water sparkled yellow and gold as if studded with topaz. Rainy and Daniel met the others on the dock, and Daniel introduced his aunt.

"You're out there on Crow Point with old Henry Meloux, is that right?" Bowers asked.

"That's right."

"You a medicine woman?"

It was asked with respect, and so she answered simply, "More or less."

"That Henry, he's one tough old bird," Bowers said. "So, is everybody ready?"

Before they could answer, a voice hailed them from the direction of the Four Seasons, which overlooked the marina. Trevor Harris came trotting toward them. Rainy was surprised to see the young man up so early, especially considering his condition the day before at the sweat. He was dressed for the cold North Country, in a leather jacket, jeans, and boots.

"Got room for one more?" he asked, nearly breathless when he reached them.

"I remember you," Bowers said. "Flew you out when we were searching for your grandfather. Trevor, right?" He shook the young man's hand. "It's okay by me. I've got room. Any objections?" he asked the others.

"Not at all," Rainy said. "I'm sure you're worried, Trevor."

"Didn't sleep a wink last night," Trevor Harris said.

Which could well have been true, because the kid looked beat.

"All right, pile in," Bowers said. "Let's get this show on the road."

They took their places, Bud Bowers at the controls, Rainy and Stephen behind him, and Trevor Harris in the very rear. Daniel undid the mooring line, stood on the pontoon, and shoved the plane well away from the dock. He climbed in, taking the seat next to Bowers. The pilot fired the engine and swung the Beaver around, nose to the open water. They glided across the lake and took to the air.

"How long to Raspberry?" Stephen called out to him.

"What takes a full day of canoeing and portaging will take this baby twenty minutes. We lucked out with the weather. Cloud cover's been so thick I wouldn't have tried this before today."

They flew northeast over Iron Lake and the reservation town of Allouette. Out her window, Rainy could see Crow Point, a mottled-green finger pointing south across the six miles of open water separating it from Aurora. She knew that Henry was there, probably burning sage and cedar and sweet grass, sending up prayers with the smoke. She found that comforting.

A quarter of an hour into the flight, she glanced back at Trevor, who was sound asleep, his head lolled back, his mouth agape. He was drooling.

"There she is," Bowers called over his shoulder a few minutes later and pointed ahead to a shimmering blue horseshoe set in a vast expanse that was a mix of evergreen and bared deciduous forest.

Bowers brought the plane down gradually. They skimmed over the very tops of the trees and dropped to the water. Rainy felt the sudden drag as the Beaver touched the lake, sending up a fine spray on both sides. Bowers motored toward the shoreline.

"That's where we camped," Trevor said, wide awake now, although his eyes were still bleary.

"Only two BWCAW sites on this lake," Bowers said. "And looks like we struck gold. I see a tent there in the trees."

He eased the plane near the shoreline and cut the engine. Daniel got out onto a pontoon and leaped to solid ground, the mooring line in his hand. He tied it to an aspen a few feet inland. He steadied himself on the pontoon and said to the others, "One at a time. Watch your footing." He helped them out and oversaw their short hop to the shore. They all made it safely, although Trevor Harris stumbled headlong on landing, and only Stephen's quick grab kept him from falling flat on his face.

They hurried to the campsite, which was deserted. They unzipped the tent flaps and found the sleeping bags and packs still inside.

"The sat phone's here," Stephen said.

Daniel checked the fire pit. "No one's burned anything for a good long while."

"Everything seems to be here except the canoe," Stephen said. "They must be out on the lake somewhere."

"I can run the Beaver around, and we can take a look-see," Bowers offered.

They piled back into the plane, and Bowers taxied them down the lake between the shoreline and Raspberry Island.

"I see a canoe," Stephen called out. "Over there." He pointed toward the big island.

"That's the other BWCAW campsite," Bowers said.

He turned the plane in that direction and eased it near the shore where the canoe lay tipped.

"That's ours," Stephen said.

They got out and secured the Beaver, then stood looking at the trees and the rock ridge that ran the length of the island and listening to the absolute silence of everything around them.

"Where are they?" Trevor asked.

"The Beaver's engine is loud enough that unless they're both stone-deaf they had to hear us," Bowers said.

"Dad!" Stephen called.

"Lindsay!" Trevor shouted.

When they received no reply, Daniel said, "Why don't we split up?"

Bowers turned left along the shore. Stephen and Harris went to the right. Rainy and Daniel headed directly inland toward the ridge. They followed a path among the pines that led them to where the sudden thrust of gray rock had created the wall. Lying on the ground at the base was a red-and-white striped stocking cap.

Daniel picked up the cap. "Look familiar?"

"I'm pretty sure it's not Cork's."

"If it's not Lindsay Harris's, the only other name that comes to mind is Waldo."

He stuffed it into his coat pocket, and they stood staring up the steep wall.

"What now?" Daniel said. "We climb?"

Rainy turned in a full circle, trying to take in everything, not just what she saw, but what all her senses offered her.

"Do you feel it?" she said.

"What?"

"It's like a rip in the fabric of this place. A violation of its spirit."

Almost immediately, they heard Stephen's distant cry. They took off in that direction, making their way as quickly as they could through the pines and the undergrowth. In a few minutes, they came to the west end of the island, where they found Stephen and Trevor standing side by side, staring at the ground.

Rainy saw it then, too, what had grabbed their attention and now made them stand there, dumb. In the shade beneath the pines, a great stain spread across the bed of needles. It was as dark as beet juice, but Rainy knew it had once been a brighter hue.

Daniel knelt, touched it, then looked up at the others. "Blood."

"Maybe from an animal?" Stephen said. "A wolf kill or something?"

"There'd be evidence of the carcass," Daniel said. "Someone bled here, bled a lot."

"Lindsay?" Trevor said. "Dear God, no."

Daniel took the brightly striped cap from his pocket. "Is this your sister's?"

"Grandpa John gave it to her. He joked that if she wore it, we'd never lose track of her." Trevor stared at the cap, then at the pooling of blood, and all the life seemed to drain from him.

They heard Bud Bowers coming through the woods, and in a moment he was with them.

"Jesus," he said. "What happened here?"

"The question of the day." Daniel stood, walked around the stain, then moved toward the lakeshore, which lay a dozen yards outside the trees. He studied the ground carefully as he went. "Here," he said. When they joined him, he pointed to a long, straight line in the dirt. "I'd bet my right arm the gunwale of a canoe left that mark."

"What's it mean?" Trevor asked.

Stephen gazed out at the empty lake and said in a tense, quiet voice, "It means that my dad and your sister weren't alone here."

Chapter 21

At first light, they hit Mudd Lake. The tall man, the woman, and Lindsay took the lead canoe. Cork and the kid followed in the other. They'd cut Cork's hands free so that he could handle a paddle. The tall man had warned him again against attempting to escape. The woman gave him a look that told him she'd love to have him try.

The kid had limped badly that morning. The tall man had looked at the stitches.

"Inflamed. Probably some infection. How's it feeling?"

"Hurts, but I'll make it," the kid had said.

"No other choice," the tall man had told him. "We'll get you looked at as soon as we're out."

On the water now, the kid sat in the stern on his pack and kept his leg stretched out in front of him and didn't lean hard into his work. That was fine with Cork. He was tired from his sleepless night and gave his own effort less than his all. As a result, their canoe slipped farther and farther behind the other.

The sun had risen and cracked the hold of the deep chill the night before. Cork felt warmed and, in a way, buoyed. He hadn't been able to spirit Lindsay Harris to safety, but he knew that he had time now to figure out a different plan. From what he'd overheard of the tall man's sat phone conversation, he understood that whoever was supposed to pick them up and fly them out was, at the moment, behind bars somewhere. Also, he'd heard the tall man mention the RCMP, the Royal Canadian Mounted Police. The party was headed north, and there was nothing north but Canada. Without a plane to fly them out, it would take a lot of paddling and a lot of portaging to get there. He looked at the blue sky and knew time wouldn't be the only thing he'd need. The good weather would have to hold, which, if winter came in the usual way, would be asking a lot.

"I've got a son about your age," Cork said. "His name's Stephen. What's your name?"

Behind him, the kid said, "Doesn't matter."

"Is that French?"

He heard the kid laugh.

"O'Connor," the kid said. "Irish?"

"Some. Anishinaabe, too."

"Shinnob? Us, too. Odawa."

"Flynn's death was an accident," Cork said. "I hope he wasn't related to you."

"He claimed to be by clan," the kid said. "Not blood. I don't know if it was true."

"I'm Ma'iingan," Cork said. Wolf Clan.

"Makwa," the kid said. Bear Clan.

"The others? Odawa, too?"

"My uncle. Mrs. Gray and Flynn, Ojibwe, I think, like you. They're from another reserve. I don't know which one. I don't know anything about them, really. Didn't even know his name was Flynn until she said it. Before that he was just Mr. Gray, like she's just Mrs. Gray. Didn't know he was her brother, either. I figured they were married."

"If you don't know them, why are they with you?"

"Fox brought them in to help."

"Fox?"

The kid must have realized he was talking too much, and Cork got no answer.

"What do you all have against Harris and his granddaughter?"

Again, the kid didn't reply.

"Kidnapping's a pretty big deal. It'll get you thrown in jail for a long time."

Cork glanced over his shoulder, and the kid gave him a dark look.

"Ever been in jail?"

"Don't talk anymore," the kid said. "Just paddle."

At the north end of Mudd, they portaged along a thread of water nearly a mile to the next lake. Cork tried to remember the lake's name and if it was one he'd been on before. But there were so many in the Boundary Waters, he couldn't pull up any recollection. The portage, however, was a new twist because it was common knowledge that there wasn't an easy way onto or off Mudd Lake. As far as Cork could tell, the tall man in the lead wasn't consulting a map. He seemed to have a good sense of the land and where they were headed.

When the sun was directly overhead, they put in to a little cove and the woman pulled food from one of the packs—beef sticks, nuts, and an orange, which she gave to the kid. They sat on the shore in the warm sunshine and ate, and for a long time no one said a word.

"Quetico by sundown," Cork said.

"Shut up," the woman said.

"Quetico?" Lindsay Harris said. "We're crossing into Canada?"

The tall man said, "The border is only a line on a map."

"*Aandi wenjibaayan?*" Cork said. Where are you from?

The tall man eyed him, and although he didn't respond, Cork knew that he understood.

"You're Odawa," Cork said. "Anishinaabe like me."

"You're *wayaabishkiiwed*," the tall man said. A white man.

"He's *chimook*," the woman said. White bastard.

"*Anishinaabe indaaw*," Cork said. I am Anishinaabe.

"In your heart?" the tall man questioned. "Would you die for The People?"

"Is that what you're planning on doing?" Cork looked at the kid. "All of you?"

"I'm gonna shut you up," the woman said and started to rise.

"Relax," the tall man told her. "The time will come, O'Connor, when the reason for all this becomes clear. I wouldn't mind having you alive to see that. You might understand. But your life, the lives of us all, don't matter much in the long run."

"My life matters to me," Cork said. "I'm sure Miss Harris feels the same about hers."

"You think we care what matters to you?" the woman said. "There are more important things at stake than your life."

"Or Flynn's?" Cork said.

"You say his name one more time . . ." the woman began.

"Leave it," the tall man said. "No more talk."

"Tell me one thing." Lindsay Harris said, a demand.

The tall man considered her. "What?"

"My grandfather, is he still alive?"

"Yes. But that might change, depending on you."

"Me?"

"No more escape attempts. If we come out of this wilderness and you're not with us, your grandfather is dead."

"Why?" Her voice was strained, taut. "What difference do I make in anything?"

"You know the bargain," the tall man said. "Do you agree to it?"

Cork watched her body, saw how rigid she held it, trying to keep her rage in check. "I don't have much choice, do I?"

"Neither do I," he told her.

The tall man looked at Cork. "The lives of this woman and her grandfather are in your hands. Will you put them in danger again?"

"I won't try to escape," Cork said. "You have my word."

"The word of a *chimook*," the sour woman said.

"All right then. We all understand each other." The tall man stood. "I'm going to check in on the sat phone."

He pulled the phone from the pack and walked away from the others.

The kid touched his knee and squeezed his eyes shut. A little moan escaped his lips.

"Are the stitches holding?" Cork asked.

"Yeah, but it hurts."

"I have a friend who makes a wonderful willow tea for pain."

"Uncle Aaron gave me some aspirin."

"Shut up," the woman snapped.

Cork couldn't tell if the hurt in the kid's eyes at that moment came from the pain of his knee or the harshness of her voice.

Lindsay leaned to Cork. "I haven't had a chance to thank you."

"What for?"

"Coming back last night. You could have left me."

"Shut up," the sour woman said.

Lindsay paid her no mind. "I'm sorry I got you into this."

"Let it go," Cork said. "My choice."

The tall man returned. "Cheval won't be getting out of jail today, but maybe first thing in the morning."

"So what do we do?" the kid said.

"Keep going. If someone comes looking for these two, the farther we are from Raspberry Lake the better."

They loaded the canoes, shoved off, and headed north. As he paddled, Cork thought, *Aaron. Uncle Aaron. And the woman's alias is Mrs. Gray*. He didn't have any idea at the moment what to do with these pieces of information, but he understood that everything you knew about your enemy was important.

CHAPTER 22

"Two canoes," Daniel English said. He knelt near the others. "The line where the gunwale lay is fainter over here, but you can see it. Whoever they were, they came and went in two canoes."

"Two canoes?" Sheriff Marsha Dross looked across the lake where the water sparkled under the midday sun. "Where are they then?"

Stephen said, "Dad and Lindsay Harris spent the night over there." He pointed toward the campsite on the mainland. "Then they must have come here."

"And either stumbled onto someone, or someone was waiting for them," Dross said.

It was hard for Rainy to look where the blood soaked the ground, but it was also hard not to. *Whose blood?* she wondered. And she prayed, *Not Cork's.*

"Bud Bowers flew the whole lake before he came to get you," Daniel said. "No sign of them."

"He also flew over the portages north and south and over the lakes at either end," Stephen said. "Nothing."

"My sister couldn't just vanish into thin air," Trevor Harris insisted.

They all looked at him silently, because that's exactly what had happened to his grandfather.

"I mean," Trevor said, "Cork was with her. He would have protected her, right?"

And again they were all silent and were careful not to look at the great staining of blood.

"Why?" Trevor said angrily. "Why would anyone want my sister?"

"Maybe it was Cork they wanted," Dross said.

But she didn't say it with any conviction, and Rainy understood why. The connection between the missing man and Cork was ancient and tenuous. The powerful connection was between the missing man and his now missing granddaughter.

Dross's walkie-talkie crackled.

"You there, Sheriff?"

"Dross here. Go ahead, George."

"I've gone over the campsite pretty thoroughly. It's just like the family said. Nothing out of order here. Nothing disturbed."

"Ten-four, George. Why don't you bring the boat over and we'll do a search of the island."

"Roger, Sheriff."

"What's the use of searching the island?" Trevor said. "They're not here."

"We need to be sure," Dross said.

She means, Rainy thought, *we need to be sure there are no bodies.*

Deputy Azevedo came across the water in a yellow inflatable raft that the floatplane had dropped when it brought the two law enforcement officers out to Raspberry Lake an hour earlier. Almost immediately afterward, Bowers had taken off again to fly over some of the other nearby lakes on the off chance he'd spot Cork and the young woman. When the deputy had joined them, they divided themselves into three groups. Dross and Azevedo took the south side of the island, Daniel and Trevor took the north, and Rainy and Stephen moved through the middle. The day had grown warm, at least compared to the cold of the night before. The island was silent in the way of the Northwoods in winter, when the birds had migrated and so many of the animals had gone into their dark, protected places to hibernate. The only sounds were the crack and scrape of their own passage as they broke through the underbrush, and the occasional cry of a startled crow, a bird that never left the North Country and was crafty enough to survive the harshest of winters.

They're not here, Rainy thought. *I would feel it if they were. And I would feel it if Cork had left his spirit here.*

As if in echo, Stephen said, "We won't find them on this island."

"We have to be certain," Rainy said.

"But you know we won't."

He glanced at her, and she felt the way she sometimes felt when her great-uncle looked at her, as if he could see all the way down to her soul. There was something unique in Stephen, and everyone knew it. Some people, the lucky ones, were born with a certainty about the path they were meant to follow. Stephen was one of these. He believed he was born destined to be Mide. Her, she'd stumbled so many times in her life, and then she'd found Crow Point and Henry. And finally Cork.

"They're gone," Stephen said. "We should be trying to figure out where instead of wasting time here."

"Henry's advice would be to stop looking and open ourselves to what's already in front of us."

They'd come to the wall of gray rock. Rainy studied the climb, trying to decide if they should attempt it. But Stephen started up without hesitation.

"Wait for me," Rainy called.

They climbed carefully and were at the top in a few minutes. Rainy stood breathing hard from the effort, taking in the view: the horseshoe of azure water, the roll of the tree-blanketed hills, the winter sun, a dull yellow in a broad sky of stunning blue. A breeze came from the west and ran along the top of the rise, carrying with it the sharp scent of evergreen.

"It's beautiful up here," Rainy said.

"Raspberry's not on one of the more popular routes through the Boundary Waters," Stephen said. "It doesn't give access to many other lakes. Those who know it love it, though."

"You've been here before?"

"Only once, a long time ago. But I have a photographer friend who comes here sometimes just to shoot this view." He turned and began to walk the length of the ridge.

They ran into Daniel and Trevor coming from the other direction.

"Anything?" Daniel asked.

Stephen shook his head. "You?"

"Only this." Daniel held out his hand. Cupped in his palm were some bits of orange peel. "There's still some fragrance to them. They weren't left that long ago."

"Someone was up here," Stephen said.

"My sister and Cork?" Trevor offered hopefully.

"Maybe." Daniel's almond eyes took in the clear 360-degree vista the ridge afforded them. "But I'm thinking that if I wanted to be certain I spotted your sister and Cork when they hit the lake, this is where I'd park myself to watch."

And so we come back to why, Rainy thought.

"Yo," Dross called up to them. She and Deputy Azevedo stood at the base of the wall below, craning their necks to look up to where Rainy and the others stood. "Anything?"

"Litter," Daniel called back. "Someone was up here not long ago, but they're gone now."

"Come on down then," Dross said. "We need to figure what next."

CHAPTER 23

They followed a twisting course. Without a map, Cork had only the most general sense of where they were in the Boundary Waters. The lake they paddled at the moment didn't look familiar. Or rather, looked like so many of the other lakes he'd canoed over the years that he couldn't say if it was one he'd been on before. He kept an eye out for landmarks that might give him an idea of his exact location, but every cliff face, every island, every shoreline seemed familiar and at the same time strange.

Sometimes he could hear a little moan escape the lips of the kid in the stern, and he knew the injured knee was giving him a good deal of pain. His mind kept working around ways to use that against these people who'd kidnapped him and Lindsay. Although he'd given the tall man his word that he wouldn't try to escape, he'd break it in a heartbeat if he was certain he could get Lindsay away from them safely. But he understood the possible consequence for Lindsay Harris and her grandfather, and for him, too, if he failed.

The pain of the kid moved him, and he admired the kid's effort to be stoic. Cork began to sing quietly:

"My paddle's keen and bright,
Flashing like silver,
Swift as the wild goose flies,
Dip, dip, and swing."

He glanced back at the kid. "Know that one?"
"I don't," the kid said.

"Dip, dip, and swing her back
Flashing like silver,
Swift as the wild goose flies,
Dip, dip, and swing."

Cork said, "It's a round that you sing as you paddle. I learned it when I was a Boy Scout. Makes the time go by. Give it a try."

"I'm not a kid," the kid said.

"The voyageurs used to sing as they paddled. Men as tough as you'd find anywhere. They knew the secret. Singing helps take your mind off the hard things. Come on, give it a try."

He sang the verses again, then said to the kid, "You start and I'll come in. Like I said, you sing it as a round."

He pulled his paddle through the water and watched the far shoreline of the lake draw nearer. It took a little while, then he heard the kid sing softly, *"My paddle's keen and bright, flashing like silver."* And Cork joined in.

They were nearing a pine-covered finger of land when Cork heard a little growling in the distance, slowly rising above the sound of his singing and the kid's. In the canoe far ahead of them, the tall man lifted his paddle from the water, laid it across the gunwales, and listened. He gestured furiously toward the pine-covered jut and dug his paddle into the lake.

Behind Cork, the kid said, "Jesus, a plane."

Cork felt the renewed thrust of the kid's strokes, and the birch-bark canoe shot forward.

"Paddle, damn it!" the kid shouted.

Cork put his back into it.

Moments before they made the cover of the point, the plane appeared over the treetops at the far end of the lake. It was a good half mile distant, flying low, flying slowly. Searching for him and Lindsay? Cork wondered.

"You do anything to attract attention, anything, and we'll kill you," the kid said. "Honest to God we will."

It was an almost hysterical statement. Not cold and calculated.

Scared. The kid was scared to death. And even a small animal when cornered and scared could inflict great harm. Cork dug his paddle into the water and gave it his all.

At first the plane kept to the north. It vanished from sight behind the pine-covered point. But the roar of the engine grew louder as the canoes hit the rocky shoreline.

"Into the trees," the tall man shouted.

Lindsay leaped out with the others in the lead canoe and ran for the shadows of the pines. Cork did the same, then heard the splash behind him as the kid stumbled getting out, and the little craft tipped and dumped the packs into the water. The kid went into the lake with everything else. The roar of the plane was almost overhead. The kid struggled to rise, making a great commotion. Cork jumped into the lake beside him and, as the kid tried to fight his way up and out, said to him, "Just relax and lie still. We'll never make it to the trees."

The kid stared at him, his eyes huge with panic.

"Lie down with me," Cork said and prostrated himself in the water.

The kid went limp and did the same. They were like small tree trunks, fallen and waterlogged beside the overturned canoe.

The plane appeared suddenly, like a great bird of prey, streaking over the treetops, dragging its broad-winged shadow across the ground. It flew directly over them, for a brief moment obscuring the sun. Cork saw that it was a floatplane, a yellow de Havilland Beaver. He was almost certain that it belonged to the Forest Service, and although he couldn't see into the cockpit, he was pretty sure Bud Bowers was at the controls. A strong part of him ached to leap up and wave his arms and call to that lean, familiar figure, a man he knew well and counted as a friend. But the circumstances were so unfamiliar, so unpredictable, so volatile that he put a clamp on all his impulses and lay still in the water, which was freezing him right down to his bones.

The plane moved south across the body of the lake and rose at the far end in order to clear the trees there. It became black and small, like a crow, then smaller, like a bit of ash, and finally was gone altogether.

Cork stood up and reached down to the kid, who, when he rose, did so with great difficulty. It was clear he couldn't put weight on his injured leg. Thigh-deep in the water, he leaned heavily on Cork for support.

"*Migwech*," the kid said. Thanks.

The others came running from the trees.

"What happened?" the tall man asked. His face was stone, his voice stern as he eyed the canoe overturned in the water and the gear that lay on the lake bottom, clearly visible in the pristine water.

The kid couldn't look at him. He hung his head. "My leg," he said. "It just gave out under me."

"Can you walk?" the tall man asked.

"I'll try."

"Come out then." The tall man reached toward him.

With the help of his uncle and Cork, the kid hobbled out and fell on dry ground. He winced and held his knee.

The woman came and knelt beside him and pulled his hands away from his torn jeans and the wound that showed beneath.

"You've broken the stitches," she said, as if he'd done it on purpose.

The tall man bent next to her. "Infected."

"I'm cold," the kid said.

"You need to get him dry and warm," Cork said.

"Right that canoe, O'Connor, and haul out those packs," the tall man said. "No use the rest of us getting soaked."

Cork did as he'd been instructed. When the packs had been laid on the ground, the tall man took the sat phone from one of them, shook off the water, and tried it.

"Dead," he said.

"Sorry." The kid was shaking from the cold so bad that he spoke in a quivering voice.

"Get him dry," Cork said again. "Get him warm."

The tall man eyed the rise at the far end of the lake where the floatplane had climbed and vanished.

"It'll be a long time before he comes back," Cork told him. "If he ever does."

The tall man looked down at the kid, and his face finally changed, softened just a little. "Let's build a fire," he said.

CHAPTER 24

They sat at the kitchen table in the house on Gooseberry Lane. Rose was peeling potatoes for the evening meal. Jenny was snapping the ends off pea pods. Waaboo was in the living room, using an old towel to play tug-of-war with Trixie. The growls of the dog and the howls of Waaboo mixed in a kind of familiar music that was oddly comforting. Rose had spent much of her life in this house with the sound of children like music in the background. She and Mal had not been able to have children, and in her own quiet home she sometimes missed all the chaos that came with little ones.

That afternoon they'd received a call from Kathy Engesser at the Sheriff's Office to say that Marsha Dross and one of her deputies had flown out to join the others at Raspberry Lake. There'd been some trouble, but the exact nature wasn't clear. She'd promised to update them when she knew more. She hadn't called back yet.

Rose watched Jenny tear at the little green pods. "Are you particularly mad at those peas?"

"I still don't get it."

"What?"

"Why Dad felt he had to go. Now Daniel's out there, too. Suddenly my wedding's taken a backseat for everyone."

"John Harris is an old friend."

Jenny tore a pod completely apart and swore under her breath. "They haven't seen each other in years."

"It's about more than that. I think Cork feels he needs to atone."

"For what?"

"Your mother. Your brother. All those poor, preyed-on kids he couldn't save after that young girl washed up on Windigo Island last year. I think maybe he feels that he's let a lot of people down."

Jenny studied the pile of pea pod ends lying discarded in a small bowl. "He never talks about that."

"Maybe he never will. That's not his way." Rose put down her potato peeler. "You know, every time I look at you, I see your mother. You look so much like her."

"Did he talk to her?"

"Not nearly as much as she would have liked. I remember her telling me once that getting him to share his feelings was like trying to pick berries off a big, thorny bush. I'm guessing that when she died, there were a lot of things he regretted never saying to her."

Jenny reached across the table and squeezed her aunt's hand. "You keep us grounded, you know. I'm glad you're here."

The kitchen door burst open. Stephen, Rainy, and Daniel swept in, bringing the cold from outside.

"Is that coffee I smell?" Daniel said.

They all tugged off their coats and hung them.

"Sit down," Rose said. "I'll pour coffee for anyone who wants some."

Waaboo came running and hit Daniel going full-bore. The man stumbled back but held. He lifted the little boy, who said, "You smell like a pine tree."

"And you smell like a dog," Daniel said.

"Cuz of Trixie," Waaboo told him.

At the sound of her name, the old dog came trotting in.

They all sat at the table. Rose gave Waaboo a little plastic tumbler of milk and a cookie, and he ate quietly as the others told of their day on Raspberry Lake, including the great spill of blood they'd found on the island.

"Search and Rescue will be out tomorrow in full force," Daniel said, shaking his head. "I don't think they'll find anything we didn't."

"Just like her grandfather," Stephen said. "They've disappeared into thin air."

"Maybe a monster ate them," Waaboo said. "There are monsters in the woods."

Jenny said, "Why would a monster eat John Harris and his granddaughter and Baa-baa?"

"I guess because he's a hungry monster. Can I have another cookie?"

"It will spoil your dinner," she said. "I think Trixie wants you to play with her some more."

Waaboo slid from his chair, picked up the old towel, which Trixie had dropped on the floor, and ran into the living room, the dog following on his heels.

"It's a good question," Rainy said. "Why would a monster eat them all?"

"And what's that monster's name?" Daniel said.

The telephone rang. Jenny answered, listened a moment, and said, "Thanks, Father Green. I appreciate your prayers. And I'll let you know as soon as we've heard anything." She came back to the table. "Word's already spreading."

"Should we call Annie and tell her what's going on?" Stephen said.

Annie, the middle O'Connor child, was in California, where she'd taken a job with a nonprofit organization in San Jose, leading groups of inner-city kids on camping trips into the Sierras. At the moment, she was in the mountains on one of those excursions.

"I think we should wait," Jenny said. "We don't know what's going on. No reason to get Annie upset and pull her away from her kids until we have a better handle on this. Okay?"

"All right," Stephen said, but it was clear his agreement wasn't wholehearted. "So what do we do? It doesn't feel right just sitting."

"I'd like to know more about this John W. Harris and his family," Jenny said. "There's a reason Harris is missing and Lindsay's been taken."

"And Cork," Rainy said.

"I think Dad just happened to be along," Stephen said. "Collateral—" He stopped himself.

They were quiet, because they all knew the blood on Raspberry Island could have come from Cork.

Daniel broke the silence. "Let's get started," he said and rose from his chair.

"Where are you going?" Rainy asked.

"To talk to Marsha Dross. I want to know what she found out when Harris first went missing."

"I'm going with you," Rainy said.

Jenny slid her chair back. "I'd like to go, too."

Daniel shook his head. "I'd rather you worked your magic on the Internet. Find out what you can about the Harris family."

"We should talk with Trevor, too," Stephen said and followed Daniel and Rainy to the door.

Rose said, "I'll have dinner waiting for you when you're finished."

They all took off, Jenny to her computer, the others out the door. Rose was left alone in the kitchen. The circumstances were certainly awful, but what she'd just experienced she understood as one of the great blessings in her life. Family. They were all different and didn't always agree and sometimes fought and knew how to hurt one another deeply, if they wanted to. But when one of them had a back against the wall, they all rallied and became a formidable whole. God, did she love them.

CHAPTER 25

They'd stripped themselves of their wet clothing, Cork and the kid. The tall man had given them each a wool blanket he'd pulled from one of the packs that had been in the first canoe so that everything was dry. Then he and the woman had gathered firewood. With a big hunting knife, he'd stripped away the outer layer of the wood, which had become wet in the recent rain, and the woman had built a fire, a good one that burned hot and sent up very little smoke. They'd strung a line between trees near enough to the fire that the wet clothing they hung there would dry more quickly.

In the late afternoon, the tall man put fishing gear into the first canoe and paddled onto the lake. Although Cork figured they'd planned on being flown quickly out of the Boundary Waters after the abduction, the tall man had clearly come prepared for the unanticipated. In the midst of all the inexplicable and confusing occurrences of the last two days, it was a small thing, but it mattered. It told Cork more about the man.

As daylight weakened, the kid sat by the fire with the blanket draped around him. He stared into the flames, his expression one that seemed to speak of sullen regret. He was still a kid, but he probably wanted very much to be thought a man. Like the tall man, Uncle Aaron. They were family. To bring a kid on an expedition like this, one that from the outset would involve kidnapping, was hard to fathom. Whatever was at the heart of their mission, it was important to them. Money? Cork dismissed that one out of hand. There'd been no ransom demanded for John Harris. Revenge maybe? Cork had seen the passion for vengeance drive even good men to horrific deeds. If revenge, then in response to what? Or it might be that the Harrises were leverage in some kind of struggle. But what struggle, and who were the forces involved?

The tall man had left the sour woman with the rifle. She sat with her back against a tree, scanning the sky as if watching for the reappearance of the floatplane. Lindsay Harris, who'd been sitting on the far side of the fire from the kid, stood suddenly and moved toward him.

"Get back where you were," the woman ordered.

"I'm not going to plot anything," Lindsay replied. "You can hear every word I say." She sat next to the kid. "You okay?"

"Cold," he said.

"Mind if I look at that knee?"

"What for?"

"I've had my share of first-aid training."

The kid drew the blanket aside enough for her to see the wound. She touched the area around it. The kid made a pained sound.

"What do you think?" he said.

"The body's an amazing thing," she said. "Good at fighting what doesn't belong inside it. But there's something even more important. When I was thirteen years old, I visited my grandfather in Costa Rica. He was designing a road through some mountains there. I got bit by a jumping viper."

"What's that?"

"A poisonous snake. It jumps when it strikes you. We were in the jungle, a long way from any clinic. Everybody thought I was going to die. Except my grandfather. He told me the only thing that would kill me was not believing."

"Believing what?"

"That my spirit was stronger than that poison. He said, 'Spirit is at the heart of everything, and there's nothing more powerful. Trust your spirit.' His exact words."

"What happened?"

"Well, here I am." She smiled. "Like I said, your body's an

amazing thing. But at the heart of everything is your spirit. Trust that."

"Stupid story," the sour woman said.

But the kid said, "I'm going to be all right." Then he said, "Thanks."

The tall man returned with a couple of smallmouth bass. While he cleaned them, the woman scrounged two forked sticks and two long, straight sticks from among the pines on the little peninsula. When the tall man was finished, he skewered the fish with the long sticks, mouth to tail. The woman pushed the two forked sticks firmly into the ground at the fire's edge and the tall man set the fish to roasting over the open flames.

The clothing had mostly dried by the time the fish was cooked, and Cork and the kid dressed for supper. Everything smelled heavily of woodsmoke. The bass were truly tasty. In the Boundary Waters, after a full day of canoeing and portaging, anything remotely edible seemed like a feast.

"You spend a lot of time in the woods," Cork said to the tall man.

"It nourishes me," the tall man said. He eyed Cork across the fire. "I'm sure you know what I mean."

"I've been coming to the Boundary Waters since before I can remember," Cork told him. "My father and mother brought me with them when I was just a baby."

"I was born in the woods," the tall man said.

"Where was that?"

The tall man smiled, as if he saw the trap, and didn't respond.

The kid said, "I don't feel right anywhere but in the woods. People, well, they just kind of make me nervous. Out here, it's just me and the spirits of the woods. I don't have to say nothing if I don't want to."

"You're talking plenty now," the woman said. Then she eyed the tall man. "Both of you."

The kid looked at her, then into the fire, and fell silent.

"Did you build the canoes?" Cork asked the tall man.

The tall man seemed to consider the advisability of answering, glanced at the sour woman, and finally said, "Yes."

"In the old way," Cork said and let his admiration show.

"My father taught me. And his father taught him."

Cork nodded toward the kid. "Have you taught your nephew?"

"Uncle Aaron—" the kid started, but the woman cut him off.

"Hush up, both of you," she snapped. "Can't you see he's just trying to get information out of us? How stupid can you be?"

"That's enough," the tall man said.

The woman looked at Cork. "I don't like you."

Cork said, "Now there's a news flash."

Lindsay Harris laughed, then caught herself and returned to her silence.

"I want to ask you something," the tall man said, looking at Cork, his eyes like glowing charcoal in the firelight. "Why didn't you try to signal that plane?"

"I know the pilot. He's a friend."

"So?"

"If he'd landed and had come to shore, what would you have done?"

"Killed him," the woman said, sounding eager at the prospect.

"Exactly," Cork said. "I didn't want to take that chance."

Night had fallen. The moon was rising, and where its glow didn't swallow the stars, the sky glittered. There was not a ripple on the lake, and across it ran a frosty-looking river of moonlight. In the summer, the woods would have been full of the sounds of nocturnal creatures—crickets, tree frogs, bull frogs, katydids, and of course the ubiquitous buzz of the mosquito. But in that shoulder season right on the cusp of winter, the woods were dead quiet. But not at all dead, Cork knew. Out there in the dark were deer and moose and mink and rabbits and a whole world of animals that didn't sleep through the cold season. Across aeons, they'd evolved into creatures that could withstand the worst of what the North Country might deliver. The spirits, as the kid had called them, of that land were powerful and enduring, and

Cork understood the awe and the kinship the kid felt toward them.

"Cold again tonight," the tall man said. "Ice on the lakes by morning, more than today. It'll slow us down."

The woman said, "We don't have much time. If we just had the damn sat phone." She gave the kid another of her cold glares.

"It will be what it will be," the tall man said. "If we have to leave the canoes and walk, we'll walk."

"Christmas before we make it to White Woman Lake," the sour woman said, then seemed to realize her mistake and looked at Cork to see if he'd caught it.

He had. And he filed that piece of information away with all the other bits he was collecting that might help him put the puzzle together before it was too late.

CHAPTER 26

Deputy Pender was at the contact desk. He buzzed them through and took them back to the sheriff's office. Marsha Dross was sitting at her desk, bent over a topographical map of the Boundary Waters. She looked up when they walked in, and Rainy saw clearly in her drawn face the deep concern she felt.

"Only one chair," she said, nodding to the empty seat on the other side of her desk. "You'll have to fight over it."

Daniel and Stephen insisted Rainy take the chair, and they stood flanking her.

"Three disappearances. And not a clue where they vanished." Dross sat back. "Azevedo's still looking. He's camping out at Raspberry Lake tonight. Tomorrow I've got Search and Rescue on it and dogs coming in, but somehow I don't think they'll turn up anything."

Rainy knew that Marsha Dross's concern wasn't just professional. Cork had hired her when he was sheriff, the first woman law enforcement officer in Tamarack County. She'd once taken a bullet meant for him. And he, in turn, had saved her life. What bound them, bound all those in the room, was powerful. They'd shared their lives with one another. They shared a common history and, in a way, a common heart.

"Whoever they were in those canoes, they were after Lindsay Harris, not Cork. The only common thread at the moment seems to be the family tie," Daniel said. "I don't want to seem cold-blooded, but Harris is a very wealthy man. What did the kids have to gain if their grandfather died?"

"A reasonable question. And one I looked into myself when Harris went missing." Dross sat back. "They inherit. They inherit everything."

"Were they close, grandfather and grandchildren?"

"I only know what I observed, and their concern for their granddad seemed real enough."

"Trevor Harris is an actor," Rainy said.

"And his sister is missing now, too," Stephen said. "If she never shows up, he's the only heir left."

"He didn't go into the Boundary Waters with Cork and his sister," Daniel pointed out. "You have to ask yourself why."

"And," Rainy added, "how was it that whoever took Cork and Lindsay knew they were coming?"

They all fell silent, mulling over these things. Then Daniel asked, "Where exactly was Trevor when his grandfather disappeared?"

"Fishing," Dross said. "Alone. Same with his grandfather. As I understand, it was a kind of contest between the two of them. Apparently Trevor bet a thousand dollars that he could land a bigger fish than John Harris. According to Lindsay and Dwight—"

"Would that be Dwight Kohler?" Stephen said.

Dross nodded. "He was their guide in the Boundary Waters. According to Lindsay and Dwight, they went entirely different directions on Raspberry Lake. Trevor paddled to the east end of the horseshoe and his grandfather headed west. An hour later, Trevor came back with a whopper of a walleye. Dwight snapped a photo of him with his prize." She got up and went to one of the file cabinets along the wall, pulled open a drawer, and drew out a photograph. She brought it back to the desk. It was a shot of Trevor Harris holding up his prize catch, a huge grin plastered across his face.

"Big fish, all right," Stephen said.

"So it would appear that Harris couldn't have had a hand in his grandfather's disappearance," Daniel said.

"That's right." Dross took back the photograph. "And the

granddaughter was with Dwight the whole time, so we didn't really look at her either."

She started toward the file cabinet with photograph in hand, but Daniel said, "Mind if I hang on to that?"

The sheriff handed it over. "I don't know what good it'll do you."

Daniel tapped the photo. "I'd like to know what bait our actor used to catch this big fish. Maybe Dwight can tell me."

"So where do you go from here?" Rainy asked the sheriff.

"The blood samples we took on Raspberry Island are being analyzed. We'll have the blood type by morning. DNA'll take a while."

"But at least you'll be able to tell if the blood type matches Cork's," Rainy said.

"Or Lindsay's. We've already secured that info. In the meantime, we'll do a thorough search of Raspberry Lake, see if the dogs turn up anything tomorrow. You're welcome to go along if you'd like."

They looked at one another, and Daniel finally answered for them. "I think we've got things here to see to. But you'll keep us posted?"

"Promise," the sheriff said.

At the Four Seasons, Nadia, the desk clerk from Romania who'd been there the day before, when Rainy and Daniel were looking for Trevor Harris, told them he'd gone out not long before.

"Dinner?" Stephen asked.

"I suppose eating is one of the things you can do at the casino," she said.

As they drove out of town toward the Chippewa Grand, Daniel said, "What kind of man gambles when his sister is lost in the woods?"

"My first guess would be someone addicted," Rainy replied.

"Another might be someone who didn't particularly care about his sister but put on a good act," Daniel said.

Rainy shook her head. "I think that's a harsh judgment. When I was with him today, I didn't get a sense of callousness. And he seemed truly alarmed today when he saw the blood."

"You're always looking for the best in people, Aunt Rainy," Daniel said.

"No. I'm always looking for what balances them, good and bad. Maybe Trevor Harris has a gambling addiction, but that doesn't mean he's the kind of young man who'd want his sister dead in order to get rich."

"But what about his grandfather?" Stephen said. "Is Trevor capable of doing the old man in? Any feeling there, Aunt Rainy?"

"I don't know how he could have been involved. He was fishing in a whole other part of the lake when his grandfather went missing. Let's talk to him before we make any assumptions. I think it's best to keep ourselves open to all possibilities."

The casino was hopping. The slots were busy, singing their siren songs to a milling crowd. Trevor Harris was at a high-stakes blackjack table. He had an enviable stack of chips in front of him. Whether he'd bought them all or had won them, Rainy couldn't have said. But in the minute or so that they stood watching before they approached him, he won and then won again, and his stacks grew. A young woman playing next to him, a redhead in a studded, black leather vest, reached out and ran her hand down his arm. When he looked at her, she gave him a big maroon-lipped smile and said, "Just trying to pick up some of your luck, honey."

To which he replied, "Take all you want, love. I've got plenty to spare."

She laughed in a way Rainy knew was meant to be seductive. Trevor Harris smiled back in a way meant to say he was interested. And Rainy worked at putting all this together in a way that might help her better understand the young man before she made any judgments. In her head, she could hear Henry advising, *Patience*.

"Daniel!"

They turned and watched a handsome man in a dark business

suit stride toward them across the casino floor. He held out his hand as he came, and Daniel grasped it when they met.

"Ben," Daniel said. "Good to see you."

"I thought you didn't gamble," the man in the dark suit said.

"I don't. Just here to talk to someone."

"Who? Can I help you find them?"

"We've found him," Daniel said. He nodded toward Trevor.

"Oh, you know Mr. Harris?"

"You know him, too?" Daniel said.

"High roller, that one."

"And quite lucky," Rainy said.

"This is my aunt Rainy," Daniel said. "And a friend, Stephen O'Connor. Folks, this is Ben Trudeau. He manages the casino."

They shook hands, and Trudeau asked in a guarded voice, "Is Mr. Harris a friend of yours, Daniel?"

"I wouldn't say that," Daniel replied. "We have a mutual family interest."

Trudeau watched Trevor Harris win another hand. "He is, as you say, extraordinarily lucky. So much so that I have him under surveillance now. He knows it and doesn't seem to care. I don't believe he counts cards, but I think he must be playing some kind of system to be winning so consistently. We just haven't been able to figure out what it is. But we will. We always do." He smiled at Daniel. "If you'll excuse me, I have things to see to. If you need anything, Daniel, just let me know. A pleasure meeting you all."

He continued across the casino floor and was lost among the machines there.

"How do you know him?" Stephen asked.

"I spoke at a conference here a few months ago, a bunch of Twin Cities businesspeople looking to invest in Native initiatives. I talked about the importance of enterprises focused on protecting the environment. Ben was extremely supportive, and we got to know each other pretty well."

"Is he Shinnob?" Rainy asked.

"Odawa. He works for a First Nations company out of Canada.

They train people to run casinos, and they consult on casino issues and management. Lots of experience, apparently."

Rainy knew that the Chippewa Grand had been through many management changes over the years. Along with the benefits of the gambling revenue had come all the dark temptations that shadowed big money. There'd been corrupt practices in the running of the casino, lingering questions about the financial records, the distributions, the hiring practices, how cleanly the games themselves were operated. Rainy almost never came to the casino. She was among those who felt it was a corruption of spirit to profit from the weaknesses of others, or even from their careless excesses. She knew, too, that there were plenty of Native folks who took the money from their tribal allotment and simply fed it right back into the same machines that had generated it.

Stephen and Daniel flanked Trevor Harris, and Rainy stood behind. Daniel put a hand on his shoulder. "We need to talk."

Trevor looked left, then right. "I'm kind of in the middle of something here."

"Something really good," the redhead sitting in the next chair said. "Shame to break his streak."

"Won't take long," Stephen said.

Trevor stood. "Mark my place, Krystal," he said to the dealer. "I'll be right back."

They walked away from the table and gathered near the bar in an area that was not so busy or noisy. Harris looked tired. They all looked tired. It had been a long and emotionally exhausting day.

"Is it about my sister?" Trevor asked. "You've got some word?"

"Nothing new," Daniel said. "We're just trying to sort a few things out."

"Like what?"

"Tell us about your grandfather."

"What do you want to know?"

"What kind of man is he?"

"Rich."

An interesting first offering, Rainy thought.

"Hard to get along with?" Daniel asked.

"Depends. There are areas neither of us go."

"I mean in general."

"He sure didn't get rich bending over backward for people."

"Enemies?"

"Probably, but I wouldn't know about that."

Rainy said, "The areas neither of you want to discuss, can you tell me more about those?"

"Look, I already gave all this information to the sheriff when my grandfather went missing. It didn't help us find him, and I don't see how that's going to help us find Lindsay."

"We're trying to see this puzzle in a different way, Trevor," Rainy explained. "Every piece, new or old, that we can put into place helps."

He thought it over and shrugged. "I disappoint him."

"Why?"

"For one thing, I'm an actor. To quote my grandfather, 'Nobody makes money as an actor.' For another, we're very different people. He's spent his life in places like darkest Africa and the Amazon and the Outback. Manly stuff. Me, I like air-conditioning and a soft bed."

"What were you doing going with him into the Boundary Waters?" Stephen asked.

"I thought, I don't know, that maybe it might bring us closer. Lindsay loves the place. And Grandpa John grew up here. Seemed like it might be a way to connect before it was too late."

"That's what you wanted?" Rainy said. "To connect on a deeper level?"

"I don't have much family. Or even a sense of family, really. That's a lonely feeling."

Daniel brought out the photograph of Trevor and his prize fish. "Did you think this might help connect?"

"Worth a try, I figured."

"Nice catch," Daniel said. "What did you use?"

"A rod and reel."

"I mean at the end of your line. Live bait? A lure?"

"A lure."

"What kind?"

"I don't remember. I'm not really much of a fisherman. That was kind of beginner's luck."

"It was a competition of some kind with your grandfather, right?"

"That's right."

"His idea?"

"Mine. He does a lot of deep-sea fishing from his homes in San Diego and Maui. Always bugging me to go with him. He's never understood that it doesn't appeal to me."

"Have you been to the Boundary Waters before?" Daniel asked.

"That trip was my first."

"What made you decide to try your hand at casting a line?"

"Honestly, I finally just got fed up with his constant sniping at me to man up."

"I understand you bet him a thousand dollars. A lot of money. Considering the nature of the enterprise, your odds weren't good."

"I never said I was a great gambler."

"You seem to be winning big here."

"Winning—or losing for that matter—goes in streaks. I'm having a good streak." He eyed Rainy. "So, how is this helping us find Lindsay?"

"Your grandfather was a distant figure," Rainy said. "At least in your life. But I believe there's an important connection between your grandfather and your sister that's at the heart of their disappearances. Do you have any idea what that might be?"

"Lindsay's not much closer to him than I am. We saw him two, maybe three times a year. The only connection any of us share is blood. I can understand why someone might have it in for my grandfather, but Lindsay? It doesn't make any sense."

"And you've given that some good thought, have you?" Daniel threw in. "Who might want your grandfather out of the way?"

"Not until Lindsay disappeared. I mean, I just thought Grandpa John might have had a stroke or something and fell into the lake and drowned or walked off into the woods and got lost. But now everything seems different."

"Whose idea was it to hire my father?" Stephen asked.

"Lindsay's. After I told her about my dream. Or vision, if you will."

Stephen nodded. "What did the vision mean to you?"

"Honest to God, I still have no idea what to think of it. I mean, it's not something I've ever experienced before."

Daniel said, "Does playing blackjack help you think about it more clearly?"

Trevor cocked his head. "What's going on?"

"I apologize if we seem to be badgering you, Trevor," Rainy said. "We're just a little desperate, and we're turning over every stone we can."

"Okay," Trevor said. "I get that. But I've got nothing to hide. And while gambling may be considered a vice by some, a lot of us just think of it as a diverting pastime. And so yes, Daniel, in a way it does help clear my head. Are we done here?"

"I think I hear Lady Luck calling you," Daniel said, not hiding his sarcasm.

"Good night then," Trevor said with a parting nod.

He left them and returned to the blackjack table. The redhead welcomed him back with a squeeze of his arm, and he took his chair and resumed his play.

"I'm no actor, but I know a little Shakespeare." Daniel's dark eyes appraised the young man, and he said, "Where his gambling is concerned, me thinks he doth protest too much."

CHAPTER 27

The tall man had bound him with tape, hand and foot, wrapped a couple of wool blankets around him for sleep, and now Cork lay next to the coals of the dying fire, listening to the sounds that the woman who hated him made as she slept and the low occasional moan of the kid, whose leg pained him even in his dreaming. Lindsay Harris slept silent as death, and Cork understood her exhaustion. The tall man made no sound, and Cork couldn't tell if it was because he slept deeply or because he slept not at all. Cork was weary in every part of his body, but sleep wouldn't come. Above him, the moon had risen, and its glow washed out the stars in a good part of the sky. The constellations still visible were as familiar to him as his own face in a mirror. The air was cold, and when he breathed upward, his breath became a momentary cloud against the heavens.

It wasn't worry that kept him awake. It was processing. He was going over everything he knew now, arranging and rearranging the pieces of information he'd gathered since Raspberry Lake. These were the same people who'd been responsible for the disappearance of John Harris. They'd been waiting for Harris and his grandchildren in the same way they'd been waiting for Lindsay and him. They'd known Harris would be on that lake. They'd known Lindsay would come back to look for him. Which probably meant that someone close to the Harrises had kept them informed. He wished he could talk to Lindsay, mine her life and even, to the extent possible, her grandfather's. There were questions Cork had now that hadn't occurred to him when Harris had first gone missing, and the answers might have given him an idea who had betrayed them. But the tall man kept them separate and would allow no conversation between them. So Cork had to go with what he knew.

They were headed to Canada, to a place called White Woman Lake. He thought he recalled a lake north of the Quetico, in a beautiful, rugged, isolated part of Ontario. He'd once fished the Manitou River near there, a marvelous flow, crystal clear and full of some of the best brown trout he'd ever angled. He believed White Woman Lake wasn't far away. What was in that part of Ontario that would involve Harris or his granddaughter? What was so important there that these people were willing to risk everything for it, including their own lives? Although he believed absolutely that they wouldn't hesitate to kill him or Lindsay if they felt it was necessary, Cork didn't think they were evil people, even the sour woman. Whatever the motive behind their actions, it wasn't selfish.

So what did drive them? He had no clue. At least not yet. But he intended to keep probing the kid, who was the weak link in all this, and listening to everything that passed between the other two. He hoped that at some point one of them would stumble and a good deal more might become clear. He had to be careful, though. The woman traveled with them but was not one of them, not family. If she'd had her way, Cork was pretty sure he'd be dead now. He wasn't certain what he could do about that except keep a wary eye on her at all times and hope the tall man didn't change his mind. Which was something he might well do if Cork tried another escape. Or if Lindsay tried. But she seemed resigned to her captivity, maybe because her life didn't appear to be on the line at the moment. Or maybe because she actually believed she might be able to help her grandfather. About that, Cork wasn't so sure.

He heard the tall man rise and watched him walk to the edge of the lake, where he stood like some solitary pine, a natural part of all that surrounded him. Cork heard his low murmuring, and although the words weren't clear, the cadence was familiar. He'd heard Meloux and Rainy speak in this same way, and he understood the tall man was praying in Anishinaabemowin. Praying for what? Or for whom? The tall man bent and cupped his hands in the water of the lake. He lifted his arms, and the water emptied from his palms, drop by sparkling drop, like falling stars. After a while, he turned back and wove his way among the sleeping figures toward his blankets. As he passed Cork, he said, "You'll be no good to us or to yourself if you don't sleep."

But Cork didn't sleep, not immediately. He thought about his children and Waaboo. He thought about Rainy. He thought that if, in fact, this was a journey from which he'd never return, there were things he wished he could have said to each of them. How much he loved them, treasured them, things they already knew, but he wished he'd said them anyway. And there was something else he wished he'd said, this to Rainy alone.

He said it now, whispered it toward the stars, as if they might hear and carry the message to her, "I love you."

The lantern wick still burned in her great-uncle's cabin. Rainy saw the light as she walked the path across the meadow toward her own cabin. The moon was high and had lit her way clearly from the road where she'd parked her Jeep and along the trail that followed the shoreline of Iron Lake. She lifted her hand to knock at Henry's door, but before she rapped, the old man said from inside, "Welcome home, Niece."

She found him sitting at his table, Ember lying peacefully at his feet. The mutt's tail wagged when she came in, but it was late and the dog didn't rise. She took off her coat and hung it and pulled out a chair and sat.

"You look like a woman who has traveled a long journey."

"I'm so tired, Uncle Henry. It smells of cedar and sage in here. You purified?"

"I had a visitor. Your aunt Leah."

"No wonder you cleansed. What did she want?"

"To wound me if she could."

"Because you wounded her all those years ago?"

"She was hurt, yes, but it was not my doing."

"Who then, or what?"

"Her youth, her vanity, her willing blindness. When she finally let herself see the truth so long ago, it split her heart open. For that, she has always blamed me."

"She's blinded herself. She's made herself believe you led her on."

"I have done my very best for nearly a century to speak nothing but the truth, Niece. I have learned that no matter how plainly I speak, there are some who hear only what they wish to hear."

"You told me she might be here to stay. Is this a woman you could abide for long, Uncle Henry?" There was a harshness to her voice. When she heard herself, heard the anger, Rainy wasn't sure if it came from her fear of the woman's intrusion on this life she'd created for herself on Crow Point, or her concern for her great-uncle, or her fear of what might have happened to Cork.

The old man ignored her question. "Did you find Corcoran O'Connor and the young woman?"

"They weren't there, Uncle Henry. It was just like John Harris. They vanished off that lake into thin air. Only this time something was left behind."

"What?"

"*Miskwa,*" she said. Blood.

The old man had been tying sage bundles. He put them aside and sat back in his chair.

"Whose?"

"We don't know. But there was a lot of it. I know I should be equally worried about the young woman, but I find myself praying mostly that it wasn't Cork's blood. Selfish."

"Human," he said. "Did you feel death there?"

"I felt a terrible violation of the spirit of that place."

The old man's eyes narrowed to slits, as if he was trying to see something at a great distance. "It makes no sense to set a rabbit snare where the rabbit will not be. Someone knew they were coming."

"That's what we've figured, too."

"Why these rabbits? And who set the snare?"

"We just came from talking with the grandson. This is a man I don't trust. I think he's weak and easily manipulated."

"If he's weak enough to be bent by others, are you not strong enough to bend him, too?"

"Maybe." Rainy laid her arms on the table, let her head fall forward, and closed her eyes. "I'm exhausted, Uncle Henry, and I'm so worried."

She felt his warm, old hands cover hers. She looked up at him and found him smiling.

"Worry, and you open the door to the worst of possibilities, Niece. Better, I think, to hope. The heart invites a friendlier spirit for its company."

"You don't ever worry?"

"Only the dead are free of worry."

"What do you do when you worry?"

"I pray and then I plan. What are you going to do?"

It was as if the touch of his hand and the warmth of his smile had nourished her, refreshed her.

"That sounds as good as anything," she said.

"This young man who bends so easily," Henry said. "Where does the wind blow from that makes him bend? That is what I would think about."

She rose and kissed the white hair on top of his head. "I'm going off to pray and to plan."

She took sage freshly bundled by her great-uncle and went to her own cabin. With a feather, she smudged the air around her and then herself. She prayed to the Great Mystery for clarity and guidance. She turned her lantern to barely a glimmer and stood at her window and looked out at the night and the moon and the stars. She didn't have an idea yet of what she was going to do, but she tried to follow Henry's advice and open herself to hope. Which had always been his advice and, in a way, had been why she'd sought him out in the first place, years ago. She'd come to him empty of hope, come running from her past, which still haunted her in the worst moments. In her life before Crow Point, she'd been a part of things that she believed were unforgivable. Joining her great-uncle had been, in its way, a last resort, one last hopeless measure.

She forced herself to stop thinking of what had been, and instead focused on the moment and on Cork. She thought, *He's out there, looking at this same sky, these stars, that moon. Let him know that I'm thinking about him, praying for him, and for Lindsay, too. Let him know that I will do everything I can to bring them back and that I won't give up hope.*

She reached toward the window, where a ghost image of her hand reached out, too. At the cold glass they touched, and she spoke aloud her final prayer that night.

"Let him know that I love him."

CHAPTER 28

By morning, the clouds had returned, and Cork woke to another gray November sky. The tall man had already rekindled the fire, and the others were stirring. They hadn't bound Lindsay with duct tape in the way they'd bound Cork. They'd told her if she tried to escape, she would only become lost in that great wilderness, and they would hunt her down, and they would not go easy on her then. She slid from her sleeping bag and tugged on her boots and said, "I'm going to relieve myself." She walked off into the woods.

The sour woman who hated Cork stood with the tall man, looking where Lindsay had gone. "Not much spirit in that one," she said. "She'll do what we need her to do." She glanced down where Cork lay and said, "When she does, your usefulness is ended."

They cut the tape that had bound Cork, and he ate breakfast with them, oatmeal and coffee. They were all quiet, the kid especially. When the tall man checked the kid's wound, he said, "The infection's spreading. But we'll be out soon and get some antibiotics in you and that'll clear it up pretty quick."

"How soon?" the kid said.

"Two days, maybe. You can make it."

The kid tried to smile. "I'll be there ahead of you."

They packed the gear and loaded the canoes. The tall man doused and buried the fire. They pushed off through a thin glaze of ice that framed the shoreline and the rocks in the shallows. Farther out, the water was still clear. The clouds had held in some of the warmth from the day before, otherwise the ice would have been an issue, a barrier. They'd been lucky, Cork knew, but he didn't believe their luck would hold. He understood enough about the tall man now to suspect that he didn't believe it either.

Behind him, the kid puffed as he paddled. Cork could feel that his own stroke was much stronger than the kid's.

"Ole walks into a beer joint and sees his friend Sven sittin' at the bar," Cork said over his shoulder. "There's a dog under Sven's chair. Ole walks over and says, 'Sven, does your dog bite?' Sven says, 'No, he don't.' Ole reaches down to pet the dog and the dog takes a big chunk out of his hand. Ole says, 'I thought you said your dog doesn't bite.' Sven says, 'That ain't my dog.'"

The kid didn't laugh and they both kept paddling. After a minute or so, the kid said, "A man walks into a bar with a frog on top of his head. The bartender says, 'Where'd you get that ugly thing?' The frog says, 'Would you believe it started as a wart on my ass?'"

Although he'd heard that joke a thousand times, Cork laughed.

The kid said, "My dad used to love to tell jokes."

"He doesn't anymore?"

"He's dead."

"I'm sorry," Cork said. "And your mom?"

"Never knew her. She left when I was too little to remember her."

"So your dad raised you?"

"Him and my uncle."

"Sounds like you must have a place in the woods somewhere. You live there year-round?"

"Yeah. It's pretty. The prettiest place on earth."

"Where is it?"

The kid was quiet, then said, "Better you don't know any more."

They made a short portage that morning to another lake, this one smaller than the last. On the other side, they were preparing to portage once again when they all stopped suddenly, lifted their heads, and listened, like an animal herd that had sensed a lion.

From far down the portage that ran through a copse of bare birch trees came the sound of someone whistling.

The tall man spoke in a low voice to Cork and Lindsay Harris. "If you say anything, you will be responsible for this person's death. Do you understand?"

He took the rifle from the woman and moved into the cover of the trees and became invisible.

In a couple of minutes, a single figure appeared on the portage, carrying a kayak, and whistling a merry tune that sounded Irish. As the figure approached, Cork discerned a middle-aged man with a full, red-brown beard and wire-rimmed glasses. He was studying the trail, his eyes downcast but his pace lively. A dozen yards before he reached the others, he glanced up and stopped dead, clearly startled.

"Well, ho," he said. "Didn't expect to see anybody in this neck of the woods."

"Hello," the woman said, not cordially.

The man approached, set his kayak down, and slid the pack from his shoulders. He held out his hand toward them in greeting, Cork first.

"Bender," he said.

"First or last name?" Cork asked, taking the offered hand.

"First name's Charlie."

"Cork," Cork said.

"Nickname?"

"Short for Corcoran. This is Lindsay."

The young woman stepped forward, smiled tentatively, and said, "How do you do?"

The kid stayed where he was and made no move to introduce himself. The sour woman stared at the stranger and said, "Mrs. Gray."

"So," Bender said. "What brings you out this time of year, and here of all places?"

"What's wrong with here?" Cork said.

"About as out of the way in the Boundary Waters as you can get."

"What brings you?" Mrs. Gray asked.

"Looking for wolves. I work for the DNR. I've been tracking a pack for the last week."

"Haven't seen any," the woman said.

"Hear any?"

"Not that either."

"Which way did you come from?"

"South," she said.

"Wind Lake?"

"I don't know the name."

The stranger looked to Cork.

"Afraid I'm in the dark, too, Charlie."

"Lost?"

"Not lost," Cork said. "We have a pretty general sense of where we are."

"And where you're going?"

"That, too."

The man eyed him with some concern. "Have you been in the Boundary Waters before? I ask because if you don't have a good map, it's easy to get lost."

"We're not lost," the woman said coldly.

"Well . . . okay then." The man gave her a halfhearted smile. He looked up at the sky, at the gray clouds. "My radio says snow maybe tomorrow. Not much, but real winter's not far behind." He brightened. "Actually, winter's my favorite time in the Boundary Waters. I generally have the whole wilderness to myself."

"You always run off at the mouth like this?" the woman said.

The man gave a small, uncomfortable laugh. "Sorry. Just haven't seen a soul in forever. Well, best be on my way."

"Good luck finding the wolves," Lindsay said.

"And good luck to you," the man said. "In whatever."

He set his kayak on the water and stowed his pack inside, but he didn't get in immediately himself. He stood for a moment eyeing the beautiful birch-bark canoes.

"I'd give my right arm for one of those." He glanced back at the others. "Did you make them yourselves?"

There was a long moment of silence. Then the kid said, "Yes."

"Works of art." Bender sighed as if he'd seen the *Mona Lisa*. "Well, like I said, best get going." He slipped into his kayak and gripped his double-bladed paddle. "Toodle-oo." He gave a final wave and was off.

They stood watching until he was far out on the lake, then the tall man emerged from the trees. He had the rifle slung on his shoulder.

"Should we do something about him?" Mrs. Gray said.

"Like what?" the tall man replied.

"We don't do something, he might give us away."

"We have three choices. We take him prisoner and he goes the distance with us. We kill him now. Or we let him go on his way and we move on as quickly as we can. Which will it be?"

The woman studied the kid, as if assessing some ability in him. "Didn't you bring him along for this kind of situation?"

The tall man slid the rifle from his shoulder. He glanced at the kid, then handed the firearm to the woman. "You think it should be done, you do it, Mrs. Gray."

She looked at the tall man, then at the distant figure in the kayak. She grabbed the rifle and walked to the edge of the lake. She knelt in a firing position and snugged the butt to her shoulder.

"You're not really going to shoot him," Lindsay said, horrified.

Mrs. Gray sighted.

"Think about this," the tall man said to her. "You miss that shot, Bender will run and we'll never catch him. We're done for sure."

The sour woman didn't respond. Cork didn't know if she would take the shot, or if she did, would be successful, but the risk was too great. He tensed himself to leap and take her down, but Lindsay was there ahead of him. She threw herself on Mrs. Gray, and they both went to the ground. When they hit, the firearm bounced from the woman's grip and the tall man snatched it up.

"Enough," he commanded.

He handed the rifle to the kid and turned to his pack. He pulled out field glasses and aimed them at Bender in the kayak. He watched a long time. Finally, he looked down sternly where Lindsay and the woman still lay tangled. "Seems he didn't see anything. Lucky for both of you. Get up and let's get going."

The sour woman pushed herself to her feet, but before she stepped away, she gave Lindsay a solid kick in the ribs. "If we didn't need you, I'd kill you right now."

Lindsay held her side and looked up at the woman. "Spirit enough for you now, Mrs. Gray?"

Which made the kid laugh.

CHAPTER 29

Sheriff Marsha Dross had called early that morning with the only good news they'd heard in a while. The blood that had been found on Raspberry Island was definitely human, but didn't match Cork's type or Lindsay Harris's. Dross was headed into the Boundary Waters to work with Search and Rescue. She invited anyone who wanted to join them. But the O'Connors had a different idea for that day.

They gathered around the table in the kitchen of the house on Gooseberry Lane. Cork's children were there, as well as Daniel and Rainy. Rose had made breakfast for them all, and they'd eaten, and now they sat sharing their information and their thoughts.

"He started out as a geotechnical engineer and worked on dams all over the world. A dam he designed in Indonesia gave way during heavy rains in 1978. The resulting flood killed hundreds of people."

Jenny was reporting what she'd discovered during her Internet search the night before.

"Harris claimed that his design hadn't been followed and also that there was graft involved in the project and construction materials weren't of the specified quality. The official report backed him up. Since then, he's personally overseen the construction of most of the dams he's built."

"What about his family?" Daniel asked.

"I know we're all wondering about Trevor," Jenny said. "But his sister is the one with the rap sheet."

Rose saw astonishment on all their faces.

"When she was a student at Northland College, she was arrested during a protest against a proposed open-pit mining operation that would have devastated part of the Porcupine Mountains in Michigan."

"The Penokee Mine," Daniel said. "I remember it. Huge money involved, but a lot of Native and environmental groups banded together and the proposal was finally abandoned. That was only a year ago."

"Got arrested, huh?" Stephen said. "I think I like this lady."

"There's more to her to like," Jenny said. "On her Facebook page, her relationship status is 'committed.' To an Odawa guy she met during the mine protests." She smiled at Daniel. "Smart woman."

"What about Trevor?" Daniel asked.

"Attended Stanford for a while but got himself kicked out," Jenny said.

"What for?"

"He set up a gambling ring on campus. Quite successful, apparently, until a number of parents complained about their kids' money going to pay debts instead of tuition. He moved to Las Vegas, which is where he lives now. His official occupation is entertainer-slash-actor. He's been in lots of Vegas shows."

"But it's clear from what we've seen that for him Vegas isn't really about the acting," Rainy said. "He has a gambling addiction."

"So maybe he's in need of money," Jenny said. "And getting rid of Grandpa—and his sister—will give him quite an inheritance to feed his addiction."

Daniel said, "If someone disappears, I'm pretty sure it's a long time before they can be declared legally dead. So Trevor has to be patient. My sense about addicts of any kind is that patience isn't one of their strong points."

"Also, that assumes something beyond addiction," Rainy said. "A cold, calculating, heartless individual. Trevor may have problems, but is he really that kind of man?"

Daniel said, "I don't have any problem assuming the worst about him. For me, the question is how he would accomplish the disappearance of his grandfather, his sister, and Cork. He'd need a lot of help in that. It would have to be someone who knows the territory, so someone local. How would he make that kind of connection?"

"And," Jenny said, "if all this is calculated and everything he's told us is a lie, how did he know about Stephen and 'monthterth under the bed'? Have you ever posted anything about that on Facebook, Stephen?"

"Are you kidding? I barely remember it. I was five."

"Trevor came by that information somehow."

Rose had been quiet, listening, trying to calm her spirit so that clarity of thought might prevail in her own mind. She offered, "What if it's a combination of many forces at work? Maybe Trevor Harris is weak, and someone has played on that weakness. As you've pointed out, if this is all part of some grand plan, he couldn't very well have accomplished it on his own. He'd need lots of help. Who would want to prey on his weakness?"

Rainy said, "That's pretty much what Uncle Henry said to me last night. Where does the wind blow from that bends this young man?"

"Someone who's after something that Lindsay or her grandfather have?" Stephen offered.

"More probably something that Lindsay *and* her grandfather have," Daniel said. "Maybe they tried getting it from Harris and couldn't, so now they've gone after his granddaughter."

"There's another possibility," Rose said. "They've taken Lindsay in order to coerce her grandfather. You might be willing to do things you wouldn't otherwise do if it meant keeping someone you loved from harm."

They digested that in silence, and Jenny nodded. "Of everything we've said, that makes the most sense."

"But it doesn't get us any farther," Daniel pointed out. "We're still in the dark about almost everything. Especially who's behind all this."

"So what do we do now?" Jenny asked.

Daniel pulled a photograph from his shirt pocket and set it on the table.

Rose saw a young man standing beside a lake holding a big fish and grinning to beat the band. "Trevor?" she asked.

"That's him with the prize walleye he caught the day his grandfather went missing. I'm going to talk to Dwight Kohler, their guide," Daniel said. "I'd like to know exactly what happened out there, the story behind how a guy who's never been to the Boundary Waters and almost never casts a line managed to land this. Forgive the pun, but there's something fishy in that story."

"I'll go with you," Rainy said.

"I want to go out to Crow Point," Stephen said. "Since Trevor screwed up the sweat, I haven't had a chance to talk with Henry about this darkness I feel. I'd like to explore it more with him."

Jenny finished her coffee. "I'm going to wake up Waaboo and get him ready for preschool."

"You all go do what you have to do," Rose said. "I'll clean up here."

She saw them off, and when Jenny had gone upstairs, Rose took her cell phone from her purse and called her husband. Mal answered in the way she loved: "Hello, light of my life."

"Oh, Mal, it's good to hear your voice."

"Whoa," he said. "Yours doesn't sound so good. What's up?"

She told him all that had occurred. He didn't interrupt.

"I can leave right away," he offered.

"At this point, it wouldn't do any good. I just thought you'd want to know what's going on. For the time being, just keep us all in your prayers."

Mal said, "There's one thing I hope everyone up there understands."

"What's that?"

"This Lindsay Harris couldn't have a better man with her than Cork. If anyone can help her, he can."

"I'll pass that along. It's a good piece of wisdom."

"I'll keep everyone in my prayers. You take care of yourself, love."

"I will, sweetheart."

She ended the call and slipped the phone back into her purse. Then she sat among all the breakfast mess that needed to be dealt with and offered a silent prayer of thanksgiving. Until she was forty, she'd believed she would never know love, the kind that Mal offered her anyway. She thought of it as a great treasure she'd stumbled upon, a blessing never anticipated, and maybe that was the best kind. She also offered a prayer in gratitude for her sister's family, which she'd always been a part of. And finally she asked for the grace to accept whatever outcome God had in mind for them all. She might have gone on in her prayers—sometimes they lasted well beyond anything she'd intended—but a knock at the back door took her from her meditations.

She found Daniel's aunt Leah standing there, looking wild-eyed.

"Can I . . . can I come in?" the woman asked.

"Of course." Rose brought her inside and took her coat, hung it, and led her to one of the empty chairs. "Can I get you something? Coffee maybe?"

The woman didn't answer. She stared at Rose with eyes hollowed into deep pits of fear. "I've seen something."

Rose sat down and took Leah's hands. "What did you see?"

As if completely disoriented, she said, "I don't know. I don't understand it." Tears filled her eyes and spilled down her cheeks. "Oh, Rose, they're dead. Hundreds and hundreds of them. All dead."

CHAPTER 30

Pakkala's Northwoods Outfitters occupied a two-story building in the center of Aurora. Both levels were filled with everything that someone intending to enjoy the great northern wilderness could possibly need—canoes and kayaks, tents, backpacks, clothing, shoes, dehydrated food, cooking utensils, stoves, fishing gear, mosquito netting, insect repellent. They sold books and games and other diversions for rainy days in the great Northwoods. They also offered guide service into the Boundary Waters.

When Daniel and Rainy entered the outfitters, Walt Pakkala, the family patriarch, came to greet them himself and offer his sympathy.

"Christ," he said, shaking his head. He was a big man with a ruddy face and a full beard, and he spoke with the accent of an old Finn in the North Country. "Cork's de last man I'd expect to go missin' out der. We been hearin' stuff. Not good. So what's really happenin'?"

"We don't know, Walt," Daniel said. "That's why we're here. We'd like to talk to Dwight, if he's around."

"Sure. In back doin' some inventory. I'll get him."

Pakkala vanished and returned with Dwight Kohler in tow. He was a tall kid, twenty years old, willowy, strong, with coal-black hair and the black shadow of a beard several days old. His eyes were piercing blue and innocent. He wore a green hoodie sweatshirt with BOUNDARY WATERS printed in white across the front. When not working for Walt Pakkala, he attended Aurora

Community College, where he took mostly photography classes. Rainy thought his work was pretty good, and a lot of his framed photos were on sale at the outfitters.

"Hey, Rainy. Hey, Daniel," he said by way of greeting. "What's up?"

"Morning, Dwight. You've heard about Cork, right? And Lindsay Harris?"

"It's all anybody's talking about this morning. Jesus, I'm sorry. It's so weird, you know. Just like John Harris."

"That's what we want to talk to you about. Walt, can we go somewhere with Dwight to talk?"

"Sure. Have some coffee on me, and grab a table. I got work to do, but you folks take your time. Give 'em whatever dey need, Dwight."

Pakkala's had a little coffee shop in one corner of the store that served up the best kolaches Rainy had ever tasted. They sat and drank coffee, and Daniel said, "We're rethinking the disappearance of John Harris."

"Duh," Dwight said. "I'm kicking myself now. Jesus, I'm thinking, what did I miss out there?"

"That's what we'd like to figure out, if we can. We believe somebody kidnapped Harris, and now those same people have taken Cork and Harris's granddaughter. They knew the family would be out there, and they knew Cork was going back with Lindsay."

"Like for ransom or something?"

"There's been no note, so we're thinking something else is going on."

"Like what?"

"We're working on that. Let me show you something." From his pocket, Daniel pulled the photograph of Trevor Harris with his prize walleye. He laid it on the table. "Tell me about this."

"Not much to tell. Trevor and his granddad took off to fish. Trevor came back with that walleye and his granddad never did come back. End of story."

"They went different directions on the lake, right?"

"Raspberry's horseshoe-shaped, you know. Trevor went down the east side, his granddad went west."

"It was some kind of contest, wasn't it?"

"Yeah. Crazy. A thousand dollars."

"Whose idea was that?"

"Trevor's. But I kind of got it. The old man, he was on that guy's case the whole time."

"About what?"

"You know, being more responsible, growing up, doing manly things. It was the kind of crap you'd give a teenager, not a full-grown adult."

"Who decided where they'd fish?"

Dwight thought about that a moment. "Seems to me it was Trevor chose first."

"Did he know anything about fishing?"

"Knew what a rod and reel were but not much beyond that. Surprised the hell out of me when he came back with that fish."

"Didn't it seem suspicious to you?"

"Suspicious? Not then. Just damn lucky."

Rainy said, "What was Lindsay doing this whole time?"

"Hanging out with me. Shooting the breeze, you know. She didn't have anything to prove. It was clear from the get-go she knew how to handle herself in the woods. Her granddad and her got along pretty well. Not like with Trevor."

"Did you see anyone else on Raspberry Lake while you were there?"

"Nobody. It's not a place many go, particularly that late in the season."

"Did anyone get any cell phone calls out there?"

"On Raspberry? Are you kidding? Sat phones are about the only things'll connect out there."

"How long were you on the lake before Harris disappeared?"

"We arrived the evening before. Had just enough time to set up camp, then dark was on us."

"What was the plan going in?"

"Three nights on Raspberry, then out. Quick trip."

"Who decided on Raspberry?"

"Don't know. It was already chosen when they hired me. I liked the idea though, because it's not somewhere I get to often. I figured we had a good chance of having the lake to ourselves. And I love Raspberry Island. A great view from the top of that palisade. I thought I might be able to take some nice shots from up there."

"Did you?"

"Nope. Harris went missing before I had a chance."

"About that fish. Do you have any idea what Trevor was using on the end of his line?"

"I sure do. I mean, when he came back with that walleye I was, like, astounded. He told me he used a Husky Jerk."

"Interesting," Daniel said. "When I asked him last night, he couldn't remember."

"Before he caught that fish, if you'd asked me, I would've said he'd be lucky not to hook his own ass."

"Did you like him?"

"Felt sorry for him mostly. I mean, he was really out of his element there. It was clear he was uncomfortable and his grand-dad was riding him and all. He wasn't obnoxious or anything, like I sometimes get." His face drew together in a sudden thought. "But you know, I did have the feeling that he was watching for something. I didn't think a lot about it then, but now, with the way everything stands, who knows?"

"Yeah," Daniel agreed. "Who knows?"

Rainy's cell phone purred and she answered.

"Rainy, it's Rose. Can you come back to our place? Leah Duling is here, and I think you need to talk to her. She's had an experience, seen something you need to hear about."

"All right. Thanks, Rose." She put away her phone. "We need to get back to Gooseberry Lane. Thank you, Dwight."

"Wish I could tell you more."

"You've been really helpful," she assured him.

As they left Pakkala's, Daniel said, "What's up with Rose?"

"Aunt Leah's at the house. Apparently, she's seen something."

"The light?"

"We can only hope," Rainy said.

"Well, I think we know a bit more now."

"What do we know?"

"That big fish. If I were a betting man, I'd bet Trevor Harris had no part in catching that walleye. Someone supplied it."

"Who?"

"No idea. But I'm pretty sure of the why. An alibi. How could Trevor have had anything to do with his grandfather's disappearance if he was out on the other side of the lake catching a prize walleye?"

When they arrived, Jenny opened the door to them. She didn't say anything, simply nodded toward the kitchen table, where Rose sat with Aunt Leah, who hugged herself as if she were cold or maybe scared. Rainy and Daniel hung their coats and sat down with the women at the table.

"Are you all right, Aunt Leah?"

She looked at Rainy, mystified. "I've never experienced anything like it."

"What happened?"

"I saw something. Something that wasn't there."

"Something you dreamed?"

"I wasn't asleep, Rainy. That's the thing. I wasn't asleep. I was in my hotel room, fixing my morning coffee. It came to me. Just came. Lucius would have said like the light that struck Saul blind."

"Can you tell us about it?" Rainy said gently.

"It didn't make any sense. But there was such a feel of great destruction about it."

"Can you be a little more specific?"

"I just stood there, looking at nothing for the longest time. I couldn't move. I couldn't speak."

"Fine, Aunt Leah," Rainy said, trying to be patient. "But can you get to what you saw?"

She stared at Rainy, then looked to Jenny and Daniel and finally Rose. Her eyes were huge, her face pale. "It was all under a charcoal sky," she began. "I stood on a cliff somewhere. I didn't recognize it. A great clap of thunder came and scared me. The air was full of white. Snow, I don't know, or maybe it was ash. And that's when I heard the screams. Terrible screams coming from below me. When I looked down, as far as I could see there was nothing but fish, flopping around on the ground. The screams were their screams. But they weren't just fish. They were fish with human heads, human faces, human voices. And they were dying. All of them dying. It was all so real, so very real." She reached out suddenly and grasped Rainy's arm. "Am I going crazy?"

In that desperate grip, Rainy felt the woman's terror, felt it as if it were her own. She spoke with great compassion. "I don't think you're crazy, Aunt Leah. This really sounds to me like a vision."

"I don't believe in visions. Not this kind. Not coming to me. Why me? And why so terrible?"

"I don't know, Aunt Leah."

"I don't want this vision."

"Yet there it is," Rainy said gently. "And you've asked a good question. Why was it given to you?"

"Given? Like a gift? It's no gift. It feels like a violation." She took Rainy's hands in her own. "Help me."

"I'll try. But I'd like to do this in my way. Will you trust me?"

It was a simple question, but the woman took a long time to answer. "All right."

"We're going to Crow Point. We're going to do a sweat."

"Not with Henry," Aunt Leah gasped.

"Not if you don't want. We'll do the sweat together, just you and me."

Rainy watched her aunt's face move through several emotions and finally arrive at acceptance.

"Good," Rainy said. "Daniel, mind taking us in your truck?"

"No problem."

"Will you come, too?" Leah pleaded to Rose. "You've been so kind."

Rose glanced at Rainy, who gave a nod.

"If it will help you, Leah, then of course," Rose said.

CHAPTER 31

For hours, they'd traveled north, following the shoreline of a long, winding lake. At midday they disembarked on a small patch of open ground that fed into the next portage. The kid, when he tried to get out and stand, collapsed and fell. This time Cork steadied the canoe and it didn't tip.

"I don't think I can walk, Uncle Aaron."

"Unbuckle your belt and pull your jeans down," the tall man said.

The kid did as instructed. The whole area around the knee was inflamed, purple-red and swollen. Dark lines like evil tendrils extended upward from it under the skin. When the tall man touched the leg, the kid winced in great pain.

"Something really nasty must've got in there," the woman said.

"We'll rest here awhile." The tall man reached into his pack and came out with a small pill bottle. He tapped out several tablets and gave them to the kid. "Swallow these with some water. It'll help the pain."

"I feel real hot, too." The kid's eyes looked vacant, lifeless.

"Probably running a little fever," the tall man said.

The others unloaded the gear from the canoes, and they all sat on the ground with the weight of the overcast sky once again heavy upon them. The kid lay down fully, his head cradled on a pack. He closed his eyes. In a short while, he was asleep.

The woman said, "We should leave him."

"We leave no one," the tall man said.

"You left Flynn."

"Flynn was dead."

She looked at the kid as if his fate was certain and the same. Then she studied the gray sky. "We're running out of time."

"We're not leaving him."

"Let me take the girl and go on ahead, then. If we push it, we could be out of this wilderness by tomorrow night."

"We go together."

"You're risking everything we've planned for."

The tall man's eyes swung to Cork, who hadn't missed a word. "We won't discuss this anymore."

The kid mumbled something in his sleep, gibberish.

The woman eyed him as she might a pile of trash. "I told you from the start we shouldn't bring him."

"What's done is done," the tall man said. "Enough."

Lindsay Harris spoke up. "What about a travois?"

"A travois?" the tall man said.

"You know what that is," Lindsay said.

"Yes."

"We could cart him on the portages. It would slow us down a little, but we'd still make distance."

Cork gave her a quick, puzzled look, and she said, "He's just a kid. And he's sick. He needs a doctor. The sooner the better."

"A travois," the tall man said and nodded.

Mrs. Gray held the rifle while the others worked. The tall man cut saplings and branches with a hatchet. He and Cork and Lindsay put the travois together, using duct tape in place of rope or twine. In a short while, they'd constructed a decent frame for the litter. The tall man stretched a wool blanket across the frame and tied it at the corners. He stood back and looked pleased.

They woke the kid and ate a meal of trail mix and jerky. The tall man took an orange from his pack and gave it to the kid.

"Are we going make it in time, Uncle Aaron?"

"We'll make it."

"I'm sorry about my leg."

"Not your fault."

"Clumsy oaf," the woman said.

"We're going to carry you across the portages," the tall man said. "Think you can still paddle?"

The kid smiled gamely. "I can do that."

They prepared to move on. The tall man double-packed, one on his back and one in front. Cork lifted a canoe onto the tall man's shoulders. Lindsay Harris took the other canoe on her shoulders. The woman hefted the third pack and carried the rifle. Cork grasped the travois by the sapling ends and lifted, and they began along the portage.

He tried to reckon where they might be now. From Mrs. Gray's comment about being out of the wilderness by tomorrow night, he guessed they were near the Canadian border, if not already across it and now into Quetico Provincial Park. He thought about the tall man's comment that a border was just a line on a map. The wilderness was the same on both sides of that line, and a man on the ground couldn't tell the difference. That was one of the things he loved about the North Country. A map, though useful in some ways, told nothing. It couldn't give in the least way a sense of the land itself, its size, which was measured truly not in square miles but in days paddling and portaging. It gave no sense of the thousand moments when a man's breath was taken away by some sudden, unexpected beauty. It offered no warning of the dangers— severe storms that blew out of nowhere, high waves that could founder a canoe, falling trees, forest fires, broken ankles, heart attack, giardia—that might await the unwary. It was untamed land, and there was not much of that left anywhere. It felt sacred to him.

The portage was more than a mile and had never been well traveled. Any earlier in the season and the ground would have been nothing but the suck of mud. As it was, the cold had hardened the muck. Which made the slog only slightly easier. They were all heavily burdened, and when they finally arrived at the next lake, they dropped their loads and sat a good while without speaking.

Lindsay finally stood and nodded toward a stand of birch. "I'm going to take care of business."

The sour woman got up and said, "I'm not letting you out of my sight." She followed Lindsay into the trees.

The tall man stood. "I'm stepping over there." He pointed toward a tangle of underbrush that made a kind of screen. "I'll be watching you, O'Connor."

"Going nowhere." When the tall man had walked away, Cork said to the kid, "You need to get up and go?"

"I'm okay." Then the kid said, "I'm sorry."

"What for?"

"This." He swept his hand down the length of the travois. "And everything else. You're a decent guy."

"I get the feeling you are, too. What's this all about?"

"I can't . . ." He closed his eyes, and Cork didn't know if it was against the pain in his leg or against another kind of discomfort. "It's important."

"I figured."

The kid seemed to be involved in some kind of inner struggle. Finally he said, "Have you ever heard of Manitou Canyon?"

Mrs. Gray hurried from the woods. "Shut up, you stupid little blabbermouth."

"I was only—"

"I said shut up."

The tall man came from the tangle of underbrush. "What's going on?"

"Your little nephew was about to blab his head off to O'Connor."

The tall man said, "You really think it would make a difference now?"

"If he knows nothing, we don't have to worry whether it makes a difference, do we?"

Lindsay Harris emerged from the trees. The woman turned to her. "You'd better be worth all this trouble."

Lindsay cocked her head and said, "Or what?"

Cork smiled, impressed by her bravado.

"You'll find out," the woman said.

"I'm so tired right now I don't really care," Lindsay said. She looked at the lake, which was so large that the far shore was invisible. A cold wind blew out of the northwest, strong enough to lift the water in waves that carried a little white along the crests. "Are we paddling across that?"

"Afraid so." The tall man drew himself up straight, but not without some effort, and said, "We'd best get started."

They reloaded the canoes and positioned themselves in them as they had before. They started across the big lake. As he paddled, Cork thought about what he knew. The kid and the tall man were family. Family was something Cork understood. It trumped almost everything. Mrs. Gray wasn't family. He began to consider if there might be a way to use this to widen the divide between his captors, enough that there might be room for him and Lindsay to make a break for it.

Patience, the voice in his head advised.

CHAPTER 32

This was her country and not her country. Rose had spent nearly two decades in Tamarack County helping to raise her sister's children while Jo had struggled to put together a law practice and Cork had gone about his duties as deputy and then sheriff. But even in those years, this was never a place that had felt to her like home. In a sense, she'd always been a stranger in a strange land. Until she met Mal and married him. Then she'd found home, which could be anywhere now, as long as it was with Mal. Driving out to Crow Point, a place she understood as sacred, she felt its familiarity, appreciated its beauty, but at the same time understood that, because she would always be a stranger, it would always contain mysteries she couldn't fathom. She knew it was different for those whose ancestry there went deep, as it did with Cork and with the Anishinaabeg.

Leah Duling said not a word, just stared out the window of the crew cab in Daniel's truck. Maybe visions did that, inspired reflection. Rose didn't know; she'd never had a vision. Because of Stephen's experiences and Henry Meloux's, she believed in them absolutely, but her own experience was of a different kind. No apparitions or omens or images delivered with startling suddenness. Hers had always been a prayerful existence, a steady journey on her spiritual path.

Daniel parked his truck on the old logging road beside Rainy's Jeep. They got out, all of them, and began to walk the trail along the shoreline of Iron Lake toward Crow Point. The day was cold and overcast, and a wind had risen out of the northwest and bit at their faces. Leah walked hunched in her wool jacket. Rose suspected that it wasn't only the chill wind that made her bend so, but also the weight of her own misgivings and uncertainty. Rose had always been especially sensitive to the pain of others, and she couldn't help but feel kindness toward this woman who'd been such a vexation.

Long before they reached Crow Point, Rose smelled woodsmoke on the wind. When they came in sight of the cabins, she saw thick gray coiling up into the air from the fire burning near the sweat lodge. They went directly to Henry's cabin. He opened the door to them as they approached.

"*Boozhoo*, Rose," he said warmly. "And *boozhoo*, Leah."

He brought them in. Leah handed Daniel her coat, and Henry led her to a chair at his table.

"Sit," he said.

She did.

He put a mug of cool water in front of her. "Drink."

She drank.

He sat down beside her and looked deeply into her eyes. "The gifts we are given sometimes come like lightning and burn us. What is left can feel like only ashes. This is true especially with a gift meant to change us."

"I didn't ask for this, Henry. I don't want this."

"The lightning has struck. You cannot ignore it."

"Why me?"

"Why not you?"

"I . . . I'm not like you, Henry."

The old Mide waited.

"I don't believe in spirits or visions. I believe in medicine."

"That is your brain talking. Speak to me with your heart."

For a long time, she said nothing. Then the little jewels of her tears appeared on the rims of her eyes, and she said, "I'm so lonely, Henry. And I'm so afraid."

Henry reached out and put his old hands over hers. "You have a beautiful heart, Leah. It is strong and it is good." He looked up at Rainy. "She is ready. The two of you will sweat together now."

They'd called ahead and had spoken to Stephen, and everything had been prepared. Rainy gave Leah a light, loose dress to wear during the sweat instead of the jeans and flannel shirt she'd come in. By the time they walked from Rainy's cabin across the meadow, Stephen had placed the heated Grandfathers in the lodge. Rainy offered prayers and tobacco. Leah did the same, though she spoke quietly and haltingly. Then she and Rainy entered, and there was nothing for the others but to wait.

Everything had moved so quickly since Stephen's arrival that Rose had had almost no time to talk to him about anything except the business of finding his father. He'd gone to the desert in search of answers. A huge question was the strength of his body. It had been nearly a year and half since the great wounding that had left him crippled, and Stephen wanted to test himself in a significantly physical way. Rose knew he was also seeking the answer to the why of that wounding. Stephen firmly believed that the hand of Kitchimanidoo was at work in all things. In the vast desert of northern Arizona, he hoped to understand what the Great Mystery had in mind for him and to find the courage to accept it.

It wasn't Rose, however, who broached the subject of his sojourn.

"What did you find in that desert?" Meloux asked out of the blue.

"Nothing at first, Henry."

"Do you know why?"

"I think so. I was looking way too hard, looking for something momentous. I got frustrated. And I was in a lot of pain."

"Body or spirit?"

"Both, Henry. But I'd set out to get to the top of that holy mesa, and if I wanted to do it, I had to accept the pain. That's when it came to me. Not a huge epiphany but an important one."

"What was it?" Rose asked.

"Everybody hurts, Aunt Rose. That was it. Everybody hurts. And if I want to be a Mide, I need to quit thinking about my own pain and think more about all those whose pain is greater than mine."

Henry's face didn't change, but he gave a nod, almost imperceptible.

The sound of Rainy singing prayers inside the sweat lodge continued, and then the first round of the sweat ended. The two women emerged drenched and steaming into the cold air outside. They were given water, and Stephen took the cooled Grandfathers from the sweat lodge and added newly heated rocks. Leah Duling looked drained, and Rose wondered if she should return to the sweat lodge for the next round. She said, "Are you all right, Leah?"

"I'm strong," the woman replied. "I can take this."

Henry said, "You have always been strong, Leah, but a sweat is not about enduring. It is about yielding."

After the new Grandfathers had had time to heat the lodge again, the two women reentered and Rainy resumed her prayers.

"What do you think, Henry?" Stephen asked.

"I do not think anything. I wait."

"Somebody's coming," Daniel said, a short time later.

Rose followed his eyes and spotted two figures walking toward them across the meadow. As they came nearer, she recognized one of them as Ernie Champoux, whom she knew from her earlier years in Aurora. He was a relative of Henry Meloux and worked, she believed, at the Chippewa Grand Casino. The man with him was a stranger.

"*Boozhoo*," Champoux greeted them all.

"*Boozhoo*, Nephew," Meloux replied.

Champoux nodded toward the sweat lodge. "Who's inside?"

"Aunt Rainy and Leah Duling," Daniel replied.

"Yeah, I heard about that woman showing up for the wedding."

"What's up, Ernie?" Daniel said.

"Got word on the rez you were out here. This here is Porky," he said.

The man who'd come with him was short, overweight, broad-faced, maybe forty, Native.

"It's really Abner," the man said. "Abner Porkman. Everybody just calls me Porky. Kind of fits," he said, looking down at his portly girth. Then he said, *"Anin."* Which, like *boozhoo,* was an Ojibwe greeting.

"Porky works security at the casino. He's got something you might want to know, about that Harris guy who seems way too lucky at the blackjack table. Tell 'em, Porky."

Porkman scratched his head and seemed less than eager to proceed. "You've got to understand, this is all kind of risky for me. I could lose my job."

"What do you want from us?" Daniel said.

"Just that whatever I tell you, you didn't hear from me."

Daniel said, "It's a promise."

"Okay. So." Porkman shoved his hands into the pockets of his jeans, as if they hid something he didn't want seen. "It's like this. I work upstairs in the casino surveillance room. We've got cameras all over the place. It's my job to monitor activity, gambling or otherwise, looking for anything that seems, you know, questionable. So one of the things we watch is someone who's winning big. We take a good look to see if they might be cheating somehow. Counting cards, maybe, or maybe in cahoots with the dealer, that kind of thing. So this Harris guy comes in a few weeks ago."

"Before or after he and his family went into the Boundary Waters?" Daniel asked.

"Both," Porkman said. "And right away he starts winning. Not every single time he sits at a table, but enough that I can't help but notice. And it's always the same dealer he wins with. So I go to Trudeau."

"The casino manager," Daniel clarified for Rose.

"I saw you on one of our cameras, talking to him yesterday," Porkman said. "Then Ernie and me got to conversing this afternoon. Why I'm here."

"What did Ben say when you told him?"

"He said not to worry about it. He was on top of it."

"That's what he told us, too," Daniel said.

"In the time I've been monitoring Harris, I figure he's won like twenty-five grand. That doesn't sound to me like anybody's on top of it. Then my shift schedule gets changed all of a sudden so that I'm never working the hours this Harris guy gambles. I think there's more going on here than meets the eye, is what I'm saying."

"Have you talked to anybody else about this?"

"I've got a family to support. This is a good job. I'm not looking to get fired."

"But you talked to Ernie," Daniel said.

"Ernie and me, we go way back. And he pointed out that if something fishy's going on and I say nothing, that could be bad, too. So I'm kinda caught here between a rock and a hard place, you know?"

"What do you think of Ben Trudeau?"

"He knows about running a casino. Things are good there, really. And he's been real good about trying to get himself involved in the rez community. I heard he goes to all the OED meetings."

"OED?"

"Office of Economic Development. They oversee all the business initiatives on the rez. And I see him at a lot of the gatherings at the community center in Allouette. But I'm thinking now that he's always asking lots of questions, you know. About the Shinnobs around here. I didn't think much about it, but now I'm thinking maybe there's more to his questions than just, you know, friendly curiosity."

"Any idea what?" Daniel asked.

Porkman shrugged. "Got me."

"Who's been dealing the winning hands to Harris?"

"A woman named Krystal Gore. New to the casino. Not from around here. When I figured what was going on, I talked to LuJean in the personnel office. She told me Krystal came here from New York. Her last job was working a casino there. An Indian casino."

"Did LuJean know why she left?"

"I could be getting us both into big trouble here."

"All this is off the record," Daniel said.

"Okay, LuJean told me her application said she wanted to be closer to family. But she's from New York State. The casino here's kind of like a small town, you know. We all get to know each other pretty well. So I asked around, and she's got no family here. Just her and her kid, a little girl."

"What about her background check?"

"Another red flag. It's missing from her file."

"Any idea who might have access to her file?"

"LuJean, of course. And Erica Feather. She's director of personnel. But we all know Erica. She's on the up-and-up."

"Who else?"

"Trudeau."

"Do you know where Krystal lives?"

"That apartment complex just south of Aurora, I think. The Pines. You going to talk to her?"

"I think that would be a good idea, don't you?"

"Like I said, keep me out of it."

"We never talked," Daniel told him.

The flap over the sweat lodge lifted, and Leah came out followed by Rainy. Leah stood uncertainly, wavering just a little, strands of wet black hair stuck to her forehead like leeches, her face drained of blood. Rainy held her up.

Henry said, "What is it, Leah?"

The woman looked at him, her eyes huge holes filled with horror.

"Oh, my God, Henry," she said. "It's the end of the world."

CHAPTER 33

Cork thought that if he were the tall man, he might believe that Kitchimanidoo had turned against him. Flynn was dead. The kid was crippled, infected, and if he didn't get help soon, maybe in big trouble. And now even nature seemed bent on ensuring that the tall man failed in his mission, whatever it was. The wind had grown powerful, bitterly cold and wet. It came howling out of the northwest, across the enormous lake, spitting sleet at them like bits of gravel that stung their faces. The waves mounted before them, capped with white foam. The tall man turned his birch-bark canoe into the wind so that the bow would cut the waves. There were a number of islands on the lake, and the tall man headed for the nearest. The canoes were taking on water. Even if they stayed afloat, the cold of the water itself could kill them all.

Cork felt the kid struggling in the stern. If it weren't for his inflamed leg and the fever, he would probably have been fine, even better than fine, in these difficult circumstances. As it was, Cork shouldered most of the responsibility for propelling and guiding the canoe. The sky was a roil of poisonous-looking clouds that turned the water black. If the canoes swamped, Cork figured he'd let the gear go and make sure the kid got to the island. Or do his best in that regard. There were no life vests on this trip, and the clothing they all wore would suck up water and become as weighty as stone. If worse came to worst, Cork wasn't sure exactly what he would do. But he suspected that if the kid died, his own usefulness on this expedition would be at an end. A single canoe was enough to get Lindsay Harris, Mrs. Gray, and the tall man wherever it was they were going.

His gloves were wet and his hands numb. His body ached from the effort and the bitter, bitter cold. The canoe was already awash in water up to his calves. With the help of the sour woman's strength, the tall man had pulled a good distance ahead, almost to the island. Cork labored, digging his paddle hard into the great swells of the lake. He glanced back and saw the kid, pale and exhausted, doing the best he could, which was pretty much just going through the motions of paddling. There was no power at all in his strokes.

Cork was still a good hundred yards out when the tall man's canoe touched land. Its occupants immediately disembarked and drew the canoe safely from the churning water. They stood on the shoreline watching helplessly as Cork fought—not only the wind and waves but the growing, terrifying realization that he and the kid probably wouldn't make it. The kid could barely lift his paddle now, and the water in the canoe was deepening by the minute.

The tall man stripped off his clothing except for his long underwear, splashed into the lake, and began swimming with sure, powerful strokes toward Cork and the kid. He disappeared momentarily each time Cork's canoe dipped into a trough, then he reappeared as the canoe mounted the wave crests. Cork was astounded by the tall man's speed and agility in the water, especially considering that the lake was only a few degrees above freezing.

The tall man reached the canoe, and as he pulled himself in, Cork counterbalanced. The tall man grabbed the paddle from the kid, shoved the gear forward to make a place for himself near the stern, and he and Cork began working together in a battle that might already have been lost.

Seventy yards, sixty, fifty, the shoreline drew ever nearer. But the canoe had taken on so much water that even its lithe construction couldn't keep it from foundering now. The lake washed over the gunwales and the canoe slipped under. But it didn't sink. Cork and the tall man continued to shove it forward, digging their paddles in as best they could. Cork was cold to the bone and had lost feeling in every part of him, but he was damned if he was going to give up. He could feel the tall man at his back and the determination there.

At last, they reached the island. Mrs. Gray and Lindsay grabbed the bow and pulled it to solid ground. Cork stumbled out, his legs numbed stumps. The tall man came behind him, dragging the kid, who looked barely alive.

"A fire," the tall man gasped to the sour woman. "For God's sake, build us a fire. We need to get Bird warm and dry."

Cork and the tall man had wrapped themselves in wool blankets and now sat beside the fire the woman had built. They were in the lee of the pine cover on the island, but they could still feel the bite of the wind as it slid among the trees. Smoke bloomed from the flames and lifted and was scattered immediately. Sleet no longer fell, but the sky showed no sign of clearing, and whitecaps continued to gallop across the surface of the lake like animals gone wild.

November, Cork thought with a leaden heart.

Bird, the kid, lay in his sleeping bag near the fire. Lindsay Harris sat next to him, gazing down at his face with a kind of maternal concern. "He's not very old," she said.

"Seventeen," the tall man said. "In the old times, he would have been a warrior long ago."

Wet clothing of all kinds had been draped over sticks stuck into the ground near the flames. An old, blue enamel coffeepot sat on the coals of the fire.

"We should have brought tents," the sour woman said, pulling her coat up against her chin.

"We didn't plan on being out this long," the tall man said.

"Your plan." She shot him an accusing look.

The tall man didn't reply.

"Tell me about Manitou Canyon," Cork said.

The tall man eyed him with surprise, then glanced at Bird

and understood. He seemed to be considering the advisability of replying.

"All of the earth is sacred," he finally said. "We should feel that in every moment no matter where we happen to be. But there are places where you can sense the presence of the Great Mystery in a powerful way, places that offer the human spirit strength and peace and a true sense of *bimaadiziwin*. You know that word?"

"A whole life, a healthy way of living," Cork said.

"That's the land where the Manitou River runs."

"Worth dying for?"

"It's my home. But even if it wasn't, the answer would still be yes."

"Something's threatening the land, the river?"

"The dam John Harris built in the narrows of Manitou Canyon."

"No more," Mrs. Gray said. "Don't tell him any more."

The tall man shrugged. "Does it really matter now?"

Lindsay said, "What do I have to with this dam? Or Cork?"

The tall man considered her question. "Have you ever tried to move a great rock? Much easier if you have a lever."

Bird stirred and opened his eyes. "I'm better," he said, but it was clearly a lie. "We should get going."

"We won't go any farther today," the tall man said. "Just rest."

Bird didn't seem at all inclined to fight that decision. He closed his eyes and was quiet awhile. Then he asked, "Can we still make it in time, Uncle Aaron?"

"That's in the hands of Kitchimanidoo," the tall man said.

CHAPTER 34

In Rainy's cabin, they took off their sweat-drenched clothing and dried themselves. As they dressed, Leah Duling moved like a woman in shock. She hadn't told Rainy or anyone else what she'd experienced, what had so stunned her and frightened her to silence. She'd spoken not another word since she uttered her horrified "Oh, my God, Henry. It's the end of the world." Sweats, if they were successful, usually resulted in cleansings that greatly relaxed those involved. Leah had come from the sweat lodge rigid and had moved as if frozen. Sweats could tax a body, and Rainy always did her best to monitor those in her charge to be certain no one went beyond her physical capability. But Leah had shown no sign of being in any difficulty. And then suddenly, it was as if she'd been stricken.

"They're waiting for us in Uncle Henry's cabin," Rainy said quietly.

Leah lifted her coat from Rainy's bed and held it against her breast and stared out the window at the meadow filled with the dead grass of November. She shook her head slowly and said, "I don't want to see him. I don't want to see anybody. I just want to go."

"Back to your hotel?" Rainy asked.

"Anywhere. I just want to leave this place behind."

"What is it, Aunt Leah? What happened in the sweat?"

Leah shook her head, this time desperately.

"Just talk to us. To me or to Henry. We can help."

She looked at Rainy, her eyes like those of someone who'd

gone through war. "No one can help. It's coming and there's nothing anyone can do."

"What's coming?"

Tears rolled down the woman's cheeks now. She stared at Rainy and finally answered, "The end of the world."

"Talk to me, Aunt Leah. Tell me what you've seen."

"Nothing," the woman replied in a dead voice. "I saw nothing."

There was a knock at the door, and Daniel called, "Everything okay in there?"

"We'll just be a moment." Rainy took her aunt's arm and drew her to the bed, and they sat together. She eased Leah's coat from her grip and laid it down. She took Leah's hands in both her own. What she tried to communicate in that touch was complete acceptance. Whatever it was her aunt held inside, whatever had frightened her wasn't so terrible that it couldn't be shared.

"What we think with our minds, Aunt Leah, can sometimes fool us. But our hearts never lie. Don't let your mind get in the way of your heart. Tell me what you feel right now."

Leah looked down at their hands, their entwined fingers. Her skin was white and thin and blue-veined and spotted. Rainy's hands were dark and strong and gentle.

"Hopeless," Aunt Leah finally said. "It's hopeless. Nothing can be done."

"What did you see?"

"Lucius was right in all his apocalyptic ranting. God is going to do it again. He's going to purge the world with water. A great flood is coming, Rainy, and it will kill us all."

"Will you come with me and we'll talk about it with Uncle Henry?"

The woman removed one hand from Rainy's grasp and wiped at the tears streaming down her face. "I didn't want this. I didn't ask for it. I want to forget it. I want it never to have been."

"It's done," Rainy said gently. "And it's not something you can run from or forget or try to throw away. It's yours, for whatever reason. Maybe we can understand why that is. Let's try, Aunt Leah. Let's try together."

Her aunt bowed her head and sat that way for nearly a minute. Then she drew herself up and turned her face to Rainy and surprised her niece by saying, "Oh, what the hell."

Henry's cabin smelled of sage and cedar. The old man was seated at his table, his face a landscape of calm. The table was laid with bread and soup. The others were there, except for Ernie Champoux and Abner Porkman, who'd left Crow Point after they delivered the information about Trevor Harris's "luck" at the casino.

"Eat first," the old man said. "Then we will talk."

They shared the meal in silence. When they'd eaten, Rose and Stephen cleared the dishes, and the others remained at the table. Meloux said nothing. In the quiet of the cabin, the only sound was the deep breathing of Ember as he slept in the corner.

"Tell me it was just a dream, Henry," Leah finally said.

"You saw the end of the world?"

"I did, Henry. The great flood all over again, water covering the whole earth."

"And everyone in the world dead?"

"I saw hundreds drowned and drowning."

"Hundreds?" the old man said. "And were you with these hundreds in this flood?"

She nodded, and tears once again began to slip from her eyes down her cheeks.

"This flood, then, was your own end, too?"

"It was the end of everyone, Henry, and everything."

"It seemed to you the end of the world," the Mide said.

"It was the end of the world," she insisted.

The old man looked to Rainy, and Rainy said to her aunt, "We see out of our own experience, Aunt Leah. It's like being in a bowl and the bowl to us seems like it's the whole world."

Leah looked confused. "What are you saying? That it wasn't the end of the world? That I just thought it was?"

"You were at the center of what you saw, what you experienced, and it seemed to you as if that was the all of everything."

Leah thought a moment and then looked relieved. "So not the end of the world?"

"I don't think so, Aunt Leah. But it certainly must have seemed so."

"It could still involve a big-ass flood," Stephen said.

"Or maybe it's nothing," Daniel said. "Maybe just a subconscious working out of some easily explainable thing in Aunt Leah's life."

"A vision can be anything," the old Mide said. "But it is never nothing."

Stephen said, "This darkness that's weighed on me, it's also made me feel sometimes like I'm drowning. I can't help thinking about the timing of these things. Why now? And I've got to tell you I think they all have something to do with Dad."

"There wasn't anything particularly threatening in Trevor Harris's vision," Daniel pointed out.

"That vision was a load of crap," Stephen said.

"Maybe so," the old Mide said. "But it might be the key to understanding everything."

"I don't get it, Uncle Henry," Rainy said. "If Trevor Harris concocted his own vision, how can that help us understand Leah's vision or Stephen's premonition?"

"Perhaps there was more truth to the lie than the liar knew."

"What kind of truth, Henry?" Stephen said.

"I think you should talk some more to this young Harris."

"We'll do that," Stephen said. "We'll nail his lying ass to the wall."

"We're going to need more leverage," Daniel said. "Maybe this woman who's been dealing winning hands to Trevor can give us that."

"Let's find her." Stephen moved from the window toward the door.

"You go on," Rainy said. "I'll stay here with Leah and Uncle Henry. But let us know what you discover."

"Can we give you a lift home, Rose?" Daniel asked.

She accepted, and the three pulled on their coats and left, heading into the chill wind of the late afternoon. In the corner of the cabin, Ember stood, stretched himself, and padded softly to Henry's side. The old Mide stroked his fur softly. Leah sat at the table, looking exhausted from her ordeal.

"You should rest," Rainy told her. "You can lie down in my cabin."

The woman stood, but she didn't move immediately to the door. She looked down at Henry and said in a tired way, "You made my life hell once before. Looks like you might do it again."

The old man smiled. "You give me more credit than I am due. But we are not finished here, Leah. Kitchimanidoo alone knows the end of this. When we see that end, maybe you will feel different."

The look on Leah's face didn't speak trust, but it also didn't show the anger that had been there when she first arrived in Tamarack County. Although she'd fought against it, and it probably confused and frightened her, Leah was changing. Which, Rainy knew, was something Henry would also not take credit for.

"Come with me to my cabin, Aunt Leah," she said. "Let's see about getting you some rest."

The woman followed her.

"She's sleeping," Rainy said, when she returned to her greatuncle's cabin.

The old man said, "Good."

"A huge flood. What could that be, Uncle Henry?"

The old man shrugged. "It was not my vision. But I think Stephen O'Connor is right about the timing. I think it is about his father. What exactly I cannot say."

Ember moved to the door and sat eyeing Rainy with a look she knew well.

"Come on, old friend. I think we both need to walk a bit."

She left Henry's cabin with the dog trotting before her across the meadow. On a day when the sky was clear, it would have been nearing dusk. Under the cloud cover, dark was descending early and rapidly. A powerful wind was up, and she leaned into it with her gloved hands deep in the pockets of her jacket. She walked to the shoreline of Iron Lake and stood amid the birches while Ember sniffed at the ground among the tree trunks. The lake had an angry look. The water was dark, bruised-looking, and raging with whitecaps. She thought about Cork. Where was he now? Out on some roiling lake, fighting the wind and the waves, the cold and the coming dark? Was that what Leah's vision of a flood was all about? If that was so, what about all those hundreds of others she saw drowning?

"Give me a vision, too!" she cried into the dark and the wind. "Show me that Cork is safe!"

She waited until her anger passed, then sang a prayer asking for the courage to accept the will of Kitchimanidoo, whatever that might be. She called to Ember and turned back to Henry's cabin, where the warm glow of a lantern was visible in the window.

CHAPTER 35

They entered Aurora just ahead of dark. The houses were lit from within by dull, artificial light. It was suppertime and the streets felt empty. Daniel drove down Oak, the main street of town. Rose sat in front on the passenger side, Stephen in back. They'd talked little on their drive from Crow Point. Like the others, Rose was deep into her own thoughts. She was thinking about the terrible time only a few years earlier, when her sister had gone missing in the mountains of Wyoming. She was recalling how hard they'd all prayed for her safe return, prayed in vain. She was afraid all their desperate prayers might once again prove useless.

"We'll drop you off at home, Rose," Daniel said.

"I'd rather come along, if you don't mind."

Daniel thought about it and glanced at Stephen, who just shrugged.

"All right," he said.

"What if Krystal's not at her apartment?" Stephen asked, speaking of the cheating dealer.

"We track her down," Daniel said. "It's a small town."

"Pull over!" Stephen called out suddenly.

"What is it?" Daniel said.

"Just pull over."

They were in the center of town, amid the shops and enterprises of the three-block business district. Daniel pulled to the curb.

"There," Stephen said, pointing across the street toward Johnny's Pinewood Broiler.

The restaurant was an iconic locale in Aurora. Johnny Papp's barbecued ribs were famous, and the Friday night all-you-can-eat fish fry was a huge favorite with the O'Connor clan. Three people were visible at a table in the window: a man, a woman, and a much younger woman.

"Ben Trudeau," Daniel said.

"The casino manager?" Rose asked.

"That's him," Stephen said. "And he's with Marlee and Stella Daychild."

Marlee Daychild was a name Rose knew: Stephen's ex-girlfriend. And Stella was her mother. Stephen and Marlee had been through a lot together. But in the way of young love, the fire had cooled eventually, and they'd both moved on. A mutual and amiable decision, Rose understood.

"What are they talking about?" Stephen said.

"Why don't you ask?" Daniel suggested.

"Just walk right up and butt in on their conversation. Right."

"I was thinking maybe you could wait here and, when they're finished, talk to Marlee and Stella. Rose and I could go ahead and locate Krystal."

"I like that," Stephen said. He got out of the truck and turned back. "If you have trouble finding her, call my cell and we'll hook back up. Otherwise, I'll meet you back at the house."

He stepped away, and Daniel and Rose drove off, heading up Oak Street.

The Pines was a recent addition to the housing market in Aurora. It was a two-story apartment complex with a faux-log finish that was meant, Rose figured, to give it the flavor of a Northwoods lodge. She thought it tacky, but not in the extreme. Although it was much too late in the season for anything to be blooming, there were flower beds along the whole front, and she decided that in summer the place wouldn't look half bad.

Daniel parked the truck in the lot, then he and Rose walked to the building entrance. Daniel scanned the names under the buttons that could buzz each apartment.

K. GORE. He pointed toward the name and poked the button for apartment number 12.

A woman answered, "Who is it?"

"Miss Gore?"

"Yes."

"My name is Daniel English. I wonder if I could talk with you for a moment."

After a pause she asked, "What about?"

"There's been some trouble at the casino."

"What kind of trouble?"

"I'd prefer to explain that when we talk."

"Who are you with?" Her voice was sharp now, and carried an edge of fearfulness.

"The Minnesota Gaming Commission."

He glanced at Rose and gave a quick smile.

For too long, there was no response from the intercom, and Rose was concerned that they might have frightened the woman into silence.

"I'll buzz you up," Krystal Gore finally said.

Inside, it was like any other modern, lackluster apartment building. Rose and Daniel walked down a carpeted hallway to the door with a brass-colored 12 attached above the peephole.

Daniel knocked and said, "Miss Gore?"

When the door opened, a slender blonde stood before them, though Rose could see that it was not her natural color. Her face was pale white, a light powdering over a foundation that tried to cover a landscape of acne scars. Her eyes were a remarkable green, almost neon. Colored contact lenses, Rose thought. Her lips were outlined in mauve and were shiny with gloss. Her fingernails were polished in a matching color.

"English?" she asked.

"Yes."

The woman's unnaturally green eyes shifted to Rose.

"I'm Rose Thorne."

"Are you with the gaming commission?"

Rose's mind didn't run to lies, so she simply said, "No," and hoped it wouldn't matter.

"What's this about?" the woman asked.

"May we come in and talk?" Daniel said.

"You got a badge or something?"

And son of a gun, Daniel reached into his back pocket and brought out a badged ID wallet, which he flipped open and flashed at the woman, who did little more than give it a glance. He closed it quickly, and back into his pocket it went.

Krystal Gore stepped aside to let them pass.

The apartment was a little messy, but not horribly so. It was suffused with an aroma familiar to Rose from all her years raising children: macaroni and cheese. A jumble of wooden blocks lay near one wall, and atop them, looking stiff and uncomfortable, sat a couple of Barbie dolls. The furniture appeared to be new but cheap, the kind, Rose thought, that might come from a rental outlet. The television was on but muted, tuned to the home shopping channel. The item front and center on the screen at the moment was a zircon necklace.

"May we sit down?" Daniel asked.

The woman waved, wordless permission. Rose and Daniel took the sofa. The cushion under Rose felt as if it had been cut from marble, and she was no more comfortable sitting there than the dolls probably were on their blocks. Krystal Gore took one of the armchairs.

"So, what's going on?" she asked.

"We're investigating allegations that some of the gaming at the Chippewa Grand Casino is being manipulated," Daniel said. "Your name has come up in that regard."

"Me?" The woman's right hand went to her breast in a dramatic show of surprise.

"We have video evidence," Daniel said.

"Bullshit," the woman shot back.

"Let's talk about one case specifically," Daniel went on, calmly but firmly. "Does the name Trevor Harris ring a bell?"

The woman's green eyes searched the room and lingered on the ceiling. Her brow furrowed and she finally said, "No."

"Slender, fair-haired, natty dresser, early twenties."

She shook her head.

"I find that interesting. Because the video we have shows that time and time again Harris wins when he plays at your table. Wins big."

"Now wait a minute—"

"No, Miss Gore, you wait a minute. When this investigation concludes, you're looking at the very real possibility of serving prison time. But . . ." Daniel paused. "We're certain that you're acting on the instructions of someone higher up. Ben Trudeau. If you help us nail him, we may be persuaded to ignore your part in the scheme."

"There's no scheme," the woman said. "I don't know what you're talking about."

"You're not from around here, Miss Gore."

"No."

"New York, right?"

"What of it?"

"I understand you left your former job to come here so you could be closer to family. Correct?"

"I need a smoke," the woman said. She stood abruptly and went to her purse, which lay on the kitchen counter. She pulled out a pack of cigarettes, lit one, and stood with her arms crossed, sending smoke from her nostrils.

"Where exactly is your family?"

"You're so smart, you tell me."

"The truth is you have no family here. You were brought to Aurora to do exactly what you're doing. Make sure that Trevor Harris wins at your table. You're pretty good at that. But you've been caught at it before. At the casino in New York where you used to work."

Which surprised Rose. How could Daniel possibly know? Then she realized he'd simply made an educated guess. The mind of a cop.

Krystal Gore stood with smoke trailing up from her as if her face were smoldering. She glared at them, her eyes like green fire. Rose figured she was lost to them, walled off by anger and probably by fear.

Then Daniel said very quietly, "We can help you. We can help you get out from under them."

"Mommy?"

The voice was slight, timid, a child's, and came from the hallway, where neither Rose nor Daniel could see.

"Sweetheart, what are you doing up?"

A little face peeked around the corner, then a whole child followed. She was dark-haired, pink-cheeked, tiny, maybe three. She wore footie Winnie-the-Pooh pajamas, and she was hiding something behind her back.

"I have some visitors, Libby. Go back to bed."

"Can't," Libby said.

"Why not?"

The little girl smiled slyly. "Drink of water."

"All right," her mother said. "A drink of water, then back to bed."

She ran the tap for a bit, then filled a small plastic tumbler. The whole while, Libby eyed Rose and Daniel, but not with fear.

"My name is Rose," Rose said.

"I'm Libby," the little girl said.

"This is Daniel," Rose said.

"Are you married?"

"Yes, dear," Rose said.

"I'm married," Libby said.

"Oh?" Rose gave her a big, pleased smile. "Who to?"

"Him." She brought out what she'd been hiding behind her back, a stuffed unicorn.

"You married a unicorn," Rose said with delight. "A very handsome unicorn."

Krystal brought the water to her daughter. The little girl dropped her unicorn, took the tumbler in both hands, and sipped.

"All of it," her mother said. "And quick now."

Libby drank the water down and handed the tumbler back.

Krystal Gore said to her guests, "Wait here, all right?"

"We're going nowhere," Daniel told her.

Little Libby picked up her unicorn and disappeared with her mother back down the hallway.

Rose could hear the soft murmur of the mother's voice. Although the woman was probably involved in whatever it was that had made Cork disappear, Rose couldn't find it in her heart to think the worst of her. She hoped the truth, when they knew it, would set them all free from what seemed like a destructive net of intrigue.

Krystal returned. Her cigarette lay in the ashtray on the kitchen counter. She picked it up, then crushed it out. "I'm trying to quit," she said. "For Libby's sake."

Although it was Daniel who'd done most of the talking until then, it was Rose who spoke now. "What's going on, Krystal?" She asked it gently, as she might of a hurt child. "How did you become involved in all this?"

The woman bit her lower lip, bit hard. Then she bent her head and began to cry. "They told me they wouldn't prosecute. They told me they would protect me."

"Who's they?" Rose asked.

"Ross Arden."

Daniel tilted his head, as if to hear better. "Ross Arden?"

"The manager of the Lake Pokegema Casino. Where I used to work in New York."

"Is he Indian?" Daniel asked.

"Seneca."

"And Ben Trudeau? He told you the same thing? That he'd protect you if you helped Trevor Harris win?"

"Yes."

"How did it happen?" Rose asked.

Krystal wiped at her tears and shook her head hopelessly. "I was behind. Behind in everything. The rent, my car payment, Libby's day care, you name it. I was so stressed, I wasn't doing my job well. Ross called me into his office and asked what was wrong. He seemed so interested, you know, so caring. I broke down and told him everything. He said he could help. I thought—" She rolled her eyes. "I thought he was going to give me a raise or something. Maybe a promotion. Instead, he asked me to help a customer win. It's not so hard, you know. He told me he would protect me. And that if I did it, he'd make sure all my back bills got paid."

She tried to take a deep breath, but with all her sobbing, it came in little gasps.

"So I did it," she went on. "I thought when it was finished, that would be it, you know? But then Ross told me he had video of me cheating and if I didn't help him some more, he would see to it that I went to jail. He said, 'Know what happens to little girls whose mothers are in jail? The little girls go into foster care. And do you know what happens to them in foster care? They get abused in every way imaginable.' He said that to me, the son of a bitch. Then he sent me out here."

Daniel asked, "Did they tell you why they wanted these men to win?"

She shook her head and wiped at her tears. "I didn't take anything for myself. Honest to God I didn't. I just did what they told me to."

"Blackmail," Daniel said.

"Yes." She leaped on that. "I didn't have a choice."

"Would you be willing to make a statement to that effect?"

"If I did, what would happen?"

"If it helps us put these people behind bars, I'll do everything I can to make sure you're dealt with fairly."

"No jail?"

"I can't promise that. But I'll do everything I can for you and Libby."

Rose saw the woman's shoulders slump and knew exactly what she was thinking: the other men had made promises, too. Why should she believe him?

Krystal stood sobbing, looking so forlorn and so broken and so alone that Rose couldn't help herself. She left the sofa, put her arms around this frightened mother, and said, "It will be all right. It will all work out fine. That's my promise to you."

"I don't want to lose Libby," Krystal said.

Rose made a promise she had no business making but every intention of keeping. "That will happen only over my dead body."

Sheriff Marsha Dross had returned that afternoon from the Search and Rescue operation at Raspberry Lake. Daniel and Rose found her in her office, working on a tuna-fish sandwich and potato chips and drinking a Diet Coke. She listened as they laid everything out for her, the sandwich sitting half eaten on the plate.

When they'd finished, she shoved her chair away from the desk. "A lot to do now."

Before she stood up, her phone rang. She picked up the receiver and answered, "Sheriff Dross." She listened, and Rose saw her eyes widen. "Thank God." She put her phone down and said with great relief, "Cork and Lindsay Harris have been spotted. They're alive."

CHAPTER 36

They were dog tired, all of them. Bird had dropped off first, right after he ate some of the meal Mrs. Gray had prepared from dehydrated vegetable soup base and wild mushrooms she'd found on the island. She'd also made biscuits. Whatever negative he might have said about her—and there was plenty of that—Cork had to admit she knew her way around a campfire. Before Bird slept, Lindsay Harris had sat with him, and Cork had heard her repeat what she'd told him before: *Spirit is at the heart of everything. Trust your spirit.* Which was something Henry Meloux himself might have told the kid.

Lindsay was the next to go. She climbed into her sleeping bag, and in less than a minute, Cork heard soft, deep breathing. The sour woman cleaned up the meal things, then crawled into her own sleeping bag. Which left Cork and the tall man eyeing each other across the flames.

"Who is she to you?" the tall man finally asked.

"What do you mean?"

"You've had chances to run, but you haven't."

"You made it clear what would happen to me. And I get the feeling you're a man of your word."

The tall man studied him. "I have the same feeling about you. Will you smoke with me?"

"I will."

The tall man stood and went to one of the packs. He bent and drew out a beaded pouch. He walked to the edge of the island, and

Cork followed after him. The wind had not abated, and Cork could hear the waves washing restlessly against the rocks all along the shoreline. The tall man pulled a clay pipe from a pocket of his coat and dipped it into the pouch.

"Let's sit," he said.

They settled themselves on the hard ground with the glow of the fire at their backs and the dark of the lake before them. The tall man hunched himself over the pipe to shield it from the wind and lit the tobacco with a wooden match. They shared the smoke in silence.

"What do you hold on to?" the tall man asked. His eyes were on the lake, though because of the dark there was nothing to see. "When you face the worst you can imagine, what keeps you from folding?"

"Belief, I suppose," Cork said.

"What belief?"

"In what I am."

"What are you?"

"*Ogichidaa*."

"Warrior," the tall man said.

"That's one interpretation. To Shinnobs in my neck of the woods, it means one who stands between evil and his people."

The tall man said, "You can't always stand against evil. Sometimes the evil is too great."

"Then a man dies trying."

"Yes," the tall man said. "A man dies trying."

"Manitou River," Cork said. "This is what you're willing to die for?"

"The river and the land it runs through."

Of a sudden, the wind seemed to double itself, and both men felt the shove of it at their backs. Sparks from the fire flew past them and died above the lake, where the water roared as if it were an animal enraged. Cork felt the cold driving through his coat and hunched himself against it.

"None of us might make it out of here," he said. "But unless he gets help, your nephew certainly won't. Mrs. Gray is right, you know. If you left him, we'd make better time."

"If you were me, would you leave him?"

"If I were you, I'd understand all the risks and how to weigh them."

The tall man shook his head. "The dangers we anticipated were very different from what Kitchimanidoo has thrown at us."

"Are you Mide?" Cork asked.

"Me? No. I don't have the spirit of a healer. Like you, I've always believed myself *ogichidaa*."

The wind let up a bit, and the tall man and Cork sat straight again.

"The dam, is that the evil you're trying to stand against?"

"The evil is greed. The dam is the result."

"John Harris, is he part of the evil?"

"He built the dam."

"What do you want from him?"

"The key to killing that dam."

"And you're willing to kill him and his granddaughter and me to get it?"

"Would you die for your home and for those you love?"

"Yes."

"Would you kill to protect them?"

"I already have."

"Then you should understand." The tall man stared into the darkness a long time before he spoke again. "It's not up to me alone."

"Who, then? Mrs. Gray?"

"Not her. You'll know soon enough." He turned and looked into Cork's eyes, and even in the dark, Cork could see the sadness there. "I hope none of you have to die, O'Connor."

"Not as much as we do," Cork replied.

CHAPTER 37

They gathered at the O'Connor house on Gooseberry Lane. Marsha Dross joined them, and they sat around the dining room table with sandwiches that Jenny had put together. Little Waaboo had gone to bed. The feeling in the room was the most hopeful and energetic it had been since Cork and Lindsay Harris disappeared. In fact, it felt to Rose like a war council.

"We got the report from a DNR guy who's in the Boundary Waters conducting some kind of wolf survey," Dross explained. "He ran into them this morning. But he didn't realize who they were until he stopped for the night and did a radio check-in. He indicated he spotted them here."

She'd laid a topographical map of the area on the table, and she pointed to a lake called Emerald, which was very near the Canadian border.

"Charlie Bender, that's the DNR guy, said there were four people, two women and two men. One of the men fit Cork's description and one of the women fit Lindsay's. Bender reported that they had, in fact, given him those names. Neither of them appeared to be in any danger or seemed threatened. Except for the fact that it was odd to find anyone so deep in the Boundary Waters at this point in the season, Bender didn't think much about it."

"Couldn't we send a plane out for them now?" Stephen asked.

"Too dark," Dross said. "The floatplane will go out first thing in the morning, weather permitting. And the report for tomorrow looks hopeful."

"What the hell is Dad doing out there?" Jenny asked. "Why didn't he say anything to this Bender?"

Dross said, "My best guess is that there were more people involved than Bender saw. Probably someone hiding, probably someone with a firearm. I can't think of another reason Cork wouldn't have spoken up."

"How many more people?" Stephen asked.

"Bender reported two canoes, so probably no more than a couple. But he also reported that the canoes were beautiful birch-bark creations. Which is a little odd, and maybe something that when we dig deeper will tell us more." Dross sat back and took a sip from a mugful of coffee. "Azevedo's the IC on this case."

"IC?" Jenny said.

"Incident commander. He's in charge of the search at Raspberry Lake. When I contacted him, I told him not to say anything to the other searchers. Until he hears from me, I want him to continue as if we don't have this information."

"Why?" Stephen said.

"Because I'm concerned someone here is in communication with the people who abducted Cork and Lindsay Harris."

"Ben Trudeau?" Daniel said.

Dross shrugged. "Who knows? There may be others."

Rose said, "Stephen, did you learn anything from the Daychilds?"

"We saw Trudeau with Marlee and her mom at the Broiler this evening," Stephen explained. "After Trudeau took off, I talked to them. Stella's worked at the casino for years, you know. In the last few weeks, Trudeau's been hitting on her, having dinner with Stella pretty regularly. He usually invites Marlee to join them. Says he doesn't have family here and claims it keeps him from feeling too lonely. Marlee thinks he really likes her mom, but he's too shy to actually date her. Me, I think there's something else going on."

"What?" Dross said.

There was an edge to Stephen's voice. "He's been asking a lot of questions about us."

"Us?" Jenny said.

"Dad, me, you. Rainy, too. You know how Marlee loves to talk. So she's told him a lot. She said Trudeau seemed especially interested in how I sometimes see and feel things. Bottom line, he's been pumping them for information."

"Why?" Daniel asked.

Stephen said, "I think he fed that information to Trevor Harris, who used it creating that crap vision of his. That's how he knew I was in Arizona and about 'monthterth under the bed.'"

"I've got a couple of deputies out right now bringing Harris in for questioning," Dross said. "If I can break him, we'll know a lot more."

"I'd love to be there for that," Daniel said.

"I want to be on that floatplane tomorrow," Stephen said.

Dross shook her head. "The only people on that plane will be the pilot, me, and some of my CIRT team." She looked them all over and finally allowed herself a little smile. "We've got a shot at bringing this to a good end."

She stood up, and as she folded the map, her cell phone rang. She pulled it out and looked at the number. "Pender," she told them. "One of the deputies I sent to pick up Harris." She put the phone to her ear. "Dross here. Did you get him?" She listened, and Rose saw her face go stony. "Keep on it and keep me informed." She slid the phone into her pocket and gave them the word. "Seems that Trevor Harris has gone AWOL."

Rainy stood alone on the dark shoreline at the end of Crow Point. The wind was a torrent out of the northwest, and Iron Lake an angry beast. She'd brought a kerosene lantern with her. Despite the protection of the glass, the flame still flickered in the currents that forced their way through the tiniest gaps. She was cold, even in her wool-lined jacket and stocking cap and gloves. But she'd been relieved of a great burden of worry. Cork was alive.

Jenny had called with the news. He'd been spotted, along

with Lindsay Harris, somewhere far north. She didn't know the Boundary Waters, not like Cork, so she had no idea where exactly Emerald Lake was. But she couldn't help thinking of it as a little like the Emerald City in *The Wizard of Oz*, a place of glittering promise. Cork was there and he was alive.

People were with him, but he didn't seem to be in any danger. She didn't know what to make of that. She'd never met a man who seemed so able to take care of himself and others. So she trusted that whatever the reason, it was Cork's choice to be there and to be with them.

The great spill of blood they'd found on Raspberry Island was still perplexing. No one seemed to have an explanation for it. But that was a mystery that would be cleared up the next day, when the sheriff and her people flew out to Emerald Lake and brought Cork and Lindsay Harris back. Rainy was a practical woman. Her belief in the power of her herbal preparations and the traditional ceremonies she took part in was based on her observations of their ability to heal the ailing body and the broken spirit. Because she was practical, she reminded herself that Cork was not out of the woods yet, quite literally, but she believed that he would be, and soon.

And then what?

With one great burden off her shoulders, another had settled in its place.

More and more since Leah's arrival, Rainy had begun to sense from her great-uncle an encouragement to move on in her own life, perhaps even to put Crow Point behind her. Uncle Henry, it seemed, believed he'd given her all he could. It was true, what he'd said, that when she came to him, she'd been in much the same predicament as Leah, so terribly lost and alone. Although she'd thought at the time that she was coming to help take care of a relative nearing the century mark, in truth, Uncle Henry had done the caring. He'd taught her more about real healing than she'd learned in any of her nursing classes. She'd hoped that with time she might come to understand how to heal herself. But that was a lesson she'd somehow missed. And now it was too late.

She was surprised when Ember gave a *woof* in warning. She turned from the lake and put her back to the wind. Her great-uncle stood at the far edge of the circle of light cast by the lantern at her feet. He looked at her calmly, but there was something about him that wasn't quite right.

"Uncle Henry?" she said.

That's when she saw the other figure, a dark shape that stayed beyond the reach of the light. All she could see of it clearly was the arm extended toward her great-uncle's back, the hand at the end of it, and the gun that hand was holding.

CHAPTER 38

Cork's wrists and ankles had been bound with duct tape before he rolled himself in the two blankets for the cold night. He waited until the others all slept soundly, waited especially long to be certain the tall man had slipped off. Then he reached carefully into the pocket of his coat and brought out a small, walnut-handled pocketknife. When the packs had gone into the water along with Bird, Cork had hauled them out. While the others saw to the freezing young man, he'd taken the knife, which he'd seen the kid put into his pack. He'd been waiting until the right moment to try another escape, but he'd finally decided there would never be a right moment. His plan was to slip away with Lindsay in one of the canoes, then head west. West would take them out of the Boundary Waters within two days. There would be roads, towns, civilization.

He'd also decided this: if the escape was unsuccessful, Lindsay would not be killed. She was too important. And Cork? Well, that would be a calculated risk. With Bird so ill and not able to help them move, he hoped the tall man would be forced to grant him a reprieve, at least until they were out of the wilderness. And how much worse off could he be then?

He worked the knife blade open and shifted the handle to his mouth, where he gripped it hard between his teeth. It took a while, but he finally cut through the tape on his wrists. He drew his legs up and sliced through the tape around his ankles. Then he folded the blade, returned it to his coat pocket, and lay for a few minutes, breathing hard, listening to be certain no one had been disturbed.

The wind had finally died. The lake had calmed itself. Only a dim light came from the coals of the banked fire. Cork rolled his head and caught sight of movement, a shade on the far side of the fire glow, a gray creep against the darker backdrop of the island pines. It wasn't the pace of someone heading off to relieve himself, as often happened in a night. The movement was like that of a hunting cat: step, pause, step.

The figure crept to where Bird lay in his sleeping bag, tossing restlessly in his fever, groaning softly. The figure knelt beside him.

It could have been nothing. The tall man, maybe, worried and checking on his nephew. But Cork didn't think so. The cat creep signaled another intention.

He threw off his blankets and leaped over the fire. He hit the kneeling figure, and together they rolled across the hard ground, away from Bird, who cried out. Cork and the figure grappled, and he felt a sting across the side of his chest. He parried the next blow with his forearm and managed to grab the wrist. He could feel the fisted hand and understood that it gripped a knife. He slammed the hand to the ground and pinned the figure under him.

"Enough!" the tall man shouted.

Beneath Cork, the woman went slack. He saw the fist open and the hand jerk away from the knife it had released. He pushed himself up and off the woman and stood.

"What's going on?" The tall man held the rifle ready.

"He was going to cut Bird's throat," Mrs. Gray said from where she lay on the ground.

"That's not true," Cork said.

"Then what's that?" The woman pointed toward the four-inch blade of a hunting knife lying near.

Bird had sat up. He looked at Mrs. Gray and he looked at Cork.

"Do you know what happened?" the tall man asked him.

"Uh-uh." Bird shook his head weakly.

Lindsay Harris lay in her sleeping bag, wide awake and watching with interest.

"I told you," the sour woman said, finally standing. She pointed toward the ground. "He was going to cut Bird's throat with that knife. He would have if I hadn't stopped him."

The tall man eyed Cork. "Well?"

"Why would I want to kill Bird?" he said. "He's slowing us down. Everyone keeps telling me I'm going to die when we get out of these woods. Why would I want to get there faster?"

"He's lying," the woman said. "He's a lying *chimook*."

"You're bleeding," the tall man said to him.

Cork glanced down where he'd felt the sting. The knife had cut through his coat, and the heavy material was staining dark. He said, "I sure didn't do that to myself."

"I did," Mrs. Gray said triumphantly. "This *chimook* doesn't know how to handle a knife. I took it from him easily."

Cork said, "If I'd wanted to cut Bird's throat, I would have used this." He dug into the pocket of his coat and brought out the little pocketknife. It was obvious he'd cut himself free, and they'd take the knife from him anyway.

"That's Bird's," the tall man said. "Where did you get it?"

"I stole it when his pack went into the water."

The tall man's eyes swung to the woman, who took a step back.

"You would kill my nephew?" He spoke quietly, but his look burned and his voice was acid. "To the enemy we are nothing. Less than nothing. They kill us with no regard. But if we kill each other, we become worse than them. Because we should matter to each other."

"The Manitou River is what matters," the woman shot back. "Not you or me or him."

"If you give your life, that's your choice," the tall man said. "But you have no right to make that choice for Bird or anyone else."

"You've been plenty ready to kill O'Connor."

"I was."

"Was?" The sour woman looked even more sour, if that were possible.

"He isn't the enemy," the tall man said.

"He sure as hell isn't going to help us save the Manitou River, now is he?"

"I don't know." The tall man looked at Cork. "I haven't asked him."

"You say one word to him, you spill the plan, and I'll kill both of you the first chance I get. You don't know what it's like, losing everything and everyone you care about. But I do. And this is my chance to make those Caldecott bastards pay." Mrs. Gray said it with such fury that spittle flew from her mouth. She turned her anger on Cork. "*Chimooks* lie to us. Steal from us. Rape us. Kill us. We don't trust *chimooks*. We kill *chimooks*."

Cork could have argued, but what would have been the use? That kind of hatred was a wall he couldn't break through, not with words anyway. He understood where some of it came from, the long, deep history of betrayal and brutality. Slaughter that approached genocide. Cultural trauma across generations. But the depth of her anger seemed to come from something more recent and personal. It wasn't just her brother's death. Somehow, she'd lost everything.

The tall man gave Mrs. Gray a penetrating look. "You try anything like that again, with Bird or O'Connor or the Harris woman, we'll leave you and you can try to get out of this wilderness alone. You understand?"

The woman met his eyes but didn't speak quickly enough.

"O'Connor," the tall man said. "There's duct tape in my pack. Get it and tape her hands."

"You wouldn't." And now the woman's eyes were like his, burning.

"One more word and I'll have him tape your mouth as well," he said.

The woman started to speak, but thought better of it.

When her wrists were bound, the tall man stepped to the knife on the ground and picked it up. He closed the blade and put the knife into his pocket. He held out his hand.

"Yours," he said.

Cork gave it over. The tall man went to one of the packs, cut pieces of gauze and tape, and gave them to Cork to bandage the knife wound.

"Uncle Aaron?"

"What is it, Bird?"

"You can leave me. I'll understand."

"And when I walk the Path of Souls and see your father, what do I tell him? That I abandoned you? No. We'll do what we came to do, and you'll be a part of it."

Bird gave a weak nod and lay back down. The sour woman returned to her sleeping bag, and the tall man sat Cork down on the blankets and bound him once again with duct tape.

Cork lay awake a long time thinking about what had just happened. He'd tried again to stand between Lindsay Harris and danger. What he'd done instead was save Bird's life. He believed the tall man would not forget that. And if it was the tall man's call, Cork thought he and Lindsay and even John Harris might stand a chance. But apparently it wasn't up to the tall man alone. There were others involved. And if they were anything like Mrs. Gray, Cork was afraid he didn't have a prayer.

CHAPTER 39

Rainy studied her great-uncle in the lantern light. Although a gun was pointed at his back, Henry showed no sign of being frightened. She couldn't ever recall seeing the ancient Mide afraid. At least for himself. His concern was always for others. Death, she knew, held no fear for him. She'd often heard him say that he was so old he thought of Death as a little brother.

"What do you want?" Rainy said.

The dark figure finally stepped forward enough that his face was visible in the light.

"They're going to kill me," Trevor Harris said. His eyes were bloodshot, all his features drawn. He looked near the edge of madness.

"Who's they?" Rainy asked.

"That's the thing. I don't know. Indians."

"We're Indian."

"You're different. Safe. I saw what you do out here. You try to help people. I need help. And . . ." He hesitated, then stumbled on. "I think my sister needs help, too."

"If you want our help, you have to put that gun away."

Trevor stared at the firearm in his hand as if it were some failing in himself that he was ashamed of. "I'm sorry," he said. "I'm just so scared."

"You don't have anything to be afraid of here," she assured him.

He considered her words, finally lowered the weapon, and shoved it into a pocket of the long, expensive coat that he wore.

"Where's Aunt Leah?" Rainy asked.

"She is still asleep in your bed, missing all the fun," Henry said with a little smile.

Rainy never ceased to be amazed at—and sometimes frustrated by—the situations Henry somehow found humorous.

"Let's go back to my uncle's cabin," she said to Trevor. "We can talk there."

While Rainy prepared tea, young Trevor sat slumped at her great-uncle's table. He looked exhausted. Henry didn't try to engage him in conversation, and Rainy thought maybe the old man was simply letting Trevor stew in the roil of his own anxieties for a while longer, to soften him further, perhaps. When the tea was ready—kava tea to help Trevor relax—she poured some for them all, then sat at the table. She looked at her great-uncle, and it was clear he intended to hold to his silence.

Trevor stared into his mug of tea. "I'm tired. I haven't slept in forever. Can I sleep here?"

"First we talk," Rainy said. "In order to help you, we need to know the truth."

Trevor shook his head and sounded bewildered. "I don't even know where to begin."

"With the Indians?"

"It goes so far back, before they ever contacted me. It's really my grandfather's fault."

Blame. Rainy thought of it like a rabid skunk. Everyone stayed as far away from it as possible.

"Tell me about your grandfather."

He looked at her with sick-puppy eyes. "Did you ever put out your arms to someone, you know, wanting a hug? And all you got in return was a cold stare? That's my grandfather. The famous Mr. John W. Harris."

"You never felt loved?"

"Not by him. From him, all I got was expectations. His favorite phrase was 'Man up.' When he sent Lindsay and me off to boarding school, he said, 'Make me proud, boy.' But it didn't matter what I did, I never could make him proud."

"And Lindsay?"

"I don't know. I only saw her a few times every year. Not enough to be close, like brothers and sisters should be. So I don't know about her and Grandpa John. I don't think she hates him like I do."

"Hate? Is that what you feel?"

He mulled that over. "Okay, maybe *hate*'s too strong. But if I disappointed him, let me tell you he was a terrible disappointment to me. Always gone building a dam somewhere, never time for us. Hell, it wasn't our fault our folks got killed."

"So you were never close. What does that have to do with these Indians?"

"I like to gamble, all right? Lindsay says I'm addicted. I think of it as a deep fascination. There's an incredible beauty in it."

"When you're winning maybe," Rainy said.

"You don't get it. You never will," he said, as if it was an argument he'd had so many times before that the thought of it bored him. "Anyway, I hit a streak of bad luck. It happens. This one was worse than any before. I owed big money to some people, not exactly patient people. I asked Grandpa John for help. He told me a man had to shoulder his own debts. I asked Lindsay. But she's got student loans like a mountain on her back. Then I get a visit one day from a man. An Indian. Calls himself Mr. Black. He says he can help me. He tells me he can square my debts and fifty grand on top of that. I ask him what's the catch. He says he wants to talk to my grandfather. That's it? I say. Talk to John Harris? Then he lays it out for me. He wants me to get Grandpa John into the Boundary Waters. He'll take it from there."

"And then what?"

"They said they would return him unharmed when they got what they wanted from him."

"Who's they?"

"No idea, but it was clear this Mr. Black wasn't operating alone and whoever was backing him had deep pockets."

"What did they want from your grandfather?"

"Search me." He took a sip of his tea. "I knew there was no

way he would go with just me. So I talked to Lindsay, gave her some bull about wanting to reconnect with the old coot. She bought it. When I told Grandpa John that Lindsay was on board, he agreed."

"Why the Boundary Waters?"

Trevor shrugged. "Got me."

"Because," Henry said, finally offering something, "a man may go missing in the wilderness for a hundred reasons. It is a mystery that may never be solved. But I think there is something else."

Trevor waited, then said with a bit of impatience, "Well, what else?"

"Emerald Lake," the old man said.

Trevor gave him a puzzled look.

"Your sister and Cork have been spotted," Rainy said. "They were seen this morning at Emerald Lake, which is pretty far north in the Boundary Waters, almost to the Canadian border."

"She's okay?" The young man seemed genuinely relieved.

"As far as we know. A floatplane's going out first thing tomorrow to locate them and pick them up."

"Oh, thank God." He sat back and looked as if a great weight had been lifted from him.

"Why did they take her?" Rainy asked.

"They told me Grandpa John wouldn't give them what they wanted. They said they needed Lindsay."

"And you gave them your sister?" Rainy made no effort to hide her dismay.

"They told me Grandpa John was fine, and that they wouldn't hurt Lindsay. As soon as they had what they wanted, they'd let them both go. And neither of them would ever know I was involved."

"And you believed them?"

Trevor wouldn't meet her eyes. "I didn't have a choice."

"We always have a choice," Henry said. "Yours was to sacrifice your sister."

"She hasn't been sacrificed, okay? Rainy just told me she's all right."

Rainy said, "Why did you think you had no choice?"

"They have evidence of everything. They told me they'd make sure it got to the cops."

"Evidence of your involvement?"

He nodded. "They taped our conversations. They kept a record of all my texts and emails. They have video of me at the casino table, obviously involved in cheating. They had me by the nuts."

"What was the cheating at the casino all about?"

"That's how they paid me. If they just gave me the money and the IRS gets wind of my spending and I have no way to account for it, I'm screwed. But if I report winnings at a casino, it's a reasonable explanation."

"So why would they want to kill you?"

"After we found all that blood at Raspberry Lake, I panicked. I mean it looked like somebody was dead. I was afraid it might be Lindsay. When I got back to my hotel, I shot them a frantic text. They replied that Lindsay was fine. But I wasn't sure if I could believe them."

"You finally wondered about the truthfulness of these people you were dealing with?" Rainy said.

"Okay, I was a little stupid. I was desperate, all right?"

"What happened then?" Rainy said.

"I told them I needed proof."

"And if you didn't get it?"

"I said I'd go to the cops."

"With what?"

"I don't know. It was just a threat. Then I go out for dinner tonight, and when I come back to the hotel, the clerk tells me a couple of guys were looking for me. Indians. I head up to my room, but as I go to unlock the door, I hear something from inside. I run for the stairs, and I hear the door open behind me. Man, I'm running like crazy. Out to the parking lot, into my car, and then just driving. I don't know where. There's nobody up here I know. Nobody I can turn to. Hell, if I just drive away, they'll find me. Whoever they are, they're powerful and everywhere. I didn't know what to do." He looked at Rainy and her great-uncle with pleading eyes. "Then I thought of you."

Henry said, in the voice he often used that could have calmed an angry bear, "And you made a choice. A good choice." He leaned toward the young man and offered an encouraging smile. "I think you are finally ready to man up."

CHAPTER 40

"Emerald Lake, Uncle Henry?"

They were waiting for the others to arrive on Crow Point. Rainy had called Daniel. He'd passed the word along to Cork's family and then had called the sheriff. They were all on their way. Trevor Harris, who'd looked exhausted to the point of collapse, had borrowed Henry's bunk and was asleep. Rainy and her great-uncle sat together at the table, talking quietly.

"You said Emerald Lake was important in why these people chose the Boundary Waters. What did you mean?"

"Not the lake itself. The route. From Miskominag," Henry said, using the Ojibwe name for Raspberry Lake. "To Amik."

"Beaver," Rainy said, translating.

"That is what our people call the lake. The whites call it Mudd. From there to Ozhaawashko-manoomin."

"Green rice?" Rainy said, translating once again.

"The whites call it Emerald," Henry said. "From there they will travel to Chi Wajiw, what white mapmakers call Mountain Lake. Then to Mooz, and finally the great Lac La Croix, in Canada."

"How do you know this?"

"When our brothers the Odawa joined us for war against our enemies, that is the route they followed. Not many remember. Whoever has taken Corcoran O'Connor and that young woman, they know the old way. They came from Canada, and to Canada they return. Whatever the reason behind all this evil, it comes from the north."

In the corner of the cabin, Ember lifted his head and looked toward the cabin door, which opened a moment later, and Leah walked in. She appeared rested, her face relaxed, her eyes brighter and emptied of fear. From the bunk came the susurrus of Trevor's deep breathing as he slept, and Leah glanced at him with surprise.

"What's he doing here?"

"My bed was taken," Rainy said. "You look much better."

"I feel . . . unburdened. Does that make sense?"

"Perfect sense," Rainy said. "Would you like some tea?"

"I'm fine, thank you." She smiled at Henry. "May I sit?"

Henry indicated the empty chair.

Leah sat and reached both hands across the table, inviting Henry to take them, which the old man did.

"You know," she said, "I thought you were the most handsome man I'd ever seen. And you're still beautiful. I don't know what's going to happen now, Henry, but I'm glad I came."

When he replied, the ancient Mide's brown eyes were as soft as Rainy had ever seen them. "You have traveled a long road, Leah. Maybe this is where it ends."

Rainy heard, and she knew that her time there was, indeed, at an end.

When she saw the flashlight beams coming across the meadow, Rainy opened the door to Henry's cabin and greeted the newcomers cheerfully. All of Cork's family were there, except Rose, who'd stayed at the house to watch Waaboo. Inside the cabin, Leah Duling sat at the table, holding Henry's hands. Asleep on the bunk was the young man who'd gone AWOL. The noise of all the arrivals didn't seem to disturb him in the least.

While they waited for the sheriff to arrive, Rainy related the things that Trevor Harris had said, which surprised no one very much. Stephen filled Rainy and Henry in on what Marlee and Stella Daychild had told them, which seemed to go a long way in explaining Trevor's "vision" of Stephen in the Arizona wilderness.

Ember, who'd been sitting patiently beside the door, rose to all fours and barked once. A moment later, there was a knock, and Marsha Dross joined the gathering. She hung her coat and was introduced to Leah Duling, then she went and stood over the sleeping figure of Trevor Harris.

"Never would have guessed," she said. "I figured he'd be half-way back to Las Vegas by now."

Rainy told Dross what she'd told the others, then the sheriff nodded toward the sleeping form and said, "Shall we invite him to the party?"

Henry said, "Let me wake him."

The Mide stood and left the table. Dross stepped aside, and Henry sat on the edge of the bunk and reached out above the rise and fall of the young man's chest. He lowered his hand until it almost touched, and he held it there for a few moments. Trevor Harris's eyes slowly opened. The first thing he saw was the face of the old man smiling down at him.

"You are needed," Henry said, as if Trevor were an important ally rather than one of the architects of whatever evil had come to Tamarack County.

Trevor sat up and looked around the crowded room, and Rainy saw fear in his eyes.

Henry said, "There is nothing here to be afraid of. These people have all come seeking your help. In turn, they may be able to help you and your sister."

The young Harris swung his legs off the bunk and rubbed his eyes and took a long, deep breath. He looked up at Henry, who smiled encouragingly.

"What do you want from me?" he asked.

"Tell me about your vision," Henry said.

"Bogus. I made it up from the things I was told. Except the Shakespeare quotes. That was my own creative addition." This last part was said with a little note of pride.

"Who told you these things?" Henry asked.

"I don't know. I got everything anonymously, through texts or emails or phone calls."

"I'll need your cell phone," Dross said. "And your computer."

"Good luck," Trevor said. "I get the feeling these people know how to cover their tracks."

"But they're slipping up," Daniel said. "We have you and we know about Trudeau."

"What's Trudeau's part in all this?" Dross said.

Trevor looked puzzled. "I don't know who that is."

"He manages the Chippewa Grand Casino. He's the one who's been seeing to it that you get your payoff."

"I don't know anything about that. I was just told to play the blackjack table and everything else would be taken care of."

Dross said, "After we have Cork and your sister safely out of the Boundary Waters, I'll pull Trudeau in and see what we can get from him."

"They will not be on Emerald Lake tomorrow," Henry said. "Look for them north, on Mountain Lake or Moose."

"How do you know?" the sheriff asked.

And the old man explained about the ancient warpath.

Rainy finally put a question to Trevor that no one had yet asked. "Why? What are they after?"

Trevor Harris said, "I don't know. I honest to God don't know the why of any of this."

"We'll know more tomorrow," Dross promised. "I swear I'll sit on Ben Trudeau until he breaks."

"Tomorrow, when Dad and Lindsay Harris are safe," Stephen said and lifted his hand as if in a toast to that near horizon.

"Tomorrow," Rainy agreed.

She looked to Henry for confirmation, but the old Mide sat in silence.

CHAPTER 41

Another hard, cold, interrupted night in the wilderness, and when Cork woke in the morning, there wasn't a place on his whole body that didn't hate him and let him know it. The cut the woman had delivered across his side stung like ants were feasting there. Cork could see that the tall man had risen early. He stood by the fire he'd long ago stoked to flame. The rifle hung from a sling over his shoulder. Cork smelled coffee and saw a pot sitting among the coals. For that alone, he could have called the tall man brother.

Cork was surprised to see that the cloud cover had broken, and its remnants were tinted by the rising sun with a burnt-orange hue. The tops of the pine trees were burnished with sunlight as well. With the clearing of the sky, the temperature overnight had dropped, and Cork could feel the freeze on his face.

The sour woman was coming from the woods, her hands freed from the tape that had bound them the night before. Lindsay Harris was stirring awake in her sleeping bag. Bird didn't move a muscle.

Cork threw his blankets aside. "Mind cutting me free?" He held out his bound wrists.

The tall man cut the tape around his wrists and ankles. Cork slowly stood up, trying not to groan too audibly.

"Not a place for sissies," the tall man said.

Cork walked to the fire and looked longingly at the pot where the coffee was boiling. "I've done the Boundary Waters all my life. If I'd been on a trip like this before, I would never have made another."

"My father lived without electricity or running water the

whole of his life," the tall man said. "The nearest settlement was a two-day paddle. Like ironwood, his muscles and spirit. There's a lot to be said for hardship."

Mrs. Gray joined them, and cast a scowl toward Bird. "You should wake him up. We need to be gone."

"There's ice on the lake," the tall man said. "We'll wait for the sun to rise higher, warm the water some, maybe weaken that ice."

"More delay," the woman said. "We should have been out of here a long time ago."

"Doesn't do us any good, speaking of what should have been," the tall man said. "We need to be talking possibilities."

"It's possible we're screwed," the woman said.

She spun away and went to the lakeshore, probably to judge for herself the truth of what the tall man had said.

Lindsay Harris crawled from her sleeping bag, and the tall man cut her bonds. She reached back inside her bag for her coat and boots, which she quickly put on. She hurried to the fire and stood with the men, her breath crystallizing in white puffs.

"Jesus, it's cold," she said.

"It will get colder," the tall man said.

Lindsay looked up where the clouds continued to thin and break and give the sky over to great channels of blue. "Not today."

The tall man nodded. "But tonight and every night after."

"Then we need to get out of here," Lindsay said, in a very practical voice.

"We'll see how the lake responds to the sun. If the ice coating is thin enough, we'll be able to move through without damaging the canoes."

Bird made a sound, a long, painful release of air. He opened his eyes and said toward the sky, "I need to pee."

The tall man walked to him and knelt. "Can you stand?"

"I can try."

He gave Bird a hand, but it was a struggle and Cork stepped in to help. Between them, they got the kid to his feet. They walked him a short way into the woods and held him while he unzipped.

"If it wasn't for this leg, we'd be at White Woman Lake now," Bird said as he relieved himself. His pee steamed as it hit frozen ground. "It's all my fault."

"No one's fault," the tall man said. "Things just happen. You get knocked down. The real question is can you stand back up."

Bird looked at the hands of the men who held him upright and said bitterly, "Not without help, looks like."

"You've given it everything you can," Cork said. "Let it go. We'll make it out of these woods, one way or another."

"It'll be too late," Bird said. "All of this for nothing."

"There's purpose in everything," the tall man said. "Though we don't always see it."

Which struck Cork as something he might have heard coming from the lips of Henry Meloux.

"Done," Bird said and zipped up.

They helped him back to the fire, where he sat warming himself and staring into the flames. The sour woman had begun preparing a breakfast of oatmeal and nuts.

"One more good meal," she said to no one in particular. "Then we're out of food."

The tall man pulled cups from his pack and poured coffee for Bird, and then some for Mrs. Gray. He filled a cup for Lindsay. There was a single cup left.

"I don't mind sharing," he said, offering it to Cork.

The sun broke through the limbs of the pines, and they sat around the fire in dappled, gold light and ate.

"I hate aluminum canoes," the tall man said. "But I wish I had them now. They'd cut across that lake without a problem."

"Why the birch bark?" Cork asked. "They're beautiful, but a lot of trouble, seems to me. Especially considering the circumstances."

"See?" Mrs. Gray said to the tall man. She looked to Cork with satisfaction. "I told him the same thing. Bring the damn Grummans."

"They're brothers to me. Brothers with wings," the tall man said. "They fly on water. And they've worked well enough before."

"Before?" Lindsay looked up from her oatmeal. "You mean with my grandfather?"

"He was easy," the woman said. "Not like you. Not like this." She glared at Bird. "And he wasn't with us."

The kid's head dropped and he stared at the ground.

"That's enough talk," the tall man said.

Cork had finished his meal. He stood and walked to the edge of the lake. The sun was high above the eastern shoreline, which lay dark along the horizon. Close in, the ice was a thin, white plating, but farther out, where the lake was deep, it was like lacquer over wood and the dark water showed clearly beneath. Cork thought that if they could get beyond the ice along the lakeshore, the canoes could probably move without a lot of worry about damage.

He heard the commotion behind him and turned to find Bird standing with the rifle gripped in his hands. The barrel was pointed at the tall man on the other side of the fire. The sour woman and Lindsay sat wide-eyed, looking on.

"Put the rifle down," the tall man said.

"No. You stay where you are, Uncle Aaron. I don't want to hurt you. You'll all be better off without me. You can get out faster. You can still save the Manitou."

"What? You're going to kill yourself?" the sour woman said. It was clear she was fully on board with the idea.

"It's the only way," Bird said.

The tall man began to walk around the campfire. His eyes never left his nephew's face. "You're not going to shoot me or yourself or anyone. That's not our way."

"Stay back."

"Shoot yourself, for God's sake," Mrs. Gray said. "Get it over with."

Bird snugged the rifle against his shoulder. The crack of the round he pulled off brought the tall man to a halt.

"I mean it, Uncle Aaron. This is the only way."

Bird's attention was fully on the tall man, and he didn't see Lindsay Harris stand silently and ease herself toward him.

Mrs. Gray said, "Sit down, you little bitch."

The kid swung his eyes toward Lindsay and shifted the rifle barrel her way. "Stay back!" His voice was desperate, and Cork wasn't at all certain that in his feverish state, the kid might not kill the woman they'd come all this way to secure.

"Bird," the tall man snapped.

The kid's eyes bounced between the tall man and Lindsay Harris. His breathing was rapid. He teetered on his feet. Panic was all over his face now, and Cork understood that he was probably capable of anything.

Then he heard it, a low, distant thrum. He said to the kid, "Wait, Bird. Listen."

They all stood stone-still, and in a few moments, they heard it, too.

The tall man spoke quietly to Bird.

"A plane," he said.

CHAPTER 42

Rose didn't go with the rest of the O'Connor clan to see the floatplane off that morning at first light. She stayed behind to take care of Waaboo and to have breakfast ready when they returned. This was such a familiar feeling for her, moving about the kitchen, seeing to the needs of others. It was what she'd done before she met Mal. She loved her husband and loved her life with him, but she missed this being part of an energy that was fluid, changing, always in motion. That's what children brought to a life. She and Mal wanted a family of their own, but they were still childless. She recalled Stephen's epiphany in the desert. Everybody hurts. That was her pain, wanting children so very much and being denied. She was almost fifty years old, on the threshold of that age when her body would naturally end any hope. So these days she didn't pray for pregnancy. She prayed instead for acceptance if it wasn't to be.

Waaboo had finished his pancakes and was on his knees on the kitchen floor rolling a Tonka truck across the linoleum, making engine sounds. Trixie stood back, alert, because Waaboo often sent his wheeled toys suddenly careening in the dog's direction. Through the kitchen windows, Rose saw Jenny's Forester pull into the drive.

"Your mommy's home," Rose said.

Waaboo abandoned his truck and leaped to his feet.

Stephen came through the door first, with Jenny right behind him. Waaboo wove around his uncle and hit his mother, when she entered, at a dead run. She was used to this wholehearted form of welcome and had braced herself. Waaboo threw his arms around her waist and said, *"Nimaama,"* which was Ojibwe for mother. Jenny wanted her son to speak the language of his Anishinaabe heritage, and she was learning it with him.

"Ingozis," she said in exuberant reply. My son.

She and Stephen shed their coats, leaving the cold of the morning on the wall pegs.

"Coffee?" Rose offered.

"I'd kill for some, Aunt Rose," Stephen said.

"Let me get an arm free, then count me in." Jenny disentangled herself from Waaboo's embrace, knelt, and looked seriously into his face. "Time to get ready for preschool."

"I want to stay home today," he said, with a little pout.

"You know who's going to be there? Bennie Degerstrom."

"Bennie!" Waaboo said, brightening in an instant.

Jenny said, "Keep the coffee hot," and went with her son to help him get ready.

"What's that delicious aroma?" Stephen drifted to the stove and peeked into the oven. "Egg bake! I love you, Aunt Rose."

"A love so easily bought isn't worth much," Rose said.

Stephen filled coffee mugs and carried them to the table. He sat down with his aunt.

"The floatplane got off okay?" Rose asked.

"Took off at sunrise. Four CIRT members."

"CIRT?"

"Critical incident response team. You know, like SWAT."

That was an acronym Rose understood. "The sheriff was with them?"

"She stayed here in Aurora to pick up Ben Trudeau when the time comes." Stephen sipped from his mug. "Should be a good day for an air search. Bud Bowers said visibility is excellent. Marsha promised to let us know as soon as they've located Dad and Lindsay Harris and have them safely on their way home."

Henry, Leah, Rainy, and Daniel had all stayed the night on

Crow Point with Trevor Harris, who adamantly refused to leave what he thought of as sanctuary. Jenny had called Daniel on her cell before they left for the marina and had promised to keep them updated as word came in from Dross.

Rose heard the television come on in the living room, and a few moments later, Jenny joined them.

"I promised him a little SpongeBob before I take him to school." She sat down in front of the mug Stephen had set for her on the table and took a sip. "Ah, nectar."

"I feel bad," Rose said. "We should be focused on you and Daniel and your wedding."

"Like we could do that with Dad lost out there," Jenny said.

"Still, this should be your time," Rose said and reached out and gently touched Jenny's cheek. "A special time."

"If something wasn't threatening us, we wouldn't be O'Connors," Jenny said.

The telephone on the kitchen counter rang. Jenny left the table to answer it. Rose watched the light dim in her niece's eyes as she listened.

"Thanks, Kathy," Jenny said. She put the receiver back in its cradle.

"What is it?" Rose asked.

Jenny stood near the sink, her hand to her lips as if to keep herself from saying something terrible.

"What is it, Sis?" Stephen said.

"That was Kathy Engesser, from the sheriff's office. About Dad." Jenny looked at them, and when she spoke again her words came in a lifeless whisper. "There's a problem."

CHAPTER 43

The plane came at them directly out of the sun, dropping toward the lake, while Cork and the others stood watching. Yellow sunlight painted the undersides of the wings and the belly and the two pontoons. It was a de Havilland Beaver, Cork could see, the kind the Forest Service employed in many ways, including the search for those lost in the Boundary Waters.

He turned, expecting to see the tall man and the sour woman making for the cover of the pines, but they stood still, their faces upturned as the plane neared. Lindsay Harris took a step forward, as if moving to greet it. Bird lowered the rifle and stared with his mouth agape. Cork spun back and watched the floatplane speeding in, less than a hundred feet above the water. It shot directly for the island, and he was afraid that the pilot wouldn't be able to pull the nose up in time, and the craft would plow right into the trees. But at the last moment, the Beaver lifted and flew above them, clearing the lofty pines and banking in a long curl that brought it around again into the sun. It slowed and dropped, and the pontoons touched the lake, sending up a white spray. It taxied across the water toward the island. By then, Cork knew why the others hadn't run for cover. The plane wasn't from the Forest Service.

Behind him, he heard the woman shout, "Cheval!"

The engine cut out, and the plane eased toward the rocky shoreline. A man exited, a man whose French name fit him admirably, a great draft horse of a man. He was Native, with long black hair, a broad, smiling face, and a nose that look flattened less by nature than by brawling. He stood on the pontoon with a rope in hand. Mrs. Gray ran to the edge of the water, and the man tossed the rope. She grabbed the line and pulled until the pontoons touched the rocks, then the man jumped ashore.

"A little late, but here I am," he said with a big grin. He opened his arms as if he expected the woman to hug him. If that was the case, he was disappointed.

"You son of a bitch," she said. "Because of you we almost died out here. You and your booze."

"A man has his pleasures, Mrs. Gray. Otherwise, life's not much worth living, eh?"

The tall man came forward and shook the pilot's hand. "Glad you could join us, Andre."

Cheval looked past the tall man. "Where's Mr. Gray?"

"We lost him." The tall man didn't elaborate.

A passenger climbed from the plane onto a pontoon. He was Native, maybe thirty, dressed in clean jeans, a plaid wool mackinaw, and new-looking boots.

"Who's that?" the tall man said.

"Calls himself Indigo," the pilot replied.

"Where'd he come from?"

Cheval shrugged. "Just showed up. Fox said we're gonna work with him."

The man leaped ashore. "*Boozhoo.*" He smiled and held up a hand.

"*Boozhoo,*" the tall man replied, but not with a smile. "Understand you're going to work with us."

"That's right. Fox sent me."

"Why?"

"You'll have to ask him that." He nodded toward Cork. "I see you didn't kill him."

"Should have," Mrs. Gray said.

"He's more valuable to us this way," Indigo said. He turned his almond eyes to Lindsay Harris. "So you're the one all the fuss is about."

"How's my grandfather?" she asked.

"Alive when we left this morning. Whether he stays that way is going to be up to you."

"What do you want from me?"

"You'll find out soon enough." Indigo looked at the tall man. "We need to go."

"As soon as I've hidden the canoes."

"Leave them. Leave everything."

"I don't want anyone finding my canoes. I'll come back for them later."

"The law sent a plane out this morning to look for these two," Indigo said. "If we don't get out of here now, we could be spotted."

"I'm not leaving my canoes for someone else to find."

"All right. Stay with them. The rest of us are flying out now."

Bird said, "We're not going out until my uncle says so." He leveled the rifle barrel on Indigo's chest.

Indigo held up his hands in placation. "Easy, kid. We're on the same side here. We're all in this together. If you want to save your precious river, we should go now."

"We do what my uncle says we do."

"We hide the canoes," the tall man said.

"I'll give you a hand," Cork offered.

While Cork and the tall man carried the canoes well into the pines and covered them with brush, the others loaded the gear into the plane. The pilot and Lindsay Harris helped Bird aboard. The tall man extinguished the fire and covered the ash and char with dirt. He stood back and studied their night's camp.

"From the air, it'll be impossible to tell that anyone was ever here," he said, satisfied. "Now we fly."

Indigo held a roll of silver duct tape. "Your hands," he said to Cork.

Cork looked at the tall man, who said nothing. He held out his hands, wrists together, and Indigo bound him.

"Now you," Indigo said to Lindsay Harris, and he bound her, too.

The tall man helped them both into the plane and secured their seat belts before climbing into the row behind them, along with Mrs. Gray. Bird lay in back, on bedding made from the sleeping bags and blankets. Indigo untied the tether line and climbed in beside Cheval.

When they were airborne, they climbed rapidly. Cork watched the lake below disappear and the vast expanse of the great wilderness open up below him. They continued to ascend until the lakes became like sapphires spilled on green velvet. They headed northeast into a sky that was clear before them.

"Will we be too late?" Bird asked weakly from the back.

"Not too late yet," the pilot said.

"But in the end, it's going to depend on Harris. Grandfather and granddaughter," Indigo said over his shoulder. Then added, "And maybe a little bit on O'Connor."

Mrs. Gray smiled at him. "You don't mind giving up a little *chimook* blood, do you?"

"Use that word one more time, and I'll throw you out of this plane," the tall man said.

They lapsed into silence then. Cork glanced at Lindsay, whose face was turned away, watching the wilderness glide below. He wondered what she was thinking and if she was afraid. From the beginning, and through all the hardships and the outbursts of violence, fear hadn't been something he'd seen in her. What he'd observed was determination, patience, strength. There was much to admire in the young woman, and he resolved that whatever the outcome for him, he would do his best to see that she survived this ordeal.

They flew for over an hour. Then the tall man said to the pilot, "Gordonville first."

"Gordonville?" Indigo said. "No. We go directly to the lodge."

"My nephew's sick. He needs a doctor."

"We drop the girl and O'Connor at the lodge, then you can find a doctor."

The tall man said to the pilot, "What'll it be, Andre? Do you take orders from this Indigo now? Or are we still clan?"

The pilot laughed and glanced at the man sitting next to him. "If Aaron says we fly to Gordonville, we fly to Gordonville."

"I don't think so." Indigo reached under his coat and drew out a handgun. Cork could see that it was a Glock.

The pilot looked at the gun and laughed again. "What? You'll shoot me? And we all crash? What a good plan that is."

The tall man said, "A stop at the clinic in Gordonville will delay us only a little. You told my nephew we're on the same side. I don't know you, Indigo, but if that's true, you'll put the gun away."

Indigo returned the Glock to the shoulder holster from where he'd pulled it. "We fail," he said, "it's not on my shoulders."

"We fail," the tall man said, "or we succeed, it's only because Kitchimanidoo wills it to be so."

Cork watched Indigo give his head a little shake as if what he'd just heard was nothing but ignorant claptrap.

They banked to the east, and in a few minutes, Cork saw a small lake materialize. It lay at the mouth of a deep canyon carved by the tumble of a white-water river. The Manitou, Cork was pretty sure. A little town lay on the shore of the lake. There was a sand beach at the edge of the town. Cheval brought the Beaver down onto the water and taxied toward the beach. The tall man got out and stood on the pontoon. As they neared the beach, the tall man leaped onto the sand and used the tether line to draw the plane gently to shore. A sign had been posted on the beach indicating there was no lifeguard on duty, swim at your own risk. The tall man tied the line to the signpost.

"Everybody out, so we can unload Bird," Cheval said.

Indigo had pulled his Glock from the holster. As Cork and Lindsay disembarked, he cautioned, "You try anything stupid, you're dead. Both of you."

The tall man and Cheval helped Bird out. The kid could barely walk, and he hung between the two men.

"We'll take him to the clinic," the tall man told Indigo and Mrs. Gray. "Then we'll be back."

Before they left, Lindsay put her hand on the kid's arm. "Remember what I told you, Bird?"

He nodded weakly. "Spirit is at the heart of everything."

"You're going to be fine." And then she did something surprising. She kissed his cheek.

The tall man and Cheval shuffled down the beach, burdened by the weight of the hobbling Bird.

"Back in the plane," Indigo ordered.

Cork and Lindsay Harris turned to obey. But Mrs. Gray, sour to the end, stayed on the beach, looking where the tall man, Cheval, and Bird had gone.

"Fools," she muttered. "Stupid, stupid fools."

Chapter 44

They met Sheriff Dross in her office, crowding into the small room. Rose sat, but the others stood in varied and uneasy poses as Dross explained the situation.

"Bud Bowers flew over every lake that Henry mentioned was on the old warpath. Flew over them several times at different altitudes. He didn't see a thing. No sign at all of Cork and Lindsay and whoever they're with."

"They could have been hiding," Jenny said.

"That's certainly a possibility," Dross said. "So what Bowers did was to move away from each lake for a while, then come back in the hope of catching them out on open water." She shook her head. "I think that if they were ever there, they've gone now."

"If Henry says they were there, they were there," Stephen said.

"Then someone pulled them out," Dross said.

"Pulled them out?" Jenny said. "How?"

"The same way we planned to. A floatplane."

Rose said, "Where have they been taken?"

"My guess would be deeper into Canada," Dross said. "That's the direction they've been headed all along."

"And that's what Henry said about the warpath," Stephen pointed out. "That it led to Canada."

Jenny's brow furrowed. "Why Canada?"

Dross put her hands on her desk and pushed herself up. "I think it's time I had a little talk with Trudeau."

* * *

The day had started with a break in the cloud cover. The sun had appeared, and the dead grass of the meadow on Crow Point had seemed to come alive again with a golden brilliance. Rainy's spirits had revived, too, as she waited for word that Cork and Lindsay Harris were safe.

She'd prepared breakfast for Henry and for their guests, then Daniel had received a call from Jenny, telling him that the CIRT team hadn't been successful in their mission. Cork and Lindsay Harris were still missing. After that, she went for a walk alone and took a towel with her.

She crossed the meadow and followed the lakeshore to the place where Wine Creek emptied into Iron Lake. The bottom was sandy, and a tiny half-moon of a beach curled to one side. The spill of the creek kept the water there ice-free well into the winter. She dropped her towel on the sand, disrobed, waded into the frigid lake naked, and submerged herself. It was like being in the angry grip of an ice giant. She fought her body with her mind, worked to calm her rebellious, cramping muscles, focused on moving beyond all the alarming messages of the flesh. She endured this self-imposed torture for several minutes, and it was only when she knew that she would not break and run that she rose up and slowly exited the lake. She dried herself carefully, dressed, and stood at the edge of the water, letting her mind and body enjoy the sense of being fully alive and, for a little while, empty of concern. It was a discipline she'd learned from Henry.

She didn't think of herself as a weak woman, but she knew that love had opened the door to a fear outside herself. Love let in harpies of worry that beat their wings against logic and courage and could drive a person mad. Although he seemed never to show it, even Henry admitted to being harassed occasionally by these demons. But somehow he found a way to keep them at a harmless distance. She wondered if she would ever achieve that wonderful old man's strength of spirit or his wisdom.

Everything in her life, in the life she'd created for herself on Crow Point, seemed to be on the verge of collapsing. Everything she'd come to love seemed about to be taken from her. She didn't believe that the Great Mystery was a spirit of punishment, but even in the calm of that moment, she heard an old, vindictive voice in her head that told her this was retribution for all she'd run from, all those ancient sins. But the calm of the discipline stayed with her, and as Henry had advised, she let that withering voice speak without giving it power.

She felt she was no longer alone and turned to see Daniel coming from the direction of the cabins. His face wore that determined look it took on whenever he was focused on some essential mission. He was a young man for whom duty was important: his work as a tribal game warden on the Iron Lake Reservation, his relationship with Jenny and Waaboo, his responsibilities to his larger family and to his people. He was not unlike Cork in this respect, and Rainy thought about the old saw that women marry their fathers. But Daniel was his own man, very different from Cork in many ways: a published poet, a reader of literature, a partner who could appreciate Jenny's deep desire to write and would support her in that journey. As she stood watching her nephew approach, she retained a good measure of the calm that the discipline of the icy plunge had given her, and she realized that even in her worry, the worries of them all, as a family they remained greatly blessed because whatever the outcome, they would still have each other.

"I'm sorry to break in on you like this, Aunt Rainy, but I got another call from Jenny. Marsha Dross is rounding up Ben Trudeau for questioning and she wants Trevor Harris there. I thought you might want to come along."

"Thanks, Daniel. I'd like that."

Daniel watched her pick up her towel, then he eyed the crystal water. "You really went swimming?"

"Not swimming exactly," she said. "Waking up. Focusing."

"Jesus," he said in a voice tinged with awe. "Wouldn't a cup of coffee do as well?"

"Let's go," Rainy said. "Maybe we'll finally get some answers."

But at Henry's cabin, it was clear that Trevor Harris had other ideas. He sat on the bunk with his arms crossed and his face pinched.

"Uh-uh." He shook his head like a recalcitrant child. "I'm not leaving. I show up in public and I'm a dead man."

"You've been watching too many gangster movies," Daniel said.

"They don't know I'm here. As soon as they see me with you, they'll know, and then there's no place to hide. I'm not going."

"Oh, you'll go," Daniel said. "One way or another."

Henry said, "I will go, too."

Rainy saw the young man's face change just a bit, grow a little less fearful, less set in its look of refusal. She wondered if her great-uncle's decision was because he thought his presence might bolster Trevor's flagging courage.

Henry made it clear that wasn't the case. "I would like to talk to this Trudeau myself," he said.

Leah said, "I should go, too. Back to my hotel for a change of clothes, at least."

Daniel held out his hands toward Trevor Harris, as if to show they hid nothing. "There you have it. Everyone's leaving. You want to stay here by yourself? You've already made it clear these people are everywhere. Who's to say they won't show up at this cabin while you're all alone?"

The young man's eyes flew to the windows, then around the small room, and finally settled on the door. "You don't have any locks?"

"Here, everyone is welcome," Henry said.

"My gun?" Trevor's voice was taut with mounting panic. "Where's my gun?"

"In a safe place," Henry assured him. "But a gun is no protection from what stalks you."

The young man looked at him without comprehension, then looked to Rainy as if for an explanation.

"What threatens you is your own fear," she told him.

"Christ, you'd be afraid, too, in my shoes."

"I am afraid," Rainy said. "We're all afraid."

Trevor shook his head and nodded toward Henry. "Not him. I want to stay with him."

"Then come," the old man said gently.

CHAPTER 45

Ben Trudeau sat at the table in the interview room of the Tamarack County Sheriff's Office. Rainy could see him from her side of the one-way glass. Cork's children were there with her. Henry, too. Trevor Harris had been asked to wait in the sheriff's office until Marsha Dross finished her questioning of Trudeau. It was clear that Deputy Pender, who was videotaping the interview, thought the observation room was way too crowded, but it wasn't his call. The sheriff entered the interview room, bringing with her a couple of disposable cups filled with coffee. She set one of the cups in front of Trudeau and then sat at the table herself. Trudeau had a pleasant smile on his face, as if he and the sheriff were just going to have a friendly chat. Which, in fact, had often been the case. Trudeau had become well liked, well respected in his short time in Tamarack County, and genial meetings over coffee were part of how he'd connected so quickly and so easily.

"Thanks for coming in this morning, Ben."

"Always at your service, Marsha." He glanced around the room. "Though this is a little different."

"I'll get right down to it. We've received some rather disturbing reports about the casino operation, Ben."

"Really? What kinds of reports?"

"Specifically, cheating at your blackjack tables."

"We watch that very carefully, Marsha. I can assure you that no one slips anything by our security people."

"Apparently, Trevor Harris has," she said.

He nodded thoughtfully, and his face took on a serious look. "We're watching Harris closely. He's a big winner right now, but gambling is all about odds, and sometimes odds can swing in a startling direction for a while. They always swing back eventually. I can assure you that Harris won't enjoy this winning streak of his much longer."

"We've had a report that you've interfered personally with the surveillance of Harris's activities at the casino."

"Really?" He looked genuinely surprised, then gave a little shrug. "In an operation as large as the Chippewa Grand, you're always going to have a disgruntled employee or two who will do their best to sully the operation and throw some dirt, especially at those of us in charge. You've been sheriff here a lot of years. You've never had to deal with an underling who had a chip on his shoulder?"

"Trevor Harris has confirmed that his winning is more than just luck."

The genial demeanor dropped away, and Trudeau said, "He's accused someone at the Grand of colluding with him to cheat the casino?"

"Yes."

"Tell me who it is, and I'll see to it that she's dealt with. I'll see to it personally."

"She?"

He faltered, then regained his composure. "The majority of our dealers are female."

"Does the name Wes Greenfield mean anything to you?"

He thought a moment. "No."

"I had a conversation less than an hour ago with Greenfield. He's with the New York Bureau of Criminal Investigation. Do you know the Lake Pokegama Casino in New York?"

"I know it's one of the casinos the company I work for manages."

"A man named Virgil Stark won over sixty thousand dollars there in the space of a couple of weeks. Does that name ring a bell?"

"I can't say that it does. But big winners aren't unusual in the course of operating a casino. As I said, the odds always swing back. I'm sure if you were to follow up, you'd find that this Virgil Stark has probably lost everything he won and more."

"He won the money by cheating. And he isn't spending any of it at the moment. He's in jail. He's been charged in the murder of Richard Axton."

Trudeau gave a small, quick smile. "If a man is a cheater, maybe it's only a short step to being a murderer, too."

"So cheating is one way to win, yes?"

"I suppose it's possible. But not in the casinos I run, I can assure you."

"Richard Axton was a Canadian citizen accused of human trafficking. He was alleged to have dealt primarily in the trafficking of Native women and children. He'd been investigated by the RCMP and New York's BCI, but nothing had come of those investigations. No charges were filed on either side of the border. Then Mr. Axton was murdered."

"A man like that." Trudeau gave his shoulders a little shrug, and finished, "As ye sow."

"Stark has told investigators that he was paid to kill Axton. It was a hit. His payment came in the form of winnings at the casino, some of it prior to the hit, some of it after. A down payment and then a settling of the bill."

Trudeau's face showed no change.

"The woman who dealt that man his winning hands has given a sworn statement confessing to her part in the payoff."

"Given to whom?" Trudeau said.

"Me. She works at the Chippewa Grand now. A dealer there. In that statement, she confessed to doing the same thing here with Trevor Harris. And she's implicated you."

Trudeau folded his hands in his lap and his face was a blank.

"Trevor Harris was paid to deliver his grandfather and his sister into the hands of kidnappers. Why?"

"If, in fact, that's true, I have no idea."

"Between the evidence that's coming in from the New York investigation and the statements we're collecting here, we have enough to hold you on suspicion of conspiracy to commit kidnapping. Maybe even murder."

"Then I think it's time I asked for a lawyer," Trudeau said calmly. "Don't you?"

That's when Henry stood up and said, "I will talk with this man."

Deputy Pender knocked on the door of the interview room and called the sheriff out. Dross excused herself and came to the observation room, where Henry repeated his request. She thought it over.

"What can it hurt?" Daniel said.

Dross glanced at Trudeau, who sat in his chair in the interview room looking not uncomfortable in the least.

"What the hell," she said with a shrug.

She left with Henry, and a moment later, Rainy saw the door of the interview room open. Henry entered alone. The sheriff joined the others in the observation room.

"*Boozhoo,* Benjamin Trudeau," the old man said.

"*Boozhoo,* Grandfather."

"We have not met, but I know of you."

"And I know of you, Grandfather."

Henry sat at the table. "Will you smoke with me?"

"I will."

The old Mide took a small leather pouch from one of his two shirt pockets and a slightly larger beaded pouch from the other. From the beaded pouch he drew out a carved stone pipe. From the leather pouch, he took a bit of tobacco and filled the pipe. He plucked a tiny box of wooden matches from the front pocket of his pants and lit the tobacco. He smoked and offered the pipe to Trudeau, and they shared it in silence. When the tobacco had become ash, the old man tapped it into his palm, added the ash to the contents of the leather pouch, put the pipe and the tobacco back where he'd pulled them from, and sat with his ancient, spotted hands folded on the table.

"I would like to tell you two stories," Henry said.

"I would like to hear them, Grandfather."

"When I was a young man, much younger than you, I often went with my uncle when he guided men into the great wilderness to the north, Ishpeming. My uncle was a fine hunter and he knew that wilderness well, and loved it as a man loves his home. One autumn, he led two hunters into Ishpeming. I went with him. It soon became clear that it was not the animals of the forest they hunted. These men were looking for gold. When we became aware of this, I asked my uncle how he could do this thing that might end in a great wounding to the spirit of Ishpeming. He told me that if these men found what they were looking for, he would kill them. He was not a violent man. He knew that to do such a thing would deliver a terrible wound to his own spirit. But because of his love for that beautiful place, he was willing to do this thing."

The old man fell silent, and the two of them sat for a long while without speaking.

"That's all?" Dross said.

"Patience," Rainy counseled.

"Did he kill these men, Grandfather?" Trudeau finally asked.

"They did not find gold," the old man said.

"Why do you tell me this story?"

"Because I think you are a man who will understand."

"The other story, Grandfather?" Trudeau asked.

"When I was a child, the woods here were still full of wolves," Henry said. "They are remarkable creatures, not unlike human beings in many ways. We think of them as our brothers."

"I am Odawa, Grandfather. We think the same."

The old man nodded and went on. "I once watched a gray wolf stand between his pack and a charging bull moose. The moose was huge, many times larger than the wolf. His antlers were like great hands with long, sharp fingers. Those antlers lifted the wolf and threw him. The wolf rose and again stood between the angry moose and the others of his pack. The moose charged and lifted him up on those antlers and threw him again. And again the wolf rose and took a stand. While the wolf and the moose went at this time and again, the others of the pack circled and finally attacked the moose from many directions, and together they brought that enormous creature down."

The old man ceased speaking, and both men sat in silence for another long while.

"Henry knows something," Dross said. She looked at Rainy. "What does he know?"

"Wait," Rainy said. "And maybe we'll see."

"That is an interesting story, Grandfather," Trudeau finally said. "The point?"

"When one wolf takes a stand against a great danger, others follow. Only in this way do the smaller creatures prevail. I think you understand this."

"I do, Grandfather."

"Do you know that Corcoran O'Connor is Ma'iingan? Wolf Clan?"

"I do." Trudeau's brow wrinkled, a ruffle of his calm demeanor. He shifted his eyes to the one-way window, where the others stood watching and listening. "And I also know that if you are the wolf willing to take that stand, you accept the sacrifice that may be asked of you."

"To protect your own, that is a noble thing," the old man said. "But not everyone is a wolf."

"There are no innocents, Grandfather. This battle involves more than wolf and moose. The sacrifices that will be asked of us all are great. My fate, or Cork O'Connor's, or even yours, is unimportant. If we continue to lose this battle, we are all doomed."

"What the hell happened in there, Henry?" Dross said. "What was that all about?"

Henry had rejoined them on the other side of the glass. Trudeau still sat at the table in the interview room, calmly finishing his coffee.

"He is not a small, selfish man," Henry said. "He has a strong spirit."

"What's this battle he talked about?" Daniel asked.

"I do not know," Henry said. "But a spider spins its web with a single thread. If we find that thread, we may follow it back to the spider."

"What thread, Henry?" Dross said.

"Ask yourself, what is it that connects these men who forced the woman dealer to cheat?"

"They both managed casinos," Dross said.

"And?"

"They're both Native," Rainy said. "And in a way, I suppose, they've fought for their people."

"What is it that connects that thread to John Harris?" the old man went on.

"Some Native interest?" Stephen said. "Some threat?"

"What does John Harris do?" the old man said.

"He builds dams," Jenny replied, then gave a little gasp. "The Internet search I did on Harris indicated he recently built a dam in Ontario. It's called . . ." She frowned, thinking. "The Manitou Canyon Dam. There was some controversy about it, I recall, pushback from a Native group."

"But it still got built?" Stephen said.

"There was big money involved, I think."

"Why kidnap Harris?" Rainy said. "If the dam's already built, what does it get them?"

Daniel thought a moment, then said, "Inside the dam. In every way."

Jenny said, "For what? Sabotage?"

"Why not?"

"But why kidnap Lindsay and Dad?" she asked.

Dross said, "Maybe because they couldn't get what they needed out of Harris. So they grab his granddaughter for leverage, and Cork gets taken in the bargain."

Deep inside, fear began to chew at whatever hope Rainy had left. If Cork was of no real use to these people, what reason did they have to keep him alive?

Jenny said, "Could I use your computer, Marsha?"

They went to the sheriff's office. Jenny sat at the desk and spent a moment working the computer's mouse and tapping at the keyboard.

"There it is," she said.

On the screen was a photograph of the Manitou Canyon Dam in the midst of construction. Below it was a photograph of a tall man, middle-aged, clearly Native. The caption under the man's photo read, "First Nations Chief Aaron Commanda." The article was about a protest over construction of the dam in the narrows at the head of Manitou Canyon.

"The Ontario Ministry of Natural Resources says the dam is one of many intended to tap the vast energy potential of Canada's waterways," Jenny synopsized out loud as she scanned the article. "But the Odawa claim the dam will only benefit the Caldecott Corporation, a South African company. That's a company that does a lot of mining worldwide. They have plans to begin an extensive open-pit operation a hundred kilometers northwest of the dam site. The Odawa contend the mine operation will pollute the Manitou River and the area around it, which is sacred to them. They petitioned the provincial government and got nowhere. They intended to take their case all the way to parliament if they had to."

"And we know how that turned out," Stephen said. "When big money's involved, the interests of Indians never matter."

Jenny swept the mouse and tapped one of the other articles the browser had brought up. There was another photograph of Aaron Commanda along with a headline that read, FIRST NATIONS CHIEF JAILED IN PROTEST. Jenny scanned it. "He's the traditional leader of the White Woman Lake Odawa, a small, unaffiliated band who occupy an off-reserve settlement called Saint Gervais in the Ontario bush." Jenny paused a moment in thought. "Saint Gervais. I've seen that name before."

"The protest didn't work," Daniel said. "Think about the flooding in Aunt Leah's vision. Does it mean they're going to blow up the dam?"

"I need to get on the phone to the authorities up there," Dross said.

Henry touched Rainy's arm. "We must go north."

CHAPTER 46

They'd sat for over an hour in the floatplane. In the west, the sky had darkened again with a swift-moving overcast.

"More fucking clouds," Indigo said. "November. I hate this month."

Cork understood, but the last thing he was about to do was agree with Indigo on anything. He held his tongue.

"Spirit's at the heart of everything?" Cork said to Lindsay.

"The best gift my grandfather ever gave me, those words, that belief. They saved me from the poison of that snakebite, they really did. And in a lot of ways since. I thought they might help Bird."

Indigo looked at his watch. "What's taking them so long?"

"He was in pretty bad shape," Lindsay said. "A couple of aspirin aren't going to do the trick."

"That kid should've known what he was getting himself into. One soldier doesn't hold up the brigade."

"You military?" Cork asked.

"Shut up" was the answer he got.

He gave it another shot. "You're First Nations. So what's your band?"

Indigo considered before responding. "Musqueam."

"Vancouver," Cork said.

Indigo seemed surprised that Cork knew this.

"Urban Indian," Cork said. "Ever go camping in the North Shore Mountains?"

"I was too busy beating up smart-ass white guys."

"Beautiful, those mountains."

"I did all my camping out in Kandahar," Indigo said.

"Afghanistan," Cork said. "What'd you do in the service?"

"Learned how to kill a guy like you a hundred different ways."

"So, nothing of much use in civilian life."

Indigo smiled. "It's coming in pretty handy these days."

Cork glanced at Lindsay Harris, who was taking in the exchange with a look of concern. She gave her head a faint shake, telling him, he figured, to cool it. He understood her fear and he shared it.

"What are you here for?" Mrs. Gray asked. She gave Indigo the same sour look she'd been giving Cork from the beginning.

"To do a job. Just like you."

"I know what my job is. What's yours?"

"I'm what you might call a facilitator."

"Of what?"

"Anything," he said with a shrug. "Everything."

"We don't need a facilitator. We've done pretty good on our own."

"You're two days late getting out of that wilderness. And one of you didn't come back," Indigo pointed out.

"His doing." She tilted her head so that her chin pointed toward Cork.

Indigo looked at his watch again.

"For an Indian, you're kind of impatient," Cork said.

"And you're kind of talkative. How about you zip it for a while."

"Here comes Cheval," Mrs. Gray said.

"It's about time."

They watched the pilot slowly make his way along the crescent of the beach. He walked with his hands in his back pockets, and Cork thought his lips were puckered, as if he might be whistling. He mounted a pontoon, opened the door, and slipped into his seat behind the controls.

"It's going to be a while," he said.

"We don't have a while," Indigo said. "We need to get going."

"We wait for Aaron. And Bird, if the doc lets him go."

Indigo reached to the shoulder holster beneath his jacket and pulled out the Glock again. "I said we need to get going."

Cheval glanced at the weapon and shrugged. "Like I told you, you shoot me, who's going to fly the plane?" He nodded toward the buildings of the small village. "And the sound of it'll get you a lot of unwanted attention from the folks in Gordonville."

Indigo reached to a pocket inside his coat, drew out a suppressor, and carefully screwed it into the barrel. He turned in his seat and leveled the Glock on Cork's chest.

"Get going or I shoot him."

Cheval gave another shrug, peered through the window, and craned his neck to scan the sky where the clouds were mounting. "I don't know him. He's nothing to me."

"Go ahead," Mrs. Gray said. "Shoot him."

Indigo seemed to consider the woman's advice, but didn't take it.

"Okay, how about this?" the woman suggested. "If you don't fly out now, Cheval, Mr. Indigo here will shoot Aaron when he comes back. Bird, too, if he's with him. We've got the Harris girl. We don't need them anymore."

"You'd kill them for a few extra minutes?" Cheval stared at her as if in shock.

Indigo nodded and smiled. "I like that idea."

Cheval said, "You do that, there's no way I fly this plane."

Indigo pointed the gun at the pilot's forehead. "Then I shoot you, too, and I just move on to the next job. This is all nothing to me. It's not my river you're trying to save."

Cork was pretty sure Indigo wasn't bluffing. Cheval must have decided the same thing. He said, "All right, we leave. But Aaron's liable to kill you when he gets to the lodge."

"If we finish this operation, he'll be forgiving. If not, we'll see who kills who."

Indigo slid from his seat and stepped outside the plane. "Mrs.

Gray, you ride up front with Cheval. I'll ride in back, keep our two guests covered."

When the woman was seated, Indigo untied the line that tethered the Beaver to the sign on the beach and stowed the rope. He shoved the plane away from shore, leaped onto a pontoon, and climbed inside behind Cork and Lindsay Harris. The engine kicked over and the propeller chugged into motion. Cheval turned the plane toward the long flat of the lake, began his run, and lifted off.

They flew for twenty minutes toward the swift gathering of clouds, following the canyon and the river that had created it.

"Enjoy the view," the pilot said. "Weather report is for snow. These clouds." He pointed west, where much of the landscape was already obscured. "Could be heavy, they say."

"The sooner we get this business behind us, the better," Indigo said.

"There it is." Cheval pointed to the right.

Below, out his window, Cork saw a steep curve of concrete at the end of the canyon. The dam there reminded him of a long fingernail that tapered down to the river. Though not particularly broad, the dam rose to an enormous height and completely blocked the entrance to the canyon. Behind it lay a lake, narrow and serpentine, that sent out little legs like a centipede into the surrounding hills. At the base of the dam stood the great block of the power station. Heavy wires had been strung on transmission towers that climbed the canyon wall and marched away among the hills to the northwest along a broad, cleared swath through the forest that resembled an endless, disfiguring scar.

"It's filling up," the pilot said. "Not long before the level will be high enough to start running water through the turbines."

"Just get us to the lodge," Indigo said and once more consulted his watch.

In another ten minutes, they dropped again, this time over a very large lake that was only a stone's throw from the Manitou River. Along the shoreline in the distance, Cork could see a small gathering of houses and other structures, a little village. Cheval brought the Beaver down onto the water and nosed it toward an inlet far from the village. Dark clouds had already eaten the sky above the lake, and the surface of the water reflected the color of charred wood. Against a solid wall of pines at the end of the inlet stood a log construction that Cork thought was probably a hunting or fishing lodge. Flanking it on either side were several small cabins. A long dock ran from the lodge onto the lake. As the floatplane approached, two men came out, walked onto the dock, and stood waiting. One of the men cradled a rifle.

Cheval cut the engine and eased the plane near enough to the dock that the man without a rifle was able to jump onto a pontoon. He took the tether rope, leaped back to the dock, drew the plane in, and secured the rope to a pylon.

Indigo leaned forward, between Cork and Lindsay. "End of the line," he said.

CHAPTER 47

"It's Canada," Dross said. "Another country. I have no jurisdiction there. I can't just up and go, and I can't sanction you going either."

Earlier, the sheriff had pulled up a map of Ontario on the computer in her office, and they'd gathered around her desk and located the dam in a remote area of the province, along the Manitou River. She'd phoned Thunder Bay, an RCMP officer named Lanny Russo, with whom she'd worked on another cross-border case. Rainy and the others had listened as Dross explained the circumstances and her concerns.

"I know it's only speculation, Lanny, but if it's true, it could be catastrophic." Dross had closed her eyes and listened. "No, no real evidence of any kind, only what I've told you." She listened some more. "Yeah, I understand. Thanks." She'd hung up. "He'd like to have more than our speculations to go on, but he said he'll check it out and get back to me. He couldn't promise anything."

That's when Daniel had made his own call, to Bud Bowers. The pilot had agreed immediately to fly them across the border, even if it got him into hot water. Anything, if it might help Cork.

"We're not looking for your approval, Marsha," Daniel said. "If the guy you've contacted sends the cavalry, great. But we all know how slow an official response can be. It could be too late. For Cork and Lindsay and John Harris. And look what's downriver from that dam. Gordonville, a town of several hundred people. If somehow the Manitou Canyon Dam goes, those folks are in real trouble. Remember Aunt Leah's vision? All those fish dying, fish with human faces?"

"What are you going to do? Fly to the dam and wait?"

"Fly to White Woman Lake, to Saint Gervais, and find Aaron Commanda."

Rainy could see how the situation twisted Dross.

"All right," the sheriff finally said. "But I'm going to let Lanny know about this, give the RCMP a head's-up. Have Bowers stay in contact. I'll give him a frequency. If I get word of anything, I'll let you know." She turned a sharp eye on Trevor Harris, who'd joined them after the interview with Trudeau. "But you, you're not going anywhere. I've got a comfortable cell for you until this is over."

Harris made no complaint and, in fact, seemed relieved.

Rose had picked up Waaboo from preschool. He was hungry—always hungry—and she'd made him a grilled cheese sandwich and poured him milk. He sat at the kitchen table, feet dangling, feeding Trixie a little bit of his sandwich now and again, when he thought Rose wasn't looking.

"Bennie said Baa-baa is a rock, Aunt Rose."

"A rock? Bennie said that?"

"He said his dad did. I told him that was stupid."

Rose had just finished buttering and seasoning a chicken she intended to bake for dinner that night. She washed her hands clean, went to the little guy. "A rock? You're sure that's what he said?"

Waaboo's eyes went to the ceiling, as if he were looking for an answer there. "Baa-baa is stone-cold. That's what he said."

She smiled and kissed the top of his head. "Your grandfather isn't a stone, little rabbit. I think he's mostly heart."

Waaboo's face scrunched up. "Like a valentine with arms and legs?"

"Like a valentine full of love," she said.

Waaboo seemed satisfied and slipped Trixie another morsel.

The kitchen door swung open, and a flurry of bodies entered, the O'Connor children, plus Henry, Rainy, and Daniel. They brought in the cold from outside, and Rose could feel a furious purpose coming off them as well.

"Canada, Aunt Rose," Stephen said without preamble. "We're on our way to Canada."

She didn't ask why, just said, "Do you want something to eat before you go?"

"Sandwiches," Stephen said. "We'll take them with us."

Jenny went to her son and gave him a hug.

Waaboo said, "Baa-baa isn't a cold rock."

The others stopped whatever they were doing.

Jenny said, "What do you mean?"

"Baa-baa is just a big heart. Isn't he, Aunt Rose?"

Jenny knelt and smiled. "You're absolutely right, little guy."

Henry sat at the table, and as Rose worked on whipping up tuna salad for the sandwiches, she listened to the old man talk to the child.

"Some people are a big heart," the old Mide said. "Do you know what else a person may be?"

Waaboo chewed his grilled cheese sandwich and thought about that. "A big mouth. That's what Mick calls Miss LaRue at school."

The old Mide laughed. "A person is also a spirit, little rabbit."

"Like a ghost? I was a ghost for Halloween."

"Did people see you?"

"I was in a sheet. So, yeah."

Jenny said, "I didn't have a lot of time to be creative this year."

"A spirit is something you cannot see," Henry said to Waaboo.

"Then how do you know it's there?"

"It shows itself in how a person acts toward others."

"David Brady hits everybody on the playground. Is he a mean spirit?"

"Maybe just a confused spirit," the old man offered. "What kind of spirit are you?"

Waaboo laughed, as if it was a goofy question. "A rabbit. I like to hop and play."

"A rabbit is a good spirit to be," the old man agreed.

Waaboo looked at his mother. "Are you going to Canada?"

"I'm staying here with you and Aunt Rose."

Stephen had left the kitchen, but he returned now with a small backpack.

"Are you going to Canada, Uncle Stephen?" Waaboo asked.

"Yes, I am." Stephen put the pack on the table and looked inside, checking the contents.

"What for?"

"We're bringing your grandpa back."

"Can I go?"

"Not this time, rabbit."

Waaboo studied his uncle. "You're a wolf."

Stephen smiled at him and waited.

"A good wolf." Waaboo looked at Henry. "You're an owl." He looked at his mother. "A mama bear." To Daniel: "A lion." To Rainy: "A flower garden." And finally to Rose: "A big warm ocean."

"Why Canada?" Rose asked as she filled the pack with the sandwiches she'd made.

"We're pretty sure that's where Dad and Lindsay Harris have been taken," Stephen said. "We're flying up. Jenny can explain it."

"You're going, too, Henry?" Rose asked. She didn't say it, but she thought that for a man of his age, something like this seemed awfully unwise.

"I did not give them a choice," the old Mide said. "I have come too far on this hunt to be left behind."

Jenny pulled Daniel aside. She whispered something to him, something loving and reassuring, Rose figured, then kissed him and let him go.

They threw on their coats, and as they headed to the door, Jenny took the old Mide by the arm and said quietly, "Don't let harm come to you, Henry. Or to them."

"A clear head is the best companion of a strong heart. I will remember this and help them remember, too."

When they'd gone, Jenny and Rose stood together in the cold draft that had come in through the opened door.

Rose whispered, "God go with them."

Behind them, Waaboo said, *"Majimanidoog."*

The women turned.

"Majimanidoog?" Rose asked.

"An Ojibwe word," Jenny explained. "It means 'evil spirits.' Devils." She went to her son and sat beside him. "Why did you say that?"

"Some people are devils," Waaboo said. "Maybe devils took Baa-baa."

He ate one last bite of his grilled cheese sandwich and fed the rest to Trixie.

CHAPTER 48

The lodge was a simple construction but sturdy and beautiful. It was built of honey-colored pine, and Cork was certain it was quite old. Inside, the main room was sparely set with furnishings constructed of the same honey-colored pine as the lodge itself: a divan, a couple of easy chairs, two small dining tables. A field-stone fireplace dominated one of the walls. Two of the walls were hung with mounted trophies, big fish and wild game. On another wall hung a large map of a lake, the lake they'd landed on, Cork figured. According to the map, it was called White Woman Lake. The map was flanked by framed photos of fishermen holding their prize catches. Aaron was in many of these, sometimes in the background, sometimes standing shoulder to shoulder with the grinning fishermen. There was not the dank, musty smell that sometimes hung in the air of old lodges in the Northwoods. The place smelled clean and felt well cared for.

On their arrival, Indigo had given over authority to one of the two men who'd met them. Now this man—slender, pock-faced, intelligent-eyed, mid-thirties, Native—invited Cork and Lindsay to be seated on the divan. The other guy who'd been waiting on the dock, a good-looking young man cradling a rifle, stood nearby, managing to appear both passive and threatening at the same time.

"Where's our host?" the man in charge asked.

"Left him," Cheval said. "In Gordonville. Along with Bird. The kid's hurt pretty bad."

"No names," the man said sharply. "And what about Mr. Gray?"

"He killed him." Mrs. Gray nodded at Cork. "We had to leave him in the Boundary Waters."

"You got rid of any identification, yes?"

"Of course," she said.

"Good. Then we're still clean. I'm sorry about your—about Mr. Gray."

Cheval went into the kitchen, and Cork heard the opening of a refrigerator door, then the closing. A moment later, the pilot returned, carrying a plate and gnawing on a leg of fried chicken. He sat at the table and ate and watched.

"Where's my grandfather?" Lindsay asked.

"You'll see him shortly," the man in charge said. "First, I want to give you the lay of the land."

He wore a down vest, fine quality, maybe REI or L.L.Bean, Cork thought. His boots were Gore-Tex. His onyx hair was pulled back in a long ponytail and held with a beaded tie. He wore gold wire-rimmed glasses, and Cork got a feel from him that was far more scholar than woodsman. A fire was burning in the fireplace. The man walked to it and turned back, so that he was framed in flames. An overly melodramatic move, Cork thought.

"Call me Mr. Fox," the man said. "If we're to save the Manitou River, we don't have much time. Every minute, the water creeps higher behind that dam. They'll be able to start running those turbines pretty soon. We need to act, act now. Which is why you're here." This last part was directed at Lindsay Harris.

"I don't understand," she said. "What can I do?"

"Talk to your grandfather. Convince him to give us what we need."

"And what would that be?"

"A way to get rid of the dam. We've asked him politely. And not so politely. But he continues to refuse to help us."

"What do you mean 'not so politely'?"

"Our well-being—yours, mine, his—is of little consequence in this. It's a cliché, I know, but the end justifies the means."

"You haven't hurt him." She looked at the young man with the rifle and said, "Tell me you didn't let them hurt him."

She said this with such vehemence and in such a proprietary way that both Mr. Fox and the young man with the rifle made no immediate reply.

"Nothing's happened to him that he won't recover from. Nothing yet," Fox finally said. "Whether it remains this way is up to you."

"I want to see him," Lindsay insisted. "Now."

Fox nodded to the young man with the rifle, but the gesture was missed because the young man was staring at Lindsay Harris with a deep look of concern.

"Mr. Brown," Fox snapped. "Fetch our guest. Lend him a hand," he said to Cheval.

The pilot looked as if what he really wanted to do was tell him to go to hell, but he put the chicken leg down and followed the young man with the rifle from the room.

Fox looked to Cork and said, "You're mixed blood, I understand, part Anishinaabe."

It wasn't a question and Cork gave no answer.

"Then perhaps you can understand the importance of what we're trying to accomplish here. Do you have any sense of what's going on?"

"You want to destroy the dam John Harris built," Cork said. Then he added with a note of sarcasm, "Indigo, Brown, Gray? The others are just colors, just shades. But you, you're something else. Fox, the wily one, is that it?"

A faint smile came to Fox's lips, then quickly vanished. "That dam is a threat to a beautiful river, and an area sacred to the Odawa on White Woman Lake. It's understandable. The spirit here is profound and powerful." He began to pace before the fire and speak as if lecturing in a college classroom. "From the first moment Europeans set foot on this continent, and every other, for that matter, they've acted as if the new land was theirs. By right of their superior God, their superior culture, their superior everything. They've justified their actions—theft, rape, slavery, murder, genocide—in a hundred ways. Our ancestors fought bravely but, in the end, fell before this white onslaught. We've been forced, like prisoners of war, onto small parcels of earth, slivers of what was once the land we shared with all other free creatures."

He stopped, turned, and faced Cork and Lindsay Harris as if they were seated at desks and taking notes. He spoke in a dramatic and practiced way.

"But we're fighting back now, meting out a justice that white laws refuse to offer, protecting Grandmother Earth from the rape caused by white greed, bringing a sense of power and purpose back to our people."

"What do you call yourselves?" Cork asked.

"We have no name. We have no real body. We have only purpose. And," he said, "we have technology." He pulled a cell phone from his pocket and held it up as if it were an exhibit at a trial. "The white man's technology turned against him."

"You're going to blow up the dam with a cell phone?" Cork said.

"We've stockpiled enough explosive here to take out a city block," Fox said, slipping his cell phone back into his pocket. "What we need is someone who understands that dam intimately to tell us where and how to plant it."

"My grandfather," Lindsay said.

"We could have pulled in another dam engineer, I suppose. But we liked the poetic justice of this," Fox said. "It will be a dam Harris both built and destroyed."

"He hasn't given you what you need," Cork pointed out.

"He will," Fox said. "We have leverage now. One way or the other, we'll get what we want from him."

Cheval and Brown returned holding a tall, grayed figure between them. The man was blindfolded. They walked him to one of the easy chairs and let him fall into it. He was a powerful man physically, but he sat with his head down, his chin resting against his chest. His face was a mottle of bruises, his lips split and with clots of blood stuck to them like black leeches.

"Oh, Jesus," Lindsay said when she saw him. "You bastards."

"He's suffered nothing he won't recover from," Fox assured her. "Yet."

At the sound of his granddaughter's voice, John Harris slowly raised his head. "Lindsay?"

"Grandpa John," she said. "I'm so sorry."

"What are you doing here?"

"Give them what they want," she said. She scooted forward, trying to get nearer to him. "Please just give them what they want."

He shook his head slowly. "Thugs."

"In our view, Mr. Harris, you're the thug. You helped destroy sacred things."

"Wasn't my intent."

"You knew the Odawa here objected to the dam. And you knew why."

He breathed a deep, ragged sigh. "I've already told you. I didn't know these things until after construction of the dam had begun. Then it was too late, out of my hands."

"We've covered this ground before and it gets us nowhere. That's why we've brought your granddaughter here. We need to move forward quickly."

A log on the fire popped with sudden force, and it was like a gunshot in the room. Cork felt them all flinch, including himself.

"What do you think you're going to do?" Harris said. Although his voice was weak, there was profound menace in his tone.

"Whatever we have to," Fox told him. "I'd prefer not to harm your granddaughter, but if that's what it takes, that's what I'll do. Or rather," he said, nodding toward Indigo, who stood off to the side with his hands behind his back in a kind of military stance, "that's what I'll have my friend here, Mr. Indigo, do. You know firsthand how he operates."

"You touch her, and I'll kill you."

"There's no need for any more violence. Just tell us what we want to know."

"If I could give you what you want, you'd have it already," Harris said.

Fox said, "We've brought someone else. Someone from your past. Mr. O'Connor, say hello."

Cork thought he would not. Fox nodded to Indigo, who took the Glock from his shoulder holster, walked to Cork, and hit him with the butt upside his head. Cork's vision went bright with fireworks. In a moment, he could see again, but now he had a headache and a loud ringing in his left ear.

"Mr. O'Connor?" Fox held out a hand, indicating Harris.

Cork said, "Hey, Johnny Do."

Harris turned his head, as if to hear better. "Corky? Corky O'Connor? Is that you?"

"Mr. O'Connor accompanied your granddaughter into the Boundary Waters in an attempt to locate you. We've brought him here for a reason." He nodded once again to Indigo.

Indigo holstered his Glock, pulled Cork roughly to his feet, marched him to the fireplace, and stood him beside Fox.

"Boyhood friends, I understand," Fox said.

He untied John Harris's blindfold. Harris blinked at the light and cleared his vision.

Fox said, "Mr. Indigo, will you demonstrate why Corky is here."

Cork didn't see the blow coming. Indigo's fist plowed into his stomach. Cork doubled over and fell to his knees.

"God, no," Lindsay cried and tried to rise.

"Sit down, Miss Harris," Fox commanded. When she obeyed, he said to Brown, "See to it she stays there."

The young man stood next to her. She glared up at him, and he reacted as if she'd slapped him.

Cork saw all this. Even with his head and gut hurting, his mind went on working, putting pieces together.

"If you continue to give us nothing, we'll kill him. Then we'll do the same to your granddaughter, but only after she's endured even more pain than you have." Fox let that sink in. "We're not cruel people. This is not how we would prefer to operate. But it's what we're willing to do, if we have to."

In Fox, Cork saw a reveling in power, which was the demon that always accompanied ultimate authority. In Indigo, he saw a cold detachment that would allow him to do anything to another human being.

"We will kill them, Mr. Harris," Fox asserted. "First your childhood friend, which is the whole point of his being here. Then your granddaughter."

Harris looked at Cork, who despite all the years that had intervened, could still see the face of the teenager he'd known and had looked up to on Gooseberry Lane. Whoever John Harris had become as a man, that admirable kid was still there somewhere.

"You don't believe me," Fox said. "Mr. Indigo, shoot O'Connor."

Indigo drew out his Glock and put it to the back of Cork's head.

"No," Lindsay cried and tried to rise.

"Restrain her, Brown," Fox snapped.

The young man blocked her way and shoved her down.

"You bastards," she shouted. "You lying bastards."

"Shoot him," the man said again, calmly.

Later, Cork would think of what happened next not as luck but as the deft and benevolent hand of Kitchimanidoo at work.

The door of the lodge burst open, and Aaron strode into the room, a rifle in his hands.

"Put that gun away, Indigo," he ordered. "Or I'll shoot you where you stand."

CHAPTER 49

Aaron's shoulders were dusted with snow, and snowflakes clung to his hair and lay melting on his face. The rifle in his hands was aimed directly at Indigo's chest. Cork looked up at the man who held the Glock to his head. Indigo's eyes were intense, excited. Cork understood that this kind of confrontation fed something in him. He was not a warrior, not like Aaron. Not like Cork. Not *ogichidaa*. Indigo was *majimanidoo*. A devil who thrived on cruelty. Among all the people of the earth, regardless of the color of their skin or their language or their culture, devils like this walked.

"Do as our host has asked, Mr. Indigo," Fox said. "Put your firearm away."

The gunman didn't immediately obey. He faced off with Aaron for a good while before he let a smile play across his lips.

"Sure," he said. "For now."

He slipped the Glock into his shoulder holster. As soon as this was done, Aaron took three long strides across the space that separated them and swung his right fist into Indigo's jaw. The man fell back against the stone of the fireplace. He quickly returned to his feet in a stance prepared for battle. But once again, he faced the barrel of the rifle Aaron held.

"You left me," Aaron said.

Indigo stood tensed, assessing the situation, the rifle, the man who held it. Finally he relaxed. "I had a job to do," he said. "How'd you get here?"

"Borrowed a truck. I have a lot of friends in Gordonville."

"Borrowed a rifle, too, looks like. The kid?"

"He'll be fine."

Fox said, "I've been told about Bird. I'm glad to hear he'll be okay. As I understand it, the same can't be said of Mr. Gray." He sounded detached. Academic. As if the dead man were something he'd just erased from the blackboard.

Aaron glanced down to where Cork still knelt on the old floorboards. "Get up, O'Connor."

Cork got to his feet.

"Over there." Aaron nodded toward the place on the divan next to Lindsay Harris.

Cork went and sat down.

"You were going to kill him?" Aaron asked Fox.

"That was my intention. The object lesson we'd all discussed. And," Fox said, his voice piqued with irritation, "we'd all agreed on. When you went to fetch Miss Harris, you were fully on board with sacrificing O'Connor, if necessary."

"I didn't know him then."

"That makes a difference?"

"All the difference in the world."

Fox nodded, thought over this turn of events, and said, "So, what do you propose now?"

"Let them talk."

"There's been nothing but talk. Too much of it. We need to act."

"Let them talk," Aaron said again. "Alone."

"You think it will make a difference?"

"We won't know until we give it a chance."

Fox's eyes moved over them all, assessing every variable of the equation he was putting together in his head. Finally he said, "Very well. Your way first." He leveled a menacing look at Aaron. "Then mine." He gestured to Indigo. "Take them to Mr. Harris's room."

Cork rose from the divan. Lindsay started up, and Brown reached down to help her. She glared at him, and he drew his hand back as if he'd been burned. John Harris tried to rise, but his battered body failed him. Cheval left the table, slipped his meaty hands under Harris's arms, and helped him stand. Then he guided Harris away, and Cork and Lindsay followed. Indigo brought up the rear.

They walked down a short hallway to an opened door. Cheval helped Harris inside and sat him on the bed. Cork and Lindsay entered, and Cheval cut the tape that bound their hands. Then the pilot backed out and joined Indigo in the hallway.

"Don't try to climb out a window," Indigo warned them. He gave a little grin, as if he hoped that was exactly what they might try to do, and he closed the door.

Lindsay went to the bed and carefully assessed the damage that been done to her grandfather's face. "Oh, Grandpa John. I'm so sorry."

"Not your fault," Harris replied.

That's when Cork said, "On the contrary, Johnny Do, I think it's all her fault."

CHAPTER 50

Rose stood at the living room window of the house on Gooseberry Lane, staring west through the bare branches of the elm in the front yard, watching as ravenous black clouds gobbled up the afternoon sky. At her back, Waaboo played with his big Duplo blocks, building a garage for his toy trucks. His mother sat at the dining room table, at work on her laptop. Trixie lay under the table with her head on her paws, watching Waaboo and his trucks from a safe distance.

Although Rose had done her best to put the fate of those she loved into God's hands, that didn't mean she didn't worry terribly. When her sister had disappeared, how many times had she prayed for Jo's safety only to have Jo taken from her in the end, taken from all those who'd loved her and had prayed for her desperately. Faith was not an easy thing. Even as she told herself that God always had a plan, her heart was troubled and afraid, and she whispered, "Please, dear God, keep them all safe."

A car pulled to the curb, and Leah Duling got out. She stood for a moment as Rose now stood, eyeing the storm clouds eating a good deal of the sky.

"Leah's here," Rose announced.

Leah turned her back to the coming storm and walked to the house. "I couldn't wait alone in my hotel room," she said when Rose opened the door to her. "Is it all right that I came?"

"Of course," Rose replied.

The two women exchanged a hug, and Leah shed her coat, which Rose draped over the newel post of the stairs.

"Hello, little rabbit," she said to Waaboo.

He looked up from his Duplos and his trucks. *"Boozhoo."*

Trixie found the woman's entrance interesting enough to trot from under the table and receive a vigorous patting from the visitor. Jenny said a simple "Hello, Leah," and went back to her work.

"I was just going to make some coffee," Rose said. "Will you have some?"

From a kitchen cupboard, she pulled down dark roast beans to grind.

"I've never had a kitchen of my own," Leah said. "Not really. This is very nice."

"And very old," Rose said. "Cork's grandparents built the house. Cork grew up in it and his children, too. A lot of love and worry soaked into these walls."

"This was your home for quite a while, as I understand it."

"I helped raise the children. Some of the best years of my life were spent here."

"No children of your own?"

"We haven't been blessed. I'm getting to the point where I'm believing we never will."

"Don't forget Sarah and Abraham in the Bible."

"What about you?" Rose asked.

"No children," Leah replied. "Which, in a way, was good. We were always on the move, living under primitive conditions. And Lucius, while he was a good missionary, wouldn't have made a particularly good father. He could be awfully impatient, and sometimes thoughtlessly cruel."

Just the opposite of Henry Meloux, Rose thought.

"I was married to him, but it was never a marriage of passion," Leah went on. "Across all those decades, Henry was never out of my heart. I feel as if I've been preparing my whole life to return to him. Is that crazy?"

"When I first met my husband, Mal, I felt the same way, as if my whole life had been leading up to that moment."

Their conversation was cut short when they both heard Jenny say from the dining room, "Huh?"

Rose poked her head out the kitchen door. "What is it?"

"Something's been troubling me all afternoon." Jenny's eyes were intent on the laptop screen. "White Woman Lake. That name. I knew I'd heard it before. Come here, Aunt Rose, Leah. Take a look at this."

The two women left the kitchen and went to the dining room table. They stood looking over Jenny's shoulder. Rose's niece had pulled up a page from the Internet with the heading NOTES FROM THE NORTH COUNTRY.

Jenny said, "While I was researching Lindsay Harris, I came across this blog she'd been posting ever since she was a student at Northland College. She wrote about her life there, her thoughts on all kinds of subjects, and also about the protests over the pro- posed Penokee taconite mine that got her arrested. It's passionate and not badly written. But take a look at this later entry."

Rose read silently from the blog post, which was dated more than a year earlier. It contained none of the diatribe Jenny had indicated, but was instead a lovely recounting of her meeting with a young man as a result of the protests and her arrest. His name was Isaac McQuabbie. He'd traveled from Canada to lend a hand in whatever way he could with the battle against the proposed Penokee Mine. He'd read about the protests and about her arrest, he'd told her, and had come because of her, because of her courage. She was taken with him. Lindsay had posted a photo of the two of them together.

"He's a hunk," Leah said.

Then Rose found the part that had made Jenny take particu- lar notice. McQuabbie was from a small First Nations settlement called Saint Gervais, which stood on the shore of White Woman Lake.

"White Woman Lake," Rose said.

All three women stared at the screen in silence.

"An incredible coincidence?" Rose offered.

"Right," Jenny said. "He's Native, eco-minded, he admires her courage. And she just happens to be the granddaughter of the man who designed the dam his people had worked so hard to keep from being built."

Rose and Leah sat down, flanking Jenny, and they read almost a year's worth of blog posts, from Lindsay's first meeting with Isaac McQuabbie to her eventual decision to follow him back to McGill, where he was doing graduate work. The posts were a mix of diatribes concerning threats to the environment, meditations on the magnificence of nature, and reveries about her life with Isaac. Very soon after she arrived at McGill, however, the posts ended.

The three women sat back and looked at each other. In the living room, Waaboo made a roaring engine noise and ran his largest truck into the Duplo garage he'd built, exploding the block structure.

"He targeted her," Jenny said.

"But look at how she writes about him," Rose pointed out. "It sounds like genuine love to me."

"On her part anyway."

"You can't fool a woman forever," Leah said. "He must have felt something."

"So much the better for the people behind all this. More incentive for her to . . ." Jenny paused.

"To what?" Rose asked.

"I don't know. We've been blaming Trevor for everything. But maybe they planned it together."

"He told us everything and never said a word about Lindsay being involved."

"So either he's a good liar or a good actor. Or . . ." Jenny drummed her fingers on the tabletop as she thought. "Maybe he's her unwitting pawn."

"I'm not sure I follow," Leah said.

"I'm not sure I do either. I'd like to talk to Trevor."

Jenny got up, went to the phone on the stand beside the staircase, and dialed.

"Hi, Kathy? It's Jenny O'Connor." She closed her eyes and nodded. "I know. Listen, Kathy, is Marsha in? Could I talk to her? Thanks." She looked up at the ceiling. Her foot tapped a mindless rhythm on the linoleum. "Marsha?" She listened. Quite a while. Then said, "Oh, my God." She looked at Rose and shook her head. "Well, look, I might have another piece of the puzzle. But I need to talk to Trevor Harris. Can I do that?" She nodded. "Ten minutes, then."

"What was that 'Oh, my God,' about?" Rose asked when Jenny had hung up.

"Lanny Russo from Thunder Bay got back to her. He's been in touch with investigators from some national security organization in Canada. It sounds like this thing is big. Really big. I've got to go."

"I'd like to be there, too," Rose said.

"Go," Leah told them. "I'll watch Waaboo, if you'll let me. Just keep me informed."

Jenny and Rose waited with Marsha Dross while Deputy Pender fetched Trevor Harris. Jenny filled the sheriff in on what she'd learned from the Internet. Dross pulled up the site herself and scanned Lindsay's blog.

"She's too smart to be taken in easily," Dross said. "If it's what you think, and I've got to tell you, I'm right there with you on this one, then at the very least, she's a coconspirator with her brother. But like I told you on the phone, this is looking like part of a much larger scenario."

She explained what she'd learned from Russo. The NSCI—the RCMP's National Security Criminal Investigations—had been looking into a series of incidents that had occurred across Canada in the past two years. In the Cascade Mountains east of Vancouver, a high bridge on a rail line that serviced a controversial copper and molybdenum mining operation which abutted Native land had collapsed unexpectedly. The subsequent investigation revealed that the bridge support had been weakened by an explosive charge.

The cost of replacing the bridge was estimated to be too high to justify continuing the mine. No one had claimed responsibility, and the RCMP investigation was still open. In that same province, a pump house on a highly controversial oil pipeline that threatened the rare all-white "Spirit Bear" of the Great Bear Rainforest was demolished by an explosive device only weeks before oil was scheduled to begin flowing from Alberta's tar sands to a port facility on the coastline of the Inner Passage. In northern Quebec, a company granted a government permit to log on land within the Ottawa River watershed, over objections from the local Anishinaabeg, was beset by dozens of incidents of equipment sabotage, so much so that the operation had nearly ground to a halt and armed personnel were required for protection. A politician from the Maritimes, a staunch advocate of nonderogation legislation which would strip First Nations of many treaty rights, was killed when his Mercedes missed a turn on a winding seacoast highway and plunged two hundred feet into the surging Atlantic.

"There are other incidents as well, enough to alarm the NSCI."

"What are they thinking?"

"They believe it's all part of some coordinated First Nations quasi-military initiative. An indigenous vigilante group. The NSCI has been trying to pin something or someone down, but so far the group has successfully eluded them. Apparently they communicate through throwaway cell phones and hide their Internet activity with sophisticated technology. Encryption, that kind of thing."

"Given what they're fighting against, I could almost applaud them," Jenny said. "If it weren't for Dad."

Pender stepped in with Lindsay's brother in tow.

"Sit down," the sheriff said.

Harris took a seat.

Dross said, "We need a few more answers, Trevor."

He tried to look confident, but it was clear to Rose that he was worried. Not just for himself, she hoped.

"Whatever you need," he promised.

"Did Lindsay have any part in planning your grandfather's abduction?"

"I already told you how it happened. She had nothing to do with it."

"Who exactly approached you?"

"Like I said, an Indian. In Las Vegas."

"How did he know your situation?"

Harris shrugged. "I assumed, you know, that it's a gambling community. The Indians have casinos, too. They probably all talk."

"Was Lindsay aware of your situation?"

"When I got way behind and my markers were called in, I told her."

"Hoping for some help?"

"I knew she didn't have money. Grandpa John paid for college, but when she headed up to school in Canada, she was on her own. School loans and such. Mostly I was just keeping her in my life."

"That was it? Just maintaining lines of communication?"

"Okay, well, I guess I hoped she might put in a good word for me with Grandpa John."

"She had a better relationship with him?"

"She was more like him. Outdoorsy and all. And, you know, motivated. They didn't have heart-to-heart talks or anything like that, but I knew she had a better shot at getting something out of Grandpa John than I ever would."

"So, she was well aware of your situation, of its desperate nature."

Harris frowned as the light dawned. "You're not suggesting she's somehow involved in this?"

"Who proposed the plan to you?"

"I told you. The Indian in Las Vegas."

"Did he have a name?"

"Black."

"That's all?"

"Mr. Black. That was it."

"And he laid out the whole thing for you? Going into the Boundary Waters, the kidnapping, the whole ball of wax?"

"Uh-huh. All I had to do was get Grandpa John to agree."

"But you and your grandfather were never on the best of terms?"

"You got that right."

"So it was clear that you'd need your sister's help to convince him. Is that something Lindsay would have known?"

"Sure. We've talked about Grandpa John. Like I said, neither of us relate to him particularly well, but he's always seemed fonder of her. She's, you know, a fighter. I just disappoint him."

"Did she ever mention a man named Isaac McQuabbie?"

"Yeah. Big part of the reason she went to school in Canada."

"Did she ever mention where he was from?"

"Canada," he said, as if it were a stupid question.

"Where in Canada?"

"Got me."

"An Odawa settlement called Saint Gervais on White Woman Lake. It's the home of Chief Aaron Commanda."

"So?"

"He led the fight against the dam your grandfather built."

The change came to his face slowly. Rose watched as his head cocked at an angle, and his mind went over things, and pieces fell into place.

"The Boundary Waters. She knows the Boundary Waters well," he said. "I figured it was just, you know, a coincidence. But when I think about it, she was on board with the whole thing really quick. She didn't even question that I wanted to get closer to Grandpa John. And when he had to cancel the first date, she seemed really upset. More than me, and I was the one with everything to lose." He shook his head. "Or so I thought."

The sheriff said, "Canada's RCMP thinks the kidnapping of your grandfather and the apparent kidnapping of your sister are part of a broader conspiracy by First Nations people. We think"—

she indicated Jenny and Rose—"that your sister is involved with them. Your part in this may well have been her manipulation."

"Lindsay?" He seemed ready to laugh at the idea. "She's all Goody Two-shoes. She doesn't have the brains or the balls for something like this. It was all my idea." But his face changed and he suddenly seemed not so sure. "I mean, hell, if what you're saying is true, why didn't she just come out and tell me?"

"Maybe she was trying to protect the people she's working with. Or maybe she was trying to protect herself. If everything went south, the blame would rest on your shoulders alone, even in your own mind."

"No. That's not Lindsay." He thought about it some more. "That little bitch," he finally said. "And to think I've been worried sick about her."

Which was not exactly how Rose would have characterized what she'd seen coming from the young man.

The sheriff said, "Deputy Pender, take our guest back to his cell."

"Come on, Harris," Pender said and escorted the man out.

"What now?" Jenny asked.

"I need to get this information to Lanny Russo," Marsha said. "And we need to let your family know what they might be flying into."

CHAPTER 51

Lindsay Harris stood with her arms crossed over her chest, as if protecting herself from harm. In the room where her grandfather had been held and brutally interrogated, she seemed to have lost all her courage.

Cork said, "I thought you were extraordinarily calm, given our circumstances, something I was more than willing to chalk up to your strength of character. Because I see that kind of strength in you. But things felt off. Sometimes a little, sometimes a lot. That ridiculous cap you wore into the Boundary Waters that made you look like Waldo, for example. What a perfect beacon, even in a thick mist, for someone who might be watching for us. Then there was the night I tried to save you, and you stumbled and cried out. It could have been an accident, but not when your life might depend on it. It was done to alert the others."

Lindsay made no reply. Her grandfather simply gazed at her out of his damaged face.

"When it looked as if we might be stuck out there with a kid who couldn't walk, you came up with the idea of a travois. A good, reasonable suggestion. And one, I suppose, that could have come from a genuine concern over Bird's condition, because I believe you really cared. But I think it was more that you wanted to be moving, to be out of there, because you had your own agenda."

She would not look at her grandfather or Cork. She stared at the floor and listened.

"There's clearly something between you and Mr. Brown out

there. You have some history together. And finally, you accused them of being lying bastards. What did they lie to you about? What did they promise in return for your help?"

She walked to the window and stood facing the glass. Outside, snow was falling. When she finally spoke, she kept her back to Cork and her grandfather.

"You were supposed to give them what they needed, Grandpa John. You were supposed to tell them how to permanently disable the dam. They would have followed your instructions, the Manitou River would have been saved, you would have been set free, and no one would have been harmed."

Snowflakes settled on the windowpane and melted immediately, sliding down the glass like teardrops.

When John Harris spoke, it wasn't in anger. He simply sounded tired to the bone. "Even if I could, I wouldn't have given them what they want. Which isn't just to disable the dam, Lindsay. That maniac Fox wants to blow the whole thing up. That would send a thirty-foot wall of water down Manitou Canyon, moving at maybe sixty, seventy miles an hour. There's a small town at the end of the canyon, Gordonville."

"We were there," Cork said.

"Then you could see that if that wall of water hit Gordonville carrying tons of rock and debris, it would seem like the end of the world to the people there. I'm not sure anyone would survive."

Lindsay turned, and the tears that ran down her cheeks were copious and real.

"So they did this to you. Oh, Grandpa John, I'm sorry."

"How did you get involved in all this?" Harris asked.

She wiped at her cheeks. "I met a man. A fine man."

"Mr. Brown," Cork said.

She nodded. "At Northland College, after I was arrested. We fell in love. He told me about his home, about the Manitou River, about the devastation your dam would cause."

"What devastation?" Cork asked.

"The electricity that dam generates will power an enormous

open-pit mine operation near the headwaters of the Manitou River," Lindsay told him. "That mine will destroy the whole eco-system there, and kill the river in the process."

"It never dawned on you what a coincidence it was that you and Mr. Brown should just stumble onto one another? You, the granddaughter of the man who designed the dam, and him, one of the people fighting against it?" Cork shook his head.

"Kismet, I thought," she replied feebly.

"Love blinds, Corky," Harris said.

Cork thought this was an interesting statement coming from the man who, if what Lindsay had told him was true, had been unable or unwilling to give his grandchildren the love they'd craved from him.

"How did these people approach you?" Cork asked. "Through Brown?"

"His name is Isaac," she said. "Isaac McQuabbie. One of his professors at McGill read about my arrest and sent him. He was supposed to, you know, woo me and seduce me into helping them. But we fell in love for real."

"Fox is that professor?" Cork asked.

"Yes."

"What's his real name?"

"Robert Baker. He's Wahta Mohawk. He promised no one would be hurt."

"And we've seen how well that's worked out. Was the whole kidnapping thing his plan?"

"We planned it together, him and Isaac and me. Isaac's people were kept in the dark about my part in all this. No one outside the three of us was to know about my involvement. That way, when it was all over, Isaac and I could go back to our lives, go on fighting the good fight together for the things we believe in. It sounded right, you know. It sounded possible."

"Whose idea was it to have Aaron and the others kidnap you?"

"Mine," she admitted.

"And your brother knew nothing about all this?"

"He thinks it was all his idea. That was Fox's suggestion. He knew about Trevor's debts."

"How?"

"They seem to know about everything. They're very organized that way. Fox pointed out that if it all went south, it would be Trevor's head on the block, and I'd still be free to fight for the things I believe are worthwhile. My brother's never been about anything but himself. So it didn't seem like a bad idea to me. That sounds terrible, I know, but I didn't really think anything like this was going to happen."

"Why me?" Cork said. "Why involve me?"

"When Fox communicated to me that Grandpa John wasn't giving them the information they needed, I suggested they use me as leverage. But I couldn't just vanish. For the same reason he couldn't have just been taken. The motive might be too obvious. We needed time to prepare properly for disabling the dam. Fox hoped the obfuscation, as he liked to call it, of simply vanishing in the wilderness would keep anyone from looking in the right direction for a while. Enough time so that we could complete our mission.

"Also, they knew about you and Grandpa John, friends a long time ago. Like I said, they know so many things. They thought you might give them another kind of leverage."

"Kill me first so that your grandfather would know how serious they are?"

"That wasn't how it was supposed to be. And we were up against the wall, in a way. All this was supposed to have been done two months ago, but Grandpa John couldn't leave his precious project in Africa. The lake kept rising and pretty soon would be high enough to feed the generator turbines, and it would be too late." Anger welled up and seemed to overpower her regret. "You told me once that spirit is at the heart of everything, and I've always believed you. What the hell is at the heart of your spirit now, Grandpa John? How could you build that monstrosity? It's so wrong."

"I know," he said.

His reply clearly caught her by surprise. "Then why did you do it?"

"I didn't."

"I don't understand."

"When the people from Ontario's Ministry of Natural Resources approached me about a dam across the Manitou Canyon narrows, I was deeply involved in a much bigger, more complicated project."

"The Okobongo Dam," Cork said.

"Exactly." He shot his granddaughter a guilty look. "The kind of dam I thought could be my legacy to the world. I didn't want to be bothered with something as small-scale as the Manitou Canyon project. So I gave it to one of my assistants. He did the on-site groundwork, created the design. I simply reviewed everything and signed off. My company built it, but it's really another man's dam."

"So you don't know it well enough to know its weakness," Cork guessed.

"I told Fox there was no way they could blow up the dam. There's so much concrete it would take a nuclear device." He looked up at Cork. "But it may have a weakness. Not in the dam itself. The narrows is the problem, the rock that anchors the dam."

"Looked pretty solid to me when we flew over it," Cork said.

"It's part of the Canadian Shield, the oldest and sturdiest exposed rock in North America. It's igneous, of volcanic origin, and was the first part of this continent to rise above the sea. It's been untouched by the subsequent encroachment of oceans in the nearly four billion years since. General thinking is that it would be a great anchor for a structure like a dam.

"But the Manitou Highlands, which the canyon is a part of, is an anomaly. It's experienced a more recent volcanic episode, a molten upthrust millions of years ago that lifted it above the surrounding area. In that uplift, the rock around the narrows of the canyon was significantly fractured. Its integrity was compromised."

"You're saying the dam is anchored to broken rock?"

"That's a gross simplification, but essentially correct."

"No one knew this?"

"They knew. They just didn't care. The narrows of Manitou Canyon is the most convenient location for a dam to provide power to Caldecott's Highland Mine, a hundred kilometers to the northwest. The mine's scheduled to begin operation pretty much as soon as they can get the dam turbines running. So, when documentation was sent to the Ministry of Natural Resources, there was no mention of the fracturing."

"Who was responsible for the documentation?"

"My man. The engineer who designed the dam. He no longer works for me, by the way. After construction began and I heard about the protests from the Odawa, I came up here myself for an on-site inspection. It didn't take me long to see evidence of the fracturing. You have to know what to look for, but it's there. I pinned my man to the wall, and he admitted that he'd been paid well by Caldecott to ignore the fracturing issue, to falsify the reports. I went to Toronto, talked myself blue at the ministry, submitted a formal report warning of the danger the dam presented if the rock gave way. I was totally ignored. The influence of Caldecott, I assume. So they completed the dam over my objections."

"It's going to give way at some point?" Cork said.

"I can't say for sure, but the possibility is certainly there. I wanted to do further geologic testing, further inspections, but every attempt was thwarted."

"Caldecott's greed," Lindsay said, two words filled with so much anger that the air in the room seemed poisoned by them.

"So the dam may give way eventually," Cork said. "Is there anything these people could do that might help that along? Sounds like they have a good stockpile of explosives."

"I suppose they could plant significant charges on either side of the narrows. It might further the fracturing already there, enough that the pressure of the backed-up water would shatter the rock and take the dam down with it. It's a very long shot."

"Maybe we should offer it to them," Cork said.

"What?" Lindsay gave him a shocked look.

"Wasn't that what you wanted?"

"To disable the dam, yes. Not sign the death warrant for every-one in Gordonville."

"All right, here's the situation," Cork said. "I'm already dead. I've seen and heard way too much. But the minute your grand-father's blindfold came off, he was dead, too. He saw everyone, can identify faces. And now he knows everything. If we leave this room and offer them nothing, they'll carry through with their threats. They'll kill me first. Then they'll put the gun to your head, Lindsay. And because there is, in fact, a remote possibility of accomplishing what they set out to do here, my guess is that your grandfather will give them the information they want. They'll do what they set out to do. And then they'll kill you both. Probably Indigo and Fox will kill everyone involved here, just to make sure they leave no loose ends."

Silence was their uncomfortable companion. The snow fell harder, and the window glass became a flood of melted flakes.

Then Cork said, "I have no intention of letting them carry through with their plan. But if we play along, we might buy us some time while we figure a way out of this."

CHAPTER 52

They flew north along the edge of the heavy cloud cover. Daniel sat up front with Bud Bowers. Henry and Rainy occupied the two seats behind them. Stephen sat in the very back.

There'd been little talk since they taxied away from the marina in Aurora and lifted off from the sparkling surface of Iron Lake. They'd watched the cloud bank to the west spill toward them across the sky. The air had become turbulent, buffeting the little de Havilland. Periodically, Bowers checked in with Thunder Bay, the nearest weather reporting frequency, and kept his passengers updated.

"Kenora's already snowed in," he reported. "The storm's moving really fast. I don't know if we're going make it to White Woman Lake before everything there is socked in."

Rainy stared out her window. They'd long ago crossed the Canadian border, but the nature of the land below had changed little. It was a great arboreal wilderness, and the boundary lines politicians had drawn on maps were meaningless. Those lines might change. Who knew? But the land itself had been as it was for millions of years and would continue for millions more. There was comfort in this, in the knowledge that whatever humans did, in the very long run their impact was small when compared with the vast patience that was the spirit of the earth. But it was only small comfort when she thought about the danger Cork was in. Cork and Lindsay Harris and her grandfather.

She saw Bowers put a hand to his headset.

"This is Alpha Bravo three four seven. Go ahead."

Bowers listened for a while. The plane made a sudden lurch to the left. Bowers dropped both hands to the control yoke.

"I read you, Sheriff. I'll let them know."

Over his shoulder, Bowers said, "I've got some interesting information to pass along. Seems the sheriff believes that Lindsay Harris may have been in on this from the beginning. In cahoots with whoever took her grandfather. The sheriff's advising a good deal of caution in your dealings with her.

"Also, we're diverting. We're going to make our landing at Gordonville, which is a little town east of White Woman Lake. A contingent from RCMP will meet us there. They don't want us going to White Woman Lake on our own. A direct order from the Canadian authorities."

"Screw the authorities," Stephen said.

"Not gonna happen," Bowers said. "We're already in hot water. If we ignore that order and something really bad goes down, who knows what we might be looking at? Jail time? At the very least, there goes my job. Gordonville is only forty miles from White Woman Lake. If the RCMP and the weather allow it, we fly there. If not, you'll have to find alternate transport. Sorry, folks. Best I can do."

"How much longer to Gordonville?"

"Half an hour more or less." Bowers looked toward the looming cloud bank to the west. "May be nip and tuck with that storm."

The turbulence got worse, and Bowers had his hands full. Rainy began to wonder if the little plane might be torn apart by the forces outside. She glanced at her great-uncle. Henry bounced lightly, like a twig on water, and nothing in his ancient face looked disturbed. She marveled at the strength that kept him so anchored to a peaceful center. She studied the sky. To the east, it was still clear, the sun bathing the land below. To the west lay an angry rush of roiling clouds painted in shades of black and gray. Life, she thought. Always a clash of opposites. Was there ever any real end to that great conflict?

"There it is," Bowers said.

Out the window, Rainy could see a tiny settlement on the edge of a small lake. It lay just below the mouth of a long, narrow break in the hills to the west, which were cloaked in cloud and precipitation. A river threaded its way out of all that dismal gray. The Manitou, she guessed. They touched down on the lake, and Bowers eased the de Havilland to a little beach near the edge of the town. Daniel got out and secured the floatplane to a sign posted on the shoreline. As he did so, a vehicle appeared from the town and approached them, driving along the beach itself. It was a white Chevy Tahoe, with the RCMP insignia painted across the side. The Tahoe drew to a stop and a lone officer got out. He stood watching as Rainy and the others disembarked, then he came to greet them.

"Constable Rudy Markham," he said and held out his hand.

Markham was a round little man of perhaps forty, with a ruddy face and eyes that seemed better suited to an affectionate but not very bright family dog. He wore a thick walrus mustache, which at the moment, was dabbed with what looked like hot dog mustard.

Daniel took the proffered hand and introduced the others. Then he asked, "Where's the rest of your team?"

"Team?" The constable looked confused.

"They told us an RCMP contingent would be meeting us."

"That would be me," the constable said. "It's a one-man detachment here in Gordonville. But we've got an incident team coming up from Thunder Bay."

"They've left?"

"Not yet. They're waiting for someone from CSIS to arrive."

"CSIS?"

"Canadian Security Intelligence Service. Another branch of the Crown. Apparently they've been conducting their own investigation into the activities of the Warrior Cohort."

"Warrior Cohort?" Daniel said.

"The people they think are behind all this. A First Nations terrorist network of some kind."

"How long until they get here?"

"Once they get started, it would normally take three hours." The constable looked at the cauldron of the sky and what was bubbling there. Snowflakes had begun to spill out of that dark, swirling mass. A strong wind had risen, and within it was carried the cold certainty of a storm. "But this weather coming in is sure to slow them down. So . . ." He gave a shrug.

"We can't wait," Daniel said. "What if they blow the dam?"

The constable wiped at his mustache and studied the mustard smear on his glove. "As I understand it, you don't know for sure that's what these people are up to. And, hell, Aaron would never do that."

"Aaron Commanda?"

"Yeah."

"You know him?"

"Everybody around here knows Aaron. And Aaron knows that if he blew that dam, the water would come roaring down the canyon and wipe out Gordonville."

"What if Aaron isn't in charge of whatever's going down?" Daniel said. "Your NSCI folks believe there's a much larger network involved. This Warrior Cohort, whoever they are, might not care about the good citizens of Gordonville the way you and Aaron do. We need to leave for White Woman Lake, and we need to leave now."

Markham thought about that. "Any idea how many of them there might be?"

"No clue."

The constable's clear, simple eyes considered the hills to the west and the mouth of the canyon, which lay a stone's throw from the town. "I tried to call the night watchman up at the dam before I came out to meet you folks. Couldn't get through. I just figured the phone line was down. Happens sometimes when a storm sweeps in." He shook his head, took a deep breath, and pulled himself up, as if to make himself a bit taller. "This is what I'm going to do. I'm going to drive to the Manitou Canyon Dam and secure it, if I can. Then I'll worry about Aaron and White Woman Lake."

"Just you, Constable? Look, we flew up here to help."

"I can't take responsibility for your safety."

"We're not asking you to," Daniel said. "And think about this. What if you get up there and discover you need backup to save that dam? Wouldn't it be best to have it already with you? I'm a trained law enforcement officer. I brought my service weapon, and I know how to handle it."

The constable chewed on his mustache while he weighed Daniel's words. "All right," he finally said, but not decisively.

Rainy said, "I'm an excellent shot."

The others looked at her with surprise. This was a new piece of information to all of them. Except, apparently, Henry. She'd never told anyone about this part of herself, part of the someone she'd once been, but nothing was hidden from him.

"If I have to, I will shoot to kill. It won't be the first time." Again to the obvious amazement of those present. Except Henry. She was relieved when, despite their surprise, no one asked her to explain.

"I get my deer every year," Bowers offered. "And I'd draw a bead on a man, if it would save Cork."

"I don't know about this." The constable looked suddenly overwhelmed and completely unsure.

"The lives of everyone in Gordonville might be at stake," Daniel said. "We don't have time to stand here and argue."

The constable tugged nervously at his mustache. "I'll need to check in with Thunder Bay."

"Know what they'll do?" Daniel said. "They'll order you to stand down until they arrive. And if they arrive and find that the town's been destroyed along with everyone in it, probably us included, they'll blame you officially because you knew about the danger and did nothing. You want that to be your legacy here, Constable?"

The officer thought that over.

"Alternatively," Daniel went on, "you can secure the dam and report that to them. Maybe a commendation'll come from it."

"I . . ." the constable began, then hesitated. "I guess so," he finally said. He eyed Henry. "We'll be a little crowded. I think you'd best stay back, old-timer."

"A mouse would take up more room," Henry said.

"No disrespect, gramps, but a mouse would be of more use to me than you."

Rainy said, "Henry needs to be there."

"Right," Daniel and Stephen agreed together.

Constable Markham was wearing a dark blue ball cap with a maple leaf on the crown. The wind gusted suddenly, throwing a flurry of snowflakes at the gathering. The constable's cap lifted off his head and tumbled across the beach. He ran for it, snatched it up, and settled it firmly on his head. He marched back to the others, trying, Rainy thought, not to look like a complete doofus.

"Okay," he said with authority. He nodded to Bowers. "You stay here. We might need that floatplane of yours before this is all over. We're going back to my office and gear up. What's the frequency on your plane's radio?"

Bowers told him, and the constable gave him the frequency he'd be using on the radio in his Tahoe.

"Stand by, and if you hear us holler, you come flying," the constable said.

Bowers looked up at the storm clouds that had already enveloped Gordonville and the lake. "Not sure I'll be able to help."

"Then get the word to those who can." The constable turned and, as if commanding troops, said, "Follow me."

CHAPTER 53

Fox stood with his back to the fireplace and listened as John Harris explained the situation of the Manitou Canyon Dam. Fox had probably heard some of it before, the part about the dam itself being a hopeless target. The possibility of blowing the rock that served as anchor on either side was a new and, judging from the look on Fox's face, intriguing twist.

"There's no guarantee it will work," Harris said. "But in my opinion, that's the only chance you have of bringing that dam down."

They'd all gathered in the main room. Cheval and Mrs. Gray stood beside the map of White Woman Lake that hung on the wall. Cork and Lindsay sat together on the divan. Behind them, still holding a rifle, loomed Brown, whom Cork now knew as Isaac McQuabbie. Harris was alone in a chair. Aaron stood near him, the rifle still in his grip. Indigo was tending to the fireplace, using an iron poker to move and resettle burning logs.

"If it works," Fox asked, "will it go right away?"

"It might. I can't say for sure. But it will certainly screw with the integrity of the dam. Its viability will have to be completely reassessed. They'll have to cease filling the reservoir behind it. At the very least, your Manitou River will be given a reprieve."

"What do you think, Mr. Indigo?" Fox asked his cohort.

Indigo rose, the iron poker still in his hand. "I think he's telling the truth. If he isn't, we can still kill O'Connor." He gave Cork a pleasant smile and lifted the poker in his direction.

"All right. Let's get started," Fox said.

"We need to get word to Gordonville," Aaron said.

"Why?" Fox seemed surprised by the suggestion.

"If that dam goes, those people will be wiped out."

"Many of those people helped build the dam."

"It was a good-paying job," Aaron said. "Rare up here. I don't hold that against them."

"And some of those people in town are relatives," Isaac Mc-Quabbie protested. "We're not killing family."

"In this war, sacrifices will be necessary," Fox said. "Mr. Gray understood that."

"It was Flynn's choice," Aaron said, emphatic about the man's real name, as if it gave his death weight and meaning. "That's something you haven't offered those people in Gordonville."

"And I don't intend to," Fox said. "If that dam goes and those people are killed, the message it sends to Ottawa is all the more powerful. I thought you wanted the dam gone. Otherwise, why am I here?"

"You're here because it serves your own purposes," Aaron said. "Don't give me a lot of crap about caring about us. Before we set off those charges, we send word to Gordonville. That's all there is to it."

"You'll never be a true warrior, Aaron."

Without warning, Indigo swung the poker and clipped the tall man a glancing blow across the side of his head, not hard enough for serious damage but enough that he dropped his rifle and fell back upon the floor. Cheval jumped to his feet, but Indigo had his Glock out.

"Don't anyone move," he said.

Isaac McQuabbie raised his rifle. "Drop your gun, Indigo."

Indigo didn't.

"I thought you were one of us," Fox said.

"I'm not like you," Isaac said. "I just want to save the river. You promised no one would get hurt."

"Things change." Fox slowly bent and reached for the rifle Aaron had dropped.

"Don't," Isaac said.

Fox ignored the warning and lifted the rifle while Isaac stood wavering.

"You can shoot me, or you can shoot Mr. Indigo, but you can't shoot us both," Fox said. "If you kill me, Mr. Indigo will shoot you, then he'll shoot Ms. Harris. We don't need either of you anymore. If you choose to shoot Mr. Indigo, then I'll be the one to kill you both. If, on the other hand, you put that rifle down, I promise no one gets shot. We do our work tonight, and we're gone. The choice is yours."

The struggle of decision was clear on his young face, but Isaac finally set the rifle on the floor.

"All right," Fox said. "We've got a lot of work ahead of us tonight."

As Fox had indicated, they'd stockpiled plenty of high explosives. In one of the empty cabins, there were cases of dynamite, TNT, and C-4. Stacked against one whole wall, like sandbags in a bunker, were sacks of ANFO, ammonium nitrate. There were boxes filled with boosters, detonators, caps, and fuse coils. Two new Cobra gas-powered rock drills stood in a corner, with a dozen carbide bits arrayed on the floor around them like goods in a bazaar.

John Harris decided on the dynamite. "Considering the conditions we'll be working under, it's the safest choice," he explained.

Fox and Indigo, always with their weapons at the ready, kept a watchful eye as the others loaded a pickup parked near the cabin. When the truck bed contained everything Harris thought necessary, Fox said, "Okay, everyone back into the lodge."

After they'd assembled, he said, "We'll need lots of muscle tonight. Harris, Cheval, O'Connor, Aaron, you're coming."

"What about the rest of us?" Isaac said.

"You, your girlfriend, and Mrs. Gray will stay here."

"No," the sour woman said. "I want to be there. It's what we came for, what Flynn died for."

Fox studied her and finally said, "All right."

"So Lindsay and me, we just stay back and wait?" Isaac said. The young man clearly liked that idea.

"Yes, but in the cooler in the kitchen."

"What?"

"Dress warm," Indigo said with a grin. "We might be a while."

After they'd donned their coats and gloves and stocking caps, Lindsay and Isaac were herded into the small walk-in cooler.

"If we don't freeze, we might suffocate," Lindsay said.

"There's plenty of air for a few hours. That's all we'll be gone," Fox assured them. "This is just a little insurance, so we know you won't be tempted to interfere."

Before the door was shut and locked, Lindsay looked beyond Fox to where her grandfather stood. "I'm sorry," she said again.

"Forget it," John Harris said. "It's on my shoulders."

Fox shut the door.

"I'll never see her again, will I?" Harris said.

"Don't be such a Debbie Downer," Indigo told him. "All this goes well, who knows? You both may be lying in the Maui sun next week. Let's go."

They took two vehicles. Cheval drove the pickup, transporting with him Mrs. Gray and Indigo. Aaron drove a new-looking black Yukon, Cork at his side, hands bound with duct tape. Fox sat in back with Harris, whose hands had also been bound. Fox held a threatening handgun.

They followed a gravel road that skirted White Woman Lake, then tunneled east through thick forest, roughly paralleling the course of the Manitou River. Snow fell heavily, and Aaron moved the Yukon slowly because the road was rough and twisting and because the snow sometimes made the way ahead difficult to see. With the storm, night had come early. The taillights of the pickup stared back at them out of the dark and the falling snow like the eyes of a demon.

"I'm sorry we dragged you into this, O'Connor," Aaron said as they bounced over the rugged road.

"How'd they talk you into it?" Cork asked.

"We didn't have to talk much," Fox said from the back. "A very nice convergence of mutual interests. The people of White Woman Lake wanted to save their sacred canyon, and we wanted to make a statement to those blind fools down in Ottawa."

"There you go with that 'we' again," Cork said. "Who are you?"

"The RCMP has taken to calling us the Warrior Cohort. I like that. And who are we? We are the Native underground. Indigenous people fed up with feeling powerless. And not just here in Canada. Thanks to modern technology, the only good thing White people gave us, this war is worldwide."

"Terrorism," Cork said.

"Justice," Fox replied.

John Harris asked, "How exactly is destroying the Manitou Canyon Dam justice?"

"It was sold to the Canadian people as part of the nation's great push to become the world's leader in producing hydroelectric power for its citizens," Fox explained. "But the truth is that almost none of the electricity those generators produce will ever reach a Canadian household. It was built to power Caldecott's Highland Mine, a mine that will eventually dwarf any open-pit iron operation on this continent. Am I right, Aaron?"

Aaron nodded. "It'll devastate the Manitou Highlands. It'll kill the land and almost certainly contaminate the Manitou River and everything downstream."

Fox said, "The Caldecott Corporation, of course, insists that it will have in place all kinds of safety measures to keep that from happening. But we all know about that kind of promise. You know the Mount Polley Mine in B.C., O'Connor?"

"Never heard of it," Cork said.

"The ecosystem of the entire region was contaminated by heavy metals from the spill of a massive holding pond there. The same thing with the spill at Caldecott's West Caribou Mine in Alberta. Their high-tech holding ponds ended up releasing billions of liters of slurry into the Caribou River. The leakage has poisoned hundreds of First Nations people in Fort Saint Antoine. You can ask Mrs. Gray about that, eh, Aaron?"

"Her entire family is sick because of it, Cork. Dying," Aaron said.

"But have the Canadian people learned any lessons?" Fox went on. "I look at the Manitou Canyon Dam and this new Caldecott mine, and I think not."

"And you find justice in blowing up the dam and killing the people in Gordonville?" Harris said.

"The world paid very little attention to the spills in B.C. and Alberta. Know why? Nobody died, or at least not immediately. It was Grandmother Earth who suffered. When Gordonville is destroyed, people—White people—will notice. And something will be done."

"Do you know what will be done?" Cork said. "They'll simply spend a great deal of time and effort hunting you down."

"If they find me and kill me, they'll have accomplished little. In Iroquois myth, there are creatures called *kanontsistonties*. They're disembodied, flying heads that wreak vengeance. That is the Warrior Cohort. No body but many heads. In this, one man is nothing."

The pickup ahead suddenly pulled off the road onto what looked like a logging trail.

"What the hell?" Fox said. "Follow him."

Aaron turned off the road, too. The pickup ahead stopped and killed its lights.

"Turn your lights off," Fox said.

In less than a minute, a vehicle passed on the road they'd just left, heading toward White Woman Lake.

"Any idea who that was?" Fox asked.

"Somebody from Saint Gervais probably," Aaron guessed. "Heading home before the storm locks them out."

"All right. Get us back on the road."

Half an hour later, an electric haze appeared through the gloom of the night, like a light in the swirl of a snow globe. They came to a place where a great upthrust of rock burst from the forest cover. It was split as if with an ax, and in the narrows of that divide lay the Manitou Canyon Dam, brightly illuminated. Cork recalled from the earlier flyover that it wasn't a particularly broad dam and tapered as it dropped toward the power station at its base, where the river continued cutting its way down Manitou Canyon. Behind it, the rising water of the new lake pressed against the massive concrete formation. The surface was brilliant topaz where it caught the light, then quickly faded to black and finally disappeared altogether behind the curtain of the falling snow.

The pickup stopped at a place where the rough road from White Woman Lake met the smooth pavement of the road that came up along the canyon from Gordonville. The Yukon stopped behind it.

Indigo left the pickup. Fox lowered his window, and Indigo leaned in.

"One truck in the parking lot. The night watchman. I'll take care of him," Indigo said.

"That'll be Harold Welles," Aaron said. "Don't kill him."

"Is he Indian?"

"No."

"Then what do you care?"

Aaron opened his door and stepped out.

Fox said, "What do you think you're doing?"

"I'm going with Mr. Indigo."

Fox pointed the big handgun at him. "I'm warning you."

"Shoot me and you give us all away. I just want to make sure about Harold."

Fox weighed this and finally gave a nod. "But don't get any ideas about trying to call Gordonville. Mr. Indigo took care of the phone line earlier today."

"Let's go, Aaron," Indigo said. "You first. And stay ahead of me."

It was a long twenty minutes until they returned. Between them, they carried a man's body. They tossed it in the back of the sole pickup in the lot, and Indigo climbed into the bed and bent over him for a couple of minutes. Then he and Aaron walked together to the Yukon.

"Not dead," Indigo said. "But out good. I bound him up tight. He's going nowhere soon."

"Okay," Fox said. "Let's blow this dam."

CHAPTER 54

"I don't know a lot," Constable Markham said as he negotiated the winding road that followed the Manitou Canyon west out of Gordonville. "Those guys in Thunder Bay, they hold on to info like it's money from their own pockets. Never mind I'm all the law there is out here."

"What exactly do you know?" Daniel asked.

A fierce wind funneled down the canyon, driving blinding snow at the Tahoe. Rainy had endured more winter storms than she could possibly remember, but this one was different. Although she knew it was ridiculous, this storm felt like an adversary, something bent on keeping her from Cork.

"These people we're facing, if they're really up there, aren't like an organized group or anything," the constable explained. "The guys at NSCI are calling them the Warrior Cohort, whatever the hell that means. Here in Canada, they're First Nations. Other kinds of Native people elsewhere, I guess. They don't have any sort of hierarchy, apparently, and no formal organization. They communicate entirely electronically. Emails, texts, Instagram, phone calls, all from sources difficult or impossible to track. Sounds like they never meet face-to-face. Sort of modern guerrilla warfare, you might say. If it hadn't been for you, NSCI wouldn't have any idea about the threat to the Manitou Canyon Dam."

The road ahead curved suddenly, and as Markham fought to make the turn, the Tahoe drifted on the pavement. The river loomed dark at their side. In the brief sweep of beam from the headlights, Rainy could see angry white water leaping over boulders in the channel.

"Jesus," the constable whispered under his breath. "This is going from bad to worse."

"How much farther?" Stephen asked.

"Twenty kilometers from the town to the dam. So maybe twelve more ahead of us. New road, this. Before they built the dam, it was all washboard gravel. Only thing up that way was White Woman Lake and Saint Gervais. Mostly floatplane visitors up there, flying into the lodge to fish the lake or the upper Manitou. Only ones who ever really used the road were Aaron and the other Odawa."

"What do you think of the dam?"

The constable shrugged. "Doesn't do us any good. Hell, all that electricity'll be going to Caldecott's Highland Mine. Aaron and his people are sure the mine'll pollute the river, and it probably will. That's one of the big reasons they're upset. It's a special place to them. Sacred, you know. I get what they're saying. I love this river, too, but what do any of us matter?"

"A little bee matters, when it stings," Henry said.

"Yeah, and Aaron tried to sting. What did it get him? Nothing but a few days in jail."

"And the knowledge that he fought," the old man said.

Markham shook head. "Look, there's such huge money involved in this and so many powerful people in Ottawa, a regular guy doesn't stand a chance."

"That does not mean a regular guy should not try."

Inside the Tahoe, it was quiet for a moment. Then Constable Markham said, "You're right, old-timer. Right as rain."

"His name's Henry," Rainy said.

The bull moose came out of nowhere. Or rather, the curtain of snow kept it hidden so that when it was suddenly revealed in the headlights, standing in the center of the narrow road, broadside to the Tahoe, Markham had no chance to avoid a collision. Rainy saw the great animal turn its head. It seemed to observe the inevitable with amazing calm.

Constable Markham hit the brakes at the same moment the Tahoe hit the moose. The impact jarred them all, and they were shoved forward against the restraint of their seat belts. Up front, the air bags deployed. There was a shattering of glass from the windshield. The Tahoe jerked to a stop, and for a long moment the only sound was the crackle of hot metal and the hiss of steam.

Markham finally said, "Is everybody okay?"

"Yeah," said Stephen, who sat in back with Rainy and Henry.

"Okay, here," Daniel said. He was up front with the constable.

"Uncle Henry?" Rainy asked. In the sudden dark, she could barely see.

"I am all right, Niece."

They got out one by one. Markham pulled a couple of big flashlights from the gear in the back of the Tahoe, and Rainy stood with the others as they inspected the damage. The front end of the vehicle was crushed, as if it had hit another vehicle head-on. In the flashlight beams, tendrils of gray steam rose up from under the crumpled hood.

"There goes my transport budget," Markham said.

"Uncle Henry?" Rainy called, because she was suddenly aware that he was not with them.

"Here," she heard him say.

Daniel swung a flashlight beam in the direction of the old man's voice. There was the Mide, kneeling beside the fallen bull moose, which lay on its side at the edge of the road. The animal wasn't dead yet. Rainy saw the great bellows of its lungs working and heard the suck of air through its nostrils. She also heard the voice of her great-uncle, whispering. She took a step toward him.

"It would be best if you all stayed back," the old man said quietly.

He rose and stepped away. A moment later, the moose trembled, struggled up on its impossibly gangly legs, and stood, as if gathering its wits. It turned its face to the flashlight beams, shook its body, gave a warning snort, then trotted off down the road toward Gordonville and disappeared into the storm.

"My God," Markham said. "The hell with the Tahoe. I should be driving one of those."

Daniel turned back to the ruined vehicle. "What now?"

"I radio Gordonville, if the radio still works, and we wait for a tow."

"What about the dam?" Stephen said.

"What do you want me to do?" Markham replied. "Fly?"

"We can walk," Rainy said. "How much farther now? Maybe ten kilometers? A couple of hours?"

"I'm with you," Daniel said.

"And me," Stephen chimed in.

"Maybe you should stay here, Uncle Henry," Rainy suggested.

"Like a moose," the old man said and thumped his chest. "I will go."

"Give me a minute," Markham said. "Let me try the radio, see if I can get an update to Gordonville and Thunder Bay."

He slipped back into the Tahoe. A minute later he slid back out.

"Nothing," he said. "And there's no cell phone service out here. So we're on our own." He returned to the rear of the Tahoe and began pulling out gear. "I've only got two vests. I'll wear one, you wear the other." He gave the armor to Daniel. He took out two rifles and a box of cartridges. He gave a rifle to Rainy. "I figure you'll provide cover fire if we need it. You better have told the truth about handling one of these."

Henry said, "Her eye and her heart are true, Constable Markham."

"All right, then." The Mountie settled his cap on his head. "Guess we've got a dam to save."

They began walking up the road, with only the vaguest notion of what might be coming at them down Manitou Canyon.

CHAPTER 55

The drills worked perfectly. The bits ate quickly into the rock and, with the extensions, reached a depth of five feet in less than ten minutes per hole. Harris guessed at the drill pattern.

"Look, I guarantee nothing," he said to Fox. "A blast like this really needs to be well considered. There are dozens of factors that come into play."

"We don't have time to consider dozens of factors," Fox said. "This will have to do."

Aaron, Cheval, and Cork took turns operating the drills, while Fox and Indigo oversaw everything with weapons at the ready in their hands. Harris marked each drill site and, along with Mrs. Gray, helped change bits and extensions as needed. When the holes were prepared, he packed the charges and connected the detonating wire.

"It's been a long time since I did this kind of hands-on work," he said.

"Always good to know what guys on the front line have to do," Indigo replied. And there was that hateful grin again.

When they'd prepared the wall on the west side of the dam, they moved all the materials and equipment to the east side and began there.

In what should have been a quiet interrupted only by the moan of wind, the screech of the drills was surreal and offensive. Rock dust mixed with the sweep of blowing snow, and in the glare that lit the dam, Cork felt as if he were in a vision of hell. He'd been watching for an opportunity to make some kind of move, but Indigo and Fox were alert and careful and gave him nothing.

When the holes had been drilled and Harris had begun to ready the charges for that wall, Fox said, "O'Connor, Cheval, haul your drills back to the pickup. Indigo, you go with them. Harris, Aaron, you stay here with me and Mrs. Gray."

Indigo waved his Glock and said, "After you, gents."

Cork and Cheval hefted the drills onto their shoulders and marched off the dam, leaving Harris and Aaron with Fox to finish the blast preparations.

The labor of drilling had been hard, and Cork had worked up a sweat that soaked his clothing. Now the wind drove the cold across the rising lake and his body stiffened.

Cheval said, "I'm too old for this kind of work."

Behind him, Indigo said, "You're just about as old as you're ever going to get, my friend."

They were near the night watchman's pickup in the lot when Cheval slipped and fell. The drill tumbled from his grip, and he lay sprawled on the ground, holding his knee.

"Goddamn ice," he said.

Indigo said, "Pick up the drill."

"Twisted my knee," Cheval complained. "Not sure I can even walk."

"Get up and give it a try."

"I need a hand up."

"O'Connor," Indigo said.

Cork lowered his drill and set it in the snow. He glanced at Indigo, whose eyes at the moment were intent on Cheval. The Glock was also aimed in that direction. Cork launched himself. But Indigo anticipated the move. He easily stepped clear of Cork's attack and stood grinning.

"I can read you like a book, O'Connor. You, too," he said to Cheval. "I'd hoped to get those drills to the truck before I took you both out. Guess I'll have to finish that job. Just as soon as I finish this one."

Indigo seemed to consider which man to shoot first. Before he could decide, a red blooming appeared in the center of his forehead just a split second in advance of the rifle report. The look on Indigo's face was of utter surprise. Then he collapsed, dropped like a rag doll, and lay with the back of his head exploded, his blood staining the snow.

Cork scanned the dark beyond the snowfall that was illuminated in the dam lights. A moment later, three figures emerged from the direction of the Yukon and the pickup parked along the road. As they neared, he recognized Lindsay. Then Isaac. And finally Bird, who was walking only with Isaac's help. In his right hand he held a scoped rifle. His face was pale and his features pained.

"I would have shot him sooner," Bird said. "But you guys were in the way."

"How'd you get here?" Cheval asked.

"I borrowed a truck in Gordonville," Bird explained. "Found these two locked in the cooler at the lodge. They told me everything."

The vehicle that had passed on the road, Cork realized.

"Where's Grandpa John?" Lindsay said.

"Still on the dam," Cork told her.

"My uncle?" Bird said.

"With him. Fox and Mrs. Gray, too."

Isaac looked at the drills on the ground. "You finished?"

"They're finishing now."

"They're really going to blow the dam?"

"They're going to try," Cork said. "And if that dam goes, Gordonville goes with it."

"That's not what we wanted," Bird said.

"You may have to kill another man," Cork told him.

"Fox?" The young man's face looked old and grim. "I can do that."

"Then let's go."

Cheval grabbed the dead man's Glock, and they moved carefully toward the dam. The wind drove the snow in a shifting, blinding curtain before them. As they approached the place where the thick, horizontal concrete met the vertical east wall of the narrows, the three men and the woman still on the dam were revealed. Cork saw Harris place something on the dam wall and step back. Fox picked up the object.

"Do you think you can get a shot from here?" Cork whispered to Bird.

"I'll make it work," Bird said.

"Not unless you have to. Stay here, all of you except Cheval. You come with me," he said to the big pilot. "And bring the Glock."

As they neared the men on the dam, Cheval asked, "How are we going to explain Indigo?"

"Probably badly," Cork said. "That's what the Glock's for."

When Fox saw them, everything about him went on alert.

"Indigo?" Fox asked.

Cork said, "Do you know about the Anishinaabe belief in the Path of Souls?"

"I know it."

"Indigo's on his way."

Fox considered this. "Makes no difference."

"Oh, but it does," Cork said. "Cheval."

The big man showed the Glock.

Fox nodded but didn't seem concerned. "The detonator trumps all." He held up his hand, and in it was what looked like a small electronic device. "You can't kill me quick enough. So, my question is this. Do we all go up with the dam?"

They stood a long moment, the only sound the moan of the wind as it pressed into the canyon. Then came the crack of the high-powered rifle. Simultaneously, the arm that Fox had lifted and that held the detonator jerked back and a great chunk of flesh and bone below the elbow vanished. Another rifle crack followed, and Fox dropped with a hole through his heart.

Before any of the men could move, the woman swooped down, snatched the detonator, and ran toward the other side of the dam.

Cork heard another crack of the rifle, but the woman kept on running. The next rifle shot brought her down but didn't stop her. She crawled to the cover of the wall that topped the dam, out of rifle sight, and moved into a sitting position.

"Run!" Cork cried.

They fled, ran clear of the dam and the eastern wall. Lindsay rushed out of the blind of snow and embraced her grandfather. Bird was beside her, and Aaron paused a moment to put a hand on his nephew's shoulder.

"We've got to keep moving," Cork shouted.

When they reached the road and the parked vehicles there, they crowded together behind the pickup and peered over the bed.

"Maybe she's not going to do it," Harris finally said.

"Or maybe she's dead," Cheval offered.

In the next moment, they were both proved wrong.

CHAPTER 56

It was a wet snow and clung to their coats as they trudged along the road up the canyon toward the dam. Flakes caught on Rainy's lashes and melted and dripped into her eyes, now and again blinding her momentarily. The wind was powerful out of the west. The night was terribly dark. But for the beams of the flashlights that Constable Markham and Daniel held, it would have been impossible to see their way.

Henry plodded at her side. As she had so often, she marveled at her great-uncle's spirit, his perseverance, his silent determination, and even his calm, which came to her despite the fierce wind that blew against and between them. She took strength in his strength.

And all the while as she pushed forward, she visualized Cork waiting for her. Safe. Unharmed. She imagined embracing him, feeling that comfortable, familiar warmth envelop her. The grizzle of his unshaved face roughing her cheek. His lips, always a little chapped in winter, against her own.

"Can't be much farther," Markham called over his shoulder. "Damnation, this is a long way on foot."

"You okay, Uncle Henry?" Daniel said. He was ahead of them, walking beside Markham. He spoke loud to be heard above the wind.

"I have walked in worse," the old man said. "And most days I still walk farther than I will this day. It would take more than a winter storm to hold me back, Nephew."

The Mide stopped suddenly, and because of that Rainy did.

And then Stephen and Daniel. And finally Markham. The constable turned back and said, "What is it?"

Henry said, "Listen."

Rainy heard nothing but the cry of the wind. She closed her eyes, blocked out her other senses, and turned her whole self to listening. Then she heard it, too. A great rumbling from up the canyon, distant at first but growing louder with every second. It was preceded by a torrent of wind more violent than anything the storm had yet produced, as if something huge and terrible was approaching and pushing the air before it. She opened her eyes and found herself staring into the face of Markham, illuminated in the glow of the flashlight. His eyes were huge and white and filled with terror. He opened his mouth, but nothing came out.

It was Stephen who spoke for him, spoke for them all. He said simply, "Oh, shit."

CHAPTER 57

The ground shook as if in an earthquake. The concussive effect was a hurricane wave that rocked the pickup and hit Cork's eardrums like blows thrown from a heavyweight. His face was peppered with a shotgun blast of hot grit. The night became instantly black, and for a moment, he thought he'd been blinded. Then he realized it was simply that the lights, which had illuminated the dam, had gone dark.

A roaring filled his ears. He wasn't certain if it was the effect of the blast or the sound of water rushing from the new lake down the canyon. In his mind's eye, he could see the deadly torrent, a great churning, uprooting trees and tossing boulders about like toy blocks. If it was the roar of water and John Harris had been correct, Gordonville and anyone between it and the dam stood no chance.

A flashlight came on. Aaron swung the beam across them all. He said something, but his words were lost in the terrible roar. He showed the light on his face and mouthed: *Are you okay?*

They all nodded, then Cork asked, "The dam? Is it gone?" Except, he couldn't hear his own voice.

Aaron shook his head and gave an exaggerated shrug.

Cork took stock of everyone around him. They all stood as if paralyzed, their eyes glazed. In the glow from the flashlight, their faces looked as if they'd all broken out in some terrible rash. His own felt abraded and tender from the blast of grit.

Aaron touched his arm and jerked his head in the direction of the dam.

Cork nodded and followed him, and the others fell in behind. The explosions had spread rock debris across the parking lot, and they walked carefully among great rugged chunks of stone. Aaron swung the beam of the flashlight across the pickup that had been parked there. The glass had been blown out of every window. In the pickup bed lay the night watchman, covered in dust and grit, still unconscious, but he seemed otherwise unharmed. They moved on and came to where the eastern wall of the narrows had collapsed. A mountain of rubble blocked their way, and somewhere under it lay the crushed remains of Robert Baker, the man who'd called himself Fox. Aaron shot the flashlight beam toward the body of the dam beyond, but the swirl of dust was too thick to be able to see if the whole structure still stood intact.

The roaring in Cork's ears had begun to abate, and as he made his way with Aaron and the others over the rubble, he could hear, faintly, the clatter of rocks as they tumbled away underfoot. Aaron played the light beam across the whole of the concrete edifice. Enough dust had settled to see what they'd all been wondering about. The dam across the narrows still held. Aaron swung the light toward the block structure of the power house below. It lay buried under tons of rock now. The surface of the Manitou River glinted in the light beam. The water was mud brown from the dirt and dust that it carried, but the flow was neither more nor less than it had been before.

Together, they walked to the edge of the west wall debris, making their way among big chunks of fragmented gneiss. Like Fox, Mrs. Gray was somewhere beneath all that tonnage of shattered stone. The great pouring of concrete under Cork's feet felt remarkably stable, and he had two reactions to that. One was relief that nothing would immediately threaten Gordonville and the people there. But the other was a profound sense of failure and, with it, sadness. What the dam had been meant to do, it still would, eventually. Caldecott's Highland Mine would get its electricity. And the great efforts of Aaron and the others to save what they loved would be in vain.

He finally heard the first voice since the explosions had deafened him. It was Bird.

"All for nothing," the kid said.

"No," John Harris told him. "The dam's been compromised. It didn't give way today, but it might tomorrow or next week or a month from now or a year. Even the greed of powerful people can't change that."

"Can they reinforce it or maybe even rebuild it?" Aaron asked.

"They'll want to try," Harris said. "There's a lot of money involved. But I swear to you, I'll do my very best to see that doesn't happen."

Lindsay looked lost. "What do we do now?"

Aaron said, "I'll drive down to Gordonville and report what's happened, alert them to the danger."

"No, I'll do that," Cork said. "The rest of you might want to go back to the lodge and get your stories straight. And think about a lawyer. The questioning by the RCMP is bound to be brutal."

Aaron considered Cork's offer and said, *"Migwech."*

They returned to the parked vehicles. Cheval gave Cork the keys to the pickup truck. "What will you tell them about us?" the big man asked.

"I've been thinking about that," Cork said. "I believe that I'll tell them the truth. Or as much of it as a man who's been blindfolded can."

"We didn't blindfold you," Isaac said.

Cheval laughed. He clapped Cork on the shoulder, a blow from a gentle bear. "You're a good man, O'Connor."

Cork turned to Harris. "You have some decisions to make, Johnny Do."

Without hesitation, Harris replied, "Like you said, Corky, what can a blindfolded man tell them?"

Bird limped to Cork. "I'm sorry about . . . everything. It wasn't anything personal, you know."

"I know."

The kid reached out and offered his hand. Cork took it easily.

Aaron accompanied Cork to the pickup.

"It's not over," the chief of the White Woman Lake Odawa said.

"Until we walk the Path of Souls, it never is."

"The canoes I left in the Boundary Waters. I wouldn't be unhappy if you retrieved them and kept them."

"I'll do that," Cork said. "But only until you're ready for them to come back to you."

"*Migwech, niijii.*" Thank you, my friend.

They shook hands. Cork got into the pickup and headed down the road that followed the canyon.

The figures emerged from the whirl of snow, trudging along at the edge of the pavement. Cork saw the beams of their flashlights first, then their bodies, brilliant in the headlights. He was absolutely amazed to see the faces of Stephen, Rainy, Daniel, and Henry. With them was a man sporting a walrus mustache and an RCMP cap.

Cork brought the pickup to a stop and stepped out. Because they were blinded by the headlights, they couldn't see him until he came forward. When she recognized who it was, Rainy's face lit up with a radiance that filled Cork's heart with a great, burning love. She ran to him, threw her arms around him, and planted a long kiss on his lips. She pressed her cheek to his face, and he could feel how rough his unshaved cheek was against the welcome softness of her own. She pulled back and looked at him, and her eyes were full of tears.

"I'm okay," he said. "Really."

She touched his face. "Good. Because you look like hell."

The others surrounded him and hugs were exchanged, then Cork faced Meloux. The old man studied him head to foot, his dark eyes unreadable.

"You were the last person I thought I'd see here," Cork said.

For a long moment, the Mide didn't speak. Then: "You are different. Have you lost something?"

Cork laughed. "Almost my life, Henry."

"No, Corcoran O'Connor." The old man sounded satisfied. "That was gone from you for a while, but I think you have found it again."

They introduced Constable Markham and explained their presence. Cork told them about the dam.

Markham said, "I could have sworn I heard a flood coming down the canyon. Then nothing happened."

"Might have been the echo and re-echo of the blasts," Cork said. "Or maybe it was the whole damn canyon shifting. Who knows?"

"I'm going to have to commandeer that vehicle you're driving, O'Connor. I'm still going to White Woman Lake, see if I can secure things before that deployment from Thunder Bay arrives."

"You won't have any trouble there," Cork said. "I'll come along, if you don't mind."

Daniel raised a hand. "Us, too. Otherwise, we're stuck in a snowstorm in the middle of nowhere."

"Might as well. We've come this far together," Markham said. "I'll drive, though. In the back of the pickup, everybody. Except you, old-timer. Why don't you sit up front with me? It'll be rough going."

Cork thought the Mide might say something that would put Markham in his place. Instead, Meloux smiled graciously and said, "You are kind."

Markham shrugged, but it was clear he was pleased. "I try to be. Doesn't everybody?"

Cork sat in the pickup bed and snuggled against Rainy.

"Not everybody," he said quietly. "But enough."

CHAPTER 58

The wedding took place on a surprisingly warm Saturday in mid-November. The ceremony was held at the O'Connor home on Gooseberry Lane. It was a small affair, with only the immediate family and closest friends in attendance. Daniel's sisters and brother had come from Wisconsin. Leah Duling was there, of course. Father Green from St. Agnes shared the duties of presiding with Henry Meloux.

The house had been decorated with daisies, Jenny's favorite flower. Everything smelled of sage and cedar. Annie O'Connor had returned for the ceremony. When she'd learned about everything that had happened, she'd forgiven her siblings for keeping her in the dark, but she'd made it clear that if they ever did something like that again, she'd stake them both over an anthill and cover them with honey. She and Stephen smudged the guests as they arrived, offering them each a daisy to hold during the nuptials.

Jenny wore a simple white dress, which she'd embroidered herself with little butterflies around the hem. Daniel was dressed in dark pants, a white shirt, and a vest decorated with beautiful beadwork, a gift from his family.

Mal had arrived the day before, and Rose sat with him, holding hands. Her heart was filled to overflowing with gratitude. Her prayers had not been in vain. Everyone she loved had returned home safely. When it was time, she and Mal stood and came forward as sponsors for Jenny, as was the Ojibwe tradition. Rainy and Leah stepped up for Daniel. Rose stood with tears running down her cheeks as Jenny and Daniel exchanged the vows they'd written. Father Green delivered a blessing and then Henry spoke. His words were Anisihinaabemowin. Rose had no idea what he said, but it flowed like music from Henry's lips, and it was clear from the effect that it had on Jenny and Daniel and Rainy and many of the others that it was beautiful and meaningful. Then Meloux spoke in the language that Rose and the others who were not Anishinaabe could understand.

"This is what I have told them. Go now together into the world and embrace the life the Creator has always imagined for you. And remember the gifts of the Seven Grandfathers. These will help guide you to a good life, which we call *bimaadiziwin*. Teach your children these gifts, and their children, so that they are never forgotten. *Minwaadendamowin*, which is respect. *Debwewin*, which is truth. *Aakodewewin*, which is bravery. *Nibwaakawin*, which is wisdom. *Miigwe'aadiziwin*, which is generosity. *Dibaa-dendiziwin*, which is humility. *Zaagidiwin*, which is love. Hold these gifts in your hearts, Jennifer O'Connor and Daniel English. And may this life you create together only add to the beauty of this world which Kitchimanidoo has imagined for us all."

At the end, Rainy and Rose, with the help of little Waaboo, placed a colorful wedding blanket around the couple, and Jenny and Daniel kissed. With that, they were wed.

There was to be a big reception at the community center on the Iron Lake Reservation. Everyone on the rez had been invited, and lots of folks from Aurora were coming. There would be Ojibwe drummers and a band made up of Daniel's friends. When he wasn't dancing, he planned to sit with them and play his accordion.

Rose couldn't have been happier if she'd given birth to these children herself. But there was an edge to her happiness. She'd always been regular as clockwork, but her period was late. She'd also been having trouble sleeping and had begun to put on a little weight. These were all, she knew, classic symptoms of meno-pause. The end had finally come to any hope for having a family of her own.

As the house began to empty, she spotted Henry Meloux standing alone near the closed patio door, watching her with a curious look on his face. He inclined his head, and she walked to him. He reached out and took her hands. His old palms were warm and wrinkled, but she could feel great strength there. He looked deeply into her eyes.

"Something has changed about you," he said.

The old Mide missed nothing, she thought. "I'm entering my change of life, Henry. Menopause."

The old man shook his head and smiled so large and beautiful and radiant that his whole face was like a second sun. "I do not see an ending. I see a beginning. I believe that you and your husband will return here within the year."

"For something special?"

"A naming ceremony."

"A naming ceremony? For a new child? Jenny and Daniel's? That's wonderful news, Henry."

"Not theirs."

She studied the old man's shining eyes and suddenly she understood. She was afraid to dare that it might be true. Yet, she had never known Henry to be wrong about a thing like this.

"It might be a good idea to tell your husband," the old Mide suggested.

In a daze of happiness, she turned. As if her feet had wings, she flew to Mal.

Cork stood alone in the kitchen. He'd stepped away from the gathering, not at all certain if he wanted anyone to see his face, his eyes especially, which were blurred with tears.

November, he thought. For much of his life, it had been a month full of nothing but loss and darkness and despair. But this day it was different. November had changed. Or maybe it was him. He wondered if this had been Jenny's intention all along. To offer him something different, something hopeful in a month that so often had felt hopeless. He would ask her, when the time was right.

It had been a remarkable month. The viability of the Manitou Canyon Dam was being officially reviewed. True to his word, John W. Harris was very public in his condemnation of the project. That his own granddaughter had been a part of the plan to render the dam inoperable was huge news, and the world seemed to be listening. But as Harris had said amid the swirl of dust atop the dam, there was such big money involved that it would be a battle, and God alone knew who would prevail. He'd secured the best legal defense possible for his grandchildren, and for Isaac McQuabbie, all of whom had been released on bail. If the media reports were any gauge, popular opinion was falling hard on Lindsay Harris's side and the side of the White Woman Lake Odawa.

Chief Aaron Commanda and his nephew Bird had vanished. No one in Saint Gervais had the slightest idea what had become of them. Or at least that's what the Odawa there were telling the investigators from the NSCI and CSIS. Everyone in the settlement swore that Andre Cheval had not been absent at all the day the dam had been attacked. Down in Gordonville, no one could say conclusively that the floatplane they'd seen when Aaron had brought his nephew into the clinic belonged to Cheval. As far as Cork knew, neither the NSCI nor the CSIS had been able to find evidence nailing Cheval to any involvement in the Manitou Canyon Dam Affair, as the media had dubbed it.

Ben Trudeau, who'd been indicted on several charges, had maintained his silence in regard to any part he might have had in the kidnappings. He was being represented by a Cherokee attorney who had a reputation for finding a way to clear her clients' names. The attorney was mute, of course, about who was footing the bill for Trudeau's defense.

As for the others who'd been involved, Cork had learned a good deal about them. Robert Baker, a.k.a. Mr. Fox, had been a kind of golden boy in the First Nations community. He'd been a Rhodes Scholar at Oxford and was a member of the Canadian Bar Association. Before joining the faculty of the McGill Law School, he'd been involved in a number of high-profile uphill legal battles, working to protect the rights of First Nations people. Cork understood why, in the end, dynamite must have seemed like a quicker solution.

As for Indigo, his real name was James Sparrow. He'd been a member of the Canadian Armed Forces, decorated during his service in Afghanistan, but mustered out as the result of an altercation with a Canadian Army officer that had involved a young Afghan woman. Sparrow's defense had been that he was protecting the woman. The officer had contended that he'd been the one to intervene to prevent Sparrow from sexually assaulting her. Instead of taking the case to prosecution, the military had simply made it go away by discharging Sparrow for misconduct.

Mrs. Gray's real name was Mona Fournier, and Mr. Gray—Flynn—had truly been her brother. Everything Fox had said about her family and the hundreds of other First Nations people of Fort Saint Antoine poisoned by the spill from Caldecott's West Caribou Mine was true. Cork, who'd fought so hard on so many occasions to protect his own family, couldn't find it in his heart to condemn these people for the bitterness that had led them to be a part of the Manitou Canyon Dam Affair.

Krystal Gore, the dealer who'd been instrumental in the payoff to Trevor Harris, had been granted immunity in return for her testimony in the case. She and her daughter had been sequestered somewhere secret, and Cork had been led to believe they would enter the witness protection program to keep them safe from the Warrior Cohort.

He'd been staring at the linoleum, lost in his thinking. He looked up and found Henry Meloux standing in the doorway, studying him patiently.

"What is it, Henry?"

"For several winters, the worry I have felt for you has been heavy on my heart. That weight is gone now. You finally understand what it is that offers you peace as *ogichidaa*."

Cork thought about this and decided it was true. "I learned

something from Aaron Commanda. He's also *ogichidaa*, Henry. I saw him give everything he could in order to stand between evil and what he loved. He accepted that the rest was out of his hands."

"To have tried and been true in your heart, that is all any human being could ask of you or that you could ask of yourself. I am proud of you, Corcoran O'Connor." The old man smiled broadly. His eyes might even have been a little wet. "I will leave now," he said, "and go dance and make a fool of myself, because that is what joy is for."

Rainy saw her great-uncle come from the kitchen in a kind of haste, which was odd for the old man. She was concerned, and she went to the kitchen to see what might have happened. She found Cork there.

"I just saw Uncle Henry hurrying away."

"He's going to dance," Cork said with a smile. "That's all. Us, too, I hope."

"He's okay? You're okay?"

"The best."

She kissed him. "I could have told you that. In fact, I have. You just haven't heard me."

"I hear you now. So, as I understand it, Leah is staying on at Crow Point. Henry is her life now."

"That's the plan," Rainy said.

"And what about you? Two women out there seeing to one man's needs? Sounds to me like a recipe for disaster."

"I'm going to give her my cabin. Although it was never really mine to give. It's been a good place for me, but I guess it's time I moved on."

"Where? You haven't talked to me about this."

She laid her head against his chest. She could hear his heart.

"You've been a little busy lately. And I haven't come up with a good plan. I could live with my daughter in Alaska, I suppose, until I've figured things out. I don't see her or my granddaughter enough."

Cork lightly kissed her hair. "There's something I've been thinking about. But, like you say, I've been kind of busy, so I haven't had a chance to talk to you about it."

"What's that?"

"I've been thinking you could stay here. With us."

"That would certainly get a lot of tongues wagging."

"Not if you were my wife."

She looked up into his eyes. "Is that really what you want?"

"I wouldn't ask if it wasn't." He studied her and his face clouded. "It's not what you want?"

"There is so much about me you don't know, Cork."

"I know what's important to me. I love you, Rainy. Isn't that enough?"

She could have argued, because in her head she wasn't at all certain of the answer to that question. Instead, she spoke from her heart. In the sunlight of a November afternoon, with the last sounds of the wedding party still filling the house on Gooseberry Lane, she said to the man who loved her, "Yes."

CHAPTER 59

Cheval's de Havilland Beaver, fitted with skis now instead of pontoons, touched down on the snow of a clearing deep in the Manitou Highlands. The sun was a great, blinding face of light beaming down out of a sky so clear and blue its beauty was almost painful to behold. The Beaver taxied toward the edge of the thick alpine forest where Aaron Commanda and his nephew Bird stood awaiting his arrival. The trees wore a mantel of clean white, and in the hills of the highlands the snow was already calf-deep.

Cheval brought the plane to a stop and killed the engine. He got out and greeted Aaron with a bear hug, then gave Bird the same.

"What's the word?" Aaron asked.

"The river's got an indefinite reprieve," Cheval reported. "The Caldecott Corporation's probably going to throw money at everyone and everything, but nothing's moving forward at the moment." He grinned at them. "If this was the old days, Caldecott would have a bounty out on your heads. As it is, you're the folk heroes of the moment."

"Folk heroes?" Bird said, and smiled as if this pleased him greatly.

"There's a defense fund being put together for you," Cheval said. "And get this, John Harris has contributed a hundred thousand to it. He says he'll give more if needed."

"They'll have to find us first," Aaron said.

Cheval looked at the hills, an inviting mottle of green needle and white snow that stretched unbroken as far as the eye could see. "I wouldn't mind staying here with you for a while. There are a lot of people, strangers, in Saint Gervais these days."

"Things will settle down," Aaron said. "Maybe then we'll come back. In the meantime, Bird has his rifle and the woods are full of game."

From the plane, they unloaded two big Duluth packs filled with supplies.

"This is the last load I'll be bringing in now. But I put a sat phone in one of those packs," Cheval said. "Use it if you need me."

"You should go," Aaron said. "Dark comes early now."

They waited as Cheval taxied across the clearing and lifted off. They stood watching until the plane was no larger than a tiny chickadee held in the vast palm of the sky. Then Aaron shouldered a pack, and Bird shouldered the other, and they began to snowshoe back through the forest the way they'd come.

The trail led them to an old cabin on a high ridge, one that Aaron's grandfather had built. Below them lay the Manitou River, silver in the sunlight, threading its way among the hills of the highlands. Gazing down at that broad, clear run of water, which had been there since long before human memory, Aaron understood what his ancestors must have felt when they first stumbled upon it: the spirit of the Great Mystery in everything it touched. He felt, as they must have felt, the deep certainty of that spirit in his own body, in every breath, every thought, every heartbeat. And he was grateful beyond words.